MEND
MEDICINE
MAN

For Margie

A NOVEL BY
CAROL TILLOTSON

Best Wishes from Carol Tillotson 1-6-94

WINDMILL PUBLISHING
CITRUS HEIGHTS, CALIFORNIA

MENDOCINO MEDICINE MAN

Published in the United States by Windmill Publishing, P. O. Box 4367, Citrus Heights, California 95611-4367.

Cover art by Ken "Rainbow Cougar" Edwards of Longmont, Colorado.

Printed in Sacramento, California by Griffin Printing, Penny Hancock, Account Executive.

First Edition: September 1994

ISBN: 0-9642919-0-8

THE COVER ARTIST

Ken Edwards {"Rainbow Cougar"} is a member of the Colville Confederated Tribes of Washington State. He graduated from the Institute of American Indian Arts High School in Santa Fe, New Mexico and earned an Associate of Fine Arts degree from IAIA {Institute of American Indian Arts}. He has received several top awards at major art shows. Ken is also a storyteller and oral historian and is very much in demand with his repertoire of over one thousand stories which increase cultural understanding.

ACKNOWLEDGMENTS

After almost three years of working on this novel, I wish to thank the many, wonderful people who have helped me along the way.

My first debt of gratitude goes to my beloved husband, Don Tillotson, who shared my journey through the agonies and ecstasies of writing. On countless, long nights, we discussed his brilliant ideas which led to the uniquely innovative twists and turns in the plot.

I am also eternally grateful to my son, Eric Tillotson, who gave unstintingly of his time and vast, literary talent to critique the entire novel, including the first, rough draft, the numerous rewrites and, finally, the finished version. With his unerring eye for detail, he gave me invaluable advice as to form and phrasing.

With deep appreciation, I offer thanks to my son, Shaun Tillotson, and his lovely wife, Doctor Jennifer Dufour. Both of them were always there for me in my hour of need. When reviewing my work, Shaun had the uncanny knack of visualizing a scene and instantly knowing whether or not it rang true. His intelligent, perceptive suggestions are evident throughout the book.

I also give heartfelt thanks to my son, Darren Tillotson, and his wonderful wife, Eileen, whose genuine enthusiasm for my writing inspired me to continue.

With the utmost respect and gratitude, I thank Mr. Hubert Herrmann, the president and chief editor of the Payson Area Writers' Society in Arizona. With his extensive educational background, I felt deeply honored that he offered to critique my manuscript. He was both kind and generous in his praise of my work, while at the same time offering excellent suggestions to improve the entire novel. His help was beyond measure and I will be forever grateful to him.

DREAMS

by Eric Tillotson

Sleeping, I dream
Dreams deeper than sleep
Thicker than thought
Of what, I know not
Always elusive, just out of sight
Like a thief running through the night
Yet, dimly I perceive
In this chilling dream
Hair of flame
And eyes of green!

CHAPTER 1 BLACK EAGLE

High upon a windswept plateau, a primitive medicine man sat before a crackling fire with his arms outstretched toward the sky, carefully repeating a sacred chant. Deeply engrossed in the ritual, he barely felt the chill of the early July evening. As the sound of his chanting echoed across the land and the sparks from his fire spiraled toward the heavens, he finally completed the sacred rite and slowly stood to look out upon the lush valley spread before him. In the waning light, his dark eyes carefully scanned the outer perimeter of the huge valley, searching for the slightest sign of the two warriors who were late in returning from a dangerous expedition. One of the warriors was his beloved grandson, Black Eagle, and the other was called Lion's Claw. They had left earlier in the day with a hunting party and, at the end of their hunt, had chanced upon some strange tracks left by trespassers crossing their land. While the rest of the group headed for the main camp, the two, young warriors had been sent to check on the intruders and discover the cause of the unusual tracks, but night was falling and they were long overdue. Just before the spreading darkness made it impossible to see, the tall, old medicine man caught sight of the two warriors as they erupted from a thick group of trees, then rode hard across a long meadow. With a sense of relief welling up, the old man followed them with his eyes until they once again disappeared into the forest; only then did he climb down from his favorite plateau and return to his tribe to announce the warriors' safe return. Even while he was making

1

his announcement, Black Eagle and Lion's Claw were slowing their horses to a walk as they entered the village with the pride and decorum expected of two such well decorated braves. They looked neither to the right nor the left, ignoring the cheering of the people and pretending not to notice the admiring glances of the eligible young maidens. Instead, they deliberately picked their way through the crowd and headed directly for Chief Grey Cloud, who stood patiently in front of his tepee. He motioned for silence and the people instantly ceased their clamor. He spoke to the two warriors. "I am pleased that you have safely returned to us. What have you learned about the strange tracks and the people who have chosen to cross our lands without first seeking our permission?"

Black Eagle spoke first. "Great Chief, hear my words and believe them, no matter how strange they might sound! The trespassers are different from any tribe you have ever known. Their skin is so light in color that they appear sickly. They have red, brown or even yellow hair! And the tracks are caused by something they drag behind strange-looking horses with long ears! Instead of riding those horses, some of their people ride in the huge things that are being drug!"

The people gasped in disbelief! Lion's Claw interrupted. "No, it's true! Believe his words! And they do the strangest things; they bring many animals with them, instead of hunting them as they need them. They appear to be fearless; they make no attempt to cover their tracks. They even travel through the open, unprotected areas, instead of keeping to the forested lands."

Chief Grey Cloud pondered these words carefully before making his decision. "I believe it would be wise to rid ourselves of these trespassers. Perhaps their fearless ways are meant to scare us off our own lands.

2

Because of their foolish arrogance, we have the opportunity to strike first! We will show them the meaning of true bravery! At tomorrow's first light, we attack. Let none escape!"

The people cheered his decision and began celebrating. They danced late into the evening while the sounds of their chanting and drums echoed through the valleys of their land.

There was a deathly quiet in the early July dawn. The eastern sky was beginning to show streaks of fuchsia and deep purple. The pre-dawn chill hadn't yet released the land. Black Eagle was lying flat amidst the grasses that lined the ridge, peering down upon the strange people in the valley just beneath him. Several of them were heading toward the river, while others milled around the camp. The smoke from their fires floated gently in the breeze, covering the entire scene in an ethereal haze. In spite of the chill, Black Eagle was bathed in sweat! Although he had already seen twenty summers, he had never fought people such as these. Something about them sent a chill down his back!

At that moment, the savage cry of the War Chief filled the air and Black Eagle was caught up with the rest of the war party, his own cries mingling with theirs. Mounting his horse with a single leap, he rushed headlong down the steep incline with the other warriors. They descended in a huge dust cloud, the earth churning beneath the horses' hooves. Although the people in the valley tried valiantly to defend themselves, their weapons were no match for the overwhelming numbers and sheer ferocity of the Indians. A little girl watched in horror while her father tried desperately to remove a lance from his stomach. He never even saw the warrior who scalped him. While he took his last breath, he saw his daughter taken captive.

With her baby in her arms, a young mother raced

toward the shelter of the deep forest. Almost there, she heard the thundering hooves of the Indian pony closing upon her. Her heart pounding furiously, she could feel the steam from the pony's nostrils on her neck and then the warrior was upon her, ripping the baby from her arms and smashing its head against a tree! As she started to crumple into a dead faint, he caught her and threw her across the pony in front of him. With a shrill cry, he raced back with his first captive!

The woman's husband saw her being carried away and ran in their direction. Black Eagle cut him off, leaping upon him from his horse. His momentum sent them both sprawling to the edge of a small plateau which dropped sharply down a steep, rocky incline to the river below. Wrestling for position, Black Eagle felt the bitter taste of fear rise in his throat as he struggled against the incredible strength of his enraged enemy. Raising his knife, he managed to slash the white man's bulging shoulder, but he appeared undaunted as he knocked the weapon from Black Eagle's hand. Then, with a murderous bellow, the crazed husband picked up Black Eagle and threw him off the cliff! The young warrior catapulted straight toward the sharp rocks below! Just before he would have hit them, a mysterious haze thickened about him and he could see nothing! Slowly, a face appeared out of the mists and he found himself looking into beautiful, green eyes filled with tears. A lovely, young, red-haired woman was trying to comfort him......

......Waking in a cold sweat, Jacob shuddered with premonition as the familiar dream slowly released him. Why else would this dream continue to haunt him, except to serve as some dreadful omen? His grandfather, the great medicine man, Lone Elk, had explained to him that their ancestor, Black Eagle, was trying to warn him of some extreme danger. Filled with

4

a sudden, desperate need to leave the reservation, Jacob quickly dressed and headed for his Jeep. The wind whipping through his hair, he drove without any conscious idea as to where he was going. Lost in a turmoil of emotions, he soon arrived at his favorite plateau. Stepping out of the Jeep, he stood amidst the tall grasses and looked up at the stars glittering in the heavens. Only then did his soul feel at home and he once again began to know some measure of peace. Comforted by these familiar surroundings, his thoughts slowly returned to his conversation with Lone Elk. As Jacob considered his grandfather's explanation, he knew only that his heart still ached for the lovely, red-haired woman of his dreams.

CHAPTER 2 JACOB

Standing amidst the tall grasses of his favorite plateau, Jacob looked out upon the vast, lush valley spread before him. It was his birthplace and it was called Round Valley, an apt name since it was completely encircled by mountains. Located in Mendocino County in northern California, the remote and sparsely populated valley contained the small town of Covelo and the Round Valley Indian Reservation. Most of Jacob's friends and, of course, his grandfather still lived on the reservation. Reminiscing about his grandfather's beliefs, Jacob remembered being told about his own birth night. Lone Elk had described to him, with great pride, the unusual omens which had preceded his birth. Now twenty-seven years of age, Jacob was lost in thought as he recalled his grandfather's account of that day......

......The date was September 1, 1966. The morning showed no sign of relief from the sweltering heat wave which had already lasted for almost three weeks. Lisea had risen earlier than usual, planning to take a walk before the heat of the day became unbearable. Taking care not to waken her husband, she stepped gently from the cabin and started up the trail that wound around Williams Creek. The trail took her up a steady incline for about half a mile, then forked sharply down to the right to a secluded glen. Heavy with child, Lisea was breathing hard by the time she reached the glen. With a sigh of relief, she stretched out upon the welcoming coolness of the damp grass. She had never felt so in harmony with the Earth; she awaited the

7

birth of this child with a serene happiness, secure in the knowledge that the child would be a boy. She also knew that he would be very special, that his life would hold great importance, for he was the Chosen One! She knew this to be true, because she had been so informed by Lone Elk and his predictions were never wrong.

Tired from her climb, Lisea fell into a gentle sleep......

Dreaming of her warrior son, she saw him as a young man riding a fierce stallion, black as the darkest night! He was galloping along a familiar trail at breakneck speed, when suddenly the trail ended at a steep cliff! Unable to stop in time, both horse and rider hurtled over the edge into the blackness!

......Startled into wakefulness, her chest heaving with apprehension, Lisea tried to fathom the meaning of the dream. She wanted to find Lone Elk and discuss this with him. Slowly rising, she felt uneasy, as though someone or something were watching her. Standing silently, she looked across the clearing and into the trees. Draped across one of the branches was a huge mountain lion staring down at her. Their eyes met for a long moment that felt like eternity. She froze with terror! She knew better than to run, so she just watched him and awaited the inevitable. His eyes never leaving hers, he leapt effortlessly from the tree and slowly approached her. He was halfway across the clearing when she heard her husband calling to her. Hearing the sound of yet another intruder in his domain, the ferocious cat stopped dead in his tracks. He threw back his head, an eerie scream erupting from his throat, and retreated into his forest.

Lisea could hardly stand; her legs threatened to buckle beneath her. She finally found her voice and called to her husband. He ran up the last part of the trail and rushed to her side. Sobbing, she collapsed in

8

his arms.

"Lisea, where have you been? I've been worried sick! Didn't you hear me calling?"

She stared into his dark eyes, so filled with concern. "Caleb, I'm sorry. I didn't mean to worry you. I only went for a walk; then I fell asleep in my favorite place. Oh, Caleb! There was a mountain lion, and......" Suddenly, she felt a sharp pain that brought her to her knees!

Caleb knelt down to hold her. "Lisea! What's wrong?"

She answered with a visible effort. "I think my labor's starting."

He scooped her into his arms and carried her the rest of the way. In pain, she stared up at the darkening sky. It took a moment for her to realize that storm clouds had blown in. The heat wave was broken; there was the unmistakable smell of rain in the air. Her son would be born in the midst of a storm! This was a good sign. It would bring him power! As Caleb carried her into the cabin, she wasn't at all surprised to find Lone Elk waiting inside. Of course, he alone would already have known that today would be the birthing day!

Lone Elk had brought with him two of the tribal women most experienced in childbirth. Rachael and Maria felt deeply honored to assist on such an auspicious occasion. Indeed, the entire tribe had already begun preparations for the name-choosing ceremony and the festivities to follow.

As her last pain subsided, Lisea realized that she had never had any breakfast. "Maria, please bring me something light to eat; I'm starved! The pains are still far apart; I'm sure it will be all right."

"Little Mother, it would not be wise to eat right now. It would only make you sick. You must trust in my advice; I have seen many births and this is only your first."

Lone Elk interceded. "Maria, this is a special birth and the food will not harm her. Bring her something." Maria hesitated. "Right now!" he boomed. She gasped and scurried to prepare something. Lisea reached her hand out to Lone Elk, thanking him wordlessly. He held her hand tightly to his chest, leaned over and whispered something in her ear. Then he cleared his throat and said, "Caleb, your son is about to enter this world and we must leave the cabin or he will think it's too crowded and he might decide not to enter!"

Caleb laughed and walked over to Lisea. Smiling down at her, he thought she had never looked more beautiful. "Beloved one, I'll wait outside with Lone Elk to hear the first cries of our son." Then he kissed her and walked outside with his father. As he closed the cabin door behind him, a flash of lightning split the sky and the rumble of distant thunder echoed throughout the valley!

The day wore on with an agonizing slowness. For Lisea, it was as though time stood still, as though life itself had become one constant pain. She was feeling so weak; if only she could rest, but they wouldn't leave her alone.

"Lisea! You have to keep pushing; the time is near. Don't you want to see your son?"

"Rachael, go away. I can't push anymore! Let me rest for a while and then I'll try again. Please, go away!" She was starting to slip into oblivion when Rachael abruptly slapped her face. She came to her senses with an angry start and began to curse Rachael when an overwhelming wave of pain claimed her body. She pushed with all her might while wave after wave of excruciating pain encompassed her.

"Lisea! Just one more push; he's almost here!"

One last exhausting push and then she heard his cry. It was the last sound she ever heard.

The baby's cries mingled with the roar of the thunder. The night sky was lit by a profuse array of lightning strikes and the thunder claps were deafening. In the midst of all this, a giant falcon was silhouetted as he swooped down on an unsuspecting field mouse. In an instant, he flew away, his prey clutched in his talons. Caleb had been watching all this when the sound of his son's cries finally reached him. As he headed for the cabin door, Lone Elk grabbed his arm. "Caleb, you saw what happened to the field mouse; while some are born, others must die. Rejoice in your son! He will be strong like the falcon!"

Caleb jerked his arm away and ran into the cabin. Rachael and Maria were crying and couldn't meet his eyes. He knew, but he couldn't accept it. He held Lisea in his arms, rocking back and forth, crying silently. "Please, God, let this be only a dream. Give her back to me!"

Lone Elk gently placed his hand on his son's shoulder. "Caleb, we live the dream. Reality will come soon enough."

CHAPTER 3 FIRST AWAKENINGS

Watching his son with a mixture of love and amusement, Caleb was struggling to appear stern and disapproving. Little Jacob was celebrating his fourth birthday and had just tackled a small guest for trying to sneak away with one of his new toys. Caleb had to pull Jacob off of the little boy, who was crying loudly and obviously regretted the error of his ways.

"Jacob! He said he's sorry and he won't do it again. Now make up and be friends! Remember, son, there is no toy that is more valuable than a friend."

......Those words echoed in Jacob's mind as he lay amidst the grasses on his favorite plateau, reminiscing about his childhood. He remembered the birthday incident like it was yesterday. He had learned an important lesson that day and he never forgot it. In fact, he had never forgotten any of the lessons that his father had taught him. Caleb had been an exceptionally caring father; he had tried with all his heart to make up for the loss of Jacob's mother. He hadn't been able to give his son wealth or an easy life, but he had instilled in him all the right values and attitudes. He had taught Jacob to be proud of his Indian heritage and never to forget that his true name was Falcon......

During his teen years, Jacob had been the brunt of some malicious remarks regarding his tribal name, but the remarks were never made twice by the same person. Jacob's fighting skills had left some in awe and others in extreme pain, but all were left with respect for the amazingly strong young man. He had inherited his father's dark, good looks and coal black eyes, but he was taller, just over six feet, and leaner. He was much stronger than he appeared, as certain muscular opponents found out the hard way.

The young ladies of his school saw him in a different light. He had a way of looking at them as though he could see into their very souls. More than one thought she would drown in his dark eyes. There was a lovely young lady in particular who wanted much more than just gazing into his eyes. Her name was Elizabeth Stanton and she was the only daughter of the local sheriff. Although Jacob was cool and aloof toward most of his admirers, he felt especially drawn to her and had invited her to the Senior Ball. She had accepted, but still had to confront her father.

"Daddy, I'm so happy! I've been invited to the Senior Ball by the handsomest boy in the whole senior class! Oh, Daddy, all the girls are so jealous of me; I just can't believe it!"

Her father chuckled and gave her a hug. "Well, Darlin', I can believe it. Any boy in his right mind would be honored to take you to that dance! Just who is this fortunate young man?"

"You remember Jacob, don't you? He was the star quarterback on our football team. Remember how you used to cheer for him?"

Her father suddenly looked worried. "Pumpkin, that was different. Of course I cheered for him; he was one Hell of a quarterback! But he is an Indian. Did you forget that ? It's all right to speak to them, but you really shouldn't date one of them! You've got to think about your reputation!"

Elizabeth started to cry. "I don't care if he is an Indian! He's a wonderful person. You just don't know him. He's intelligent, considerate and a gentleman! Please, Daddy! It's only a dance. You know you can trust me!"

"Sweetheart, of course I trust you! I just don't

know if I can trust him. Indians are different from us. They have wild blood in them. What about all his fights? Can't you see how savage he really is?"

"Daddy, I swear to you that nothing will happen! Please don't forbid me to go out with him. If I can't go with him, then I just won't go at all!" She started to cry again.

"All right, Elizabeth! You can go with him. Just quit crying. But God have mercy on him if anything happens to you, because I sure as Hell won't!"

......Jacob rolled on his back on the soft grasses of his plateau. 'Good Lord!' he thought to himself. 'Could that dance actually have been ten years ago?' He removed his shirt and used it as a pillow. He felt the warmth of the early June sun on his bare chest. It reminded him of that June evening with Elizabeth......

They were lying on a blanket of soft grass and he felt a very special warmth against his bare chest, quite different from that of the sun. It was a tingling sort of warmth which came from her bare breasts caressing his skin. They were both completely undressed, but neither felt the chill of the evening. There was a fire burning in both of them that refused to be ignored! Jacob rolled her over on her back and parted her legs with his own. Rubbing his male hardness slowly against her, he kissed her long and deeply, his tongue insistently probing her mouth. Then, he brought his lips down to her shapely breasts, kissing them lightly all over and then gently sucking each nipple. Elizabeth sighed and stroked the small of his back, then lowered her hands down to his taut buttocks. Shivering with desire, Jacob slowly moved his hand toward her private area, leaving a trail of goosebumps on her soft skin. She moaned aloud as he began to stroke the silken hair of her inviting mound. Staring into his hypnotic black eyes, she felt her very soul slipping away as she succumbed

15

to the thrill of his touch. Sensing that she was as ready as he, Jacob mounted her with one quick hard thrust! She cried out at the brief moment of sharp pain, but then gasped at the extreme pleasure of being so filled by him. With every stroke, the throbbing pulsations intensified until the two young lovers entered a plane of ecstasy they could never have imagined! Silhouetted by a myriad of sparkling stars, Jacob stared down at Elizabeth, his dark eyes glowing with an inner fire. Gazing into those obsidian eyes, Elizabeth thought he looked for all the world like some kind of conquering hero. Sighing, she pulled his face down to hers and kissed him tenderly, clinging to him as though she would never let him go.

Jacob would never forget that night; it was his first encounter with real passion and the experience had filled him with wonder. He would also never forget the turmoil that followed. After graduation, he and Elizabeth continued to see each other, causing her father extreme distress.

"Honey, I think you and Jacob are spending far too much time with each other. You're both too young to date so exclusively. Why don't you go out with some other boys for a change? What about that nice Jason Bradley? You used to date him."

"Daddy, can't you see that I'm in love with Jacob? I don't want to date anyone else! We're almost eighteen and I'm going to marry him, with or without your consent!"

"What?!!? Have you lost your mind? No daughter of mine is going to marry a Goddamned Indian! You mean he actually had the nerve to ask you to marry him?"

"Not yet. But he's going to if I have anything to say about it!"

Glaring, he slapped her hard across the face!

"You're not going to have anything to say about it! Get to your room and stay there!"

Sobbing hysterically, she fled to her room and locked the door. Her father ran out the front door and jumped into his Chevy Blazer. He knew exactly where to find Jacob at this time of day; he had a summer job working at old man Benson's ranch. Right now he would be cleaning out the stables. Driving with a vengeance, he cursed Jacob every minute of the way. Screeching to a stop, he jumped out and ran toward the stables. Hearing the noise, Jacob turned toward the door just as it crashed open. "Mr. Stanton! What are you doing here?"

"Don't you Mr. Stanton me, you fucking Indian asshole! What the Hell makes you think you've got any future with my daughter? You're not to see her again! Do you understand me?"

"Wait a minute! We're both almost of age. You can't stop me from seeing her!"

"Oh, yeah? We'll see about that! How's your old man doin'? I hear things are kinda rough for him right now. It wouldn't be too difficult to stick him with a phony drug rap. Picture this, asshole! Your dad caught with the goods, tryin' to make a quick buck. Maybe you'd better think twice about seein' my daughter again!"

In a split second, Jacob was upon him, hitting him so hard he loosened two of his teeth. Then he picked him up from the ground and slammed him into the railing. "You worthless piece of shit! I'm not going to see your daughter again, but only because I don't want to be near anyone related to trash like you! And you'd better remember this; if you ever do anything to my father, there won't be enough of you left to bury!"

Jacob never saw Elizabeth again. He couldn't bear the thought of looking into her soft blue eyes one last time and then forcing himself to walk away. It would

17

be entirely too painful for both of them. Eventually, he heard that she had been sent to another state to live with her aunt. For the longest time, every thought of her was like a knife in his heart, but he knew he had made the right decision. He was well aware that her father would have gone to any extreme to keep the two young lovers apart. He would even have carried out his threat against Jacob's father. And Jacob could never allow that to happen, regardless of his deep feelings for Elizabeth. Besides, he was very young and he knew there would probably be many women in his life, but only one father as wonderful as Caleb.

CHAPTER 4 VIEW TO FOREVER

Jacob awoke with a start! He had fallen asleep in the soft grasses of his own private plateau. This was his favorite place in the entire world. Although he knew the land really belonged to all of the people, in his heart, he somehow felt as though he alone owned this beloved mesa. It was almost as if his ancestors had bequeathed it directly unto him.

The sun was in its final decline of the day; soon it would be dusk. The last rays of the sun painted the clouds in vivid shades of pink and purple. He stood and stared into the vast horizon. It occurred to him that his entire life was finely intertwined with all the mountains and forest spread before him. Memories flooded his mind as he recalled his countless forays into this cherished wilderness. As a young boy, he had explored several of the easier pathways, having mock battles with his homemade bow and arrows. By his older teen years, he had gained extensive knowledge of the forest lands surrounding his tribe's reservation. He had often used one of old man Benson's horses and explored the hidden recesses of the land. No one alive knew the territory like he did!

Since the dawn of time, the forest had given and taken life at its own dictate. Eons ago, early man had battled one another for control of the hunting grounds. Generation after generation fought the same battles for the same basic reasons. Then man became civilized. He committed his atrocities for less valid reasons, such as bigotry, jealousy and greed!

In a sense, the forest was like a strong warrior,

knowing countless secrets, yet divulging none. Only the most dedicated and persistent would ever untangle any of its numerous mysteries. The most recent events hidden by the forest included romantic trysts with various lovers, rapes, murders and unaccountable disappearances. But the most insidious secret of them all, unless checked, would have a devastating effect on thousands of people. Jacob, in his twenty-seventh year, chanced upon this dangerous secret quite by accident......

......He was riding his favorite horse, Tomahawk, through one of the more remote areas. Tomahawk was an outstanding quarterhorse, just over sixteen hands in height, perfectly proportioned and beautifully trained. He was black as the darkest night and had an intimidating manner. Jacob was the only one who could ride him. They had been out all day and twilight was approaching. He knew he should be heading back because dark falls quickly in the mountains. It seemed as though one minute it would be dusk and the next minute it would be pitch black! He was just descending Shale Mountain when he noticed a wisp of smoke about two miles to the north. He decided to check it out and make certain that some careless camper didn't light up the whole forest. Being wary by nature, he approached the area without using any trace of a trail. Actually, the region was so remote that the only paths he had found were those made by animals. However, just to be on the safe side, he even avoided them. As he picked his way through the denser part of the forest, he noticed that it was unnaturally still. There was no birdsong and the smaller animals seemed to be in hiding. He leaned over and whispered to his horse. "Be extra quiet now! We're getting close and something just isn't right!" The horse was so attuned to Jacob's body language, that he tensed up whenever Jacob did. He knew instinctively to move with great caution; his ears were pointed forward to catch the slightest hint of danger. Their descent was very slow as they approached a tree-covered knoll overlooking a small valley below. Jacob looked at the land beneath him in astonishment. Where before there had been only irregular forest growth, there was now very regulated growth, done in careful rows, obviously planted by man. Even without being close enough to identify it, he knew it could only be marijuana. As he realized this, he broke into a sweat; he must be in extreme danger! Thank God he hadn't gone any farther! The crops were probably surrounded by booby traps. He looked all around the edge of the valley, searching for some kind of camp. Just a few hundred yards to his right, he saw what appeared to be a rustic shelter. He could barely make it out in the declining light. It had been built in such a manner as to almost blend into the forest. Slowly retreating back into the thicker foliage, he spotted a sudden movement off to his right. He heard voices and then two riders came within view. He froze! They hadn't seen him yet, but soon would as they came closer. In order to leave this knoll, he would have to cross a small clearing; they were bound to spot him in any case. They were undoubtedly armed and he was not. Jacob had no choice but to run. Digging his knees into Tomahawk's sides, horse and rider burst from the protective cover of the knoll and raced up the mountain toward the crest! The two riders stared, open-mouthed.

"Matt! Who the Hell was that?"

"I don't know, Jim, but we better catch up with him damned quick!"

They spurred their mounts and raced after him with a vengeance! Their horses were fresher and they were steadily gaining. Jacob had just mounted the crest and was starting down the other side when he heard a bullet ricochet against a rock! He caught sight of a main trail just ahead and spurred his horse into a gallop. He looked back. Jesus Christ! They were getting dangerously close! He couldn't keep dodging bullets indefinitely! As they approached the Rattlesnake Bar area, Jacob remembered that a less used trail would soon intersect this one. He veered off on the new trail with the two riders hot on his heels. Tomahawk was breathing hard; Jacob knew he was running out of time. "Come on, just a little bit farther! We're almost there!" They rounded a bend and the trail ended at a steep drop-off! In a heartbeat, they hurtled over the edge into the blackness!

Matt and Jim reined their horses in hard. They were barely able to stop in time. Matt was panting. "Holy shit! That crazy son of a bitch is dead for sure!"

"You got that right! One thing's for sure; I ain't goin' over the edge to check it out! What're we gonna tell the boss about this?"

"Just tell it like it happened! We caught some crazy asshole snoopin' around, chased him off a cliff and he bought the farm!"

Peering over the edge, all they could see was a black emptiness down below. They listened carefully, but the only sound they could hear was the bubbling and splashing of the stream at the bottom of the ravine. From nearby, an owl hooted. Matt shivered. "C'mon; let's get outa here. That sucker's dead meat!"

Some distance below, Jacob and Tomahawk were safe within a small cave just off the narrow ledge upon which they had landed after sliding through thick pine needles down the steep incline. Jacob's knowledge of the land and trails had undoubtedly saved his life! He waited quietly for about ten minutes, checking Tomahawk's legs to make certain he was uninjured, then cautiously left the cave. The ledge wound around the side of the mountain for about a quarter of a mile and then hooked up with the main trail again. Wearily, he headed home. This had turned out to be a much longer day than he had planned. While he rode, he thought about what he should do. He wasn't about to tell the sheriff, since he was a staunch enemy. Besides, it wouldn't surprise him at all to find out that Stanton already knew about the crops. It was quite possible that he was on the take, especially considering that Stanton had the reputation for being aware of almost everything that was going on in his jurisdiction. Otherwise, just how in the Hell were these guys moving their shipments out of the mountains without getting caught? Even if the sheriff were innocent, Jacob would much prefer to take care of the drug dealers by himself. He'd make such an example of them that it would be a cold day in Hell before anyone would ever again dare to grow that garbage in his forest!

While Jacob rode slowly along, his mind raging with a turmoil of angry plans, a young woman in a place far removed from him was equally distressed by her own problems. Bitterly pacing back and forth, Shannon was torn between wanting revenge against her unfaithful husband and a deeper desire to save her marriage. In the end, she would come up with a solution which would greatly complicate Jacob's life.

CHAPTER 5 SHANNON

Leaning over the upstairs balcony, Shannon looked out at the city lights of downtown Sacramento. It was almost midnight and Larry still wasn't home. This was beginning to happen all too often. She found it hard to believe that his evening appointments had anything at all to do with his insurance business. He was entirely too flirtatious to be trusted! When they entertained, Larry always permitted his gaze to linger on any attractive women just a little longer than he should. Most of the women quite correctly considered his look an invitation and some of them came on to him, even in front of Shannon.

She remembered their very last argument all too well......

It was just after their most recent party and Shannon was sitting on their bed in tears. "Why do you always have to humiliate me in front of my friends? Can't you flirt on your own time?"

"Honey, I wasn't flirting! I was just being friendly to our guests."

"Of course you were! But only to the foxy, female guests, right?"

"Why do you always have to twist everything? Socializing is good for my business! Since you're a Realtor, I'm sure it's equally good for yours. You, of all people, should understand that! Besides, don't you realize how much I love you? I wish you'd quit worrying about other women. You're the only one who means a damn to me! Come here."

He pulled her into his arms and tried to kiss her,

but she turned her face away, too angry to kiss him. She tried to break away, but he held her in a tight embrace. With one hand gripping both of hers, he used the other to caress her breasts. In spite of her anger, she felt her nipples harden with desire. She hated the effect he had on her! It always ended like this! They never settled anything. He felt her will dissolving and released her hands. He pushed her down roughly on their bed and began to untie her bathrobe. She half-heartedly tried to stop him.

"Please don't! I'm tired. I just want to go to sleep."

Laughing, he quickly removed his clothing and climbed onto their bed, looming over her with a knowing expression. "The real problem is that I've been too easy on you lately. What you need is some good, old-fashioned, rough sex! When I get done with you, I guarantee you'll get a good night's sleep!" Seizing her wrists, he leaned over and kissed her so hard that he bruised her lips. Moaning, she tried to twist out of his grip, but it was too late! Forcing her legs apart, he mounted her with one savage thrust while she lay there, trembling.

......Remembering back to that evening, a confusing mix of desire and resentment blunted the sharpness of her anger. She couldn't understand the strange hold he had over her. Most of the time, his treatment was gentle, almost mundane, and almost always over with too quickly. He saw to his own needs and all but dismissed hers. But, every now and then, he would brutally take her against her will! And, much to her private shame, some desperate inner need of hers was satisfied only on those occasions. In spite of the pain, his wild abandon at those times added an excitement that left her breathless. It helped to make up for his dreadful lack of duration. And she sensed that

26

it was always better for him than it was for her, so why did he need other women? She had sworn a thousand times to leave him, but he had always charmed her into staying. She finally decided that something had to change, or she really would leave him, once and for all.

They both had a two-week vacation coming in July. Shannon thought it would be a good idea to go someplace completely new and really get away from it all. She was determined to avoid the party scene altogether during those precious two weeks. She craved a tranquil setting, something to bring them closer together. Perhaps a trip to the mountains would be the solution. In a primitive forest setting, maybe she would finally be able to express her needs in a way that he would understand.

One of her clients had just recently told her about a guided wilderness tour in the northern part of the state. She and her husband had gone last year with two other couples and she said it was the most fun she'd ever had. She told Shannon that the program only accepted six people at a time to go on the tour. At first, she had thought that was strange, but then she decided that it had probably turned out to be more fun as a result. With less people, everything seemed more primitive and back to nature. She had given Shannon a number to call and told her to check it out.

The more she thought about it, the more she liked the idea. But what two couples should she invite? The first to come to mind were Tony and Caitlin Salerno. Now there was an interesting mix. Caitlin was Irish and Tony was Italian. Talk about two hot-tempered people! It was amazing they got along as well as they did. Caitlin's nickname was Cat and it was somehow fitting. Although, with her hot temper, Shannon thought she should have been called Wildcat! She remembered the look on Cat's face on an occasion when Larry was busy making a fool out of himself with a pretty, young lady at one of their parties. Cat's eyes had radiated a look of pure disgust and contempt! Shannon laughed at the memory of that menacing look. It was undoubtedly Larry's great, good fortune that he wasn't married to her; she tended to get violent when she was angry. At least she wouldn't have to worry about sparks erupting between those two on the trip!

Another couple she'd like to invite would be Eric and Elaine Taylor. They had been neighbors and close friends for over two years. Elaine would be another safe choice, because she only had eyes for her husband. Even after two years of marriage, Elaine still couldn't believe that Eric had actually chosen her for his wife. She was attractive in a quiet way, but Eric was devastatingly handsome! He was built like a Greek God, had dark, laughing eyes and a wonderful personality. He was always the life of the party. To know him was to like him. Even Shannon had to restrain herself from staring at him. God, he was so tempting! But she would never betray her friend or her husband, so she put the idea out of her mind. She was determined to make her own marriage work. She had invested three years of her life in this marriage; she was willing to give it one last chance.

CHAPTER 6 ERIC

Sweating profusely, Eric brought his workout to an end. He had completed extra sets of each exercise and was feeling very pleased with himself. A certain amount of self-discipline was required to adhere to such a rigorous workout schedule, but he was determined to stick with it. He enjoyed the overall feeling of well-being accomplished by his strenuous efforts, but he was especially happy about the admiring looks he received from young women! He had even caught his lovely neighbor, Shannon, staring at him in that hypnotic way of hers. Whenever their eyes met, she seemed quite uncomfortable and would quickly look away. If only he knew what she was thinking! She was undoubtedly the most beautiful woman he had ever known. Apart from the physical attraction, he found himself drawn by her sense of honor and dignity. Her bearing was regal, making her appear almost unapproachable. They were both married and he knew he had no right to feel this way about her. But she projected such a vulnerability that he was unable to quit thinking about her. He sensed an intense yearning within her, so strong that her very need seemed to cry out to him for relief!

Feeling guilty over his desire for Shannon, Eric began to think about his relationship with his wife. Technically, Elaine was the perfect wife. She tried to please him in every possible way. Even with a full-time job, she managed to do all the house cleaning and cooking. He felt a little ashamed that he was unable to return the depth of her love. In the beginning, her submissive, adoring attitude had made him feel like some kind of hero. Her entire world revolved around him. He couldn't remember exactly when his feelings toward her began to change, but, somewhere along the way, they did. They had only been married a little over two years and already he felt smothered by her constant devotion to him. Even their sex life was hindered by her attitude. He never knew if she were truly satisfied; she would never have let on to the contrary. He somehow sensed that sex was not high on her list of priorities anyway. She was rather quiet by nature and definitely not very passionate. He was always the one to instigate any sexual overture and he suspected that a great deal of her response was feigned.

Relaxing in his Jacuzzi, Eric felt relieved that Elaine had gone to stay with her mother for a couple of weeks. Her mother had undergone surgery and her request for help gave the two of them some much needed, separate time. Eric stepped out of his bath, dried off and wrapped his towel around his waist. Since it was an unusually warm evening, he decided to relax on his balcony for a while and enjoy the fresh air. Out of habit, he looked over at Shannon's house. His pulse quickening, he noticed that she was pacing back and forth on her own balcony. He looked down into their driveway and saw that Larry's car was missing. He thought to himself, 'Another late business appointment, hmmm? Yeah, right!' He couldn't believe it. A wife like Shannon, and he was fooling around! If only he had found her first and had succeeded in persuading her to marry him, he would never have taken a chance on losing her. There are millions of women on this planet, but only one Shannon! She always appeared so ladylike and dignified, but there was a latent sexuality about her that could not be camouflaged. He could only imagine making love to her; the very thought was overwhelming! On a whim, he decided to call her, in

30

spite of the late hour. He wasn't even sure what to say. He just wanted to hear the sound of her voice.

After ringing over six times with no answer, Eric was about to give up when Shannon breathlessly answered the phone.

"Hello! Larry, is that you?"

"No, Shannon. It's me, Eric! I'm sorry to disturb you so late at night. It's just that with Elaine gone, I was feeling lonely. I noticed your lights on and thought maybe you and Larry could come over and cheer me up. I didn't realize Larry was out, but the invite still goes for you. I've got some old videos we could watch, or do you think Larry would mind?"

There was a long silence on the other end. "Shannon? Are you still there?"

Her voice filled with bitterness, she finally responded. "Yes, I'm still here and I'd love to come over! I could stand some company, myself. And I really don't care if Larry minds or not! I'll be right there."

Eric shakily hung up the phone. He couldn't believe his good luck! He threw some clothes on, quickly straightened up the living room and set out a bottle of wine and two glasses, all the while thinking, 'Dear God, don't let me blow it! I may never get a chance like this again.'

He saw her walking up the front steps and opened the door even before she could knock. They just stared at each other for a long moment and, this time, she didn't look away. She hesitantly stepped inside and he closed the door.

"Come in the living room, Shannon. I've set out some good wine for us. You look like you could use a drink."

"I don't need a drink, Eric. I need a new life! Larry's probably out with some bimbo again and I'm fed up with him! I just can't take it anymore!" She started to

31

cry and walked into his welcoming arms.

"Don't cry, Shannon; he's not worth it! He doesn't deserve a woman like you! Why don't you leave him? You could have any man in the world. You don't have to take his crap!" He held her gently, lightly stroking her back.

"Eric, you're such a good friend! I'm sorry to burden you with my problems. I'm just going to have to work this out by myself. Maybe I should go." Her voice held a note of desperation.

He tightened his hold on her. "Don't go yet! The last thing you need is to sit alone in an empty house. Stay with me for a while; I guarantee I can cheer you up."

She turned her tear-streaked face toward him and looked at him with such a hunger that he just had to kiss her! Their kiss was long and devouring. Without another word, he picked her up and carried her into the bedroom, kicking the door shut behind him. He set her down and they stood for a moment, watching each other silently. She unbuttoned her dress and let it fall to the floor. Slowly removing her bra and panties, she let them fall to the floor, also. Shivers racked his body as he saw her in all her naked glory. Then she started to unbutton his shirt. While she opened his shirt, she began to cover his chest with soft kisses. Lightly moaning, he ripped the rest of his clothes off. Then she held his hard member in her hands, stroking it gently. He began to fondle her full breasts, when suddenly she fell to her knees and took his throbbing shaft into her mouth. She ran her tongue all over it and began to suck vigorously. He thought he would die of the pleasure and could barely contain himself. Then she released him and stood up to give him another long, hungry kiss. Sighing, he picked her up and placed her on the bed. He lay down beside her and started kissing her all over.

With gentle hands, he explored every inch of her beautiful body. Reaching down, he put his finger inside her and stroked that secret place of hers, driving her insane with desire. She moaned with pleasure, then pushed him on his back and climbed on top of him. For the first time in her life, she was the one in control! Very deftly, she seized his pulsating manhood and slid it inside herself. She rode him with an uncontrollable lust! Leaning over him, one of her breasts brushed against his lips. He grabbed both of them, held the nipples together and sucked on them both at the same time. She groaned softly and then neither one could wait another moment. They came together in an electrifying thrill that seemed to last forever!

Finally, they collapsed in each other's arms. Eric continued kissing her gently and held her as though he couldn't bear to release her. Shannon had never realized it could be like this. Sex with her husband was either boring or painful, never this beautiful or satisfying! When Larry was done, he usually just rolled over and went to sleep. Now she had another problem to face. Sex with Eric was pure Heaven! But she wasn't sure if she really loved him and her conscience wouldn't permit her to carry on an affair with him. She certainly felt no remorse regarding her unfaithful husband, but she had no right to hurt Elaine. She tried to gently disentangle herself from his arms.

"Eric, that was truly fantastic, but it was still a mistake. We can't ever do this again! We can't risk hurting Elaine."

He held her even more tightly, refusing to let her go. "Shannon, don't leave! Can't you see that I'm in love with you?"

She placed her fingers over his lips. "You're confusing love with lust! Eric, it's late. I have to go home." She kissed him one last time and rose to leave.

Eric knew he couldn't keep her against her will. But she was wrong! It was love! And he didn't know what to do about it. He only knew that she had captured his heart and soul for all time!

The two of them had been so lost in rapture that they never heard Larry's car pull into the driveway. Larry had quietly entered his home and tiptoed into the bedroom, so as not to awaken Shannon. When he discovered, much to his surprise, that she was not in bed, he searched the house for her. It finally dawned on him that she was gone. Instantly irritated, he began talking to himself. "Where in the Hell could she be at one o'clock in the morning?" He walked back outside and saw that her car was still in the driveway. "She's probably mad at me for staying out so late. I'll bet she's taking a late-night walk just to worry me." He looked up and down the street and noticed the lights were still on at Eric's house. He saw the shape of a woman silhouetted against a curtain in the upstairs bedroom. He laughed. "Well, well! I didn't know Eric had it in him. Hell, I don't blame him! With the old lady gone, why not have a good time? Life's just too short to spend it with one woman!" Standing in the shadow of the big oak tree in his front yard, he took one last look in that direction and saw an incredible sight! Shannon, his Shannon, was walking down the front steps of Eric's house!

CHAPTER 7 LARRY

Shaken to the core, Larry rushed back through the shadows into his home without being seen by Shannon. He quietly closed the door and leaned against it, his mind in a raging turmoil. He broke into a severe sweat and suddenly felt sick to his stomach! Until this moment, he hadn't quite realized how much Shannon meant to him. Suddenly, all the other women seemed like a complete waste of time. Dear God! What if he actually lost her? What an idiot he'd been, stroking his ego at her expense. The final cost would be his, of course. His instincts warned him not to confront her, to pretend that he suspected nothing. As he heard her approaching their door, he ran to their sofa and lay down on it, feigning fatigue. He heard the front door open and watched Shannon enter the room. She looked disheveled and distraught. Trying to appear calm, he slowly sat up. "Hi, Honey! I didn't know you were still up. I guess it was too warm to sleep, huh?" He walked over to her and gave her a hug. "I'm glad to see you, Sweetheart. I missed you."

He tried to kiss her, but she averted her face. She wouldn't meet his eyes. "I'm sorry, Larry. I don't feel well. I thought a walk in the fresh air would do me some good, but it didn't help much. I'm really tired; I'm going to bed. I'll talk to you in the morning." She turned and went upstairs to their room.

Larry sat back down on the sofa, holding his head in his hands. He wondered if it were already too late for him. She must have been pretty miserable to actually have an affair! She just wasn't the type for it. It was completely out of character. And with Eric, of all people! Even he wouldn't have considered playing around with a neighbor. It was way too risky! No wonder she had looked so distraught. Damn! He should have seen it coming! He wondered just how long this had been going on. God, he'd like to kill that bastard! To make matters worse, he would have to pretend they were still friends. He knew that pressing the issue at this point would only increase his odds of losing her. He'd rather die first!

Larry thought back to their wedding day. Shannon had been so exquisitely beautiful in her bridal gown, his heart had ached with happiness! That day was only three years ago. How had things managed to change so much in such a short time? He remembered how Sherri, one of the girls at his office, had started flirting with him. He had been flattered and one thing soon led to another. It seemed like such harmless fun at the time, but it had evolved into his first affair. He recalled how guilty he had felt and, after a while, he'd broken up with her. After that, there had been a random series of affairs and each time his feelings of guilt had lessened. He rationalized that men, after all, were not monogamous by nature, and what she didn't know couldn't possibly hurt her. How wrong he had been! He was just beginning to realize the depth of her despair. Somehow, women always knew. They didn't need any proof; they just knew!

He went upstairs to bed and held Shannon in his arms while she slept. He would have to find a way to make everything up to her. It was a long time before he was able to sleep.

Shannon awoke with a start and looked at the clock. Oh, my God! It was eleven in the morning already! Eric's wife, Elaine, was arriving today and they were supposed to meet him at his house at noon! The three of them had planned to pick her up at the airport. She shook Larry. "Wake up! We're going to be late! It's almost noon! Come on! Wake up!" She shook him again.

Larry groaned and rolled over. "I'm too tired! Let's call him and tell him we can't make it."

"We can't do that! What would Elaine think? Did you forget that we're all supposed to go out to dinner afterwards? This has been planned for a long time. Get up!"

She tried to push Larry out of bed, but he grabbed her and pulled her to him. "All right! I'll get up, on one condition. Where's my kiss?"

She tried to pull away, but he was too strong. Trapped, she gave him a light kiss, which he turned into a long one. Then he released her. Confused by his tenderness, she headed for the shower. Maybe there was hope for them after all. Well, she would soon find out. This was the day she would invite Eric and Elaine on the trip. Even after what had happened, she still wanted their company. She was confident that she could control the situation. She refused to acknowledge, even to herself, that she secretly yearned for another interlude like last night.

Dreading the ordeal looming in front of him, Larry finished dressing and tried to prepare himself for making small talk with that bastard! The thought of them in bed together made his stomach churn with bitterness! Maybe taking a wilderness trip together wasn't such a bad idea, after all. If he could just get Eric alone, he'd shove that jerk off a cliff! If only he could erase from his mind the picture of them wrapped around each other. He knew he'd better try, or he'd never get through the day.

Shannon looked at her watch. "Larry! It's almost noon. Aren't you ready yet?"

37

He walked silently up behind her, putting his arm around her waist. "I'm right here, Sweetheart. Let's go."

She was both pleased and surprised by his change of attitude. She felt even guiltier about last night. She smiled at him and, holding hands, they walked over to Eric's house.

Eric saw them coming and quickly went outside to meet them. With a short greeting, he hurriedly ushered them into his car. It was difficult for him to meet their eyes, so he decided to rush things along. As they began their long drive to the airport, the tension was so thick, it could have been cut with a knife. All three of them started to say something at the same time and then they all became silent at the same time! Eric laughed nervously. "So, Larry, what have you been up to? I haven't seen you around lately."

"Oh, just the same old stuff." He couldn't resist the opening. "I'll bet I know what you've been up to, though."

Eric reacted with a start. "Huh? What are you talking about?"

"It's all right, Eric. You don't have to play dumb with me. After all, when the cat's away, the mice will play! Why don't you level with me? With Elaine gone, I'll bet you've been a bad boy! Go ahead; tell me I'm wrong."

Shannon choked and then found her voice. "What's the matter with you, Larry? You can't speak to Eric like that!"

"Relax, Honey. I'm only kidding. It's just man-talk. Right, Eric?"

Feeling intensely uncomfortable, Eric visibly paled. He gave Larry a long, menacing look in the rear-view mirror. "Yeah, right! Just man-talk. We guys understand each other, don't we, Larry?" Eric decided that two could play this game. He also decided he'd better get Shannon alone and find out just how much Larry actually knew. He reasoned that he probably didn't know everything, or he wouldn't just be playing word games. Maybe he was just suspicious, since he was such a playboy himself. He could see that it was going to be a long day!

It was early afternoon when they finally pulled in to the airport. It hadn't been an easy trip. They were about fifteen minutes early, so they found some seats and settled in to await Elaine's arrival. Larry kept giving strange, unfathomable looks to Eric. The look on Eric's face was grim. Worried, Shannon looked from one to the other. She couldn't believe how Larry was acting! He couldn't possibly suspect anything, or could he? Unable to cope with the tension, she excused herself and headed for the restroom.

Glaring at Larry, Eric burst from his seat and confronted him. "Listen up, Jerk-off! What's with all these Goddamned looks of yours? If you've got something on your feeble mind, you'd better spill it right now!"

"What's the matter, Eric? Feeling guilty?"

"Look who's talking! If anyone should feel guilty around here, it's you! What in the world would I have to feel guilty about, anyway? Anything I've done is more than justified and I'd happily do it again. In fact, I'm planning on it! And there's not a damned thing you can do about it, you weak piece of shit!"

"We'll see about that! You think you're pretty tough, don't you? But a gun is a great equalizer! Understand, Hotshot? You'd better get one thing straight right now; the only way you'll ever get Shannon away from me is over my dead body!"

"That's just the way I'd prefer to do it! But I won't need a gun!"

They both turned as they heard Elaine calling.

39

Shannon returned just in time to see Elaine rush into Eric's arms and give him a long kiss. Something burned in the pit of her stomach. Wait a minute! How could she be jealous? She kept telling herself that she didn't really love him. Besides, Elaine was her friend. She glanced over at Larry and caught him staring at her in the strangest way; he seemed almost vulnerable. She hurried over to Elaine and gave her a big hug. "I'm so happy to see you! It seems like you've been gone forever."

Elaine positively glowed. "I've missed you, too. It's so good to be back! I'm starved; where are we going to eat?" She was too overjoyed to notice the hostilities.

Eric and Larry looked at each other, both silently acknowledging an unspoken truce. Shannon sighed, grateful for the temporary relief. "I thought we might eat at Benihana's. It's a really fun place to eat and the food's great! I know you'd enjoy it, Elaine. By the way, it's our treat!"

"Thanks, Shannon. It sounds wonderful!"

The general atmosphere and entertaining way in which their meals were served kept them too busy to think about their problems. They all had a good time in spite of themselves. Shannon knew she had made a wise choice in restaurants. However, she was dreading the long ride home.

During the first half of their drive, Elaine had been telling them all about her visit with her mother and sisters. She turned to Eric, feeling a little embarrassed. "Goodness! I've been doing all the talking! Tell me what's been happening while I've been away. Anything exciting going on?"

Larry responded. "Yeah, you might say that! At least I think it's been pretty exciting around here lately. Don't you think so, Eric?"

Flushing angrily, Eric replied. "Yeah! But not as

exciting as it's going to be!"

Elaine looked puzzled. "What are you guys talking about?"

Shannon quickly interceded. "They're talking about our big surprise for you, Elaine. We're all taking a vacation together in the mountains!"

Looking bewildered, Eric tried to interrupt, but Shannon wouldn't allow it. "Shut up, Eric! Let me tell her about the trip. It's going to be very exciting! We're going on a guided wilderness tour in the northern part of the state. Tony and Caitlin are going too, only they don't know it yet. We wanted to tell you first. Just think, Elaine! Sleeping under the stars, swimming in secluded rivers and horseback riding through the forest. I can't wait! I can just smell that mountain air already! Well, what do you think?"

Elaine was thrilled. She hugged Eric. "Oh, Honey, what a wonderful surprise! When do we leave? What should I pack?"

While she happily babbled on, Eric gave Shannon a soul-searing look in the rear-view mirror. His eyes were so filled with yearning and frustration, that she felt pierced through the heart. 'Dear God!' she thought, 'What have I done?'

CHAPTER 8 IL ITALIANO

It was a warm Saturday afternoon and Tony Salerno was relaxing in his favorite place, the hammock stretched between two trees in the large backyard of his Citrus Heights home. He had just finished mowing his lawn and the fragrant aroma of newly-cut grass was wafting on the light breeze. He reveled in the comfort of the swinging hammock, the delightful perfume of the June flowers and, especially, the glorious peace and quiet of the day. This happy interlude had been made possible by his wife, Caitlin. She had taken their adorable, but noisy, twins to a matinee. Thank God for small favors! Now he had time to mull over the invitation they'd just received from Shannon. Actually, the idea of a two-week vacation in the mountains sounded like Heaven to him. The problem was with Cat; she hated leaving their sons behind, but there was no way they could go. Her sister had already agreed to watch them, so they didn't have to worry about a baby-sitter. But Cat had strong opinions about the importance of family vacations. In fact, they had spent the morning arguing the point and they would probably spend the evening continuing the debate. Sometimes, Tony thought all they did was argue. He tried to recall how it was with them in the beginning, when they had found more pleasant ways to spend their time. Lost in thoughts of the past, Tony slowly dozed off......

As he slipped into the hazy realm of dreams, he recognized the Caitlin of his youth approaching him. She was tall, slender and had long, light brown hair. She was a little too thin, with a pleasant, almost pretty

43

face and legs that went on forever. It was the legs that appealed to him the most; he wanted to slide his hand up between her legs, her inviting legs. He reached, almost there, and reached again; then he was falling through the mists, drifting......

He landed with a crash and woke up cursing. "This Goddamn piece of shit hammock! That does it! I'm all done falling out of this thing. I'm getting a new one! I don't care what Cat says!"

The sound of laughter reached his ears and he turned, startled into abrupt silence. Damn! It was Shannon. How Embarrassing!

"I'm sorry, Tony. I didn't mean to startle you, but it was so funny. One minute you were reaching out and the next minute you just toppled out on the lawn! I couldn't believe my eyes. Are you all right?"

"Yeah, yeah! Rub it in, why don't you? I'm just the local clown, right?" His pride hurt, he stood, half glaring at her, still dusting himself off.

"Now, Tony, don't get mad! I was in the neighborhood and just dropped by to see what you two had decided on the trip."

She was always amazed at how quickly he became irritated over the smallest things. At least he was equally quick to calm down and return to good spirits. She really liked Tony; he was one of the very few, truly good people she had ever known. He would give you the shirt off his back if he thought you needed it. Cat was very different from him; when she got mad, she stayed mad. You wouldn't want her for an enemy. And she was very practical; if she gave you the shirt off her back, she'd probably charge you for it!

"Well, Tony, I hope you two have decided to go. It just wouldn't be the same without you!"

Tony knew she meant it. They had always been the best of friends. He'd always heard that men and women couldn't really be friends; they were either lovers or enemies, nothing in between. Bullshit! He knew better than that. He and Shannon had been best friends for years. Of course, every now and then, he had sort of fantasized about her, but, what the Hell! That's all it had ever been, just a fantasy. She was still his best friend and he'd challenge anyone to say otherwise!

"Listen, Kitten, I'm dying to go! You know it's always been my fondest dream to die with a fishing rod in my hand! But Cat thinks it's a sin to take a vacation without the kids. So, the only answer I've got for you is that we're still fighting about it!"

"Maybe I should talk to her, Tony. Would it do any good?"

"No, I don't think so. You'd better let me handle it; you know what a hothead she is. But don't worry. She might win most of the fights, but I'm damn well gonna win this one!"

After Shannon left, Tony decided to check out his motorhome. Maybe it would help his cause if he made sure it was extra clean and ready for a long trip. As he stepped into the Winnebago, a wave of pleasure washed over him. This thing was a real beauty! He kept it in such good repair, it really didn't need a cleaning. It was his pride and joy! Although they had owned it for three years, it still looked brand new. Sitting at the spotless table, memories flooded his mind. He remembered that first summer after buying it......

Cat and the kids were spending two weeks with her folks back in Maryland. He had never gotten along with her parents and had flatly refused to go. They'd fought and fought about it! She screamed and cried, but he remained adamant in his refusal. It was one of the few times he didn't back down. In the end, he was left with a very angry wife and a glorious two weeks to spend all alone with his precious Winnebago!

At first, much to his surprise, he felt a little lost without his family. He didn't quite know what to do with himself. He found himself confronted by that one flaw which is common to all marriages, the good and the bad, namely the loss of one's individuality. Even in the best of marriages, people usually feel less than whole without their mates. Everything in life has its price and that feeling of loss is part of the cost of true commitment.

After spending a few days fishing, Tony became restless. He decided to drop by the local bicycle store and check on a part for his son's bike. He had been in the small store many times and knew the owners quite well. It was a popular place for a lot of young families, especially the men. They were all drawn to the owner's wife, Nicole. She worked part-time at the business, mainly on weekends. The store was fairly busy during the week, but on the weekends, it was like a beehive and Nicole was the queen bee! She was French and had an exotic look about her, with her long, dark hair and deep green eyes. She was very dignified, almost aloof, but when she finally deigned to look at you, she made you feel like you were the only person in the world who mattered. Over the last several months, the one she had been watching was Tony. He was both amazed and flattered by her attention; after all, hers was the face that haunted his dreams on many a long night. But why him? She could have anyone, literally anyone! It wasn't as though he considered himself unattractive, but he knew there were many men, much better looking, all competing for her attention. Tony felt both proud and somewhat bothered by the envious looks on their faces. Meanwhile, he didn't quite know how to respond to Nicole. After all, her rather oblique looks didn't exactly signify an open invitation, but merely offered the suggestion of one.

There was a mixture of emotions churning within

him and he needed to sort them out. First in importance, he knew he didn't want to risk a divorce and not just because he was a staunch Catholic. He truly loved Caitlin and his sons and would never leave them. He had indulged in a few affairs along the way, but only in those that were popularly known as one-night stands. He had never permitted himself to become emotionally involved with another woman. Secondly, he had a strong conscience and Tom North, Nicole's husband, was a very good friend of his. Tony often dropped by the store after work just to visit with him. How could he betray such a good friend and still live with himself? His third consideration was Nicole, herself. There was so much more to her than just physical beauty. Technically, there were many women more beautiful than she, but none who could capture a man's attention the way she did. When entering a crowded room, noisy chatter would abate, as though by some imperial decree, and all heads would turn in her direction. Her charisma was that strong and there was something else about her, something elusive that defied definition. He was unable to pin down that mystical quality; he only knew that he desired her to the point that he was afraid to think about her. His instincts warned him away from her; he knew her allure was dangerous, that he could easily fall in love with her. She would never be a one-night stand. Yet, when in her presence, he could feel his will power crumbling. Today, checking on that part for his son's bike, he realized that it was only an excuse. He had been drawn there, like a magnet, hoping she was working that day. He approached the counter and felt the back of his neck tingling. He turned around and found her watching him in that beguiling way of hers. She got up from her desk and walked slowly toward him. His mind blanked! He couldn't think of one word to say to her; yet, at the same time, he was unable to look away from her penetrating gaze. Stepping uncomfortably close to him, she spoke, almost in a whisper.

"It's good to see you again, Tony. You've been missed."

He swallowed hard. "It's good to see you again, too. How've you been?"

"I've been fine, Tony, just fine. Could I ask you a favor?"

"Of course! Uh......anything! Just ask!" He was stumbling over his words and felt foolish.

"Tom's at a business conference and will be gone all week. Unfortunately, I've had some problems with my car and had to drop it off at the shop for repairs. I could really use a ride home tonight. Some of the guys have already offered their assistance, but you're the only one I trust. How about it, Tony?"

His will was not his own; he was completely mesmerized by her. Nervously, he answered. "Sure, Nicole, I'd be glad to. What time do you want me here?"

......Tony should have known better than to tempt fate. After all, whatever Destiny wants, Destiny takes!

CHAPTER 9 LIAISON

Tom and Nicole North lived down a secluded country lane in El Dorado Hills, a small, attractive community in the foothills east of Sacramento. On a heavily-treed five acre parcel, they had built a lovely, Mediterranean-style villa that wrapped around a giant oak tree. They chose this location because they thought it would be a perfect place to raise children. But that was four years ago and so far Nicole had been unable to conceive. She had endured every possible test, always with the same results; there was nothing physically wrong with her. Tom had promised numerous times to have himself tested, but somehow managed never to keep his appointments. He always had a good excuse and was definitely going to take care of it next month, always next month! Meanwhile, one year disappeared into the next.

Nicole had every reason to believe that the problem was with her husband. She strongly suspected that the reason he was forever missing his appointments was that he couldn't bring himself to face the probability of being infertile. In most relationships, there is usually one who loves more than he or she is loved. In this case, it was Tom; he cherished Nicole more than life itself. He was so afraid that she would leave him if he were unable to give her children. Although he had never actually voiced his feelings, Nicole understood exactly how he felt. With her European heritage, she would never have considered pushing the matter any further. According to her upbringing, a good wife does not cause her husband to feel less than a man; instead, she finds other, more subtle ways to solve her problems.

Nicole had been aware for some time that Tony was attracted to her. Of course, she was also aware that most men were drawn to her, but Tony was the only one she would consider to father her children. She chose him for a variety of reasons. First, he was intelligent, handsome and of good character. Second, he was happily married and a devout Catholic, so she wouldn't have to worry about breaking up his marriage or her own. After all, she really did love Tom and had no wish to leave him. But she desperately wanted children and she wanted Tom to believe they were his own. Since he would probably never be tested, he would assume the children were his. Her third and last reason was that she wasn't a loose woman. She didn't think she could go to bed with just anyone. Out of all the men she knew, Tony was the only one she sincerely liked and admired. He had only to walk through the door to brighten her day. He had such a wonderful sense of humor! Very often, when she had been downcast, he would sit by her desk and tease her into laughter. He could remove the clouds from a rainy day!

Speaking of rain, Nicole looked out the window of her store and could hardly believe her eyes. It was early June and the day had begun unusually sunny and warm, but now, at six in the afternoon, raindrops were splashing against her window. What an unexpected change in the weather! She had worn only a light, summer dress. Looking outside, she shivered in anticipation of the cold. She saw Tony pulling in to the front of the store; he was right on time. As he was getting out of his car, she quickly locked the front door. He walked over to her.

"Nicole, where's your coat? Aren't you freezing in that thin dress?"

"I didn't bring one, Tony. The day started out so

warm, I didn't think I'd need one."

She couldn't stop shivering. He removed his jacket and wrapped it around her shoulders, allowing his arm to linger just a little longer than necessary. She continued to shiver, but not from the cold. As Tony opened the door for her, their eyes met for a brief, electric moment! They both looked quickly away. Tony walked around to his side and got in. Fumbling with his keys for a few, tense seconds, he finally managed to start the motor. Leaving it at an idle, he slowly turned to look at her.

"What about dinner? Are you hungry? We could eat somewhere before I take you home."

Nicole flushed slightly. "No thanks, Tony. I'm not really hungry yet. Besides, I have plenty at the house. We could eat there, if you want."

"Sounds great! Anything's fine with me."

While they drove, the temperature dropped dramatically; the driving rain changed to hail and pelted the windshield relentlessly. The violence of the sudden storm awed them into silence. About halfway to the villa, the intensity of the storm lightened almost imperceptibly. Tony broke the silence.

"Nicole, you've been unusually quiet. There's something wrong, isn't there? Why don't you tell me what it is?"

"You're very perceptive, Tony. That's one of the many things I like about you. There is something wrong, terribly wrong, but I don't quite know how to broach the subject without offending you."

"Nicole! You could never offend me! You can tell me anything, ask me anything. My God! Aren't we friends?"

"All right! But first promise me that I won't lose your friendship no matter what I ask of you. And that you'll never repeat what I'm going to say to you. Swear

51

it!"

"I promise! Now tell me this terrible secret of yours."

"Tom is unable to get me pregnant and I want children. He refuses to be tested, but I have been and I know the problem is not with me. I need a good man, one that I like and trust, to father my children. You're the only one I would consider."

Tony was shocked into silence. Nicole was afraid to look at him. She should have known better than to suggest such a thing! She wished she could take back the words.

They pulled into her driveway, the tires crunching against the wet gravel. As he came to a stop, she reached for the door handle. Tony grabbed her arm, pulling her to him. "Don't you want to hear my answer first?"

Nicole felt a chill go through her body. "I thought......"

Tony interrupted her with a kiss, long and sweet. "The answer is yes!"

Overwhelmed by a mixture of relief and anticipation, her eyes filled with tears. All at once, his last inhibitions removed, Tony felt extremely protective of her. "Don't cry, Nicole. Everything will turn out just fine."

His kindness only made her tears flow more freely. Turning her face up toward his, he began to kiss away her tears. Nicole hadn't been this happy in years. She ceased her crying and hesitantly returned his kisses. Tony groaned with pleasure. "Nicole, I sure hope you meant for something to happen today, because I'm about as ready as I'll ever be!"

He grabbed her hand and placed it on his crotch. Caught off guard, she instinctively tried to remove her hand, but he wouldn't let her. She could feel his throbbing shaft through his Levis and forced herself to stroke it. She had never been unfaithful and hadn't expected it to be this difficult. She felt herself both attracted to him and a little afraid of him, all at once. Not trusting her voice, she smiled at him and motioned him into the villa. He got out and rushed around to her side. Opening her door, he helped her out of the car. They walked up the steps to the massive front door. This time it was her turn to fumble with keys. She dropped them and they both bent over at the same time to retrieve them. Laughing nervously, Tony took the keys and opened the door. Looking pale, Nicole just stood there, as though in a trance. Tony knew the rest was up to him. He picked her up and carried her inside. She was so light, it was like lifting a feather. Still holding her, he walked toward the stairs. "Where's the bedroom?"

"It's upstairs. Put me down, Tony. I can walk." Silently, they climbed the stairs. Tony glanced inside the first bedroom. She quickly grabbed his arm. "No! Not that one! That's our bedroom! I can't......I mean......"

"Calm down, Nicole. I understand. Where's the guest bedroom?"

"Follow me. It's over here."

She turned into the furthest bedroom. It was beautifully decorated, all done in soft pastels. Seeing how nervous she was, he tried to soothe her.

"We don't have to do anything right away, if you don't want to. I could come back another time."

"No, Tony! Please don't leave. We have to get this over with. I mean......"

He laughed and held her close again, stroking her back. "It's all right; I understand. Let's just lie down on the bed together and get comfortable. Remember, we're not going to do anything until you're ready."

The storm had brought an early darkness with it so that Nicole felt more at ease removing her clothes. Even in the dim light, Tony was awed by her petite beauty. She was small, but perfectly proportioned. Slightly embarrassed, she quickly slid under the covers. Tony hastily threw his clothing aside and slid in beside her. This was all just too good to be true; he felt that he must be dreaming! She reminded him of a fawn, so easily frightened was she. Proceeding slowly, he held her gently and covered her with light kisses. He was so gentle with her that she felt herself relaxing. Even more, she felt herself responding to his caresses. She put her arms around him and rubbed her breasts against him. He shuddered violently as he began to squeeze her breasts. He felt her nipples harden and lowered his mouth to suck on them. He could feel himself losing control; he didn't know if he could wait much longer. Reaching down, she began stroking his swollen member. Tony yelled out loud, "Oh, no!" He quickly seized his throbbing shaft and tried to mount her, but it was too late! Before he could manage to put it inside her, he found himself coming all over the outside of her soft, inviting mound. "Oh, God! I'm so sorry, Nicole! You must think I'm an idiot! Are you sure you want me to be the father of your children?"

Nicole laughed and held him gently. "Tony, it's perfectly all right! Actually, I feel quite flattered that you desired me so much that you were unable to wait. That's the nicest compliment I've ever received!"

Tony felt greatly relieved. "Well, anyway, I guess it's a great ice-breaker! I'll bet neither one of us will be quite so nervous next time."

After Tony had gone home, Nicole lay awake in her bed for a very long time. Thinking about the evening, she realized that certain things would never again be the same for her. The smell of a man's leather jacket, a violent hailstorm, the fragrance of a certain after-shave, all these things would forever remind her of Tony. Life was strange. Just when you thought you had everything figured out, life would throw you a curve. This entire arrangement was supposed to be only a quick cure for her problems, but it just wasn't that simple. She wasn't supposed to have any deep feelings for him, but when he held her close and kissed her tenderly, she realized that he had captured at least some small portion of her heart. She would never again be able to regard him as only a dear friend. And what about Tom? She knew she still loved him deeply. Until now, it had never occurred to her that you can indeed love two men at the same time. She was so confused. She had known women who bragged about various affairs and claimed they had no real feelings for the men involved. They said they just used them to spice up their otherwise dreary lives. She had hoped an affair would be equally simple for her; there was no room in her life for complications. But there was no denying the feelings that engulfed her while she was in his arms. She was a woman afflicted with deep emotions. For her, lovemaking would always go hand in hand with love.

In spite of everything, Nicole was still determined to go through with her plans. More than anything, she wanted her own children. She called Cathy, her part-time helper, to fill in for her for the rest of the week and the weekend. Tom wouldn't be home from his trip until Monday, so she felt safe. The weather had cleared up nicely and she and Tony made plans to head for the mountains. Tony carefully provisioned his Winnebago, picked up Nicole and they left early in the morning for an experience neither of them would ever forget.

They were driving up Interstate 50, which begins in Sacramento and crosses over the mountains into Nevada. They were on the California side, heading for the campgrounds near Wrights Lake, when Tony came up with a better idea. "Nicole, the campgrounds are likely to be crowded. We might even run into someone we know. I know of a more secluded area, closer to the summit. Shall we try it?"

"You're right, Tony! I should have thought of that."

When they were close to the summit, Tony pulled off on a side road which wound around the side of the mountain for miles and then he turned off on a dirt road leading to a very secluded meadow, surrounded on three sides by heavy forest. They parked on a nice level spot and got out to stretch their legs. The mountain air was intoxicating and provocative. What is it about forest odors that turn a person's thoughts to sex? Whatever it is, they were both immediately affected and, without a word, climbed back into the Winnebago. They stood by the bed for a few moments, hungrily kissing each other. After hurriedly undressing, he lifted her upon the bed. Climbing in beside her, he spread her legs apart. This time, he was taking no chances! He would make certain she was ready. He gently spread apart the soft lips of her private area and put his tongue inside her as far as he could. He stroked her over and over with his tongue until she moaned in desperation. "Please, I can't wait any longer!" He quickly mounted her, pumping himself into her again and again. "Now, Tony, now!" He could feel her coming as he filled her with his seed. Breathing hard, they clung to each other. "My God, Tony! That was so wonderful!"

He stayed inside her for a long time, kissing her over and over again. For the first time in his life, Tony knew what it was to make love with a truly passionate woman! Like Nicole, Tony also didn't want any emotional complications in his life. But he also knew that he didn't ever want to give her up. Oh well, he'd have to cross that bridge when he came to it. Meanwhile, he would be kept happily busy trying to impregnate her. Their time together was blissful, literally filled with lovemaking. Tony wouldn't have thought it possible to complete the act of lovemaking so often; they just couldn't seem to get enough of each other. Although neither of them knew it, by the time they left for home on Sunday night, Nicole was pregnant!

Sleeping late the following morning, Tony was awakened by the sound of his phone ringing. Not fully awake, he answered in a sleepy voice.

"Hello, Tony's not in at the moment, so please leave a message at the beep."

"Tony! Quit fooling around! This is Cat and I'd like a ride home from the airport, if you can find the time!"

Now he was fully awake! "Cat! What are you doing back so soon? It's only Monday! You were supposed to stay until Friday. Where are you calling from?"

"Tony, is your brain working yet? I said I'm at the airport. Now get your ass out of bed and get the Hell over here! By the way, I've been trying to reach you for the past five days. I think you're going to have a lot of explaining to do when I get you alone. Now hurry up!"

She hung up before he could say another word. Tony jumped out of bed, muttering to himself while he threw his clothes on. "Jesus Christ! This is all I need!" All the way to the airport, he kept trying to think of a plausible explanation for his absence. He decided the most believable story would be that he simply took off in their new Winnebago and explored some mountain roads.

As he pulled into the airport, he saw Cat and the kids waiting right out in front. The minute he got out of

57

the car, he was assailed by the twins. They were so happy to see him, they almost knocked him over as they leaped into his arms! He hugged them both, set them down and walked over to Cat to give her a kiss. She looked strained. "Tony, I'm very tired. Let's just get home as fast as we can."

The drive home was filled with the chatter of his children, but Cat was noticeably silent. After reaching their home, unloading their luggage and getting the kids settled in, Tony noticed that Cat wasn't in the house. He walked outside just in time to see her stepping into their Winnebago. Then he realized he hadn't yet had a chance to clean out the motorhome. What if Nicole had dropped an earring or, worse yet, what if Cat noticed certain, unmistakable spots on the bedsheets? Starting to panic, Tony rushed inside after Cat, only to find her methodically searching the motorhome. She turned toward him and gave him a scathing look. Tony broke into an intense sweat! "What are you looking for, Cat? Can I help you find something?" She stopped her search only long enough to give him an even more menacing glare, but she still didn't speak. Having completed her search of the kitchen area, she moved to the bed. Tony rushed to her side, grabbed her by the arm and spun her around to face him. "This has gone on long enough! Just what in the Hell are you looking for? Answer me!"

"What's the matter, Tony? Afraid of what I'll find?" She jerked her arm away from him and pulled back the top sheet. With an angry gasp, she turned toward Tony and slapped him hard across the face! She had found what she was looking for!

CHAPTER 10 DISCOVERIES

The past three years hadn't been easy ones for Tony and Caitlin. It took quite a while, but she had finally forgiven him for what he had claimed was only a brief interlude with someone who hadn't mattered to him at all. It was fortunate for Tony that she hadn't noticed the remarkable similarity between him and one of Nicole's two children. The younger one was an adorable, one-year-old, little girl, who was the image of Nicole. But the older child, a two-year-old boy, strongly resembled Tony. Although Caitlin seemed unaware of the resemblance, it wasn't lost on Tom. He had known for some time that the children weren't his. Even more than the question of looks, Tom was aware that Nicole had been behaving differently toward him for a long time. It was just after he had returned from a business conference over three years ago that he first noticed her unusual behavior......

......She had always been a passionate woman, but suddenly seemed different during their lovemaking, somehow more reticent. He couldn't put his finger on it, but she just wasn't the same. She appeared to have a generally guilty air about her. Tom was bewildered; she had never acted this way before. Then, a few weeks after he had been home from his trip, Nicole began to suffer from morning sickness. The thought of pregnancy hadn't occurred to him; he'd assumed it was the flu. Upon returning from an appointment with her doctor, Nicole approached him hesitantly with her news.

"Tom, you were wrong. This isn't the flu. Can you believe it? I'm pregnant!"

59

Tom was simultaneously shocked and thrilled. "Nicki! Oh, my beautiful Nicki! You've just made me the happiest man in the whole world!"

He picked her up and danced around the room with her. Laughing, she begged for mercy. "Tom, put me down! You're making me dizzy."

He set her down very gently and held her, looking into her eyes with such adoration, she was instantly besieged by another wave of guilt. Her eyes filled with tears. "Tom, does it mean that much to you?"

"Darling! Of course it does! Doesn't it mean as much to you? I thought you wanted children more than anything in the world! Aren't you as happy as I am?"

"Oh, yes! I'm very happy! I just meant, you know, we've had so much time alone with each other......I was afraid you might resent the baby! I mean......"

She was stumbling over her words and seemed quite agitated. He should have realized then that something was very, very wrong. However, blinded by his love for Nicole and his extreme joy in her wonderful news, the only feeling he had was complete rapture. Only after their son had his first birthday, did Tom begin to doubt Nicole. Tony, Caitlin and their twins were among the guests at the birthday party. Nicole had gone into the kitchen to bring out some more refreshments and Tony had followed her. Tom thought nothing of it at the moment, but then he decided to go in the kitchen for some more ice. As he entered the doorway, he found the two of them wrapped up in a passionate kiss! They were too engrossed to notice him and he quickly retreated. Suddenly, he could no longer hear the noise of the party; all he could hear was the sound of his own heart hammering in his ears. As though in a fog, he slowly became aware that someone was calling his name. Shaking his head to clear the mists, he realized that it was Caitlin!

"Tom, are you all right? You look like you've just seen a ghost! What's the matter?"

He tried to appear calm, but his voice was shaky. "Nothing! Nothing at all. I was just feeling a little queasy; it must have been something I ate."

"That's good. You had me worried there for a minute. Well, excuse me, Tom. I have to find Tony; we're supposed to be leaving."

She turned toward the kitchen. Tom quickly grabbed her arm and pulled her along with him. "I just saw Tony walk out in the front yard. Come on; I'll walk out with you." He'd managed to buy Tony and Nicole some time and had averted what would have been a very ugly scene.

For the time being, Tom succeeded in acting nonchalant and even tried to convince himself that she had only been flirting at the party, that it couldn't really have been serious. In the end, he couldn't stand the suspense. He had to know the truth, once and for all! About four months after the party and without Nicole's knowledge, he forced himself to make an appointment to be tested. This time he kept the appointment! Once the result of the test arrived, he was not at all surprised to find that he was indeed infertile, but he was devastated by the ramifications of the knowledge. Numbed by the absolute certainty of Nicole's infidelity, he drove home without even remembering the act of driving. Wondering how on Earth he would ever cope with this knowledge, he was greeted at the door by a very exuberant Nicole.

"Darling! Guess what? I'm pregnant again! Isn't it wonderful?"

Stunned by still another shock, Tom did his best to retain his composure. He reached out and hugged her, but this time he didn't dance around the room with her.

"Nicole, that's terrific news! Now I won't have to worry about Tommy Jr. being an only child."

"Oh, Tom, I would never have considered such a thing! After all, it would take a very selfish woman to let the discomforts of pregnancy take precedence over the happiness of her child! Believe me, I would never have allowed that to happen."

"I believe you, Sweetheart. I'm certain there's absolutely nothing you wouldn't do to ensure your child's happiness."

Something about the way he had phrased his words gave Nicole cause to worry. She found herself looking for double entendres in everything he said. Deciding to forget about it, she told herself she was probably just being paranoid. Somehow, she would have to learn to cope with her terrible feelings of guilt.

However, as time went by, Tom was the one who succeeded in the art of coping. In spite of everything, he knew that Nicole sincerely loved him and that he truly loved her and the children. After all, their only other alternative would have been adoption. At least, these children were half Nicole's. That was more than enough reason to love them; he didn't care where the other half came from. In the evenings, when he cuddled the two little ones on his lap and Nicole snuggled up next to him, he felt as though he held the world in his arms. In one respect, he was almost grateful to Tony. Without him, he wouldn't be holding these beloved babies at night, or waking the next morning to their adorable smiles. By all the standards that matter, Tom would be their true father. He would be the one to wipe away their tears, celebrate their joys and teach them right from wrong. Besides, he was far from being the only man to raise children that were not of his own seed; it's just that the others rarely knew it.

CHAPTER 11 TIME

In the warmth of the early June evening, the three couples were sitting in Shannon's living room, discussing their plans for the upcoming trip to the mountains. While the sun was making its final descent of the day, Shannon opened the French doors leading to the brick patio, allowing the sweet aroma from her flower garden to float inside and mingle with the various scents of the ladies' perfumes. In the soft twilight, the sound of the crickets seemed unusually loud. Louder still was the laughter and chatter emanating from the room.

They were all laughing at Tony's account of a previous attempt to master the art of horseback riding......

During the time that he was courting Caitlin, she had expressed an interest in learning to ride. He suggested going to a nearby stable and renting a couple of horses for the day. Once they were there, the horses brought to them for inspection appeared old and worn-out. Tony felt insulted.

"I would appreciate it if I could ride one that wasn't on its deathbed!"

"Wait a minute, pardner! You told me you were both beginners. These horses might look a little tired to you, but they're exactly what you need to start out on."

"I'll be the judge of that! Either you can bring me one with a little more life in him or you can forget the whole thing!"

"Take it easy, friend! We aim to please around here. Lively you want, lively you'll get!"

As the stable-hand turned to pick out two others, Caitlin grabbed Tony by the arm and whispered to him. "Tony, I don't want a lively one; I'll settle for one of these tame ones."

Tony quickly yelled to the man. "You only need to bring one fresh horse; the lady's gonna stick with one of the deadbeats!"

"Tony! Did you have to put it like that? Jesus! How embarrassing!"

The stable-hand brought out a young gelding, a beautiful bay with a blaze on his forehead. Tony was more than satisfied; the animal seemed downright frisky! He reached out to pat the horse on his nose, causing the bay to arch his neck, prick his ears forward and stare down at Tony.

"This one will do just fine! Saddle him up and one of those deadbe...... I mean, one of those tame ones."

"Yes Sir! I'll have 'em ready in a flash." While he saddled the horses, he could barely contain a smirk. "I do have one suggestion, Sir, if you don't mind. The bay is pretty fresh and he hasn't been out for a run yet. You really should ride him in the arena before you take him out in the open."

"I don't think that will be necessary; he and I will get along just fine. I'm afraid there's been a little misunderstanding about my ability to ride. You see; the lady is a real beginner, but I used to ride horses on my Grandpa's farm when I was a kid, so I don't think there'll be any problem."

"Tony! You told me it was only an old mule you used to ride and you said you could barely get it to move."

"Cat, I was exaggerating! Besides, how difficult can it be? I'm sure it's just like riding a bicycle; once you've ridden, you can do it again."

"Sir, excuse me, there's just one more thing I'd like to say. I think I should remind you of our safety policy here. If you choose to ride a horse other than the one we recommend, then you ride at your own risk."

"Jesus Christ! You're really worried about this, aren't you? Well, I think you're in for a surprise."

As it turned out, Tony was the one in for a surprise. No sooner had he mounted the bay, than it took off like Hell bent for leather! Tony was almost unseated at the offset, barely managing to hang on to the saddle horn. While they screamed across a large, open meadow, Tony's curses could be heard a mile away. "Whoa, you stupid, Goddamn horse!" The bay did everything but laugh at him. What Tony didn't realize is that a horse instantly knows what kind of rider is on his back and the intelligent bay was well aware that he could get away with almost anything with this particular rider. The bay circled the meadow twice at full gallop; it was a miracle that Tony had thus far succeeded in maintaining his seat. Then the horse turned and raced back toward the corral! Tony's hands were frozen on the saddle horn; he never even tried to pull back on the reins. His eyes were huge as he saw the corral looming closer and closer. He pictured himself plastered against the railing! The bay screeched to a stop just short of crashing into the fence and unceremoniously sent Tony tumbling end over end across the railing. He landed with a hard thud that knocked the wind out of him! He just lay there, spread-eagled in the dust, gasping for air. When he was finally able to sit up, he was mortified to find Cat and the stable-hand laughing so hard they could barely stand!

......After Tony finished relating his memories of that death-defying experience, his audience was doubled over with laughter!

"Well! Thanks a lot! I guess everyone thinks my ordeal was pretty funny. Everyone except me, that is! I wish you'd all keep in mind the fact that I could have been killed, paralyzed, or whatever! That's why I want to suggest an alternative to a horseback vacation. Why don't we backpack instead? God knows it would be safer!"

Eric groaned out loud. "Oh, Tony! Come on; don't wimp out on us now! The arrangements are all made; we've already sent them our money. For Christ's sake, we don't even know if we could get a refund! Besides, isn't it about time you got over your fear of horses? Jesus! You're a grown man and I see little kids riding them all the time."

Elaine broke into the conversation. "Eric, don't be so hard on him! He's absolutely right; he could have been severely injured, or worse. I was a little hesitant to bring it up, but I'm somewhat frightened of horses, too. Let's all be honest with each other. Who wants a horseback vacation and who would prefer to backpack? I think we should take a vote."

They all began to talk at once, until Larry managed to drown them out with his deep voice. "Quiet! Let's have some quiet, please! Here! Everyone grab one of my business cards and write your preference on the back. Then, toss them in this bowl and we'll have a fair vote."

When everyone was done, Larry handed the bowl to Shannon for the count. She carefully put the horseback votes on one side and the backpack votes on the other. "Well, it looks like the horseback riders win, four to two!"

Feeling contrite, Eric turned toward Tony. "I'm sorry about coming on so strong there. I didn't mean to sound rude, but I really think we're all going to have a great time on this trip. I just want us to give it a chance!

We ought to all get together before the trip and spend a weekend practicing our riding. That way, we'll be prepared for the real thing. Well, what do you think?"

"It looks like I don't have much of a choice. I've been out-voted, even by my own wife! Thanks a lot, Cat! Well, I guess I'll just have to make the best of it. And you're right about practicing; we'd all better do that. Anybody know of a good place to ride?"

Shannon had a surprise for all of them. "As a matter of fact, I do know of a good place. I love to ride horses, so, off and on for the past year, I've been riding at a place called the Briar Patch. It's a working dude ranch located just northeast of here and it's not too expensive. They accept guests on the weekends and they have trail rides, barbecues, lessons, just about anything you could name! Why don't we all plan on going next weekend?"

They all started talking at once again. Larry had a worried look on his face. "Quiet! Come on, guys; I'm trying to say something. I know next weekend is the last weekend before the trip, but there's no way I can make it. Shannon, don't look at me like that! Did you forget about my company's annual meeting at the Sheraton in San Francisco? There's no way I can get out of going and you know it!"

Shannon immediately felt guilty. Her first thought was that he probably had some bimbo lined up for the weekend. She had completely forgotten about his meeting. For once, he wasn't lying. "I'm sorry, Honey. You're right; I forgot all about it. Well, I guess the rest of us will just have to go without you. You're already a good rider, so I don't think you need the practice, anyway. Let's have a show of hands. Who's able to go next weekend?"

The only other person not free for the weekend was Elaine. "This is terrible! I've never actually ridden before, so I really need the practice, but my best friend from my college days is getting married on Sunday, and I'm her matron of honor. I can't possibly get out of it! But there's really no reason why the rest of you shouldn't go. I'll just have to learn on our vacation and hope you'll all be patient with me."

Eric was unsuccessfully trying to hide his pleasure at the thought of spending time with Shannon without Larry or Elaine around. Elaine didn't notice, but Larry did. All through the evening, Larry was aware of the looks flashing back and forth between Eric and Shannon, like lightning strikes during a summer storm. If you weren't looking for it, you probably wouldn't notice it, but Larry was constantly watching them.

Caitlin stood up and stretched her legs. "Well, I guess everything's settled. Mmmm, those flowers of yours smell so good! You're lucky to have a green thumb, Shannon. I can't make anything grow!"

The three couples drifted out onto the patio. The sweet aroma of the hyacinth was especially strong and the jasmine was almost intoxicating! The western skyline was painted a deep red by the disappearing rays of the sun, almost the exact shade of red as one of Shannon's carefully tended, velvet-red roses. The serene beauty of the soft, summer evening, the exotic fragrance of the various flowers, even the chirping of the crickets all served to lull the small group into a shared sense of peace and harmony. In a setting such as this, a person's deepest, subconscious thoughts and feelings tend to creep ever so subtly into the conscious mind. It was no coincidence that all six members of the group became silent at the same time. Each of them was lost in thought.

Tony worried about the son and daughter who would never know him as their father. And try as he would, Nicole was never really out of his mind or his heart. They say time heals all wounds. What bullshit! He knew he'd go to his grave loving that woman. Surely the worst thing that can happen to a man is to love two women at the same time!

Seeing the hurt look on Tony's face, Caitlin felt a familiar tug at her heart. She knew all too well that Tony's so-called 'brief interlude' was anything but that. She wondered who the woman was and why Tony was unable to forget her. She didn't know for whom she felt sorrier, herself or Tony. She knew he had ended the affair, but she also knew how badly he had been hurt by it. Tony was a good man and she was confident that he really loved her and the children.   But she was also aware that he must have cared deeply for the other woman. Surely, the cruelest thing that could happen to a person would be to love two people at the same time. She was grateful that it had never happened to her. She knew that time was supposed to heal all wounds. She couldn't understand why it was taking so long for Tony.

Shannon had also noticed the sad look on Tony's face. She wished she knew what was bothering him. He was such a dear friend; she hated to think of him being unhappy. She certainly hoped his life wasn't as complicated as hers had become. Sometimes she felt hopelessly confused. She used to worry constantly about Larry's preoccupation with other women; she had been so afraid of losing him. Now, all of a sudden, he showered her with constant attention and affection. And he almost never went anywhere without her. She used to dream of receiving such devotion from him, but, now that she had it, it just didn't seem all that valuable! She had always thought of herself as unique, someone who had the right set of values. Maybe her self-perception was wrong. Perhaps she was just like everyone else, always wanting what she thought she couldn't have!

Was that why she couldn't get Eric off her mind? Because he belonged to someone else? She didn't think she actually loved him, but, dear God, she was unable to quit thinking about him. Every time she looked at him, she could feel his arms around her and still taste his kisses. She could feel herself grow moist, just being in the same room with him! She knew time was supposed to cure everything. She wondered just how long it would take for her to quit wanting him.

Shannon was so busy thinking about Eric that she never realized she was being carefully scrutinized by Larry. He felt deeply saddened by the knowledge that her thoughts were not of him. He had tried everything he could think of to win her back, but he strongly suspected that he was wasting his time. Her expression was so revealing that he knew exactly what she was feeling whenever she looked at Eric. She had desire written all over her face! He was amazed that the others didn't seem to notice what was so blindingly obvious to him. He was at a loss as to what to do next. What he'd really like to do would be to kill Eric! Even if he could manage it without getting caught, it wouldn't do any good; it would only serve to make a martyr out of him and then she'd never forget him. The only hope he had was time itself. Eventually, time would cure everything. He just had to hope that it wouldn't take too long.

Eric was standing with his arm around Elaine, but his thoughts were of Shannon. She looked unusually beautiful this evening; he hadn't been able to keep his eyes off her. Every time he looked at her, he tasted her kisses all over again, felt his hands on her full breasts, felt himself inside her. God, he wanted her so much! Would he ever be able to forget her? He doubted it. He'd always heard that time cured everything. He knew better. Time could never cure him of wanting her!

70

Of the entire group, only Elaine was completely at peace with herself. Feeling secure in Eric's arms, she sighed contentedly. Elaine truly personified the saying that 'ignorance is bliss'. She didn't have the foggiest notion as to Eric's true feelings. Years ago, in a very troubled childhood, she had learned to protect herself by taking everything at face value. She never allowed herself to probe too deeply into matters of emotional import, because she didn't want to discover anything unpleasant. Therefore, she never had to worry about time curing anything. In fact, she thought that she and Eric had all the time in the world!

CHAPTER 12 THE BRIAR PATCH

Saturday morning dawned with a rosy glow in the eastern sky as the sun peeked around a brilliant, white, cumulous cloud. Eric slowly awoke to the lovely melody of a thrush serenading him from outside his open window. Still in a state of half-sleep, he was just emerging from the mists of a dream. There was something wonderful about the dream, but he couldn't recall exactly what it was. It was slipping out of his reach; he tried to bring it back, but it was too late. The tantalizing dream continued to fade until it was completely gone and he was fully awake. All of a sudden, he realized that today was Saturday and he was about to embark on a trip more wonderful than any dream. Just imagine, a whole weekend to spend with Shannon! He stood up and stretched, walked over to the window and looked out upon a glorious new day. The whole world seemed new to him; he felt reborn. Whistling happily, he headed for the shower. Momentarily interrupted by the sound of Eric's whistling, the thrush cocked its head and listened, then continued with its song, creating a beautiful harmony. As the sun climbed higher, the morning sky changed from a pale blueish-gray with rose accents to a deep, vivid blue. Eric was absolutely correct. It was going to be a beautiful day!

Tony and Caitlin were on their way to pick up Eric and Shannon. Halfway there, Tony started complaining.

"Shit! Wouldn't you know it? I left my sunglasses home. And the sun's so Goddamned bright, I'm going blind!"

"Relax, Tony. They're right here. I picked them up for you on my way out the door. You always forget them!"

"What do you mean, 'I always forget them'? I don't always forget them! Are you trying to start a fight or what?"

"Tony! Shut up and drive! God, I get so sick of your constant griping. I'm not going to let you ruin this weekend. So just shut up and drive!"

They finished the trip in a tense silence. As they pulled into Eric's driveway, he was just locking his front door. He climbed into their car with a big smile on his face. "Perfect timing! Well, are you two ready to head for the hills and ride some wild broncos?"

Tony scowled. "How in the Hell can you be so happy this early in the morning? I'd appreciate it if you'd kindly wipe that smile off your face."

Eric laughed out loud and grinned at Cat. "One of those mornings, huh? Just how long does it usually take for him to get friendly?"

Cat groaned. "Are you kidding? Who said he ever gets friendly? I'll have you know, you're seeing his good side!"

Tony pulled into Shannon's driveway, turned around and glared at Eric. "If you can spare the time from picking on me, perhaps you'd be nice enough to get Shannon out here. And would you please take long enough for me to beat up my wife?"

"Sure! Anything for a buddy! Just honk when you're ready to go."

Eric rang the bell, but received no response. He tried the doorknob and found it open. Tapping on the door, he slowly opened it. "Knock, knock, anyone home?" Receiving no answer, he quietly walked upstairs toward her bedroom. Her door was ajar and, as he hesitantly peered through the doorway, he saw her reflection in a mirror. She was using her hair dryer; that was why she hadn't heard him. She turned it off and stood, clad only in a bra and panties. As she caught sight of him in the mirror, he stepped into the room. They just looked at each other for a long moment; she didn't seem at all surprised to find him in her bedroom. Then Eric realized it had been no accident that both doors were unlocked. In half a heartbeat, they were wrapped in each other's arms. While they hungrily kissed, the incessant sound of Tony's horn finally reached them. Shakily, Eric released her. "We'd better go, Shannon. They're waiting in the car with the motor running. You know how impatient Tony is." Weakening, he grabbed her and devoured her with one last kiss.

Reluctantly, Shannon pushed him away. "Eric, you'd better go downstairs before one of them comes inside. Besides, I don't know what I'm thinking. We both know this is impossible!"

Eric just nodded, not trusting his voice. He looked her up and down one last time, indelibly imprinting the vision of her perfect beauty upon his mind. Then he rushed down the stairs and out the door to the car. As he climbed into the back seat, Tony turned toward him and half-glared.

"Glad you could make it! I thought we were supposed to be in a hurry! Where's Shannon?"

"Cool it, Tony! She's almost done. You know how women are; no matter what time you tell them to be ready, they're bound and determined to make you wait!"

"Well, excuse me! I'll have you know I was ready before Tony was!"

"Pardon me, ma'am; I stand corrected. However, Cat, you must know you're not exactly the average woman and Tony is definitely not the average man!"

"Wait a minute!" They both protested in unison.

At that moment, Shannon walked outside and

locked her front door. They all turned to admire her. She was truly a vision of loveliness in a soft, pink sundress. Giving them all a radiant smile, she climbed into the back seat with Eric.

Tony just shook his head in despair. "Jesus, another smiling early-bird! If you two don't cut it out, I'll make you both walk."

Eric and Shannon looked at each other and burst into laughter. Without realizing it, Tony had eased the tension between them and the trip to the Briar Patch was spent in pleasant conversation. Tony was like that; he could remove the clouds from a rainy day.

Finally, they were approaching the main gate of the huge ranch nestled in a lovely valley amidst the Sierras. In order to enjoy the view, Tony decided to stop for a short while, so impressed was he by the majestic beauty and magnitude of the place. They all climbed out of the car and stretched their legs while Tony got his camera. He motioned the three of them to stand in front of the gate. Eric stood between the two women with an arm around each one. The picture to be later developed would capture for all time the look on Eric's face when, at the last moment, he glanced at Shannon.

From the front gate, the road continued for a full two miles to the main house. It was a huge, three-story, Victorian mansion, surrounded on all sides by a large, inviting veranda. Not too far away were some attractive bunkhouses for the help. A little farther still, was the largest barn Caitlin could possibly imagine. Completely in awe of the place, she just stood for a moment, staring. She considered it the warmest, most welcoming estate of its kind she had ever seen. "Shannon, you must be mistaken. There's no way a place this grand could ever be inexpensive!"

Shannon had to smile at the looks on all their faces. "Don't worry, Cat, it will be for us. You see, we're scheduled for a two-day trail ride, which includes sleeping out in the open tonight. It would have been expensive if we were sleeping in their rooms, but we're not doing that."

"I didn't know that! I thought we would be using their lodgings. If I had known, I'm not so sure I would have agreed to come. I hate doing without a shower and......certain, other facilities."

"I know. That's why I didn't tell you until just now. Don't you understand? We need to get used to roughing it! Did you think we would have showers on our two-week vacation? If you can't stand it for one night, how are you going to stand it for two weeks?"

"Okay, you're right! I guess I'm just going to have to get used to it. Well, let's check in, shall we?"

Tony put his arm around her. "C'mon, you spoiled city gal. I'll walk you up the stairs."

Shannon looked at Eric, who'd been quietly watching her the whole time. "What? No complaints from you?"

"You'll never hear any complaints from me, Shannon."

It was fortunate they had left as early as they did; their trail ride was scheduled to begin in twenty minutes. They had just enough time to check in and prepare to leave. They all changed into their riding clothes and joined the large group waiting out by the corrals. The Trailmaster stepped out of the huge barn, walked over to the corrals and stood before the crowd. He never had to worry about getting anyone's attention. His size alone guaranteed that! He was approximately six feet, four inches tall and had a naturally muscular build. He never actually worked out, but, to look at him, you would have sworn that he did. He was thirty-five years of age and in his prime. His real name was Jack Daniels, so of course he had acquired the nickname of 'Whiskey'. He was constantly out in the open and his face showed the abuse caused by the elements. No-one would have described him as handsome, but he had a strong, animal magnetism and such an air of supreme confidence, that women considered him extremely desirable. The men considered him dangerous. He never had to worry about the help not taking orders; none of them was brave enough to cross him.

"Welcome to the Briar Patch, folks! My name is Jack Daniels, but you might as well call me 'Whiskey'; everyone else does. I know you're all going to have a great time here. The reason I know this is because I'm going to make certain that it turns out that way. My job is to see that everything goes smoothly, so, if any of you has any complaints along the way, don't hesitate to tell me about them. Whatever the problem may be, large or small, I guarantee I can handle it. All right, let's get started. The first thing we're gonna to do is separate the bunch of you into two groups. Number one will be those of you who know how to ride, but not very well, and number two will be those of you who are good riders, or at least think you are. Group number one, line up over there to the left, and group number two, line up over there to the right. Now folks, it's not that I'm the suspicious type, but it's been my experience that sometimes people misjudge themselves. Every once in a while we get someone in the experienced group who actually belongs in the beginners' group. So, everyone in group number two has to take a little test, just so's I'll be satisfied in my own mind that they'll be okay when they're out ridin' on their own. You see, the beginners absolutely have to stay with me on this trail ride, but the ones I think can handle it will be allowed to roam around on their own, so long as we all meet at the base camp in time for supper. Now I want all of you to take a gander at that large corral over there. That's right, the one with all the obstacles set up in it! Anyone who wants the freedom to ride around on his or her own is gonna have to show me that they can manage that obstacle course. All you have to do is make it twice around the arena by jumping the hurdles and avoiding the rest of the obstacles without gettin' thrown. Let's get cracking! Who wants to be first?"

There was a lot of shuffling and low murmuring within group number two. Apparently, no-one wanted to be first. Noticing that Shannon was watching him expectantly, Eric winked at her and stepped to the front of the line. "I sure hope you've got a good horse for me; I'd hate to wear out a poor one on this little exercise!"

"So you figure you're the man for the job, huh? Well, today's your lucky day! I always give the spunkiest horse to the first volunteer." He turned to one of the hands. "Miguel, bring out Chico for this brave young man."

"Si! Right away, Boss!"

The entire crowd gasped in unison as a magnificent, sixteen-hand quarterhorse was led in their direction. He was jet-black with a star on his forehead and four white socks and he was the picture of strength and vitality. Miguel was having a difficult time keeping Chico at a walk. The proud, young gelding pranced toward them, kicking out with his back legs every few steps just for the joy of it! Eric looked at him skeptically, then approached him with a confident air. He patted the horse and spoke soothingly to him at the same time. "All right, Chico, you and I are going to be good friends, right?"

After they entered the arena and closed the gate, Eric took the reins and motioned Miguel away.

"But, Senor, I must hold onto the horse while you mount. This horse es muy dificil to control. Es la verdad, Senor!" Whenever Miguel was nervous, he tended to slip back into his native language.

"Don't worry, Miguel! Everything's going to be just fine. I've been around horses all my life. The tougher, the better, as far as I'm concerned!"

Still unwilling to release Chico, Miguel looked at Whiskey, appealing to him for help.

Whiskey nodded for him to leave. "Well, fella, I can see you have plenty of guts. Now let's see if you can keep 'em from gettin' splattered all over the arena!"

Talking to the horse in a low, steady tone, Eric mounted him in one smooth, deft motion. Chico reacted as though someone had placed a hornet's nest under the saddle. First, he reared, pawing the air with his front legs! Eric instantly leaned forward, forcing him down. Then, Chico simultaneously began bucking and violently twisting in a circular motion! As they careened toward the railing, someone in the crowd screamed! Eric jerked his leg out of the way just as the wild-eyed gelding crashed into the fence! Barely keeping his seat, he forced Chico's head in the opposite direction, causing him to snort and rear up again. In fact, he reared up so high that he almost went over on his back! This time, Eric not only leaned sharply forward, but also whacked him over the top of the head with his fist! Now Chico hunched up and started to buck in earnest! The crowd watched, horrified. Cat was white as a sheet and Tony was drenched in sweat as this brought back horrible memories of his own terrifying ride. Shannon was both terrified and thrilled all at the same time. Miguel was wringing his hands and talking to himself in Spanish. But Eric was an incredibly talented rider, and he outmaneuvered the lathered quarterhorse at every turn. Finally, his sides heaving from his violent outburst, Chico stood in the still-churning cloud of dust, breathing hard, but resigned to obeying the commands of this particular rider. Of course, he would still test the next person to try him out. He always did! It was just part of his nature.

As is often the case with spirited, strong-willed horses, once their will has been mastered and they acknowledge the control of the rider, their performance is usually outstanding!   Such was the case with Chico.

Eric leaned over and whispered in his ear. "Well, boy, now that you've had your fun, let's show 'em what we can do!"

As the crowd stood, spellbound, horse and rider flew effortlessly over the hurdles and whipped around the obstacles as though they weren't even there! The ride was executed so flawlessly and with such speed, that it appeared to be over in the blink of an eye! Eric finished his performance by bringing Chico's front legs up high and spinning around with him! The show he put on was so electrifying that the entire crowd broke into spontaneous applause!

"All right, folks, settle down! It was quite a show, but it's over now.   Time to get back to business." Whiskey was a little irritated by the way Eric had managed to steal the show. He was used to being the center of attention and he didn't appreciate being shown up by a city boy, no matter how clever he was! Well, the trail ride was just beginning and a brash young man like that would undoubtedly overstep the bounds, sooner or later. He would enjoy forcing him back into line, nicely, of course, but firmly.   The others in the group were allowed to ride around the arena on much tamer horses. After careful deliberation by the Trailmaster, the people were separated into their correct groups and given their final instructions with a map of the entire area. Theoretically, there should be no possibility of anyone getting lost.

Whiskey rode to the head of the crowd and turned around.   "We're burnin' daylight! Roll 'em out!"

With those words, he put his horse into a light canter and the two groups followed behind him and several of his men, with Miguel bringing up the rear, still muttering to himself. "Madre de Dios! These foolish gringos! Will they never learn?"

As they rode down the trail, Eric and Shannon were talking and laughing with Cat and Tony. Their conversation was continually interrupted by other riders congratulating Eric on his triumph in the arena. He was also being covertly admired by several young ladies in the group.

"Shit! Look at those women droolin' all over you! How's it feel to be a hero, Mr. Macho?" Tony was grinning widely at the discomfort he was causing Eric.

"Tony, shut up! Do you have to talk so loud? One of those women turned and looked right at you; I know she heard you!" Cat looked like she wanted to crawl under a rock.

Eric flushed and looked at Shannon. "Let's get away from this noisy crowd for a while. Remember, we're part of the experienced group. We're allowed to ride on our own whenever we feel like it, unlike a certain loud-mouthed beginner, whose name I won't mention!"

With that parting shot, he glared at Tony and started to lope towards a steep, heavily-wooded hill. Shannon looked at Cat, shrugged her shoulders and took off after Eric.

Eric had to slow down to let Shannon catch up with him. She was riding a paint mare by the name of Moraya. Although the mare's name meant 'wind', she was anything but fast. In fact, her most endearing quality was her stability, not her speed, which was only in the medium range. Eric had been allowed to ride Chico, since he had proven himself to be such a superior horseman. Usually, Whiskey only used Chico to scare the pants off the first volunteer for the test ride in the arena. This ploy of his served as an excellent tool for separating the men from the boys, so to speak. Once the crowd witnessed what was usually a case of the volunteer getting thrown, many of the so-called experienced riders would subtly join the beginners' group, thereby greatly relieving Whiskey of his concerns about the safety of any marginal riders. However, Eric had thrown him a curve; he hadn't expected to witness such expertise! The only other rider he considered as good as Eric was himself. But then, there was that woman riding with Eric. What was her name? Oh yeah, Shannon! She was also a damned good rider, not to mention unusually good-lookin'! She looked like she'd be good at a few other things, too. He'd sure welcome an opportunity to get to know her better!

Sitting on their horses at the top of the heavily-wooded hill, Eric and Shannon looked down upon the picturesque valley where the ranch was located. The riders spread out far below them appeared very small from this height. Watching them ride along, kicking up streamers of dust as they rode, made Eric feel as though he had stepped back in time. In fact, time itself had no meaning here. The scene before him belonged to a bygone era. He looked further down the valley at the charming Victorian mansion and could easily imagine himself and Shannon as the owners of this lovely ranch. What a wonderful life that would have been! No telephones, no cars, no crowds, no rat-race, no stress! Just him and Shannon, whatever children they would have had and all of nature at their fingertips. What he wouldn't give to have had that life, living in a time when a man was really a man, drawing on his strength and hunting skills to provide for his family, each day dawning fresh and new, with the possibility of unforeseen adventures. He looked at Shannon and saw her drinking in the scenery with a thirst to match his own. She was so engrossed that Eric realized she shared his thoughts and had also retreated to that happier, more peaceful time. He somehow sensed that they also shared an abiding strength, an innate ability to survive, no matter what the odds. She was truly the woman with whom to cross life's river. If only.........

Shannon slowly emerged from her own private thoughts of a past life. She would have sold her soul for such a life, living in a time when a woman was more than just a woman, a time when a marriage would have meant a true partnership, when both husband and wife would have had to share life's responsibilities in order to survive. Larry and Elaine would have hated such a life; it's doubtful that either would have survived the physical hardships intrinsic to such an era. But Eric would have had the strength, both physical and mental, to conquer whatever problems he might have encountered! Shannon had only to look in his eyes to see the inner strength that radiated from him. Oh yes, he was truly the man with whom to cross life's river. If only.........

The sudden nervous sidestepping of their horses brought them both out of their reverie at the same instant! Horses have that uncanny ability to recognize the slightest sign of danger before a human is ever aware of it. If Eric and Shannon hadn't been so busy daydreaming, they would have noticed the change in their horses' stance, their ears pricked sharply forward, their general edginess. By the time a horse begins to sidestep, almost prancing in place, and throws its head back and forth while lightly snorting, the danger is usually imminent! Eric looked hastily around and noticed they were not in a good position for a hasty retreat. They had ventured to the far edge of the wooded knoll in order to look out over the valley. Unfortunately, the descent from this location was very steep. He and Chico might succeed in the attempt, but he had grave doubts about Shannon and Moraya. The only safe route would be to retrace their steps leading to this point, but they might not be lucky enough to have that option. It would depend on whatever the danger might be, which was evidently lurking somewhere along that forest trail. While these thoughts flashed through his mind, the horses were beginning to show extreme signs of panic. Their eyes were wide with fear as they frantically tossed their heads, paced back and forth and neighed to one another! Both Eric and Shannon were intensely staring into the forest in a concerted effort to locate the danger. It seemed to both of them that time was passing in slow motion as they strained to hear any unusual sound. After what felt like an eternity, they heard a muffled crashing. Something was definitely moving in their direction. The crashing became louder and louder, until, suddenly, two small bear cubs erupted from the underbrush!

Shannon laughed aloud in her relief! "Oh, Eric! Aren't they adorable?"

"Shannon! There's nothing funny about this! Don't you understand? The mother bear has to be very close! We're in real danger! Whatever happens, you stay behind me and when you get the chance, run for it! I'll try to buy you some time!"

"I'm not leaving until I know you're safe! We'll just both have to run for it!"

"Shannon! You'll Goddamn well do what I tell you!"

The bone-chilling roar from the mother bear cut their conversation short! For a moment, they both just stared, horrified! The bear loomed before them like a monster. It didn't seem possible that an animal could be that large! Even the horses were momentarily paralyzed. Then the bear advanced, roaring even louder and clawing the air, as though to show them what she intended to do to them. The horses wanted to bolt past the bear, but Eric knew there wasn't enough room to get safely around. He forced Chico to turn and face the steep edge. Then he yelled to Shannon. "We don't have any choice! We have to go over the edge! Keep Moraya's head up slightly and lean far back in the saddle. Don't worry, we'll make it!" Then he positioned himself between Shannon and the bear, which was steadily advancing. "Now! Go now! I'll be right behind you!" Shannon tried desperately to force Moraya over the edge, but the fear-crazed horse wouldn't budge. The constant roaring of the mother bear had crippled the horse's will to move. Eric lashed at her hind quarters with his quirt, to no avail. The bear was almost upon them, her mouth foaming as she snarled her protest of their invasion into her domain. Eric knew they were running out of time. He forced Chico right alongside of Moraya, grabbed the reins and literally pulled her along as he and Chico bolted over the edge! Scrambling and sliding through the rocks and brush, Eric had to hold Chico back ever so slightly in order for Moraya to keep up. He glanced back at Shannon and saw that she was leaning far back in the saddle, her face tense with concentration. Then he looked further up and saw the bear watching them from the top, still roaring her defiance! With about a third of the distance still to go, they suddenly found themselves in some very slippery shale. The horses instinctively sat on their haunches and slid the rest of the way!

After a seemingly interminable and almost uncontrollable ride, Eric and Shannon sat on their still shaking horses at the bottom of the knoll and just looked at each other for a while. So attuned were they, it was unnecessary to speak. Eric was relieved by the way she had handled the dangerous descent and Shannon was thrilled by the way Eric had taken charge and protected her, literally bringing her down the steep hillside and out of danger. She was filled with admiration for him! Eric smiled at her and brought out his map to check for the nearest lake. They both turned in the direction the group had taken, just in time to see the last streamers of dust as the riders slowly disappeared from sight. Eric motioned Shannon to follow him and they headed in the same direction. Judging from the map, he figured they would reach the nearest lake in just over an hour. Shannon smiled happily at him; she would follow him anywhere.

They rode slowly on their way to the lake, sparing their horses and themselves. As they approached a lookout point from where they should be able to see the lake, Eric noticed Shannon looking nervously over her shoulder.

"What's the matter? Did you expect the bear to follow us?"

"Not really. It's just that I feel uneasy in general. I guess I'm not used to this much quiet. Until that incident with the bear, I don't think I actually understood how very alone we really are, or how vulnerable!"

"Shannon, I hope you realize that you're one hundred percent safe with me! I would never let anything happen to you!"

Looking into his dark eyes, she felt her fears vanishing. Her eyes misting over with happiness, she found it difficult to speak. She gave him a tremulous smile and raced him to the lookout point. Eric quickly overtook her and they stood at the edge together, looking down upon Half Moon Lake. The beautiful, crescent-shaped lake mirrored the blue of the sky and was very inviting, especially considering the warmth of the day.

They brought their horses down to the water's edge and allowed them to drink, then tied them to a couple of nearby trees. Without a word, they both stripped down and dove into the delightfully cool water. While they playfully splashed and ducked one another, they were completely unaware of the eyes watching them from a dense thicket! Whiskey had left one of his hands in charge and backtracked to check on these two. He had correctly guessed that they would stop off at the nearest lake and he had settled in to wait for them. His wait had paid off! He had known all along that Eric would eventually break the rules and swimming in the nude was definitely against the rules! Breaking cover, he quietly walked to the water's edge, his eyes never leaving Shannon. Laughing, she splashed Eric one last time and turned to race him to the shore. Standing in ankle-deep water, she caught sight of Whiskey staring at her and screamed! Angrily, Eric rushed to catch up with her and stood in front of her, covering her naked body with his own!

"What the fuck are you doing here? You'd better get the Hell out of here until she's dressed!"

Whiskey nonchalantly sat down on a tree stump and continued to stare at them with an arrogant leer.

"Apparently you two can't be trusted to mind the rules, so I don't think I'll be lettin' you outa my sight. I'll just wait right here 'til you're dressed and take you back to camp with me."

With a dangerous snarl, Eric rushed him headlong and leaped on top of him, knocking him off the stump and onto the wet ground. Eric sat on him, slamming his fist into his face over and over. Shannon screamed and ran to grab his arm.

"Eric! Stop it! You're killing him!"

Whiskey took quick advantage of her intervention to roll out from under Eric and kick him in the stomach! While Eric doubled over, trying to catch his breath, Whiskey came up from behind and locked his arms around his neck, choking him! Gagging, Eric clawed at his arms, desperately trying to dislodge them. Shannon jumped on Whiskey's back and sank her teeth into his shoulder, drawing blood. Cursing, Whiskey released Eric and stood up, with Shannon still wrapped around his back. Finally shaking her off, he shoved her down on the ground and turned back to Eric, who was just getting his wind back and trying to stand. Whiskey kicked him in the groin and belted him in the jaw with an audible thud! As Eric fell, his head hit hard against a rock, knocking him almost senseless! Shannon screamed and rushed to him, kneeling to hold him. Whiskey reached down and grabbed her by her hair, pulling her up against him. She kicked at him and raked her fingernails across his chest, leaving a trail of blood. Yelling, he slapped her across the face!

"So you like it rough, huh? Well, that's just fine with me! I'll show you just how rough it can get!"

With that, he tossed her over his shoulder and carried her into the thicket where he had been hiding. Then he threw her roughly to the ground and hurriedly removed his pants. Shannon knew what was coming. All she could think was, 'When he's done, I'll kill him! I'll find a gun and I'll kill him!'

Throwing his pants and boots aside, he knelt down, grabbed her ankles and dragged her toward him. Shannon broke free with one foot and kicked him squarely in the nose! While he held his hands over his face, reeling with the pain of a broken nose, she tried to scoot back out of reach. Whiskey got up and staggered toward her.

"Don't even bother tryin' to escape! You ain't goin' anywhere 'til I'm done with you!"

He threw himself on top of her only to be savagely ripped away and thrown to the ground! With his lustful passions aroused, he had failed to notice that

Eric had come out of his stupor. Enraged by what he saw, Eric fell upon him and pounded him over and over again, quitting only when Whiskey was unconscious. This time, Shannon made no attempt to interfere.

Finally, Eric stood and slowly walked over to Shannon. She lay on her side, her face hidden in her hands, sobbing quietly. Kneeling down, he gently pulled her into his arms, stroking her hair and comforting her without any words at all. Eric instinctively knew that sometimes, silence was the best medicine.

After a while, Shannon and Eric walked back to the lake and cleaned themselves. When they were dressed, they returned to the thicket and looked down on Whiskey. His face was completely unrecognizable and he lay dangerously still. Horrified, Shannon turned away and tried to control the urge to vomit.

"He's dead, isn't he? I knew it! You killed him! And I didn't even try to stop you! Oh, God! What are we going to do now?"

She fell to the ground and started crying hysterically. Eric pulled her back to her feet and shook her.

"Stop it! He's not dead! I just felt his pulse; he's going to be all right. Shannon! Did you hear me? I said he's not dead! Now pull yourself together!"

Struggling to compose herself, Shannon looked up at him with a tear-streaked face.

"What are we going to do with him? We can't just leave him here. In a couple of hours, we're all supposed to meet at the base camp for supper! You look all right, but he looks horrible! How are we going to explain his appearance?"

"We're not! He can do his own Goddamned explaining whenever he shows up! I strongly doubt that he'll admit to spying on us and attacking you. As far as I'm concerned, we never saw him."

"You mean we're just going to leave him here, in that condition? My God, Eric! We can't do that! What if a bear comes along and kills him? He's completely defenseless!"

"Quite frankly, I don't give a shit what happens to him! In fact, I'd just as soon finish him off myself! How can you feel this way, Shannon? He certainly didn't worry about how defenseless you were, did he? Now listen to me! We're leaving him here and that's the end of it! Get on your horse; it's going to take a couple of hours just to reach the base camp."

Taking one last look at Whiskey, Shannon reluctantly followed Eric. After they'd both mounted their horses and turned them back to the main trail, Shannon thought about everything Eric had said. He was probably right about leaving Whiskey behind. If they had all returned to the base camp together, they would have played Hell trying to explain the situation. Besides, Whiskey struck her as a saddle tramp, just someone who drifted from job to job, probably getting fired quite often, due to his bad temper and frequent fights. On the other hand, did that make his life any less important? She had been raised to value life, all life! In spite of what he had done, she considered it wrong to leave him in danger. And God knows this country is filled with danger! She was amazed by Eric's violent reaction and complete lack of remorse. She had never suspected he was like that! Maybe it was just the effect of being in the wilderness; it could make one feel so alone and vulnerable. That was probably what it was like in the frontier times, people driven to extreme actions in order to survive. Perhaps she was judging Eric too harshly. After all, wasn't she equally guilty? During one point in the attack, all she could think of was killing Whiskey!

Shannon wasn't the only one lost in thought. Eric

was already thinking about the explanation he'd have to make to Tony and Cat about his bruised face. He'd just say that he ran through some branches escaping from the bear. Yeah, that should work! Then he recalled the feeling that had washed over him like a wave while smashing in Whiskey's face. It had felt so good! He wished he'd killed that bastard! Better yet, he wished he had tortured him to death! Seeing him attack Shannon had put him in an uncontrollable rage. Even now, he'd like to return and finish the job. If only he weren't trapped by society's stupid rules! What he wouldn't give to have lived in the frontier times, when a man could mete out justice as he saw fit and take his chances on the consequences! What an effect the wilderness had on a person! It made you realize how nature really intended for you to live, free to make your own choices and act on your own decisions. Eric realized he had never felt more alive than when he was attempting to flee from that bear and, even more, when he was savagely pounding Whiskey into oblivion! Breathing the fresh mountain air, Eric felt invigorated and confident in his own abilities. He suddenly felt that anything was possible. He looked at Shannon, more determined than ever to make her his own.

About half way to the camp, they came to a fork in the trail. It was apparent that the group had gone to the left, but Eric wanted to see where the right would take them. He gave Shannon a questioning, eager look. She nodded her assent and smiled at him. If that wasn't just like a man, always wanting to know what lay over the next hill. They cantered up the light slope; even the horses seemed excited, almost as though they knew something good was waiting for them. The trail led up to a crest and followed along the ridge for a while. They held the horses in check, riding very slowly to enjoy the panorama spread before them. As far as the eye could see, there was row after row of mountains, valleys, streams and lakes. Nature had bestowed the tallest of the mountains with a hat of fluffy, white clouds. In contrast, the sky was the most vivid blue they had ever seen. Shannon wondered how it was possible for this land to seem so savage and terrifying one moment and so utterly serene and beautiful the next!

Chico whinnied to Moraya and she returned his call. They were both doing a little dance in anticipation of the lush grasses which were just a little further down the trail. Eric laughed at their eagerness and gave Chico his head. Shannon followed suit and the two horses loped the rest of the way. When they reached the thickest of the grasses, they dismounted and let the horses graze for a while. Hand in hand, they walked to a nearby stream and sat on a large boulder, watching the water wind its way around the rocks.

"Shannon, we haven't really talked about it yet. Are you all right? I mean........."

"I know what you mean. You want to know if an experience like that is going to turn me off for all time, right? The answer is 'no'. I'm tougher than that, Eric. I thought you already knew that. Besides, he didn't actually rape me. Thanks to you, he only came very close." Struggling through some inner turmoil, she lowered her eyes for a moment and spoke softly. "It seems as though you're always saving me from something terrible. That horrible man, the bear and possibly even my husband. I see you as quite the hero!"

Gently raising her face, he kissed her tenderly.

"I'm no hero, Shannon. I'm just a man in love, a man who will cherish you for all eternity!"

Her eyes glowing with happiness, she leaned over and kissed him. Wrapping his arms around her, he turned the kiss into a lingering, passionate one. They slid from the boulder and stretched out on a blanket of thick grass. He very gently placed his hand beneath her clothing and lightly cupped her breast. She held her hand over his and pressed down, letting him know he didn't have to be quite that careful. Smiling happily at her, he kissed her again, even more passionately. As he slowly removed her clothing, he was entranced by the beauty of her perfect body. Then he removed his own clothing and threw it aside. She felt the heat from the sun warming her skin. It was such a heady freedom to lie naked beneath the deep blue sky. Then she felt the heat from his body as he lay on top of her, warming her to an infinite degree. He began to nuzzle her breasts, sucking first one nipple and then the other, causing her to moan softly in her need of him. As he slowly filled her with his engorged manhood, her world began to spin out of control, until there was only a blazing fire which consumed them both. Lost to the flames of passion, they came together in a searing heat!

Unwilling to release one another, they remained intertwined for a while, as lovers will. The sweet smell of the buckbrush wafted through the air, the perfect scent for such a tryst. Savoring their time together, they lingered as long as possible. Neither of them would ever forget the beauty of their surroundings, nor the delicious aroma of nature's own sweet perfume.

Moraya's soft nicker reminded them that it was time to go. They had completely lost track of time and would undoubtedly be late in reaching the base camp. They hurriedly dressed, mounted their horses and returned to the main trail.

"We'd better hurry, Shannon! We've got to beat Whiskey back to the camp! I don't want him spreading any wild stories about us!"

"He wouldn't dare! He's probably scared to death of what we'll say about him! I only wish we could turn

94

him in to the authorities, but there's no way to do that without advertising our affair."

"You're right about that, but at least he didn't get away without some real punishment! I gave him a beating he'll remember the rest of his life! We'd still better hurry; it's getting late!"

Having been well-rested and well-fed, Chico and Moraya were more than willing to lope along the trail at a fair speed. They made better time than Eric had expected and arrived just in time for supper.

"Well, it's about time you two showed up! We were about to send out a search party! Where the Hell have you two been all day?"

"Shut up, Tony! Can't you see he's been hurt? Eric, get down and tell us what happened!"

One of the hands stepped forward and took their horses so they could relax and enjoy their food. Shannon walked over to the chuck wagon to get their plates while Eric explained the bear incident to Cat and Tony. She returned with their meals just in time to hear Cat's response.

"Good Lord! That must have been terrifying! You're both lucky to be alive! I've always heard there's nothing more dangerous than a mother bear."

"Cat's right. You two were really lucky! It's hard to imagine running into a mean, mama bear and coming out of it with only a few scratches and bruises from tree branches. Now see, Eric; if you weren't such a damned hot-head and had stuck with us, instead of runnin' off, it never would have happened!"

"Shut up, Tony! And quit being such a jerk! You're the only person I know who would chew somebody out after an experience like that! I'm sorry, Eric. I keep trying to teach him some manners, but it never seems to do any good. By the way, while you were gone, we've had some excitement of our own.

95

Before we even got here, Whiskey said he had to check on something and took off by himself to God knows where! He left one of the hands in charge and said he'd be back before supper. Miguel says he's never late and nobody has any idea what's happened to him. Did you two see any sign of him along the trail?"

Eric and Shannon looked at one another for a long moment and then both shook their heads.

"Shannon and I had our hands full with that bear for a while. If Whiskey passed our way at all, it must have been when we took a detour to get away from the bear. Anyway, we definitely haven't seen him!"

While Eric was talking, Miguel kept staring at him. Everyone else believed Eric's story, but Miguel was unusually perceptive and he knew something was very, very wrong. For one thing, he knew his boss extremely well and he knew without a doubt that he would have returned by now, unless something terrible had happened to him. For an ordinary man, there might have been the danger of tangling with a ferocious bear or mountain lion. But Miguel knew that Whiskey was no ordinary man; the only harm that could have befallen him would have been caused by another man. And Miguel thought Eric had a guilty air about him! He had noticed the look that passed between Eric and Shannon and he felt in his gut that their story was a lie. He decided to saddle his horse and backtrack until he found Whiskey; he was determined to find out what had happened to him!

Miguel was just about to mount his horse when Whiskey slowly drifted into camp. There was an audible gasp from those who first saw his face. Miguel rushed to help him dismount, but Whiskey angrily brushed him aside. His lips were so swollen, he could barely speak. He dismounted very slowly and motioned for Miguel to take his horse. Looking neither to the left nor the right, he headed directly for his own tent and retired for the evening, giving no explanations to anyone. Before taking Whiskey's horse away, Miguel just stood there in the heavy silence and glared at Eric for the longest time.

"Jesus Christ! What the Hell was that all about?"

"Shut up, Tony! Let them eat in peace, all right? I'm sure they're too tired to talk right now. C'mon, let's go set up our tent."

Cat had her own opinion as to what might have occurred, but she wasn't going to discuss it with anyone, especially not Tony.

Later in the evening, Shannon and Eric laid their sleeping bags out in the open. They didn't want a tent over their heads, separating them from the night sky. When the sun's last rays disappeared into the horizon, darkness fell upon the land like a mantle. Since there was no moon, the night was a deep, velvet black, the perfect enhancement for the myriad of stars which sparkled like diamonds suspended in the heavens. Eric and Shannon fell asleep to the soothing sound of crickets chirping and the hooting of a nearby owl.

The next sound they heard was the clang of the breakfast gong, waking them as the first rays of the sun appeared in the eastern sky. Eric looked over at Shannon, who was still not quite awake, wondering that she could look so impossibly beautiful this early in the morning. She was one of those rare, lucky women, who don't need any makeup to enhance their natural beauty. He gently shook her awake and was rewarded by one of her radiant smiles. Cat was standing in front of her tent and saw the look that passed between the two of them. She quickly stepped back into the tent, wishing she hadn't seen them. She had long suspected how they felt about one another, but she didn't want to know for sure. She still hadn't fully recovered from Tony's affair and she certainly didn't want to become involved in any

97

of her friends' intimacies. A love affair between close friends and neighbors would invariably blow up in everyone's face. She didn't want to be around when the explosion took place and she definitely didn't want to be put in the position of choosing sides. She valued her friends far too much for that!

The morning passed uneventfully. Whiskey had breakfast in his tent and generally avoided everyone. With a beautiful new day in front of them, the rest of the group looked forward to an enjoyable ride back to the ranch. The entire two-day ride was a circuitous one and the last part would lead through a section of deep forest, eventually ending at the back side of the ranch. Whiskey took the lead along with two of the hands; the rest were interspersed at regular intervals between the riders, with Miguel bringing up the rear, as usual. Eric thought it best if he and Shannon stayed with Cat and Tony for the remainder of the trip. He didn't want to chance anything else happening to Shannon. Not that Whiskey would try anything again, but you just never knew for certain with his type.

As they began their ride, they slowly gained in altitude. The air seemed a little fresher and just slightly cooler. There was the delightful odor of cedar mingled with the pungent aroma of the tarweed. Tony sighed happily as he took in a deep breath. He was in a rare, good mood.

"Yessiree! This is the life for me! What d'ya think, Babe? Don't I look like I was born on a horse?" He pulled his hat down at an angle and gave Cat a cocky grin.

"I don't know, Tony. I think maybe you look more like the horse's ass! What do you two think?"

Shannon smiled at both of them. She was pleased to see them so happy and joking with one another. They hadn't been that way for a long time.

Whatever their problems were, they seemed to be working them out.

"Actually, I think you both look great on horseback. See what a little practice can do? I knew this trip was a good idea!"

"Shannon's right. You're both lookin' good! Guess what? I just checked the map and we should be crossing a river pretty soon. I think we're stopping for lunch on the other side."

"A river! What river? Nobody said anything about crossing a river! It better not be deep. I'm not in the mood to get wet!"

"Take it easy, Tony. At this time of year, I'm sure it's no more than a small stream. Anyway, it shouldn't be any problem for a guy who was born on a horse!"

"Yeah, right! I knew I should've kept my big mouth shut!"

At this point, the trail turned sharply to the left and made a slight descent as it led to a fair-sized stream. They all stopped and watched while the riders at the front of the line allowed their horses to drink and then crossed easily to the other side. Tony looked relieved as the horses pranced through the water with their hooves kicking up a fine spray. "Hey! I don't know what I was so worried about! That water's not too deep. This oughta be a snap!"

Feeling brave, Tony decided to go before Cat and his friends. When he reached mid-stream, his horse suddenly stopped and started pawing at the water. He began to circle and continued to paw at the water. Tony was perplexed, but Eric knew exactly what the horse had in mind.

"Tony! Pull his head up! Quick, before he rolls!"

His words were wasted. Tony couldn't hear him over the splashing of his horse. He thought the animal just wanted a drink, so he gave him his head. That was a big mistake! Instead of drinking, the horse began to kneel down in the water. Suddenly realizing what the horse was about to do, Tony tried desperately to pull his head up!

"Get up! You stupid, rotten, flea-bitten piece of shit! Get up!"

Unable to deter him, his horse lay completely down in the water and Tony barely had time to jump off of him before he rolled over on his back! Dismayed, disgusted and thoroughly soaked, Tony glared as Cat, Eric and Shannon dissolved in laughter.

"Yeah, that's right! Have a good laugh! I'd like to know why in the Hell everyone thinks it's so funny when some stupid horse gets the best of me!"

"Oh, come on, Tony! If it happened to someone else, you'd be laughing right along with the rest of us! Where's your sense of humor?"

"That's easy for you to say, Eric, since you're never the butt of the jokes! You're too busy being a Goddamned hero!"

Finished with his roll in the water, Tony's horse got back on his feet and Tony led him across the stream and up on the opposite bank. The others quickly crossed over without incident and tied their horses to some trees. Eric started to walk over to Tony, but Cat restrained him.

"Let me talk to him first. I think we need some time alone. Tony has a lot of pride and, well.........let's face it, Eric. Sometimes you're a hard act to follow!"

Speechless, Eric just stared at her! He looked over at Shannon and found her nodding in agreement with Cat.

"She's right, Eric. It must be very difficult for him to always stand in your shadow."

"I had no idea he felt that way. We've always been the best of friends. I never realized there was a problem. Maybe I should talk to him."

"No! Let Cat take care of it. She knows how to handle him. Besides, what would you say? Would you apologize for being stronger and better looking than he is? The biggest favor you can do him is to just pretend that his outburst never occurred. And don't worry! He'll come around. He is your friend, after all, and I'm sure he'll manage to overcome his jealousy. So come on; let's go eat our lunch!"

After lunch, the riders began the last leg of their journey. The trail narrowed and climbed at a much steeper angle. About two miles further, the trail leveled off and they found themselves traveling through the thickest part of the forest. The dense growth made their surroundings seem like a primeval jungle. The trail wound through moss-covered pines and firs; vines hung low from some of the branches. The sun had quickly faded from view and it became increasingly dark. The air turned abruptly cooler. There was a damp, musky smell emanating from the forest. It was as though they had entered another world. There was absolutely no birdsong; the quiet was almost deafening. By some remote instinct, no-one spoke. With their ears pricked forward to catch the slightest sound, even the horses remained silent. As they traveled, single-file, Eric couldn't shake the feeling that something was about to happen! He carefully looked around, alert to any possible danger. Finally, it dawned on him that it was simply the effect of the forest itself. Surroundings such as these served as a constant reminder that Mother Nature was still the most powerful force on the planet, unquestionably the most formidable foe mankind would ever encounter. Unless treated with the utmost care and respect, she could easily make the world uninhabitable for humans and permanently remove them from the face of the Earth!

CHAPTER 13 THE HOMECOMING

The trip home from the Briar Patch was rather subdued. Tony and Eric were pointedly polite to each other, both determined to salvage their friendship. Cat was also very careful in speaking to Eric and Shannon, making certain not to let on about her suspicion of their affair. However, Shannon knew something was wrong, just by the look on Cat's face and from her inability to look her in the eye while they were talking. A man can often deceive another man, usually with apparent ease, but a woman can almost never deceive another woman. Women, as a whole, are far too perceptive; they have that uncanny ability to recognize the most infinitesimal change in a person's expression, the slightest difference in a person's mode of speaking, even a minute change in body language. Therefore, Shannon quickly understood that Cat had some inkling as to their affair. She also understood that Cat had no intention of saying anything about it. She felt extremely grateful to have such a good, caring friend. In a way, Shannon felt a deep sense of relief, for she would now have the opportunity to take Cat into her confidence and pour out all her troubles. She really needed someone to talk to and who could be better than wonderful, sensible Cat?

As evening approached, Shannon looked out the car window and saw the first, bright star in the western sky. As the star glimmered and winked at her, she was momentarily transported back to her childhood and the memory of an old rhyme came back to haunt her. 'Star light, star bright, first star I see tonight! I wish I may; I wish I might, have the wish I wish tonight!' If only wishes could really come true, she knew exactly what she would wish for, that she had met Eric first and married him instead of Larry.

Eric looked over at Shannon and smiled. There was such a look of longing on her beautiful face; he knew it could only have to do with the two of them. She was still unwilling to use the word 'love' with him, but it didn't matter; she showed her love in countless other ways. A woman like Shannon could never succeed in hiding her true feelings. Thank God for that! The only thing that worried him was her misguided sense of loyalty. After everything Larry had put her through, she had absolutely no reason to feel any loyalty toward him at all! He realized that she considered their upcoming trip a last chance for her marriage, whereas he considered it his final opportunity to convince her to divorce Larry. For two cents, he'd prefer to throw Larry off a cliff and be done with him, once and for all! Suddenly, Eric realized that all his thoughts were centered on Larry, Shannon and himself; he hadn't given any thought at all as to what he would do about Elaine. He regarded that as the toughest problem of all! What on Earth could he possibly say to her to lessen the blow that he was planning to leave? Even if Shannon refused to leave Larry, Eric knew that he could never stay with Elaine. Now that he had finally known the ecstasy of true love, he could never again settle for less. As an act of kindness, he decided that he would wait until after their vacation to tell her the news. Yeah, right! It would be an act of kindness, all right, for himself! It would simply postpone what he knew would be a heart-wrenching confrontation.

Tony glanced at Cat as she dozed in the front seat. He was glad they'd had this opportunity to get away from the kids for a while. She always felt guilty about leaving them, even for a short time, but he knew they really needed more time alone, just for the two of them. This weekend had been wonderful; she was so different when she was away from the twins, so spontaneous, more like the young girl he'd married. He loved her so! He knew he could never have left her, even if Nicole had been willing to marry him. Jesus! Not Again! Even at times like these, the memory of Nicole would creep back into his mind, always with the accompanying pang in his heart! How could he love two women so deeply, yet in such different ways? He loved Cat for the wonderful, decent person that she was; he couldn't stand the thought of losing her! But whenever he thought of Nicole, it was as though his very heart were being crushed, so severe was the pain of living without her! He loved her with a passion that went beyond words; in her presence, everything and everyone disappeared, with only her beautiful face and gentle ways filling his mind and soul. He sincerely wished he had never met her; to love someone to that degree was unbearable. The worst part of such a love was the utter impossibility of ever recovering from it.

Cat was the only one who'd been able to sleep on the way home. She drifted in and out of various dreams, with the last one being extremely frightening.

......She was walking along a mountain trail, with a haze surrounding her. It was the middle of the night and she had only the moonlight to guide her steps. The trail was very steep, winding around the edge of the mountain. As she walked, vines grew across the trail, getting thicker and thicker, causing her to stumble. Something was following her and she tried desperately to run, but the vines were circling her ankles and she couldn't break free! She bent over to untangle the vines, but they wove themselves around her wrists and held her fast! Whatever was chasing her was crashing down the trail, gaining on her! Unable to escape, she strained to see what it was. Then, all of a sudden, she could just make out the form. Something huge, outlined by the moonlight, was bending over her. She screamed! The creature shook her, and she screamed again!

......"Cat! Wake up! You're dreaming! Wake up!" Eric continued to shake her until she awoke.

"Oh, my God! I just had the most terrifying dream! I was in the mountains and I was being chased by some horrible creature! I don't even know what it was. I couldn't get away; I was trapped. And then you were shaking me! Oh, Eric! Do you think it was some kind of premonition, some omen that perhaps we shouldn't go on our trip?" From the depths of her terror, Cat was still shaking.

"Cat, it was just a dream. We've all had our share of scary dreams. Tell me this; have you ever had one of your nightmares actually come true?"

"No, of course not! But this was so real! I just can't shake the feeling that we're in for some real trouble!"

Eric couldn't help laughing. "Relax, Cat. You don't have a thing to worry about. What we're really in for is the time of our lives!"

Tony reached over and grabbed her hand. "He's right, Honey. We're goin' to have a great time. So quit worryin' already! Besides, you're not gonna be alone on some mountain trail. In fact, you're not gettin' outa my sight, Babe! So, what d'ya think of that, huh?"

Cat started laughing, too; it was contagious. They were all laughing, except Shannon. She'd had some premonitions about this trip, also, but not in the form of nightmares. It was something else, something intangible. She couldn't put her finger on it; it was just a feeling she had. Oh well, she'd just have to play it by ear; she wasn't going to let some vague feeling ruin their vacation.

It was late when they pulled up to Shannon's house; she noticed that all the lights were off. "Well, I'd ask you all in for a cup of coffee, but it looks like Larry's asleep. Cat, I'm not working tomorrow, so let's get together to do some clothes shopping for the trip, okay?"

"Sounds good. I'll call you around elevenish. Goodnight!"

Shannon and Eric both got out of the car. "I might as well get out here, too; I can just walk across to my house. See you two later."

Tony and Cat waved to both of them and then pulled away from the curb. As he drove down the street, he noticed Cat looking behind them. "What are you looking at, Hon'?"

Cat turned back to the front and gave Tony a long look. "Nothing, nothing at all. Let's get home; I'm tired."

Eric and Shannon stood in the shadow of the large oak tree in her front yard and just looked at each other, neither one wanting to leave. Eric pulled her to him and held her tight. She lay her head on his shoulder and drank in the smell and the feel of him.

"Shannon, my beautiful Shannon, you're going to have to make a choice, and very soon. I don't know how much longer I can stand the thought of you in bed with him! Hasn't it occurred to you that I just might lose my cool and kill him? I really might, you know."

She tried to push away from him but he held her in an iron grip, refusing to let her go.

"Please don't try to push me into a decision so soon, Eric. I'm just not ready yet! After all, I made a promise to him when we got married and I don't take promises lightly."

"Yeah? Well, maybe you don't, but evidently he does. What about his promise to forsake all others, huh?"

"Eric, stop it! I'm equally guilty! Aren't you and I still having an affair?"

"I'm so glad you said 'still'! I couldn't stand it if you said it was over! Shannon, listen to me! He's not right for you and he never will be, no matter how many chances you give him. Can't you see that it's you and I who belong together?"

Shannon looked into his dark eyes and felt her will dissolving. Dear God! Would she ever be able to quit wanting him? Instead of answering him, she reached up and gave him a long, soul-wrenching kiss. Then she turned and ran into her home. Neither one had seen Larry watching them from the upstairs bedroom window!

CHAPTER 14 CONFIDANT

Shannon was relieved that Larry had already left for work before she awoke. She was also grateful that he had been asleep last night when she climbed into bed. She just wasn't up to discussing her weekend with him. She hadn't realized how tired she was; she'd actually slept in until ten o'clock! Thank goodness she didn't have to return to work until tomorrow; she would never have made it today. She took a long, refreshing shower, reveling in the simple pleasures of soap and water. How delightful it was, after going two days without one. Taking a shower would be the one part of civilization she would truly miss on her vacation.

Just as she finished dressing, Cat called and said she was on her way over. Shannon sat in her living room, nervously wondering just how wise it would be to confide in Cat. She hoped her friend wouldn't be too judgmental. Lost in thought, she was startled by the sound of the doorbell. Quickly opening the door, she invited Cat inside.

"I'm glad you're here; I really need to talk to you."

"Oh, dear! I was hoping you wouldn't say that! I was afraid that was the real reason you asked me to go shopping with you."

"I'm sorry to burden you with my problems, but if I don't talk to someone pretty soon, I'm going to lose my mind. And you're the only one I can trust!"

"What about Eric? Can't you talk to him?"

"I had a feeling you already knew. When did you find out?"

"Does it matter? I've suspected for a long time,

but I didn't know for sure until just now."

"I hope you won't hate me for this. Believe me, I know it's wrong and I'm not proud of myself. But I don't think I'm strong enough to give him up! I never planned any of this; it just happened and now it's really gotten out of hand. The worst part is, I think I love him!"

"Listen, Shannon, I don't want you to take this as an insult, but aren't you confusing love with lust?"

Shannon let out a small, bitter laugh. "How ironic that you should put it like that; those are almost the exact words I said to him when he told me that he loved me."

"Dear God! You mean he's in love with you, too? This really has turned into a mess, hasn't it? Have you given any consideration at all to Elaine's feelings? I'm really disappointed in you, Shannon; she's supposed to be one of your best friends! How could you do something like this?"

Tears were streaming down Shannon's face; she looked at Cat beseechingly and tried to explain. "You don't understand! I just couldn't help myself! This all started on a night when Larry was out with another woman. He's been cheating on me for a long time and I just couldn't take it anymore! Then Eric called and invited me over; he said he was feeling lonely because Elaine was gone, staying with her mother. Ordinarily, I'd never have gone over to his house, alone, at that hour. But I was losing my mind! I just had to talk to someone, right then! If only he hadn't held me and started kissing me; that's what really started it all!"

"Oh, for God's sake! Don't even try to blame this on Eric! Women lead men exactly where they want them to go and then let them think it's their idea! I know what really happened and so do you. You've had the hots for Eric for some time and Larry's cheating was the perfect excuse to justify your needs! It's that simple and you know it's true, even if you won't admit it!"

Shannon sat with her head in her hands, sobbing quietly. She knew Cat was right and guilt was eating her alive. Cat was feeling guilty, too. She knew she'd been way too hard on Shannon and she knew exactly why. She was using Shannon as a means of lashing out at the 'other woman' who'd stolen Tony's affections and possessed a part of his heart for all time. She'd never found out the identity of that 'other woman', so she was taking her buried hatred out on Shannon. She sat down and also began to cry.

Genuinely puzzled, Shannon looked up at her friend through blurred eyes, wondering what was really the matter with Cat. She got up and walked slowly over to her and gently put her arm around her shoulder. "I think you need to talk even more than I do. Tell me what's wrong, Cat. Maybe I can help."

"How on Earth can you help? You're the 'other woman'! You have no idea how it feels to be the one left behind with a broken heart! Oh, sure, Larry's cheated on you, probably hundreds of times, but they were just bimbos and he never fell in love with any of them. The only thing he managed to hurt was your pride! Just how in the Hell do you think you'd feel if the man you loved with all your heart fell deeply in love with another woman, huh? I can tell you exactly how you'd feel......like second best for the rest of your life!"

Shannon just held her quietly while Cat cried herself out; sometimes words only got in the way. She finally realized what had been the problem with Tony and Cat for the last three years; another woman, one who had really mattered, had come between them. Since they were Catholic, Cat was bound to wonder if Tony stayed with her because he loved her the most, or because of his religion. How horrible that would be, to never know for sure. Suddenly, her own problems didn't seem so huge. At least, she had no doubt that Larry actually loved her; the doubt was whether or not she still loved him. She knew she cared deeply for Eric, but did she love him enough and in the right way? She didn't want to make another mistake. And what about Elaine? Could she really bring herself to cause Elaine the kind of pain that Cat was experiencing? Dear God, life could be so confusing! She didn't have any answers; she would just have to rely on time to help solve her problems.

When Cat was finally able to quit crying, she looked up at Shannon and gave her a tremulous smile. "You must think I'm a big baby! Here you come to me for advice and now you see that I can't even handle my own life. In any case, the best advice I could give you would be to do just what I'm doing; take life one day at a time and try to make the best of it."

"Cat, you're absolutely right. And that's exactly what I'm going to do, take everything one day at a time, until I finally get it all figured out. Now come on; dry your eyes and I'm going to treat you to a delicious lunch before we start our shopping."

"Wait a minute; there's one more thing I need to tell you. I'm sorry about laying such a heavy guilt trip on you about Elaine. Actually, I always had the feeling that Eric wasn't very happy with her. Don't get me wrong; I like Elaine, but she's just a little too boring for him. You know what I mean? So, when they split up, I don't want you to blame yourself. It was always just a matter of time, anyway."

Shannon smiled at her and gave her a gentle hug. "See? You've managed to cheer me up, just like I knew you would. Come on; let's go."

As the afternoon wore on and Cat still hadn't returned from her shopping trip with Shannon, Tony decided to phone Larry and see if he had heard from them.

"No, Tony, I haven't seen or heard from the girls, but you know how they are; they'll probably shop 'til they drop."

"Jesus Christ! What are you tryin' to do, scare me? Cat just better not be spending all my money! Well, I guess I'll go out and do some shopping of my own and beat her to the punch. Wanna go?"

"No can do, I've got a big report due first thing in the morning! In fact, I'd better get busy. Talk to you later, Tony."

Feeling restless, Tony called Eric and invited him to go shopping. Eric jumped at the chance to get out of the house and away from Elaine. He just wasn't in the mood to put up with her chatter. When Tony pulled up to their house, Eric was already waiting outside for him.

"Wow! Things must be pretty rough at your house for you to be waitin' at the curb. What's goin' on?"

Eric laughed out loud! "That's what I like about you, Tony, direct and to the point. Has anyone ever told you you're a nosy son of a bitch?"

"Yeah, all the time, but it doesn't even slow me down! Like I said, what's goin' on?"

"All right, wise guy! If you really have to know, maybe I'll tell you. Actually, I could use a little advice, anyway. Since you're the only guy I know with the balls to ask a question like that, I guess you're the guy I'm going to confide in. But you'd better understand it's strictly confidential! I mean it, Tony; this is no bullshit! Before I tell you anything, I have to know if you're going to have any problem keeping your mouth shut, understand?"

"Jeez! Yeah, I get it! Hey, man, if you don't trust me, then just keep your stupid secrets to yourself, okay?"

"Cool it, Tony! I'm not trying to insult you, but this is really important; it involves Shannon."

"Shannon! What about Shannon? There'd better not be anything funny going on with Shannon!"

"Oh, God! I forgot what good friends you two are! Now this is going to be extra difficult. Listen; hear me out completely before you turn rabid, okay? I'm not going to go into all the sordid details; it's enough for you to know that Shannon and I are in love with each other. Of course, she won't admit that she loves me, but I know she does. That's basically the problem; she has this hang-up about giving her marriage one last chance. Can you believe it? Larry's such an asshole! God knows he doesn't deserve another chance. All he's ever done is cheat on her and I know she doesn't really love him anymore. Tony, short of killing the bastard, what in the Hell can I do?"

"Well, for starters, you don't have to worry about me turning rabid. To tell you the truth, I've never liked Larry. I always wondered what Shannon saw in him in the first place. I try to be polite to him for her sake, but I think he's a jerk and he definitely doesn't deserve her. But what about Elaine? If you still love her, and I assume you do, then you've got a real problem. Take it from me, buddy; loving two women at the same time is Hell on Earth. I've got this friend, see; he made the mistake of having an affair with the most wonderful, beautiful woman on this entire planet. Unfortunately, he fell hopelessly in love with her. Now, mind you, he still loved his wife and kids, so he couldn't leave them. Oh sure, he was smart enough to end the affair, but it was too late! Even now, three years later, he can't forget that other woman and he probably never will."

Looking at Tony's sad face, Eric realized that the 'friend' could only be Tony, himself. So that's why Cat and Tony didn't seem too happy with each other for such a long time. He always wondered; he just never had the nerve to ask.

"Listen, Tony; I'm sorry about dumping my problems on you like this. I'm sure you've got enough troubles of your own without having to worry about mine. I guess I'll just have to wait until after our vacation for her to make up her mind. Hey! Maybe I'll get lucky and he'll fall off a cliff while we're out there!"

"Yeah! Right! Just make sure you don't help him off that cliff, okay?"

CHAPTER 15 THE CHOSEN FEW

In the darkest hour before the dawn, Shannon was tossing and turning in her bed, trapped within the shrouded realm of nightmares. She awoke with a start and clutched the covers tightly about herself as she tried to recall the terrifying dream. Unable to remember what had frightened her so, she was left only with the vague feeling that danger would find her somewhere in the wilderness. This was the fourth, consecutive night that she had awoken with that same uneasy feeling. What nonsense! She refused to let such a ridiculous, superstitious feeling ruin her vacation. She rolled over and tried to relax, but sleep was a long time coming.

Not too far away, Cat was also having trouble sleeping. Finally, just before dawn, she gave up and quietly went downstairs for a cup of coffee. In the faint chill of the early July morning, she stepped out on her patio just as the sun's first rays were peeking through the branches of the huge oak trees in her back yard. She was greeted by the sweet serenade of two beautiful, yellow-breasted meadow larks, celebrating the break of day in their own melodious fashion. Not to be outdone, a nearby mockingbird joined them and carried their song to new heights. Lost in the pleasure of their captivating rhapsody, she was unaware of Tony standing behind her, until he gently put his arms around her.

"So you couldn't sleep, either; huh, Babe? Are you still having bad dreams about this trip?"

"Not really. It's just that something's been bugging me, but I'm not really sure what it is. Maybe it's leaving the kids or just plain, old fear of the unknown. Maybe it's both; I don't know."

"Honey, you don't have to worry about the kids; your sister will take good care of them. You know she loves them like her own! And you really shouldn't worry about this trip, either. We're gonna have a great time; believe me, this is one vacation we'll never forget!"

Eric was another early riser on this July morning. He looked over at Elaine, still peacefully sleeping, with just a hint of a smile on her serene face. He wondered what her dreams were like and if she were truly so at peace with herself as she always seemed. Sometimes, she looked so vulnerable that his heart ached for her. Poor Elaine! If only life could be as simple as she obviously needed it to be. Taking care to be extra quiet, he went downstairs to prepare their breakfast. At least he could do that much for her.

As the sun climbed higher, the cool of the morning slowly changed into a true summer heat, just in time for the group to meet at Tony's and pack all their gear into his Winnebago.

"All right, gang, that's it! We've gone over our check list a dozen times, already! If any of you think you've forgotten something, then it's just too damned bad! I'm not goin' over that stupid list again! C'mon; everybody pile in. We're takin' off!"

They all climbed in and got comfortable, with Eric and Larry being carefully polite to one another. Shannon was exhausted, so she lay down on the bed and dozed through most of the trip. By the time they reached Ukiah, she was just awakening. Tony caught sight of her stretching in his mirror.

"Well, it's about time, kiddo! Get enough beauty sleep? You almost missed out! We're about to stop for an early dinner and we weren't even goin' to wake you."

Larry put a protective arm around Shannon.

"Don't you worry, Honey; I wouldn't have let you miss dinner. Just ignore him!"

With a sardonic grin, Eric watched Larry and thought, 'He's trying too hard; he'll never fool her with that stupid, solicitous act of his!'

Ever cheerful, Elaine pointed happily to a restaurant sign. "Look! There's a smorgasbord! Let's eat there, shall we?"

Obligingly, Tony pulled in and parked. "Okay, everybody out! Last one in gets the bill!"

Just as they were finishing their meals, Tony noticed that the people in the booth directly to their right were getting louder and louder. He nudged Eric and motioned him to listen. In an instant, the entire group quieted down in order to listen to the noisy bunch sitting next to them.

There was one man in particular who kept drowning out the others. Eric thought he looked like some kind of red-necked hillbilly. He was huge; he must have weighed close to three hundred pounds. He had three plates spread before him and was wolfing down his food like there was no tomorrow! Even with his mouth bulging with food, he continued to bellow his complaints. "Those Goddamn fuckin' enviramenallist assholes! Of course they wanna shut us down! They don't give a shit about us loggers! What do they care what happens to us? They git paid anyways!"

"Yeah, Tiny, yer right! Y'know what? I bet those creeps git paid extra fer shuttin' us down!"

"Just you wait 'til tomorrow. Those pricks got a big surprise in store fer 'em! They're plannin' some big political shindig right there in that little town of Covelo. Can you believe that? They're gonna drive some bigshots around, showin' 'em the so-called damage caused by clear-cuttin'. They're even tryin' to blame us fer bringin' harm to some dumb-shit spotted owls.

Figger that one out! They're more worried about them stupid birds than they are about us!"

At that point, Tiny belched loudly and pushed his empty plates to the middle of the table. "Well, I guess it's time to grab some dessert. C'mon, guys; let's go clean 'em out!"

Eric was the first to speak. "Did you hear that? Covelo is exactly where we'll be sleeping tonight! We're supposed to meet the head of the pack train there tomorrow morning. It looks like we'll be arriving just in time for some major excitement! I wonder what he meant by a 'big surprise'?"

Elaine looked pale; she wasn't her usual, cheerful self. "I don't know about the rest of you, but I've lost my appetite. I hope you've all had enough to eat, because I'd really like to get out of here."

The others nodded in agreement; they were more than ready to leave. It was a much more subdued group that climbed back into the motorhome. For a while, they rode quietly. As the sun began its descent behind the nearby mountains, their collective mood seem to darken along with the evening sky. Larry was the first to break the silence.

"I know those guys sounded like a bunch of jerks, but, when you think about it, they did have a point. I mean, how do you justify putting the needs of some owls over the basic right of human beings to have jobs? If men like that aren't able to earn their own way, they'll just wind up on welfare and we're the ones who'll have to pick up the tab. We all know the system's running out of money, so they'll probably raise our taxes in order to support those poor slobs, when all we have to do in the first place is simply allow them to earn their own living."

Eric snorted in derision; he could hardly believe his ears. "You've got to be kidding! You sound just like one of those arrogant assholes who think they're among the chosen few who should be allowed to use the Earth to their own selfish satisfaction! Since you're an educated man, I thought you might at least have something half-ass intelligent to say. Just for the record, all living creatures share the same home, namely, the planet Earth! And, yes, that does include the spotted owls. Tell me, does the phrase 'balance of nature' have any meaning at all for you? It's obvious you're not the least bit worried about upsetting that delicate balance! And what about the rain forest? I'll bet you think it's a great idea to destroy that, too, and use the land for farming! Listen; if mankind doesn't stop screwing up the environment pretty damned soon, good old Mother Nature's going to kick us all right off the planet!"

Tony interceded in order to relieve the growing tension. "Yeah, Larry, he's right. There's always something in the news about those huge, old trees gettin' whacked. And some of them were over a thousand years old! Think about it; a thousand years to grow and only minutes to get cut down! Jesus! It's downright criminal!"

Shannon was equally horrified by the destruction of the forest lands. "What really amazes me is the short-sightedness of the loggers. At the rate they're cutting down the old trees, they'll run out of them in a few years! Then, they'll still have to face the dilemma of how to make a living. What a shame they don't tackle that problem now! Then maybe we could save the forests, the spotted owls and whatever else we might be destroying!"

Caitlin had been quietly listening to all of them before adding her point of view. "You're absolutely right, Shannon! You know what? I think we could all learn a lot from the American Indians. It's obvious they were way ahead of their time! They managed to cooperate with nature, instead of fighting it. For instance, they only hunted what they needed to survive. Then came the white man, who just had to destroy the huge herds of buffalo. After screwing up our environment in so many different ways, you'd think our people would finally smarten up enough to at least save what's left of the forests!"

Seeing how strongly the group sided with Eric, especially Shannon, Larry decided this would be an inappropriate time to take offense to Eric's remarks. Instead, he thought it would be wise to defuse the situation. "I'm beginning to realize that I never gave this matter the serious attention it deserves. You've all made some valid points tonight. Hey! Take a look out the window; you're missing a fantastic sight!"

They were just approaching a scenic overlook point with a truly magnificent view of the entire Round Valley, which included the small town of Covelo. They were only minutes away from the valley floor, where they would choose a secluded parking site and sleep the night away. But first, they decided to park and enjoy the view. Bathed in an iridescent mist which gently reflected the moonlight, the remote, mysterious valley shimmered with an ethereal translucence. Standing close to the edge, Shannon drank in the beauty surrounding her and thought how unreal it all seemed. Eric stared at Shannon and thought her beauty was so perfect that it seemed unreal. Larry looked from one to the other and thought his chances of ever winning Shannon back were completely unreal. He had made up his mind about one thing; if he couldn't have her, then he'd make damned sure that Eric wouldn't either!

"C'mon, gang! That's enough gawking! We're almost there; let's get on our way!" Tony was impatient, as usual. Everyone climbed back in the motorhome and they continued their drive down the twisty mountain

122

road. Finally, they reached the valley floor and the road stretched out in front of them, taking them directly into Covelo. As they slowly drove through the small town, they noticed that everything was pretty well shut down for the evening, except for a large barn located just on the outskirts. There were some people milling around outside and some loud country music coming from the inside. Eric was intrigued.

"Tony, pull over and park for a minute. Let's check this place out. It looks like an old-fashioned barn dance! You know what? It's still early and I haven't been to a barn dance since I was a kid. I vote for joining the party! Well, what do you say? Does that sound like fun or what?"

"Okay, let's put it to a vote. Yessiree, it looks like the yeas have it! Let's go, gang. Everybody bale out and prepare to party, party, party!"

Cat was indignant. "Wait a minute, Tony! What do you think you're doing? Nobody voted except you and Eric. You can't make the decisions for everyone else!"

"Wanna bet? It's my Winnebago, so that makes me the captain and the captain gives the orders, see? C'mon, everybody; let's go!"

Shannon grabbed Cat by the arm and smiled at her. "Don't worry about it; it's all right! I don't want you two fighting about this. Whoever wants to go, can go, and whoever doesn't, can stay in the motorhome and catch some sleep. I, for one, am going to the dance and have some fun. After all, isn't that why we're here?"

Seeing how eager Shannon was, Larry knew he'd have to go, whether he wanted to or not. He wasn't about to let her go without him!

Elaine groaned to herself. She had absolutely no interest in going. She was still feeling depressed from their encounter with the loggers; the last thing she

123

needed was to be around more, noisy, obnoxious people. She detested crowds; they made her feel extremely uncomfortable. She always had the feeling that she didn't quite fit in. "Eric, I'm really tired! I can barely keep my eyes open. Would you mind terribly if I stayed behind?"

"Of course not, Sweetheart! You go right ahead and get some sleep." Instantly elated, Eric tried not to look too happy. He kissed her goodnight and stepped out of the motorhome.

In spite of her objections, Cat really wanted to go, too. She climbed out with the rest of them and they all headed for the barn. Standing in front of it were two men in western dress, watching them with obvious interest. Eric walked up to them with his hand outstretched. "Hi, there! My name is Eric and these are my friends. I was wondering if it would be all right for us to join the party?"

One of the men reached out and shook Eric's hand. "Sure, friend, you're more than welcome. This barn dance is an annual shindig and we're always happy to have company. By the way, my name is Andy and this fellow is Jeremiah."

The rest of the group shook their hands and they all started to go inside. Shannon and Larry were the last in line and, as they approached the opening, Shannon felt herself being watched. She looked to her left and saw half a dozen Indians staring directly at her. Annoyed, she stopped in her tracks and glared at them. Larry glanced nervously at them and tried to pull Shannon into the barn, but she refused to budge. With an unwavering gaze, she noticed one in particular, taller than the rest. He had been sitting on a tree stump behind the others. As he got up to see what they were looking at, the small group instinctively moved out of his way and he walked to the front to gain a better view.

The moment he saw her, he felt a shock of recognition! Her perfect figure was clad in a clinging, soft green dress. Her delicate, heart-shaped face was set off by the most vivid green eyes he had ever seen. But her most arresting feature was her thick, long, naturally wavy hair! The light coming from the barn danced in her shining tresses, reflecting the color of burnished copper. With mixed emotions, Jacob knew there could be no doubt; she was exactly the red-haired woman in his dreams!

At first, Shannon had stared back at the Indians simply because she was irritated. She didn't like being stared at and decided to give them a dose of their own medicine! But the tall one was a different matter altogether. When their eyes met, it was with a definite sense of deja vu. She knew him; she didn't know how, but she knew him. She studied his face carefully, feeling a need to memorize it. With his dark, exotic looks and lean, hard body, she found him immensely attractive. But his gaze was unsettling; she had never had a man look at her quite like he did. His eyes were so dark, they were almost black and she suddenly felt in danger of losing her very soul in them. She forced herself to break away and turned to Larry. "I'm ready now; let's join the others."

Looking back uneasily, Larry took her arm and led her into the barn. "What was that all about? Why were you staring at them? Do you know any of them?"

"No, I don't. It's just that the tall one reminded me of someone. It's nothing, really; just forget about it. Come on; let's have some fun!"

As they entered the huge barn, their senses were assailed by the pungent aroma of hay and sweat mixed together. Bales of hay had been set out for the people to sit on between dances. There were old harnesses and riding equipment hanging on the walls of the barn.

Shannon once again had that delightful feeling of stepping back in time. She and Larry looked around and found Eric, Cat and Tony standing with a group of other people, all of them encircling the square dancers and clapping their hands. The mood was contagious and the music inviting. Larry and Shannon started clapping their hands right along with the others as they all listened to the booming voice of the square dance caller.

"Grab your partners; don't be shy! Come on, gals; give 'em the eye! Sashay left and do it right now! Twirl that gal and give her a bow! Sashay right and go back around! That's the purtiest gal you ever have found! Now grab your gal right around the middle and bring her back to listen to the fiddle!"

The dancers stomped their feet and hooted out loud, all moving in perfect precision to the caller's orders. Tony grabbed Cat and hauled her out on the floor. "C'mon, Honey! This'll be a piece of cake!"

They stumbled around and messed up on the calls so badly that the crowd started laughing, but they didn't care; they were having a great time. Shannon turned to Larry. "Come on, Larry; let's try it!"

"Uh, uh! No way! I'm not going out there and make a fool out of myself!"

Eric laughed out loud. "It's a little late to worry about that, isn't it, Larry? Come on, Shannon! I'll dance with you."

Eric grabbed Shannon by the hand and pulled her along with him. They stood with Tony and Cat and formed their own little square. Pretty soon they were hooting and stomping along with the rest of the dancers. By the time the dance was over, the four of them had dissolved into laughter. Shannon couldn't remember when she'd had such good, simple fun!

The hours raced by like minutes! Before they knew it, it was after midnight. They were all sitting on bales of hay, drinking some punch, when Tony looked at his watch. "Jesus! I didn't know it was so late! I guess we'd better think about gettin' some sleep. Eric, what time are we supposed to meet that pack train guy?"

"I think he said about nine in the morning. But why worry about it? As far as I'm concerned, the night's still young!"

"Bullshit! C'mon, Eric; it's time to go!"

"All right, Captain! Your wish is our command! But tell me something; has anyone ever told you you're a bossy son of a bitch?"

Tony grinned. "Yeah, but it never even slows me down!"

Larry tapped Tony on the shoulder. "Why don't you guys go on ahead of us? I want to talk to Shannon alone for a minute."

"That's fine! Just don't be too long; I don't want you wakin' me up once I'm asleep."

The three of them went outside and headed for the motorhome, leaving Larry and Shannon alone. Larry sat quietly for a moment, studying Shannon's face, searching for just the right words. "Shannon, I know we've had our share of problems and I know I'm mostly to blame for them. But I've really been trying to make things right again and I somehow get the feeling that you're not helping as much as you could. In fact, sometimes I wonder if you even care at all anymore."

"Actually, Larry, sometimes I wonder the same thing. It's almost as though something has died in our marriage and I don't know if it can ever be revived. I think it's only fair to tell you that I consider this trip our last chance. If something doesn't change dramatically between us by the end of the trip, then I think we should separate."

Finding it difficult to speak, he took a while to respond. "Well, at least you're being honest with me. I'd like to ask you something very important. If there were someone else, would you tell me?"

Shannon took a long time answering him. "Only if I were very certain that the other man was the right one for me."

Painful as it was, Larry was grateful for her honesty. In fact, her remarks gave him at least a small ray of hope. Since she didn't mention Eric by name, that could only mean that she didn't yet consider him the right man. Perhaps he still had a chance after all. He smiled and took her by the hand. "I guess we should turn in, too. Let's go, Honey."

While they headed for the door, they were being carefully watched by a tall man with a muscular build. He seldom came into town and nobody knew much about him, only that his name was Mathias. He had a deep scar down the side of his face; except for that, he might have been considered handsome. He'd had his eye on Shannon ever since she walked through the door and he thought she was the best looking woman he'd ever seen! While he watched her dance, he drank a little more than he should. He was one of those men who become meaner as they get drunker. It would have been better for all concerned if he had been completely drunk, because then he merely would have passed out. Unfortunately, he was only at that stage where he could blame his actions on the liquor, but still had a surprising amount of control. He belligerently stepped directly in their path as they tried to leave, refusing to move so much as an inch. An open barn door covers a wide area, so Larry simply moved further to his left to try to get around him without incident. Mathias anticipated his move and, with a malicious gleam in his eye, stepped directly in front of him, once again barring his path.

Annoyed, Larry looked up at him. "Excuse me, would you please move and let us pass?"

"I really don't give a shit where you go, Bud, but I think the lady wants to stay behind and dance with me!"

"No, I don't! I'm tired and I want to go to bed!" Shannon was disgusted; she loathed drunks.

"Well, now, that's just fine an' dandy with me, Sweetheart! I'd just as soon take you to bed as dance with you!"

With that, he grabbed Shannon by the arm and started dragging her out the door. Larry rushed him and punched him hard, right in the stomach! It didn't even faze him. With one arm, he knocked Larry to the ground! While he lay there, doubled over with pain, Mathias walked over and spit right in his face! Then, holding Shannon tightly in front of him, he slowly squeezed first one breast and then the other. Tauntingly, he made sure Larry was watching. "See this, Bud? Now I'm takin' the lady home with me and we're gonna dance all night long!"

By this time, an angry crowd had gathered around them, muttering threats. One of the men from the crowd actually approached Mathias. "You'd better let her go! There's only one of you and lots of us!"

Matt laughed and spit right on the man's shiny, new cowboy boots.

"Shit! I done mopped up floors with more'n the lot of you! There ain't a man Jack among you that could beat me if I lost both my arms!"

While the man looked down horrified at his brand new boots, Matt took quick advantage of the moment

129

and knocked him flat! The crowd gasped in unison and stepped back a pace without even realizing it.

"All right! This is gettin' to be fun! Now which of you brave souls wants to be next?"

No-one answered and no-one moved.

"Hah! Just as I thought! The whole lot of you ain't nothin' but a bunch of Goddamned wimps! Maybe y'all just better get the Hell outa my way!"

With that, he started to drag Shannon toward the crowd. She struggled desperately to no avail. She looked beseechingly at Larry, who was sitting up, but making no attempt to rise. "Larry! Please! Help me!" Filled with shame, he hid his face in his hands.

As Matt shoved his way through the glaring crowd, he came face to face with a tall, strong Indian who wouldn't move. Surprised, he hesitated and stared into Jacob's menacing eyes. Matt slowly smiled and nodded, acknowledging the Indian's silent challenge. Roughly, he threw Shannon aside, relishing the fight to come. He'd been aching for a good fight for a long time. He was an extremely proficient fighter who fought fairly when it suited him and unfairly whenever he deemed it necessary, but, in either case, he was used to winning. Most of the time, it was just too easy for him. Looking at Jacob, he noted that he was tall, like himself, with a sinewy strength which he recognized as dangerous. Oh, yes, this would be a great fight! With an almost obscene grin, he suddenly charged Jacob, catching him around the waist. The two of them crashed into the screaming crowd, taking three of them down into the dirt with them. As they rolled in the dust, Jacob lifted his knee up between them and smashed it into Matt's stomach, then rolled him over on his back and began strangling him. Almost choking him to death, Jacob leaned over and whispered something in his ear. "I know exactly who you are and I'll be coming for you, all

130

of you!" Then he grinned maliciously and released him.

Gasping for air, Matt slowly rose. He stared at Jacob, not quite understanding what he meant, but feeling a chill go down his back. Then he got angry; this wasn't fun anymore! With a bellow, he charged Jacob again. This time, Jacob quickly sidestepped and struck Matt with a lightning-fast blow to the head! The punch landed with such force that he staggered and fell to his knees, dizzily shaking his head while blood sprayed from his nose. Such a hit would have rendered a lesser man completely unconscious, but Matt was incredibly strong, especially considering his intoxicated state. When he attempted to stand, Jacob grabbed him, lifted him high and then slammed him into the hard-packed ground! Within seconds, he had him wrapped up like a pretzel, holding him in an iron grip which forbade movement of any kind.

"You dumb shit! Just had to come back for more, didn't you? Don't you realize I could snap your neck in a second if I wanted to? But I'm not going to let you off that easy. Remember what I told you! I'll be coming for you, all of you, and I guarantee you won't survive our next meeting!"

Unable to sleep, Eric decided to take a short walk and get some fresh air. As he stepped out of the motorhome, he heard screams coming from a crowd in front of the barn. He ran over there, arriving just as some Indian slammed another man into the ground and held him in a bone-crunching hold. Then he released him, glaring down at him with hate-filled, obsidian eyes. Confused, Eric looked from one to the other and then noticed Shannon standing at the edge of the crowd. She was staring at the Indian, her eyes filled with open admiration. The Indian returned her stare with an unfathomable look. Her heart hammering in her chest, she took a step toward him; she wanted to thank him,

131

but Eric interceded, blocking her view.

"Shannon, are you all right? Where's Larry? What happened here? Who are those two men?"

"Eric! Please! I'll explain later! Move out of my way; I have to thank that man for helping me!" She forced herself past him, but it was too late. The Indian had disappeared. She looked around desperately, but he had vanished without a trace!

CHAPTER 16 BARRICADE

Shannon awoke early the next morning feeling as though she hadn't slept at all. The others didn't seem to have her problem; they were all sound asleep. As she lay quietly lost in thought, she wondered why her life seemed to get more complicated by the day. Just when she thought she had enough problems, especially with Larry and Eric, along came someone so intriguing that she was unable to quit thinking about him. His face had been the last one she saw before she finally drifted off to sleep and it was the first one she saw this morning. His sharply defined, brooding face with the unfathomable, coal-black eyes was forever imprinted on her mind. She wondered why he had disappeared without a word and why he had looked at her so strangely. She wanted more than anything to find him and thank him, but most of all, she just wanted to look into his eyes one more time.

Shannon looked over at Larry's peaceful face and was overwhelmed by a wave of extreme pity and compassion. How horrible life must be for a man without courage. She vaguely recalled an old saying she'd heard years ago. Now, how did that go? Oh, yes, 'The brave man dies but once; the coward dies a thousand times.' How aptly that described Larry, for he would surely die of shame every time he looked into her eyes. How sad! She realized all of a sudden that their marriage was truly finished; his cowardice was the final blow. There had been at least a slim possibility that they might have worked out their other problems, but no marriage could survive what had happened last night.

She could not live with a man who had failed to protect her and he could not live with his failure.

Involuntarily, her thoughts returned to the Indian. Now there was a man! He was certainly no coward; in fact, Shannon sensed that he somehow needed to fight. Obviously, he was living in the wrong century, for he was a born warrior! A chill went through her as she tried to imagine making love with such a man, being totally conquered by him, drowning in the black pool of his eyes!

Shannon tossed restlessly, then finally decided to get up. As she quickly dressed and combed her hair, she became aware of Eric leaning on his elbow, watching her intently. He quietly dressed and motioned her to go outside with him. As they stepped out of the motorhome, they were greeted by the first rays of the sun, peeking over the rim of the mountains which encircled Round Valley. They walked for some distance and then stood beneath a weeping willow tree to ensure the privacy of their conversation. Shannon shivered from the morning chill and Eric quickly wrapped his light jacket around her shoulders, then pulled her to him and held her tightly. Neither of them spoke for a while, both of them taking comfort from each other's warmth, when suddenly they caught sight of a flurry of movement in a nearby field. They turned just in time to see six or seven deer sail gracefully over a low fence and disappear through the trees. Eric smiled to himself, thinking of the total freedom enjoyed by the fleet-footed deer, and fervently hoped the forest lands would never be taken away from them. Holding Shannon close to his heart, he also prayed she would never be taken away from him, for he needed her like the deer needed the forest.

Tormented, Shannon buried her face in his chest, wondering how she could feel so at home in his arms and yet be so attracted to that tall, dangerous Indian.

134

She had always considered herself a one-man woman; she couldn't imagine being otherwise. She honestly thought she had finally found that one man in Eric. Holding Eric even more tightly, she wished the two of them could be completely alone with each other for at least a week. Maybe then she would be able to sort out her true feelings for him.

While she clung to him, Eric responded by kissing her deeply and passionately. Instantly filled with desire, she moaned softly, then forced herself to push him away.

"Eric, please don't! I'm so confused right now. I need time to think. I hope you understand."

"No, I don't understand! You didn't need time to think at the Briar Patch! What in the Hell has changed since then?"

Seeing his hurt expression, Shannon felt a wave of guilt and wondered what she could say to lessen his pain.

"Eric, surely you already know how deeply I care for you. And after last night's fiasco, you must know my marriage is completely over. But this isn't the right time to go into all this. I thought you agreed to wait until after our vacation for my final answer. I still have a lot of thinking to do."

"If your marriage is really finished, then what's left to think about? For God's sake, woman, tell me you love me and that you'll marry me! I'm not letting you go until you say it. I have to know, once and for all!"

"What about Elaine?"

"My marriage is as finished as yours, regardless of your answer. So don't even try to use her as an excuse!"

Sighing, Shannon realized she couldn't stall him any longer. She knew she had deep feelings for him and wasn't quite sure why she found it so difficult to use the word 'love' with him.

"All right! Since you insist on knowing right now, this is my answer. I think I love you, but I'm not completely certain and I'm definitely not ready to discuss marriage! Just the thought of marriage, even with you, makes me feel horribly trapped and I don't know why. I need to search my soul and find out exactly what I want to do with my life. I feel very confused; the only thing I know for certain is that I truly care for you."

Eric hugged her so tightly she lost her breath. "I knew it! I knew you really cared for me; I just had to hear you say it! My beautiful Shannon! I love you more than words could ever say! I can wait for you to use the word 'love' and we won't even talk about marriage until you're good and ready. Hell! For that matter, we can just live together, if you that's what you want. We belong together, now and forever, and I don't need some piece of paper to tell me that!"

Shannon hid her face on his shoulder and prayed she would never disappoint him. Deep in her heart, she feared that she didn't care for him quite as much as he loved her. If only love could always be equal! Unfortunately, that was rarely the case. With tears in her eyes, Shannon stared up at the beautiful canopy created by the weeping willow and saw the golden rays of the sun gently peeking through the draping branches, as though loath to disturb them.

"Eric, we'd better start back. I don't want the others to suspect anything just yet. I'd really like to wait until after our vacation before we tell anyone anything. I especially don't want to hurt Elaine. Don't you agree that would be best?"

"Of course! You don't have to worry; I'm not planning on saying anything until we're home."

They kissed one last time and then stepped out of the protective canopy of the weeping willow into the

136

blinding glare of the morning sun. As they walked back down the road, Eric stopped Shannon for a moment and pointed to the field across the way. They both paused long enough to watch the morning mists begin to rise from the damp ground. The sun was reflected off the patchy mist in such a way as to resemble a large, silvery, patchwork quilt floating gently just above the meadow. The crisp morning air was rich with the distinctive, sweet smell of alfalfa from nearby fields. When they were within about two hundred feet of the motorhome, a squirrel ran directly across their path and scurried up the nearest tree and out onto a limb just over their heads. Eyeing them suspiciously, he scolded them loudly for intruding into his territory. Eric and Shannon looked at each other and burst into laughter! As they continued on their way, they saw Tony walking toward them.

"Well, it's about time you two got back! You know, we just barely have time to get a bite to eat before we have to meet that pack train guy. By the way, you're both lucky I was the first one to get up and notice that you were missing. The others are just now getting up, so they don't know how long you were actually gone. I went looking for you a while ago, but you were a little too preoccupied to notice me, so I came back and decided to watch for your return. I think it's only fair to warn you that a weeping willow tree isn't as protective as you seem to think, so why don't you two cool it for a while? I'm sure we'll have enough excitement on this trip without the added worry of bloodshed within our own group."

Shannon gasped out loud. "Tony! How could you spy on us like that? I thought you were my best friend in the whole world!"

"I am your best friend in the whole world and that's why I went looking for you. Listen, kiddo; I'm trying to protect you from your own stupidity! Larry isn't blind and he isn't retarded. Don't make the mistake of selling him short. You probably don't realize it, but the man is quite capable of murder! And you, Shannon, are the one person in the world he'd readily kill for! Look; we're almost there, so let's drop this conversation for now. I just hope a word to the wise will be sufficient!"

As they reached the motorhome, the others were just stepping out of it and stretching their legs. Larry looked at Shannon and then quickly looked away, finding it difficult to meet her eyes. Elaine ran over to Eric and gave him a hug, causing him to wince imperceptibly. Cat gave Tony an oblique look and shrugged her shoulders. "Tony, I'm starved! Let's go find a place to eat, okay?"

"Cat's right! Everyone climb back in and let's hit the road!"

As they drove down the main street of the small town, the Covelo Hotel caught their eye and they decided to check it out. On the bottom floor was a small restaurant. Upon entering the charming cafe, the delicious aroma of hot coffee and sizzling bacon and eggs made their stomachs growl in anticipation. After they were seated and the waitress had taken their orders, Tony stretched happily, reveling in the pleasure of a delicious cup of coffee.

"Mmmm, this is the best coffee I ever tasted! Well, gang, what d'ya think? Am I smart or what? Even in a small town, I can always find a great place to eat!"

Eric laughed. "Tony, it's probably the only place to eat! Besides, how do you know it's great? We haven't eaten anything yet!"

"What a schmuck! I can tell by the coffee. When the coffee's great, the food's great, too! Jesus! I thought everybody knew that! By the way, you'd better check your notes again and figure out exactly where

138

we're supposed to meet that pack train guy. I know when, but I don't remember where. So get to checking, okay?"

Eric pulled out his notes and grinned at Tony. "Well, I guess you did get lucky and pick the right place. It just so happens this is where we're supposed to meet him! So I guess we can all just relax right here until he shows up, which should be in about an hour."

Their orders arrived and they all dug in. They soon discovered the food to be every bit as delicious as the coffee. Tony had been absolutely correct!

While they were enjoying their breakfasts, the cafe began to fill up. They nodded to several people they recognized from the square dance. An older man from another table approached them and spoke directly to Shannon.

"Excuse me, young lady. I don't mean to bother you, but, on behalf of the townsfolk, I just wanted to apologize to you about that unhappy incident last night. That feller was just plumb nasty and we wanted you to know that he's not one of us. Fact is, we wish we could find him so's we could run him outa town on a rail. In the old days, we would of tarred and feathered a mean critter like him!

Shannon blushed slightly. "Thank you! You're very kind, but you really don't owe me an apology. That man was just a disgusting drunk and you're not at all responsible for him. As far as this town is concerned, I think it's charming and so are the people. I knew right away that he couldn't be one of you, so please don't worry about it."

The man tipped his hat to her and returned to his table. The whole room had suddenly become very quiet and Shannon felt extremely uncomfortable.

"I'm already finished with my breakfast, so I think I'll walk around outside while you're waiting for that man to show up. I'll just explore the town a bit and meet you back here in a little while, okay?"

As she started to rise, Larry also stood. She quickly motioned to him to sit back down.

"Larry, if you don't mind, I'd rather walk alone for a while. Please don't worry about me; I'll be right back."

Once Shannon had left, everyone slowly resumed talking again. Looking around at the people in the cafe, Elaine felt a little confused.

"What in the world was that all about? Who was that man? And what sort of an 'incident' was he talking about, anyway?"

Larry's face instantly darkened and he excused himself to go to the restroom. Cat and Tony exchanged oblique looks and said nothing, both of them at a loss for words. Elaine's friends always worried about just exactly how much they should tell her regarding anything unpleasant, because she seemed almost incapable of handling any kind of stress. Weighing his words very carefully, Eric decided he should be the one to tell her what had happened.

"It's like this, Elaine. Last night, after Tony, Cat and I left the barn dance and returned to the motorhome, Shannon and Larry stayed behind to talk alone for a while. Evidently, there was a drunk who gave Shannon a hard time and some Indian came to her aid and beat the guy up. That's about all there was to it, so we didn't really think it was worth mentioning."

"Not worth mentioning! Are you kidding? What exactly do you mean by a 'hard time'? And why did an Indian have to rescue her? Where was Larry?"

Larry returned to the table just in time to hear her last questions. Glaring at her, he sat down and pounded his fist on the table. Startled, everyone in the room turned to look at him.

"Larry was busy protecting himself! Larry was

140

busy being a Goddamned coward! There! Does that answer your questions, you nosy bitch?" With those remarks, Larry jumped up, knocking over his chair, and rushed out the door before anyone could say a word to him!

With a look of rage on his face, Eric quickly stood up to go after Larry, but Tony grabbed him by the arm and stopped him.

"Eric! Let him go! He's already being punished enough! Think about it; he has to live with his shame. I guarantee you he's locked up in his own private Hell right now and I don't think he'll ever escape from that prison. So just forget about it!"

Before Eric could answer, Tony noticed a lean, hard-looking man in his late thirties standing in the doorway, staring at them with just the hint of a sneer. Still angry, Eric walked over to him and looked him right in the eye.

"Just what in the Hell do you think you're looking at?"

Not at all disturbed, he laughed out loud. "As a matter of fact, I think I'm looking at some city dudes who want to join my pack train!" With an arrogant stance, he looked them slowly up and down. "And a hundred bucks says I'm right!"

Taken aback, Eric just stood there with his mouth open, staring at the man. Tony stepped right up to him and reached out to shake his hand.

"You'll have to excuse my friend here; he's practicing using his mouth for a fly-trap!"

Laughing even louder, the man shook Tony's hand, looked skeptically at Eric and introduced himself.

"The name's Trevor Thompson, of Thompson's Middle Eel Wilderness Expeditions, and you are......?"

"I'm Tony and this is my wife, Caitlin. My friend here is Eric and this is his wife, Elaine. The other couple, Larry and Shannon, are out exploring the town at the moment."

"Well, there's really not much to explore in this town; it's very small, so they'll probably get back pretty quick. By the way, I was just in the doorway when some dude went stormin' by me! Was that Larry, by any chance?"

"Uh, yeah, I'm afraid it was. Actually, he and his wife are kind of in the middle of a spat. You know how it goes; they're probably out makin' up right now. Sorry about the trouble!"

"It's fine with me so long as it happens out here. But let's make sure we understand each other; I don't want any of that shit goin' on when we're on the trail! Comprende, amigos?"

Still irritated, Eric walked over to him and gave him a long, hard look. "Don't worry about us! We take care of our own problems! Comprende?"

Tony quickly stepped between the two bristling men. "C'mon, you guys! I think we all comprende! Besides, we're not here to argue; we're supposed to be taking care of all the last-minute arrangements."

Eric and Trevor reluctantly stepped back a pace, neither of them willing to back down. Tony motioned them to the table and they all sat down to discuss the particulars of the trip.

Shannon had reached the end of the main street and stopped to look around. She found the light morning breeze very refreshing and the town quaint and peaceful. With very few changes, it could easily have been a frontier town from another era. Shannon relished the peace and quiet; in fact, she dreaded the thought of ever returning to her hectic life in the city. Of all the places she had ever been, this lovely Round Valley somehow felt like home to her. It was almost as though she had lived here in a previous life. If only

142

there were some way to remain here after all the others had gone home.

She was brought out of her reverie by the sound of a convoy of jeeps approaching the main street. While she watched, they all parked and a group of important-looking people headed for the Covelo Hotel. She quickly returned to the cafe to find out what was going on. The large group was just being seated as she stepped in the doorway. She paused there for a moment, silhouetted by the morning sun. Eric and the others looked over at her as she stood there, the sun's rays dancing in her glorious red hair, setting it aflame with streaks of red and gold. Trevor stopped dead in the middle of a sentence and openly stared at her. As she approached the table, looking at him curiously, he was completely captivated by her emerald-green eyes, set in a lovely heart-shaped face with a flawless, creamy complexion and sensuous, full lips. He slowly lowered his eyes to take in her perfect figure, clad only in a pair of jeans and a pale green tank-top. He could hardly believe his eyes; never had he seen such a beautiful woman!

Flushing angrily, Eric stood to get a chair for Shannon and carefully placed it right by himself. He motioned for Shannon to sit while he glared at Trevor. His glare wasn't lost on Trevor, nor especially on Elaine, who suddenly looked quite ill and excused herself to go to the restroom. Feeling extremely embarrassed, Shannon turned to leave also, but Eric grabbed her by the arm and held her right there by his side, his eyes never leaving Trevor's. "Well, it looks like we've pretty much settled everything on the agenda. Do you have any other questions before you leave?"

"Just one more thing. Why don't you introduce me to the lady? Better yet, I'll introduce myself! The name's Trevor Thompson and I'll be your tour guide.

143

You must be the one they call Shannon. I want you to know that I plan on taking especially good care of you. I'll personally see to it that all of you have an unforgettable vacation.

He held out his hand to her, but Eric quickly stepped between them, preventing them from shaking hands. With an amused smile, Trevor turned to leave.

"Well, I guess that's about it, folks. Remember; we'll be meeting bright and early Monday morning."

After he'd left, Shannon glared at Eric and jerked her arm away from him.

"Eric! How could you do such a thing? Don't you realize how you must have hurt Elaine? You'd better go after her right this minute and try to explain yourself! And just for the record, I can take care of myself just fine! I could easily have handled that situation without your help!"

Looking a little ashamed, Eric left to find Elaine. With tears in her eyes, Shannon looked at Tony and Cat apologetically.

"I'm so sorry about that ridiculous scene! I just don't know what to do with him! I'm sure you're both aware that we care very deeply for each other, but he wasn't supposed to say or do anything about it until after our trip. Only then was he going to talk to Elaine about a divorce. This just can't happen right now, in front of everyone."

Cat looked at her with compassion. "Then the two of you have decided to get married? I didn't know things had advanced that far."

Shannon looked horrified. "No! I mean......I don't know if I ever want to marry again! It's just that he's decided to divorce her regardless of my decision and he wanted to spare her until after the trip."

Cat had a worried look on her face. "What on Earth can he possibly say to her now that would do any good? I mean......Shannon, you should have seen the look on his face! Only then did I realize exactly how much you mean to him. I do believe the man would kill for you!"

Tony gave Shannon a long, hard look filled with concern. "That's all you need! Now you've got two men who would kill for you! You'd better be extra careful around Larry and Eric. At this point, I'm beginning to wonder which one of them will still be alive after this trip, but I think I'll put my money on Eric! He's a lot tougher and a lot smarter! As far as this guy Trevor is concerned, I wouldn't worry too much about him. He just sounds like a big blowhard to me. Besides, I don't think he'll have much of a chance to get out of line with Eric around! The only way he'd ever manage to get his hands on you would be over Eric's dead body!"

Shannon couldn't help laughing. "Oh, Tony, you exaggerate everything! I really doubt it would ever come to that!"

While they sat enjoying one last cup of coffee, they couldn't help but overhear the conversation of the large group that had arrived in the convoy of jeeps. They were discussing the effects of the clear-cutting of timber on the environment. One of the men in particular was adamant about stopping the loggers in their tracks.

"Gentlemen, I know you're all familiar with the very serious danger facing the spotted owl due to the loggers' practice of felling our ancient forests. I'm equally certain that you're all aware of the necessity of preserving the various keystone species which hold major ecosystems together. I am proud to be in the company of such far-sighted, dedicated individuals as yourselves and I am confident that, together, we can and will make a difference. Before we embark on our physical inspection of the damages caused by the logging industry, I should warn you to brace yourselves for the devastating loss of large portions of our once beautiful and vast ancient forests. For those of you who have witnessed this continuing depletion of our proud heritage, I can only say that it is time to put an end to this travesty, once and for all, for our great-grandchildren. Hopefully, they will be able to enjoy our lovely forests, abundant with the very trees which we are so diligently striving to preserve and which, if we succeed in our endeavor, will have out-lived all of us here today."

As he finished speaking, there was a spontaneous burst of applause from the other members of his group. Tony, Cat and Shannon also stood and applauded since they were in complete agreement with everything he'd said. The rest of the people in the cafe immediately followed suit and the pleasantly surprised, grey-haired gentleman who had spoken so eloquently found himself slightly embarrassed by the standing ovation. With a gentle smile, he nodded in appreciation to his audience and rose to leave. As he and his group headed for the door, Eric and Elaine were just returning to their table. Apparently, he'd succeeded in calming her down. Eric looked at the departing group with curiosity.

"Hey, Tony, who are those people? What do you suppose they're doing here?"

"I think they're here to make some kind of an official inspection. One of them talked about the damages caused by clear-cutting. You should have heard his speech, Eric. He brought up some really good points. Well, gang, shall we all go outside and look around the town? There's no sense in waiting any longer for Larry; he's probably off sulking somewhere. C'mon; let's go!"

As they walked out the door, they noticed that both ends of the street had been completely barricaded

146

by logging trucks. There were at least half a dozen trucks at each end. The group of people that had arrived in the convoy of jeeps were standing in the middle of the road, looking from one end to the other in confusion. While they stood there, the drivers climbed out of their trucks and slowly approached them. Each one of the drivers carried a winch bar, a long metal rod used in tightening the chain binders around the logs on their trucks. These winch bars could easily double as effective weapons, should the need arise. The group from the jeeps looked apprehensive as the truck drivers steadily advanced toward them. The grey-haired gentleman decided it was time for another speech and prayed the truck drivers would listen to reason.

"Gentlemen, I sincerely hope that none of you are contemplating some form of violence! Let me assure you that it would be entirely unnecessary. I'm sure we are all reasonable men and reason dictates that we should communicate our differences to one another and strive to resolve them in a peaceful manner."

One of the truck drivers raised his winch bar in a threatening manner. "Oh, yeah? Well, listen up, Mac! We know why you're here; if you don't quit tryin' to shut down the logging industry, I'm personally gonna communicate this bar right in the middle of your face! And I'll only go that easy on you 'cause I'm such a reasonable man! How's that for peaceful manners, huh?"

With those remarks, the truck drivers continued to advance in a menacing fashion. They were joined by some of their logger friends who had also shown up to join in the protest against the environmentalists. One of the loggers decided to express his complaints in a little more detail.

"Listen, you jerks! Did it ever occur to you guys that we have to cut down the trees so we can make a

147

living? Tell me this; if you shut us down, are you gonna feed my wife and kids? Of course not! You don't give a shit what happens to us! Why don't you try to figure out some way to grow more trees to replace the ones we cut down, instead of tryin' to starve us out? I'll tell you why; it's 'cause you don't give a damn, that's why! All you guys care about is your own fat paychecks; ain't that right? Well, this is one time you're gonna have to work extra hard for your money. Fact is, after we get done teachin' y'all some hard lessons, you won't think they paid you near enough!"

By this time, the sidewalks were filled with some of the Indians from the reservation, the local townspeople, some tourists and a few other strangers. With naked fear visible on their faces, the group from the jeeps cautiously stepped toward their vehicles. In the still of the summer morning, tension held everyone in an ever-tightening grip. Even the morning breeze had retreated, leaving in its wake a dry heat to match the hot tempers already flaring like small volcanoes.

Eric looked across the street and saw Larry standing close to several of the Indians, who appeared ready and eager to fight, grateful, in fact, for the opportunity. Seeing a sudden flash of light off the roof across the street, Eric looked up just in time to see two men hide behind a large chimney. Puzzled, he turned to Tony and whispered to him.

"Tony! Did you see those two men standing on that roof? Look! One of them just peeked out from behind that chimney! They're up to something! Tony! Are you listening? I'm trying to tell you there's going to be some serious trouble!"

"Jesus! Will you shut up? Any fool can see there's gonna be trouble! Forget about the Goddamn roof! The fight's gonna break out in the street, you dummy, right in front of you! It's pretty clear we're gonna have to help out those poor guys in the jeeps. I don't think we can count on Larry for any help, but those Indians look anxious to jump into this. I sure hope they're on our side! Well, here goes nothin'!"

They both walked toward the grey-haired gentleman and stood by his side, making clear their intention to protect him. Their action caused one of the truck drivers, a big, burly man who went by the name of 'Tiny', to snort in derision. Tony and Eric remembered him from the restaurant in Ukiah.

"You two wimps really oughtn't to stick your noses where they don't belong; you're just liable to git 'em broke that way!"

Before they could answer, Jacob stepped off the opposite sidewalk and walked right up to the mouthy trucker.

"You'll have to get by me first, if you think you got the balls for it!"

Sensing that the Indian relished a good fight, Tiny stared into his malevolent, black eyes and swore he could see his own funeral in them! His resolve weakening, he stepped back a pace without even realizing it. Feeling the eyes of his fellow truckers upon him, he couldn't bear the humiliation of backing down, so he forced himself to respond to Jacob's challenge.

"Listen here! We ain't got no gripe against you Indians, so why don't you just stay out of this and save yourselves some grief?"

Watching Tiny break into a cold sweat, Jacob couldn't suppress an evil grin. At this point, more than a dozen Indians sauntered out into the street and stood behind their leader, wearing the same malevolent grins.

"Jesus Christ! What's the matter with you guys? I already told you; we ain't got nothin' against you Indians! So why don't you just butt out?"

The other truckers looked at Tiny in disgust.

149

They knew he was just plain scared. One of them whispered loudly to the others. "I don't know about the rest of you, but I've had enough of this bullshit!"

With those words, he charged the Indians. With a shout of pure rage, he raised his bar to strike at the nearest one. His target, a short, stocky Indian by the name of Oak Stump, grabbed hold of the bar and used it to send the foolish trucker sailing right over his head, landing with a loud thud. Then he wrenched the bar out of his hands and hit him over the head with it, knocking him cold. Laughing triumphantly, he threw the bar at the line of truckers, preferring the use of his bare hands against his enemies; it was always more satisfying to fight like a real warrior! Jacob gave Oak Stump a nod of approval and then turned back to Tiny, who had stepped back several more paces. Sweating profusely, he brandished his bar at Jacob, making a weak attempt to appear in control of the situation. Jacob laughed out loud as he rushed Tiny, knocking him down hard against the pavement, banging his head against it until he was senseless! He'd barely gotten to his feet when two of the loggers jumped him from behind, causing all three of them to fall to the street in a jumble. Jacob viciously kneed one of them while grabbing the other one by the arm, brutally twisting it behind the man's back until he heard a loud snap! Screaming in agony, the logger cursed Jacob with a vengeance, while the other one lay holding his private parts, groaning in pain. Dismissing both of them, Jacob quickly looked around and saw a warrior named Three Bears being held by two of the truckers while a third violently pounded him in the stomach! Before Jacob could reach him, Eric and Tony tackled the two holding him. With his hands suddenly freed, Three Bears leaped upon the one who'd been pounding him, bringing him to the ground with a loud crunch as he smashed the back of his head into the pavement. While the trucker lay dazed, Three Bears began to strangle him, pressing hard on his windpipe until he fell unconscious. Worried that he might actually kill him, Jacob motioned for him to stop. Reluctantly, the warrior released his victim and stood by his leader's side just as two, lean, hard loggers swaggered toward them, their eager expressions betraying an obvious lust for fighting. One of them brandished a dangerously long knife and the sunlight glinted from it like small lightning flashes as he smugly tossed it from hand to hand, all the while edging closer to the two Indians. With a quick glance at each other, Jacob and Three Bears rushed the two loggers, causing the one with the knife to stop short in a sudden decision to throw it at Jacob. Measuring the distance, he swiftly end for ended the blade and hurled it with deadly accuracy! In one incredibly fluid movement, Jacob managed to sidestep, snatch the knife right out of the air and hurl it back at his opponent, with the blade landing directly between his feet! The stunned logger stared down at the knife in disbelief, then looked up just as Jacob delivered a bone-crunching blow to his jaw, instantly rendering the man unconscious! Catching his breath, Jacob saw Three Bears holding the other logger in a hammerlock, slowly choking the life out of him. Seeing his leader's look of disapproval, Three Bears grinned and reluctantly released the wheezing man, who fell to the ground and weakly crawled away. As Jacob stood surveying the scene, he was joined by the rest of his warriors and they all watched with contempt as their few opponents still able to stand made a hasty retreat. Jacob decided to give them one last warning.

"If you value your lives, stay the Hell out of our forests! If I or any of my people catch you there, no white man's law will save you and no white man will ever find you!"

With those words, he turned and walked directly toward Shannon, his dark eyes boring into her very soul. With a shock, she realized he'd known all along exactly where she was standing. With her heart in her mouth, she looked up at him, still intent on thanking him, when all at once a shot rang out! Without a moment's hesitation, he threw Shannon to the ground and covered her with his own body! A second shot rang out, narrowly missing Jacob, and he quickly rolled Shannon along with himself through an open doorway and out of danger! When the dust settled, she found herself lying completely beneath his warm, hard body as she looked into the blackest, most dangerous eyes she'd ever seen! Completely captivated by the strength of his gaze, she found herself unable to utter a single word. Helplessly pinned beneath him, she could only return his unwavering stare. It was just as she had suspected; she felt herself drowning in the black pool of his eyes. In just those few seconds, he had somehow transported her to a dark, private world of his own, where only the two of them existed. She no longer heard the continuing uproar in the street; even the continued use of firearms failed to reach through the mists of this new realm in which she found herself. She was only brought back to reality when he suddenly removed his body from hers and ordered her to stay put. She nodded and lowered her gaze just for a moment. When she looked up, he had once again disappeared, leaving her with the strange sensation that it had all been a dream.

Jacob had climbed through a back window and was racing along behind the buildings. As he neared the corner of the last building, he slowed his pace and looked up and down the street leading to the one with the barricades. Finding the street empty, he quickly ran to the next corner, from where he had a clear view of the continuing riot. With a shock, he saw that two of his warriors had been shot! Keeping low, he swiftly ran alongside the huge trucks and headed toward the back of the building from where the shots had come. He quickly climbed the back stairs leading to the top of the building and quietly dropped over the edge onto the roof. Holding perfectly still for a moment, he scanned the entire area and saw nothing! He suddenly realized that the shooting had stopped. Perhaps the shooters had escaped down the back stairs before he had arrived. Either that, or they had seen him running in their direction and were hiding behind the chimney, just waiting for him to show his face. Seething with anger, his heart hammering in his chest, he stealthily approached the chimney. Listening carefully, he could hear someone breathing on the other side! As he looked at the rock which comprised the chimney, he realized that he should be able to climb to the top, giving him a definite advantage. If none of the rock broke loose and if they didn't hear him! That was a pretty big 'if', but it was the only chance he had. He decided to go for it and slowly began to climb. Just as he carefully pulled himself onto the top of the chimney, two of the rocks broke loose and fell to the roof with a loud clatter! Shocked by the noise from the falling rocks, the two men hiding on the other side of the chimney stared at each other, their faces bathed in sweat. The one named Tyler motioned the other one to keep silent. The one who couldn't control his ragged breathing was called Weasel, a most appropriate name, since he looked and acted just like one. Tense with anticipation, they nervously watched the corners. Both were fully prepared to gun down whoever might show his face. It was fortunate for Jacob that neither of them had thought to look up. It simply never occurred to them that anyone would attempt to climb the chimney. Looking down on them, Jacob carefully noted the distance between them and then jumped directly on the nearest one, who just happened to be Weasel. Just as he leaped off the edge, his body cast a shadow in front of his intended victim, causing him to look up at the exact moment of impact. The move cost Weasel his life, as the sound of his neck snapping in two broke the silence! Tyler stared with his mouth hanging open, too horrified to react in time to save his own life. In a heartbeat, he found himself being thrown from the roof, landing hard right beside the body of one of the warriors he had shot and killed. Not quite alive and not quite dead, the last sight his eyes ever beheld was that of Jacob, standing victoriously on the edge of the roof, his strong, lean body silhouetted by the sun, looking like some kind of vengeful God. Then his vision blurred and he was gone. With the exhilaration of his first kill coursing though his veins, Jacob took one last look at Tyler's crumpled body and then quickly disappeared from sight. With the sun behind him, no-one had been able to recognize him as the man on the roof and he carefully blended in with the crowd milling around the bodies on the ground. Now that things had calmed down a bit, Shannon walked out into the street and stood by Eric, who quickly put his arm around her and turned her face away from the bodies. Intent on seeing exactly what had happened, she pushed herself away from him and looked up just in time to meet Jacob's penetrating gaze. Afraid that she wouldn't have another opportunity to talk to him, she forced herself to walk directly over to him in order to finally thank him for coming to her aid at the barn dance. Eric attempted to follow her, but she cut him short with one look of warning, then nervously continued on her way.

"I wanted to thank you for helping me last night. I know this isn't the best time for us to talk, but I didn't know if I'd ever see you again. I mean......"

Her voice trailed off and she found herself stammering. She really didn't know what to say to him after that. She found being face to face with him completely unnerving. If only he wouldn't look at her that way!

Jacob took her by the arm and pulled her along with him as he walked into an empty building. Then he turned and faced her, standing so close to her that she involuntarily took a step backward.

"All right, you've thanked me! Now I want some answers. What are you doing here? And when are you leaving?"

"What!? My friends and I happen to be going on a wilderness trip led by a man named Trevor Thompson. Why do you ask? And just what business is it of yours, anyway?"

"I'm making it my business! It just so happens that you've arrived at a very bad time and you could easily wind up in an extremely dangerous situation! There's a lot going on right now that you know nothing about. It would be best if you and your friends took your vacation elsewhere. If you have any sense at all, you'll take my advice."

Shannon was bristling with anger! "If you think for one moment that you can make me cancel my vacation plans, then you're the one who doesn't have any sense at all! I don't know why I even bothered to thank you. I think you're one of the rudest people I've ever......"

Cutting her off in mid-sentence, Jacob abruptly pulled her to him and kissed her hard on the mouth, bruising her lips as he held her in an iron grip. The feel of her body pressed against his was like a sweet torture. Overwhelmed by the deepest hunger she'd ever felt, Shannon instinctively returned his kiss with such a passion that he groaned in desperation.

"I knew it! I knew you were the one!"

With those words and one last searing look into her emerald-green eyes, he once again disappeared from her sight. Stepping outside into the blinding glare of the sun, Jacob heard the wail of the Sheriff's siren as it approached the town. The truckers and loggers immediately ran for their trucks in a hasty attempt to leave. Jacob watched with disdain their cowardly retreat, then walked toward his band of warriors to join them in mourning their brothers. Halfway there, he was intercepted by Eric, who had been waiting to catch him alone.

"If you've got a minute, I'd like a word with you. First of all, I'd like to thank you and your friends for siding with us in that fight."

Jacob impatiently interrupted him.

"Let's get one thing straight right now. We weren't fighting for you; we were fighting against them! Now, what did you really want to talk to me about?"

The look on Eric's face visibly hardened.

"You don't miss much, do you? All right, let's get right to the point. I appreciate the fact that you came to Shannon's aid last night, but I don't appreciate your grabbing her by the arm and pulling her into some building with you! Do you understand what I'm saying?"

Jacob's face instantly darkened, right along with his mood.

"Just exactly what does this Shannon mean to you? Are you married to her?"

"No, not yet! But she will become my wife. You can bank on it!"

Jacob derisively laughed out loud. Then he took a long, hard look at Eric, sizing him up. He recognized that he was a good man and he almost felt sorry for him.

"I really don't think so. She's not for you."

"You can't be stupid enough to think she's for

you! You don't even know her!"

Jacob looked at him with a reserved compassion. It was clear that Eric really loved her.

"I've always known her! It just took this long to meet her and it has always been written in the stars that she is for me, even though claiming her means facing certain death!"

Amazed by the temerity of the man, Eric stared at him angrily.

"You're damned right about facing certain death; I'll see to that! Don't even think about trying to claim her; she'll never belong to anyone but me!"

Their conversation was cut short by the arrival of Sheriff Stanton and his deputy. As they surveyed the scene, Stanton caught sight of Jacob and walked directly over to him. His eyes were filled with an old hatred as he confronted him.

"I should have known you'd be in the middle of this! Anywhere there's trouble, you always manage to show up. Well, explain yourself! What have you done now?"

Before Jacob could respond, the grey-haired gentleman from the group in the Jeeps came forward to vouch for him.

"Excuse me, Sheriff. My name is James Randolph and I believe I should be the one to explain all this."

With a gasp, Stanton interrupted him.

"Are you the James Randolph I'm always reading about in the paper? The one that heads a group of environmentalists?"

"Well, yes. In fact, my group and I are here to conduct an official survey of damages caused by the logging industry and I'm afraid that's what brought on all this trouble. We were being accosted by some loggers when this gentleman and his friends literally saved our collective asses, if you'll pardon my terminology."

The entire crowd broke into laughter, which immediately served to lessen the extreme tension felt by everyone present. As further explanations were offered by various bystanders regarding the shooting, Stanton realized with regret that he would be unable to hold Jacob responsible for any of this. Looking at him with barely concealed disgust, he dismissed him.

"Go on! Get out of here! I want you and your Indian friends to clear out. And I'd better be able to find you if I need to question you. Make damned sure you don't disappear on me! Just remember; I've got my eye on you. Do I make myself clear?"

"I'm sure I'll always be a little closer to you than you realize. Do I make myself clear?"

With those words and a last, venomous look, Jacob joined his men and they pointedly remained for a while, talking quietly among themselves. Standing by two of his closest friends, Two Eagles and Running Deer, Jacob looked down upon the two dead warriors and tried to stifle the grief welling up inside him. This was not the place for mourning, not this white man's town! They would return their beloved brothers to the reservation, where they would be appropriately buried with all the honors they were due. While they were talking, Eric caught sight of Shannon and rushed over to her.

"Shannon, I think it's time we had a talk! There's something strange going on with you and that Indian. And I'd like to know just what in the Hell it is!"

"What on Earth are you talking about? There's nothing going on between us! He helped me last night and I thanked him today and that's the end of it!"

"Not according to him, it isn't! He thinks you belong to him! He claims it's written in the stars!"

Looking at her face, he realized that she knew

more than she was letting on. She could say the words, but she was one of those people who could never breathe life into a lie.

"Shannon, I know you too well. You're not being completely honest with me. Don't you realize a relationship can never succeed if it's based on lies?"

"All right! It's just that it's so hard to explain when I don't even know myself what's going on! He has some kind of hold over me and I don't know what it is. It's almost as though we've known each other from a previous life. I know it sounds crazy and of course we don't actually know each other, but we're somehow drawn together, almost against our wills. I can sense that he's somewhat afraid to be with me and there's something about him that scares me too, but I don't know what! Am I making any sense at all?"

"Unfortunately, yes. He said something about facing certain death if he claimed you. It's obvious that he believes in some Indian prophecy. I can understand his belief, because it's probably part of his Indian culture. But I don't understand your feelings. You're not an Indian! You know what I think? I think you're just physically attracted to him and don't want to admit it, not even to yourself. Well, you can quit worrying about it; I can live with the fact that you find someone else attractive, as long as it stops right there, okay?"

Shannon decided it was best to let him think whatever pleased him. The last thing she wanted was to hurt him and he would certainly be hurt if he knew how she really felt about Jacob. She was just beginning to understand how many different kinds of love one could feel. She was also becoming aware that it was quite possible to love more than one person at the same time, although never quite in the same way. She loved Eric for the wonderful, decent person that he was and also felt strongly attracted to him on a physical level.

159

Unfortunately, loving and being in love are two vastly different feelings. With Jacob, she had felt emotionally devastated from the first moment she looked into his eyes. It was as though she knew, all in that instant, that she had found her soul-mate, the one man who would ever really understand her and satisfy her in every possible way. Just thinking about him put her into such a realm of ecstasy that she could barely tolerate the magnitude of feeling coursing through her entire being. The depth of emotion was so extreme, she thought her heart would surely burst! For the first time in her young life, Shannon was truly in love.

CHAPTER 17 LONE ELK

Jacob left the small town of Covelo with a heavy heart and mixed emotions. He was greatly saddened over the loss of two of his warriors, who also happened to be two of his best friends. They had grown up together, laughed together and even fought with each other on occasion. They would be missed more than words could ever express. Jacob felt as though a part of his youth had died right along with them. In the midst of everything that had happened, he now had another problem with which to cope. In a turmoil of emotions, he was half horrified and half exhilarated that he had finally found the red-haired woman from his dreams. She was everything he had imagined her to be and more, much more! Even worse for Jacob than the thought of facing the death he had seen in his dreams was the awful knowledge that he would never again truly be his own man. He had always prided himself on the fact that he had never really relied on anyone other than himself. There had been many women along the way, but none had succeeded in laying claim to his heart. Thus he had remained free to follow whatever path he chose, without having to consider anyone other than himself. But now that he had actually held Shannon in his arms and looked into her mesmerizing, green eyes, he knew his heart and soul were lost for all eternity. Never again would he be completely free. His desperate need for her would reshape his entire future and he knew there was absolutely nothing he could do about it. Even now, all he could think about was the taste of her kiss, the feel of her body pressed against his, the green fire in her eyes! Never had he desired a woman as he desired her! She had ignited a fire within him that could never be extinguished. He sensed that she shared his passion but, for some reason, was wary of him. He wondered what she must think of him and what he would have to do to finally possess her. He suddenly realized that he didn't even know if she were already married or engaged, or even her last name. Of course, none of it really mattered; he would do whatever necessary to claim her! However, before he could decide on a course of action, he knew what he had to do. It was time to see his grandfather, Lone Elk.

Jacob drove out to the reservation to speak with the revered Medicine Man of Mendocino County, but found his cabin empty. Surprised, he approached one of the women to inquire as to his whereabouts.

"Maria, have you seen my grandfather? I need his counsel."

Maria seemed very surprised by his question.

"You mean you have not yet spoken with him today? That is very strange! He left here about two hours ago to meet you. He said you needed his advice on an urgent matter and that he would join you in a place which held significant meaning for both of you. Do you know this place?"

At first, Jacob was confused. Then, suddenly, he understood. He smiled at Maria.

"Yes, I know the place well. Thank you, Maria. You've been a great help."

Jacob ran to his Jeep and drove out to his father's old cabin by Williams Creek. As he walked by the old, deserted cabin, memories of his childhood flooded his mind. He slowly walked up the barely discernible trail of his youth, which led to a favorite, secluded glen where he and his father used to picnic. While he walked, he could almost hear his father calling to him to slow down, could almost feel his father's strong hand, holding his own small one as Caleb smiled down at his son. Dear God, how he missed his father! He would never understand why life had to be so cruel. Well, at least he still had his beloved grandfather. Sometimes he worried about him. He was getting on in years, although he would never admit it. Jacob didn't even know how old he was; his age was something that Lone Elk refused to discuss.

The trail took Jacob up a steady incline for about half a mile, then forked sharply down to the right, leading to their special glen. As he quietly approached, he saw that Lone Elk was sitting in front of a small fire with his back to him.

"Well, Grandson, it's about time you arrived. You've kept me waiting for quite a while. Come and sit with me, Jacob. We have much to discuss. You may begin by telling me all about your red-haired woman."

Jacob marveled at his grandfather's perceptive abilities and his keen senses. Jacob's step was so light that his approach couldn't possibly have been heard, not even by a much younger man. Yet, Lone Elk had somehow sensed that he was there. He even knew why he was there. His grandfather was indeed an incredible medicine man! No wonder he was so revered by all the tribe. There were many white people in the valley who had heard of his reputation, but they refused to take him seriously. Either they were closed-minded bigots or they were subconsciously frightened by his mystical abilities, a fact which they wouldn't admit, even to themselves. Jacob walked around the fire and sat across from his grandfather.

"My heart is gladdened by the sight of you, Grandfather. Too often, time has a way of separating us from those we love. I am at fault for allowing this to happen."

"I will not allow you to accept the blame for this, Grandson. It is merely the way of life. In one's quest for survival, one will often be too busy to do that which he would prefer. It has ever been thus and will always be so. Who among us can control his or her destiny? Life will often lead us upon a path other than that of our own choosing. Isn't that why you're here, to discuss the path you're about to take, even against your will?"

Again, Jacob was in awe of his grandfather's abilities. Lone Elk's vision had been steadily declining for some time, but even with his failing eyesight, he saw so much more than anyone else possibly could. Jacob was suddenly overwhelmed by a surge of love for the old man. He prayed that he would have many more years with him.

"Yes, Grandfather, that is exactly why I am here. I have found the red-haired woman from my dreams. I used to hope I would never meet her, because I thought she would only serve to verify the prophecy, which I didn't want to believe......"

Lone Elk gently interrupted him. "And exactly what prophecy would that be, Grandson?"

"Grandfather! Have you actually forgotten my dream? I wouldn't have thought it possible! I'm referring to the part where I see our ancestor, Black Eagle, thrown off a cliff to his certain death! Obviously, that was an omen that I would be the one thrown from a cliff. You were the one who said Black Eagle was trying to warn me of an extreme danger! Don't you remember?"

"Grandson, you must not allow yourself to become so agitated. Of course I remember your dream; I could never forget it. But you have misinterpreted what I told you. It is true that Black Eagle was trying to warn you of an extreme danger, but it was only that, not a certain death. It is you who must recall everything in the dream, especially the ending. Did not Black Eagle find himself being comforted in the arms of the red-haired woman? Therefore, he could not have died when he fell from the cliff. Do you not see the logic in my interpretation?"

"But, Grandfather, when he looked into her green eyes, they were filled with tears. Why would she cry unless he were dying?"

At these words, Lone Elk laughed out loud.

"Grandson, you have much to learn about women. They find as many reasons to cry as there are stars in the sky. However, their men rarely have any idea as to what it is they are crying about. Therefore, you must not allow that part of the dream to concern you. I have given much thought to your dream and I have had a very clear vision show itself to me as I sat before this fire. I have seen you and the red-haired woman together, splashing each other in a deep pool of water. You are both laughing, but there are eyes hidden behind the trees, watching you both. They are dangerous eyes, so beware! That is all I have seen, for then the vision begins to fade. Jacob, you are my only grandson and I love you deeply. Do not let anything happen to yourself. When I lost your father, a part of me died forever. All that remains of me would die with you if you should go. You must not allow this to happen. It is my deepest desire to see the great-grandchildren which you and the red-haired woman will give me."

Choked with emotion, Jacob found it difficult to speak. Finally, he was able to compose himself.

"And just what makes you so certain that I will marry this red-haired woman? What if I do not find her pleasing once I get to know her? What then, Grandfather? Would you have me marry her just so you can have red-haired great-grandchildren?"

"Jacob, this is not a subject for jokes. Choosing a

wife is a very serious matter. Besides, we both know that you already find her extremely pleasing. Is that not so?"

"Yes, Grandfather. I find her exceptionally so. I must confess that I do not understand why I feel so strongly about her. After all, I have only just met her. I know nothing about her and yet, when I look into her eyes, I feel as though I have known her all of my life. How can this be?"

"Ah, now you are beginning to make sense. Jacob, you must understand that the eyes are the pathway to a person's soul. Although the lips can tell a lie, the eyes can almost never succeed in doing so. By closely looking into the eyes of another, one can usually determine that person's character, temperament and even their intellect. Tell me; how would you describe her in regard to those three traits?"

Jacob hesitated for a moment, giving careful consideration to the question.

"I believe she is of excellent character and is highly intelligent. I think she has a fairly even temperament, although I did observe a bit of a flash temper on one occasion."

"Ah, then you have already managed to anger her. Do you consider that wise when you are trying to court the woman? What exactly did you do?"

"Grandfather! I have not yet begun to court her! Besides, I only tried to give her some good advice, which she was just too stubborn to take."

"As I have already said, Grandson, you have a great deal to learn about women. It has been my experience that they do not appreciate advice, not even good advice. Perhaps you should learn to hold your tongue until you have succeeded in courting her. And Jacob, when you gave her that first kiss, you did begin to court her, whether you realize it or not."

166

Once again, Jacob was stunned by the scope of his grandfather's knowledge.

"You will never cease to amaze me, Grandfather. Is there no limit to your knowledge? I am truly humbled by your abilities and I sincerely wish they had been passed on to me."

"Are you so certain that they have not been passed on to you, Grandson? After all, you are still a very young man, only twenty-seven years of age. I was already twenty-nine before I realized that I had any special abilities at all. When the visions first began to show themselves to me, I was thrilled. In my arrogance, I thought I held the world in my hands. It took many years for me to understand that a vision was not necessarily the blessing which I thought it to be. It is not always a good thing to see a piece of the future, especially when there is always the possibility of misinterpreting a vision and acting incorrectly on it. The best way to explain that problem to you is to tell you about the vision I had just before I met your grandmother. Have I ever told you about that part of my life, Grandson?"

"No, Grandfather, you have not." Jacob lay back on the grass, happily anticipating one of his grandfather's rare and extremely interesting stories.

"This particular vision, which was my very first one, came to me on a beautiful, spring day, when the valley was fragrant with the heady perfume of a myriad of flowers. I had gone for a walk, with no thought other than to enjoy the beauty of spring. I must have walked for at least four miles when I decided to take a rest by a lovely stream. As I sat down and leaned against a tree, the sound of the water bubbling and splashing over the rocks gently lulled me into a dream-like state. As I looked across the stream, I saw a lovely, young woman standing on the other side, staring at me. She had

167

appeared as though out of a mist. One moment, there was no-one there and in the next, she had suddenly appeared. I thought I must be dreaming, but it didn't feel like a dream. She was unusually beautiful, with thick, black hair hanging loose all the way to her slender hips, and dark eyes filled with the most inviting look. She called to me to follow her. As I stood to do so, I felt very foolish, as though I were attempting to follow a ghost, for she was still surrounded by a mist. But curiosity overcame my reluctance and I crossed the stream to follow her into the forest. As I walked along, she seemed to be getting further and further away, until finally, I lost sight of her altogether. I felt a desperation to find her and I listened carefully for the sound of her step, but all I could hear was the sound of birdsong and a light breeze whistling through the trees. At first, I felt devastated and then I felt ridiculous. My common sense told me that it had to be some kind of a waking dream. I decided to return home and swore that I would never again follow some false vision! But then, I remembered the invitation in her dark eyes and, against all common sense, continued in the direction she had taken. After walking for another ten minutes, I heard the faint cries of a female voice calling for help. I rushed forward, heading toward a steep cliff, and the cries became louder. I looked over the edge and saw a young woman holding on to a small tree growing out of a crevice. She had evidently fallen and was quite fortunate to have grabbed onto the tree instead of falling to her death. The tree wasn't that far down, but it was just far enough that she could never have climbed back to the top without help. I yelled down to her to hold on, that I would find a way to help her. I found a very long branch and extended it down to her. As she held tightly to the branch, I pulled her to the top, where she collapsed in tears. She then told me that she had been trapped there for the longest time and had almost given up all hope of being rescued. As I looked closely at her lovely face, I realized with a shock that it was the very same woman I had seen in the mist. If I had continued to regard that as a false vision, your grandmother would surely have died and you would not be here, Jacob. The path that I followed that day was not one of my own choosing, but it led me to my destiny, one which I would not change if I could. I believe your path will lead you to the same wonderful life with your red-haired woman that I had with your grandmother, Liana. I could wish no greater happiness for you than that which I have already had."

Overwhelmed by emotion, Jacob again found it difficult to speak. Although he didn't realize it, his silence said more to Lone Elk than words ever could. They sat quietly together for some time, both lost in thought as they stared at the crackling fire. As the sun began to fade in the western sky, Jacob had some questions for his grandfather.

"When you met Grandmother for the first time, did you know with a certainty that she was the one for you?"

"Yes, Jacob, I never doubted it for a moment. All it took was one look into her dark eyes. You have inherited them, you know, the very same eyes, dark as the blackest night and just as mysterious. From the moment I gazed into her eyes, she became my entire future and I felt most fortunate that she shared the depth of my feeling. The great majority of people never experience such a love as that. Your father and mother shared such a love and I believe it will be the same for you and your red-haired woman."

"But, Grandfather, she is not of our people! She is white and you must know how I have always felt about the whites. I do not want to love her! I feel trapped by my own feelings! It is just as I have always suspected;

to love another is to lose yourself! And I can't help but wonder about one thing in particular. Would you still have married Grandmother if she were white?"

Lone Elk looked astonished.

"Grandson! I am truly shocked by your question! Did I not make it clear enough how I felt about your grandmother? I would have married her if she were purple! What difference could the color of her skin possibly make in my feelings toward her? I never realized that you held bad feelings for the whites. Jacob, I hope I do not detect a note of bigotry in your voice! There are good whites as well as bad whites, just as there are good and bad people in every race! I know that my son would never have taught you prejudice! Where then, did you learn such foolishness? Surely, not from your own people? Have we not, ourselves, often been the victims of prejudice? That alone should have taught you to abhor it!"

"It is exactly because our people have been victimized for so long by the whites that I do not trust them! I thought you, of all people, would understand that, Grandfather!"

"Grandson, in order to live in harmony with other races, it is very important to see the world as a whole picture, not just in bits and pieces. I believe this whole problem of prejudice could easily be settled if man could just learn that we are all members of the same race, namely, the human race, and we all share the same home, namely, the planet Earth. Jacob, can't you see the logic of my thinking? If you are able to understand what I am saying, I mean, really understand, then you could not possibly concern yourself with the color of your woman's skin. There are only two things that should really concern you about her. One, is she a good woman, and two, do you really love her?"

Jacob looked very contrite and found it difficult to

meet his grandfather's eyes.

"I am deeply ashamed, Grandfather. I have allowed the actions of some very bad whites to color my judgement of all the others. I have been as guilty of prejudice as the very ones I have accused. As to your questions regarding the red-haired woman, yes, I believe she is a good woman and I feel very certain that I love her. But there may be other complications, Grandfather. She may already be married or, worse yet, she may not share my feelings. And even if she does, we are from two different cultures! What if we don't want the same things out of life? What if we have different ideas as to where we should live? What then, Grandfather? I can't help but wonder if life will always be so complicated."

Lone Elk could not help but chuckle at his remarks.

"Grandson, it has been my experience that life is always complicated. Did you really think that your grandmother and I were able to live in such harmony just because we were from the same culture? There are such inherent differences between men and women, regardless of their culture, that a marriage will only succeed if both are very willing to compromise. We both made many compromises, because we truly loved one another and were determined to make each other happy. I don't believe the difference in your cultures will affect you as much as you think. Perhaps, Grandson, it would be wise to get to know her better and then make your decision. Is the young lady still in town?"

"Only until tomorrow morning, Grandfather. Then, she and her friends will be heading into the Yolla Bolly Wilderness area for a vacation. They are taking a guided tour which will be led by someone named Trevor Thompson. Have you heard of him, Grandfather?"

Lone Elk looked concerned. "No, I have not

171

heard the name, but......"

All of a sudden, he quit speaking and looked as though he were in a trance. Jacob stared at him for a long time and then gently shook him.

"Grandfather! What is it? Have you seen something? Tell me what's wrong!"

Lone Elk slowly came back to reality and stared at Jacob.

"Grandson! You must also go on this trip, but do not let them know that you are there. I have had another vision and I do not like what I saw. There was a very large man running after your red-haired woman. She was screaming and she was heading toward a cliff. Then, the vision faded. Her life is in danger, Jacob! You must follow her and the rest of the group. Choose two of your warriors, only two, to accompany you. Do not look so horrified, my Grandson. My heart tells me that, at the right moment, you will know what to do. If you are able to return to me, Jacob, I hope you will have the red-haired woman with you. Go now! Make your preparations. It will be a difficult and very dangerous journey!"

They both stood and Jacob embraced his grandfather.

"Don't worry, Grandfather! I will return and I will bring her with me. You will yet have the red-haired great-grandchildren you so desire!"

Although Jacob tried to sound positive about his return, in his heart, he didn't feel quite so certain. As he walked up the darkened trail, he turned to take one last look at Lone Elk sitting in front of the glowing embers of the dying fire and fervently prayed that this would not be the last time he would ever see his beloved grandfather.

CHAPTER 18 MATHIAS

Sitting in his old Dodge pickup, Mathias had plenty of time for making plans while he waited for Trevor Thompson to show up. Trevor was late, as usual, and Matt was so angry he was talking to himself.

"That Goddamned asshole always keeps me waitin'! I oughta just leave! It would serve him right! Who does he think he is, anyway? I'm the one who makes everything work out. Hell! He just sits back and rakes in the gravy, like it was all his own doin'! Well, things are about to change around here! There's just two things I want and I'm damned well gonna have 'em. First, there's the money. I can't wait to see Trevor's face when I pull that off! He's got a big surprise waitin' for 'im on that end! Then there's that red-haired woman! God Almighty! She's somethin' else! One way or the other, I'm takin' that woman!"

Try as he might, Matt couldn't quit thinking about Shannon. He'd never wanted a woman like he wanted her and he couldn't quite understand the feelings that washed through him whenever he thought about her. The first moment he saw her was like someone stabbing him right through his heart! His physical reaction to her was so strong, it literally took his breath away! He didn't know what to make of these new feelings; he only knew that he had to have her, no matter what! He thought if he could just spend a few days in bed with her, he could get her out of his system and concentrate on his latest plan, namely, to get rich quick and get out of the business once and for all. Hell! For that matter, if she pleased him as much as he thought she would, maybe he'd just take her along with him when he left the area. Yeah, that was a great idea! He was so lost in thought that he wasn't even aware of Trevor's arrival until he felt his hand on his shoulder. Startled into reality, Matt shoved his hand away!

"You Goddamned jerk! Don't you ever come sneakin' up on me like that! You're lucky I didn't blow you away! Just where in the Hell have you been, anyway? You're only two hours late, asshole! What's your excuse this time?"

Trevor's face instantly darkened with anger, but he quickly managed to compose himself. There would be time enough to deal with Matt, but right now, he needed him. He made an attempt to sound jovial.

"Cool it, Matt! You know I'm never late on purpose! Besides, judging from the expression on your face, you were having some wicked thoughts. Wanna tell me about it?"

"My thoughts ain't none of your fuckin' business! Now are you ready to discuss the job, or what? If you ain't, then I'm outa here! I got better things to do than sit around here all day, jackin' off with you!"

"All right! Will you calm down? I was just tryin' to be friendly, but if you want to get straight down to business, then let's do it! Here's the set-up: the dudes are meetin' with me early tomorrow morning and we're headin' down the trail. Now these people requested a two-week tour, so you gotta figure a week goin' in and a week comin' out. So far, you've only worked the one-week tours, so we'd better make sure you're familiar with the longer trail and that we meet at the right spot at the turn-around."

"I told you before I don't like workin' the longer trail; it's too dangerous! It gives the dudes too damned much time to nose around and discover things."

"Bullshit! The longer tour never gave me any

174

problems I couldn't handle! So what in the Hell are you talkin' about?"

"Are you brain-dead or what? Have you already forgotten what happened the last time on a long tour? Don't look so surprised! You shoulda known Jim would spill the beans! Just for the record, he told me everything and I do mean everything. I know all about how you handle your problems and I don't like it! Maybe you just better get ahold of Jim and have him take this tour. He's too stupid to know how dangerous it is!"

Trevor gave Matt a long, hard look and wondered just how much he really knew. He was certain that Jim couldn't have had enough time to blab the news before he'd disappeared. Of course, Matt could just be bluffing; he was famous for that. Trevor was well aware that Matt was extremely sharp and very successful at outwitting others. Except for himself, of course! He had yet to meet the man who could outwit him. Feeling very smug, Trevor laughed condescendingly.

"I don't know what Jim told you, but our problems on that tour were very minor and they were solved in a flash! Why don't you just do your job and let me handle the rest, especially since you're startin' to get nervous about these things. Y'know somethin'? I'm beginnin' to wonder about you. Usually a guy doesn't get edgy unless he's lookin' to get out of the business. Could that be what's really on your mind?"

Matt gave him a penetrating look and then laughed out loud. If Trevor was hopin' to see him break into a sweat, then he had a long wait comin'. It would be a cold day in Hell before he'd let a jerk-off like Trevor get the best of him! Besides, if things worked out the way he planned, this would be his last trip, so maybe the length of the tour wouldn't really matter. Come to think of it, the longer trail just might come in handy for his plans.

"You don't wanna know what's really on my mind; it would scare you too much! Maybe I'll go on this tour after all, right after I have one last talk with Jim. Who knows? Maybe he'll decide to tag along. What do you think?"

Trevor didn't like the look on his face. Maybe he really did know too much. He decided he'd better find out.

"I guess you didn't hear the news; Jim disappeared right after the last tour. Could be you were the last one to talk to him. Exactly what did he tell you?"

Matt looked at him with barely concealed contempt. Who did he think he was foolin' with that dumb-shit question? They both knew Jim was dead! Maybe it was time to shake Trevor up a little.

"If you really need to know what he told me, then maybe you'd better ask him yourself. I'm sure you can figure out right where to find him, if you really want to. Of course, you just might have reasons of your own for not wantin' to dig him up, right?"

Trevor felt a sudden chill go down his back and gave Matt another long, hard look. He decided he'd had enough of this conversation. Sometimes he just couldn't get anything out of that bastard; he thought he was so Goddamned clever! Well, maybe this time he'd outsmarted himself. As far as he was concerned, this pretty much settled it; he'd make certain that this would be Matt's last trip, whether he was planning it or not! He gave Matt a supremely confident smile.

"That's all right. Whatever Jim told you couldn't have been all that important anyway. Let's forget about him and get back to the job. You're pretty familiar with the Rattlesnake Bar area, aren't you?"

"Yeah, why? You plannin' to use that for the turn-around?"

"Yeah, I thought it would be a good idea. One of

176

the boys was out snoopin' around last week and found a cave just off a ledge below one of the trails. It would be ideal for storin' the goods. Here, take a look at this map. See that spot right there? That's it. Do you think you can find it all right?"

"Shit! If I can't find it, it ain't there! Hey, wait a minute! I know exactly where that's at! Well, I'll be damned!"

"Yeah, I'm sure you will be, but who cares? Just exactly what are you talking about anyway?"

"Very funny! Listen; you remember a while back when me and Jim chased some dude over a cliff and he bought the farm? Well, maybe he didn't bite the bullet after all, because that's the exact spot where he went off the edge! Something tells me he knew exactly where he was goin' and he prob'ly hid in that cave until we left. It was gettin' dark while we were chasin' 'im, so I couldn't see who it was. But my gut tells me it was that damned Indian and I'll just bet I'm right!"

"What Indian? And what makes you so sure, if it was too dark to see?"

"Gut instinct! That's what makes me so sure! You should know who I'm talkin' about; he's the leader of those Indians that hang around town. You know; they call themselves the Warriors. You told the boys to get rid of their leader, but it looks like he was the one who got rid of them! Now do you know who I'm talkin' about?"

"Jesus Christ! You really think it was him? Did you actually see him on the roof?"

"No. All I saw on that roof was somebody who looked like God Almighty himself! I never actually saw his face, but I know it was him, 'cause he was the only one who coulda done the job. It just so happens I have personal knowledge of his fightin' style, since we had us a little set-to the night of the barn dance. I guess you didn't hear about that."

"I heard tell some asshole started a ruckus, but I didn't know it was you. I thought you knew enough to keep your nose clean around town! What the Hell were you thinking?"

"Oh, shut up! It wasn't that big a deal! I just had a little too much to drink and got into a tussle with that Indian. What the Hell's his name? Oh yeah! Jacob, that's it. Anyway, he shouldn't of stuck his nose in my business in the first place! All I was doin' was havin' some fun with a red-haired broad and he decided to play hero. If I hadn't been drinkin', he wouldn't of been able to stop me and I woulda had one Hell of a piece of ass that night!"

With a shock, Trevor realized he could only be talking about Shannon. As an unexpected wave of anger surged through his body, he suddenly broke into a sweat and glared menacingly at Matt.

"You dumb fuck! That woman just happens to be a member of the tour group! Do you have any idea what you almost did? You came damned close to screwing up the entire trip and that woulda cost me money! And all for a piece of tail! You'd better quit thinkin' with your dick and start using that pea-brain of yours. And you'd better get one thing straight, right now! That woman is one hundred per cent off limits! Y'got it?"

Watching Trevor's face beaded with sweat and his forehead knotted with purple veins, all rigid like they were about to burst at any second, Matt had a sneaking suspicion that he wasn't the only one turned on by that red-haired woman.

"Yeah, I got it! I guess that means she's off limits for you too, right? Unless, of course, you been thinkin' of her as your own private stock. Maybe you got some secret ideas about puttin' your brand on her. Well, well, just lookit your face! I guess I hit the old nail right on the head!"

Trevor could barely control his rage. What he wouldn't give to wipe that knowing leer off Matt's face! His hands were literally shaking with the need to strangle that bastard! But this wasn't the time for it and he knew it. With a visible effort, he slowly managed to regain his composure.

"Just for the record, this conversation isn't over with by a long shot, but I don't have time to play word-games with you right now. So pick up your map and get your ass on the trail. You don't have as much time as you think to carry out your orders, so get a move on!"

Without so much as moving a muscle, Matt continued to leer at him. He took great pleasure in tormenting Trevor and he was delighted to have found that the woman was one of his weaknesses. That knowledge was bound to come in handy! In spite of his mutilation of the English language, Matt was actually highly intelligent and there was usually a purpose behind everything he did. Early in life, he had discovered that most people were very easy to manipulate, through one type of prodding or another.

"I'll get a move on when I'm damn good and ready. If you can't stand the heat, then maybe you'd better haul your sorry ass outa here. By the way, it just so happens I agree with you about not screwin' with her while the job's still on. But, mark my words, the time will come when she'll be fair game and you might as well leave her to me. She looks like a mighty passionate woman to me and I just don't think you'd be able to satisfy her like I could. Just between us, I'm plannin' on givin' her the fuck of her life!"

If looks could kill, Matt would surely be dead. Trevor's face had darkened with a rage that would only abate with Matt's death. Sincerely afraid of what he

179

might do if he stayed for even another moment, he turned abruptly, climbed into his Jeep and headed for town. While he drove, he could only think of the great pleasure he would have in killing Matt.

Feeling very smug, Matt stared at the dust cloud raised by Trevor's Jeep as he stormed off down the dirt road leading back to town. He couldn't suppress a self-satisfied chuckle as he remembered the look of pure hatred on Trevor's face. That was exactly the result he'd wanted. He immediately felt more secure about his upcoming plans, because he would know exactly what to expect from Trevor and would be able to use that knowledge against him. That was the nice thing about enemies; you always knew where you stood with them. They were completely predictable. It was your friends you couldn't trust. In his youth, he had quickly learned that only the people you cared about could actually hurt you and he had been hurt far too many times in his life, especially when he was very young and still vulnerable. As he leaned back in his seat, lulled by the quiet of his surroundings, memories of his unhappy childhood slowly crept into his mind. He could easily picture the filthy apartment in which he had been raised. He could still smell the stench of the ever-present garbage in the small kitchen. He could almost hear his father's angry voice still screaming at his mother, while she lay sobbing on the floor......

"You Goddamn whore! I told you what I'd do if I ever found him in this apartment again! He's lucky I only threw him down the stairs; next time I'll kill the bastard! Maybe this time I'll just kill you!"

Then he picked her up off the floor and started slapping her, over and over, while she screamed and begged for mercy.

"Please! Don't hit me anymore! We didn't do anything! We were just talking; I swear it!"

180

"You lying bitch! So that's why you were only wearing your slip, huh? I guess you like to entertain your friends in your slip, right? You rotten tramp! I'm gonna fix you where no man will ever want you again!"

While he held her by her hair with one hand, he used the other to get his switchblade out of his pocket. As he held it in his hand, she stared, horrified. Matt was only six years old; terrified, he crouched down low in a corner of the room. He could still hear the sound of the loud click echoing against the walls of the small room as the blade was released. He would remember that sound for the rest of his life. When his mother saw the blade, she screamed hysterically and kicked him hard in the stomach, which only served to further infuriate him. He forced her head back and slashed her face with the knife, causing her to scream hideously one last time and then she mercifully slumped into a dead faint, while blood poured from the deep cut. His rage momentarily spent, Matt's father stared at the bloody knife with a vacant look, almost as though he were seeing it for the first time, as though someone else had committed this horrible atrocity. When his father raised the knife to stare at it, Matt mistakenly thought he was about to continue the attack on his mother. Determined to save his mother's life, he sprang from his corner and leaped upon his father's back! With a clatter, the knife fell from his father's hand, instantly bringing him out of his trance. Now his fury was directed at his six-year-old son! He wrested him from his back and threw him against the wall! From that point, everything seemed to happen in slow motion. Matt felt himself slowly sliding down the wall, about to land on the floor. While he was still falling, he saw his father looking at him with a strange hatred, almost as though he didn't recognize him, but was determined to kill him. As young as he was, Matt knew that he couldn't possibly stop his father and was certain he was going to die. Too terrified to move, he just watched him getting closer and closer, when suddenly the front door was smashed open and they were surrounded by the police, all pointing their guns at his father. That scene was forever etched on his young mind, especially the look of complete despair on his father's face while they handcuffed him. After that, Matt's life was never the same. At first, he hated his father for what he had done and hoped with all his heart that he'd never have to see him again. His wish came true. It was only a short time later that he was told his father had died in prison. As the years went by, long-suppressed feelings of guilt began to gnaw at his conscience, feelings which were continually fueled by the various affairs his mother had with a series of different men. Finally, Matt concluded that his mother was just a worthless whore who had driven his father insane with jealousy, thus causing him to commit his acts of violence. He convinced himself that his father had truly loved him, in spite of what he had done. As for his mother, she never even bothered to hide her affairs from her son. In fact, she rarely paid any attention to Matt at all. It was one of the worst types of child abuse, complete emotional neglect. By the time Matt was twelve years old, he had personally witnessed more sexual acts than he could count. There was a large hole in the wall that separated his bedroom from his mother's and he used to watch while the men would strip her down and mount her. At first, he was only curious, but then he became fascinated by all the different things they would do to her. Most of them liked to suck on her tits and a lot of them liked to eat her pussy before they mounted her. It seemed like the rougher they were, the more she liked it! She would moan so loud while they were fucking her, he couldn't figure out if it was from pain or pleasure. There was one man in particular, a tall, black man with a huge, long penis. Matt was watching intently when he tried to mount her; he was certain the man could never get it all inside her, not without killing her, anyway. While he slowly put it in, his mother moaned and groaned aloud and then, to Matt's amazement, begged for more until, finally, he had the whole thing inside her. Incredulous, Matt watched as the man pumped it into her over and over again. By the time he finally filled her with his come, his mother was writhing and screaming until Matt couldn't stand it anymore and covered his ears with his hands! He finally decided that women must like being treated roughly and he also determined that sex was about all a woman was good for. Other than that, he could see no value in them at all. He swore that he would never allow a woman to get close enough to hurt him as his father had been hurt. He'd been on his own for the last twelve years, ever since he was fifteen years old and, in all that time, he had kept his promise to himself. He had used and abused women for his sexual pleasure, but he had never allowed one to get close to him emotionally. In fact, the only pain he'd ever suffered as a result of one of his sexual affairs had occurred when he was only nineteen. He had been carrying on with a married woman in her early thirties. To this day, he could still remember the feel of her voluptuous body and the taste of her passionate kisses. She was the best fuck he'd ever had and he'd been seeing her on a regular basis, always in the daytime while her husband was at work. She was the first woman to tell him how handsome he was and he was shocked by her words. His mother had never told him he was handsome, therefore he had always considered himself average at best, another result of his mother's emotional neglect. The woman also told him he was a great lover and encouraged him to try new things. On one hot summer day in particular, he had gone to her upstairs apartment and found her with a damp towel wrapped around her naked body, trying to cool off. She told him to go home, that it was too hot for sex, but he just laughed and carried her into the bedroom. She fought him, but he thought she was just playing hard to get. While she tried to push him away, he peeled the towel from her body and threw her on the bed. Then he grabbed a couple of her scarves from her dresser and tied her hands to the bedposts. While she lay there, angry and helpless, he undressed very slowly just to torment her. When he climbed onto the bed, she kicked at him, but only managed to further arouse him. He split her legs open and mounted her with a savage thrust, causing her to yell out in pain. He continued to pump himself into her, over and over, until she was finally moaning in pleasure. She wrapped her legs around him and pulled him in tight while they came together in a steamy climax. While they lay together, breathing hard and still entwined, neither of them heard her husband enter the bedroom. Her eyes were blissfully closed while Matt was sucking on one of her breasts, when they suddenly heard the unmistakable sound of a switchblade being released! It was the only sound in the entire world that could strike instant and complete fear in Matt's heart! He found himself at an extreme disadvantage as he scrambled to disentangle himself, half-falling off the bed, just as her husband leaped across it and slashed at him with the knife! The blade caught Matt right across the cheek, leaving a deep gash! When he brought the blade up to slash at him again, Matt managed to grab him by the ankle, bringing him down in a loud crash! While they rolled on the floor together, her husband still held the knife and tried to stab Matt in the stomach. Just as the blade started to cut into him, Matt succeeded in twisting the man's wrist just enough to turn the blade away from himself and bury it deep into his assailant's chest! There was the strangest look in the man's eyes as he died without so much as a whimper, almost as though he were too surprised to utter a sound. While Matt lay panting on the floor, covered with blood, he heard the sound of sirens approaching from a distance. Someone had called the police! He jumped up, threw his clothes on and rushed toward the bedroom window leading to the fire escape, without so much as a backward glance at his lover! As he fled through the window, his last memory of her was the sound of her screams, begging him to untie her! The memory of his actual escape was blurred; it was a miracle that he had succeeded in getting away at all. He was never caught and he never returned to the city.

......To this day, he wondered what had become of her and how she had explained being nude and tied to the bedposts. By habit, he stroked the long scar on his cheek. Fortunately, women still considered him attractive in spite of the scar, but it had been a painful lesson about the importance of staying alert when fooling around with another man's property! And that's exactly how he regarded married women; in his eyes, they were just property, fair game for any man with the balls to go after them. Besides, if a man couldn't control his woman, then he didn't deserve to keep her! Of all his numerous affairs, it was the married women who excited him the most, partially because they were forbidden fruit, but mainly because of the danger. Matt was one of those men who just had to live life on the edge; it was the only way he felt truly alive!

While he reminisced about his past, his mind suddenly leaped forward to the night of the barn dance. If he closed his eyes, he could still see that red-haired woman dancing, her lithe body swaying to the beat of the music. She was smiling while she circled around, her long, flame-red hair swirling around her, the skirt of her green dress billowing up around her thighs, every now and then showing a flash of her black, lace panties. The intoxication he'd felt that night was more from her than from the liquor. He really didn't know why it should matter, but he suddenly wished he could undo the way he'd treated her that night. He could still remember the look of disgust on her face and it cut him to the quick! He didn't want her to think that he was always like that. It shouldn't matter one way or another, but it did. Christ! What was he thinking? She was only a woman! Who gave a fuck what she thought!? He lay back, lost in thought, and slowly began to doze off. As he entered the hazy world of dreams, his last vision was of her green eyes staring at him accusingly.

CHAPTER 19 THE WARRIORS

After the meeting with his grandfather, Jacob rushed to his Jeep and drove back to the reservation to meet with his warriors and decide which two would accompany him into the wilderness area. It would be a very difficult decision. No matter whom he chose, the others were bound to feel insulted by not being chosen. His warriors numbered seventeen in all and he wished he could take every last one of them. But Jacob knew better than to question Lone Elk's advice, especially since he always knew more than he let on. Well, he would just have to work it out, somehow or other, and hope they would understand. Although all of his warriors were fiercely loyal to him and extremely proficient in their fighting skills, there were two who stood above the rest, Running Deer and Two Eagles. While he drove, Jacob smiled as he recalled various incidents from their youth......

The ages of the young warriors at that time ranged from eleven to thirteen. Running Deer and Two Eagles were among the youngest of the entire group. They were also very skinny and not very tall. It was only natural that these two would gravitate toward each other for companionship and they soon became the very best of friends. Yet, in spite of their shortcomings, they were both held in high esteem by their peers due to certain very special talents. Two Eagles had the sharpest vision of them all and often saw things that no-one else was able to see. Running deer had the ability to outrun everyone in the group, much to their constant annoyance. After spending a whole summer losing races to the incredibly fleet-footed runner, they decided to challenge him to an unusual race, one where the odds would decidedly favor them. He would have to run on his own separate course, which would be filled with various obstacles. The rest of them would run on a parallel course, only without the obstacles. Like any young boy who had often been teased about his size, he was especially proud that he was able to best them in at least this one area. Confident that he couldn't lose, he grinned mischievously while he eagerly accepted their challenge.

"Go ahead, guys! Set up the toughest course you can think of! It won't make any difference; you'll never be able to beat me!"

Laughing, he raced away to find his friend, Two Eagles, while the rest of the boys plotted his downfall. One of them, a tall, thoughtful boy of thirteen, who went by the name of Owl, had come up with a clever idea.

"Listen to me! I'm telling you it will work! When he's about halfway down the course, he'll never notice the trap! All we have to do is cover the pit very carefully with thick ferns and grasses and then top it off with dirt. If we do it just right, he won't spot it in time to keep from falling into the pit! Well, what do you think?"

Hawk was in favor of the plan.

"Owl's right! It's a great idea! About halfway through the course, there's a turn. You know, right around that mound of rocks. He'll just be getting his second wind and he'll be too busy concentrating on the turn to notice the trap. I wish I could be right there to see his face when he drops into the pit!"

The boys laughed gleefully and then they all turned toward Jacob. Even at that young age, he was already their acknowledged leader. After considering the alternative, which would be to lose the race, he opted in favor of the plan.

188

"I agree with both of you. It's a great idea! Just one thing though, don't dig the pit too deep; I don't want him to break a leg. I just want to beat him for a change!"

So it was decided and they spent the rest of the afternoon preparing their trap. Running Deer had been called home by his mother and they knew he wouldn't return until the next morning, the very day of the race. So they safely worked well into the evening, setting up various obstacles which would serve to slow him down a little, but, most importantly, would distract him, thereby lessening the chance of discovering their trap.

After a seemingly endless night, the big day finally arrived. The morning dawned crisp and clear in a season called, most appropriately, Indian summer. The large meadow where the race would be held was still shrouded with a dewy mist. Running Deer and Two Eagles had risen extra early in order to check out the obstacles before the race. The morning air was so crisp, it almost hurt as they took deep breaths while trotting down the hill toward the silvery meadow. As they reached the beginning of the course, they noticed the very first obstacle, which was a sizable log that was too large to jump over and would have to be climbed instead.

"Wow! Check this out! They really are trying to slow me down! I can't believe they rolled this huge log all the way out here. I wonder where they got it?"

"I don't know, but It looks to me like you're in for a pretty serious challenge. This is only the first obstacle and it's a killer! C'mon! We'd better check out the others."

They ran ahead to the next one. It was only a long pole propped up at both ends by a pile of rocks. He'd only have to leap across it while running; it wasn't set very high, so it shouldn't be too difficult.

"Those dummies! This hurdle won't even break

my stride! C'mon! Let's go back; we don't need to check every one. This race is going to be too easy. What idiots!"

Two Eagles felt uneasy. He was very shrewd and he knew something was definitely amiss.

"Wait a minute! Don't be in such a hurry! Something is wrong here."

"What are you talking about? You're always such a worry-wart! Can't you see the only thing wrong is their lack of brains! If that's the best they can come up with, then they're just a bunch of dumb dodos!"

"Don't you get it? That's exactly what they want you to think! I'll bet they've got something big planned for you, something they don't want you to notice! C'mon! We're going to check out the whole course. Hurry up or we'll run out of time!"

Two Eagles ran on and Running Deer reluctantly followed, grumbling to himself all the way.

"What're you griping about? It's not going to take that long to check things out. You sound like you don't even care whether or not you lose!"

While they ran, they spotted three more hurdles, all relatively harmless. They were almost halfway through the course when Two Eagles stopped dead in his tracks.

"I knew it! Look at that! That has to be it!"

He was pointing to a spot where the course curved around a large mound of rocks. Running Deer still couldn't see anything, so he started to run over there for a closer look.

"Stop! Don't go another step closer! That ground looks funny; let me check it out first!"

Running Deer had stopped just short of crashing into the pit and still couldn't see anything wrong. But he knew better than to question his friend's eyesight and waited patiently for him. Two Eagles approached the area very carefully and stared at it for a while. Then he gingerly put one foot forward, easing his weight down ever so slowly, until he felt the ground begin to give way. He quickly leaped backward to safety and grinned triumphantly at his friend.

"I knew they had some dirty trick in store for you and this is it! Help me cover it up again with some more soil. I don't want them to know we found it! I wonder how deep it is? Oh well, we'll find out after the race. We're just lucky we discovered it in time!"

They quickly covered it up again and then Two Eagles walked all around the edge of the area, carefully scrutinizing the ground. Then he marked the exact boundaries of the pit with some small rocks, in such a way that the others wouldn't notice. Then Running Deer stepped back a ways, got a running start and leaped over the entire pit with room to spare. Feeling very satisfied with themselves, they smiled victoriously at each other and raced back to the beginning of the course. Fortunately, the others still hadn't arrived, so they sat down to eat some nutbread they'd brought along for quick energy. They were just finishing as Jacob and his young warriors started down the hill to join them.

"I don't believe it! You actually got here before we did! What's the matter, girls? Were you just a little too nervous to sleep in?"

The rest of them laughed hilariously at his remark. Hawk nudged Owl in the ribs and flashed him a secretive smile. Owl shoved him away and flashed him a warning look. Jacob glared at both of them and decided it was time to get started.

"C'mon, guys! Let's go! It's time to show Running Deer that his winning days are over!"

Two Eagles and Running Deer flashed each other a knowing look and howled gleefully!

"Hah! You'll never see the day that any of you can beat me, no matter what obstacles you put in my way!"

Jacob laughed confidently.

"We'll see about that! All right! Is everyone on their mark? You all know the rules; when Two Eagles shoots his arrow into that tree, we go!"

Everyone immediately became quiet. All eyes were on Two Eagles. He looked at his friend to see if he was ready and Running Deer gave him a slight nod. In one fluid movement, he raised his bow and sent the arrow flying directly to the center of the target. At the exact moment of impact, all the runners took off in a cloud of dust. They ran as though their lives depended on their speed. While they ran, they kept looking nervously at Running Deer, hoping to leave him far behind. In the beginning, they did manage to stay ahead of him, especially since he first had to climb that huge log. But once he was over it, he began to catch them at an alarming rate. He flew over the series of pole hurdles with the greatest of ease until, finally, they were all approaching the halfway point. By this time, they were all about even and they were happily anticipating his fall into the pit. Just as Running Deer came into the danger zone, he caught sight of the boundary markers and sailed completely across the entire pit. As they watched him soar around the mound of rocks and disappear from their view, they all came to a stop and looked at each other, puzzled. Jacob was disgusted.

"Great job, guys! Who was the moron in charge of covering that pit?"

Bristling with indignation, Hawk stepped forward.

"I was! I don't know what happened, but I know I did a good job!"

Jacob glared menacingly at him.

192

"Evidently it was too good! Just in case you didn't notice, you made it so strong he was able to run right over it!"

Hawk was starting to get angry.

"That's impossible!"

"Oh yeah? I'm going to walk over it myself and show you just how impossible it is! And you'd better Goddamn well pray that I fall in!"

Furious, Jacob rushed over there and stepped right on top of the cover. To his amazement, he found himself crashing straight through to the bottom of the pit! While he and the others were stunned into absolute silence, Two Eagles and Running Deer broke that silence with their hysterical laughter. They had both circled around and hidden behind the huge mound of rocks, showing themselves only when they heard Jacob fall noisily into the pit.

......Jacob couldn't help smiling to himself as he remembered that humbling experience. It was the first and last time that anyone had ever gotten the best of him. He never again made the mistake of under-estimating his opponent! In fact, that was exactly why he was worried about taking only two of his warriors into the wilderness area with him. He was well aware that his enemies were extremely dangerous and he didn't like the idea of being outnumbered. He was sorely tempted to sneak them all into the danger zone with him, perhaps just a few at a time. While he weighed the consequences of going against Lone Elk's advice, he finally reached the reservation. As Jacob came to a stop and climbed out of his Jeep, he noticed that the tribal fire was lit and his warriors were standing around it, almost as though they had been expecting him. Two Eagles and Running Deer were the first to approach. Watching the two of them, so tall and muscular, he found it difficult to believe they had ever

193

been so short and so skinny. Who would ever have thought they would turn out to be such strong, handsome men? There were only two things that hadn't changed about them. Running Deer was still the fastest runner he'd ever seen and Two Eagles, with his outstanding vision, was still unsurpassed with the bow and arrow. He was proud of them both. They were more than friends; they were the younger brothers he'd never had.

"What's with the fire? Did you call a tribal meeting without me?"

Running Deer smiled at Jacob and addressed him by his tribal name.

"No, Falcon. We would never do that. Early this morning, Lone Elk told us that you would arrive at this hour and that we should light the fire in preparation for the meeting you would call."

Jacob wasn't at all surprised.

"Of course! I should have known that he would have things already prepared! Well, what else did he tell you? Do you know why you're here?"

"He only said that it involved something very dangerous and that you would explain the rest. Does this mean you've decided it's time to take care of those marijuana growers?"

"Let's just say my plans for them have been slightly updated. I was only waiting to find out how and when they were planning to take out their next shipment. Well, I think I just found out. Has any of you ever heard of a man by the name of Trevor Thompson?"

Owl was the first one to step forward.

"Yeah! I've heard of him. Doesn't he run some kind of wilderness tours for vacationers?"

"Yeah, that's the man! He and his hired hands guide people into the Yolla Bolly and out of it. It makes you wonder what else they might be bringing in and taking out. Think about it! They might just be bringing supplies in for the growers and taking shipments out on the return trip. While we've been wondering how they were doing it, I believe they were operating right out in the open."

"Well, I'll be damned! It never would have occurred to me to check them out. I think they've been in business for a long time."

"I'll bet they have! And a very profitable business at that! Well guys, after I check them out to make certain they're as guilty as I suspect, I think we should pay them a surprise visit! How about it, girls? Is everyone here ready to kick ass?"

They all hooted and hollered at Jacob's remarks! Three Bears walked over to him and grabbed him in a bear hug.

"Falcon, I don't care if you are our leader. You'd better watch out who you're callin' a girl!"

In the flash of a moment, Jacob wrapped one of his legs around one of Three Bears' and brought him down hard, breaking out of the bear hug at the same time! Then he laughingly helped him up, while the others assailed him with an onslaught of questions. He held his hand up, motioning for silence, and attempted to answer them.

"Enough! If you'll all be quiet, I'll explain exactly what we have to do. Unfortunately, this won't be as simple as I'd like, since we also have those vacationers to worry about. We're going to have to make certain they don't get hurt."

With an incredulous look, Two Eagles stared at Jacob.

"Are you crazy? They're just a bunch of white people! Who cares what happens to them? Let them take their chances! I'm not risking my life for any of them! We're going to rid our forests of those damned

195

drug dealers once and for all and I wouldn't be a bit upset if we got rid of the whites right along with them! Since when did you start worrying about whites anyway? I thought you felt the same about them as I do! Are you going soft, or what? You're sure not the Falcon I remember!"

There wasn't a sound as the entire group stared at Jacob. Seeing the skeptical looks on the faces of his warriors, Jacob suddenly realized that he was, in large part, responsible for their feelings of prejudice. What a fool he'd been! He was their leader; he should have known better! He should have realized that they would follow him, even in attitude. With words alone, his grandfather had shamed him into realizing the error of his ways. Could he possibly do as well as Lone Elk? Somehow, he would have to find the right words and help them learn to cope with the bad whites without hating all of them.

"I wish I were as wise as my grandfather. If I were, I wouldn't be in this Goddamned mess! All right, here goes! Out of all of us, I was probably the guiltiest when it came to hating the whites. By my bad example, I probably influenced some of you into the same, senseless prejudice."

Looking puzzled, Two Eagles interrupted him.

"You can't be serious. You're not the reason I hate the whites; they are! Have you forgotten how they've treated us all our lives?"

"No, I haven't forgotten how some of them treated us, but it wasn't all of them, was it? I'll bet everyone of you can remember being treated nicely by at least one white person, right? And I really doubt that any of you can deny having been cruel to them, even when they didn't deserve it! Well, I don't hear any denials; could I possibly be right?"

They were all watching him with bewildered looks

196

on their faces. He just didn't sound like the leader they remembered. Seeing their reaction, Jacob was beginning to lose patience.

"All right, enough of this crap! This is the way it's going to be! From now on, we're only against the bad whites, not all of them. Understand? And remember this! If you're not with me, then you're against me. So you'd better make up your minds right now where you stand! We've got a job to do and part of that job will involve protecting some innocent whites! If anyone has a problem with that, you'd better let me know right now!"

Once again, there was complete quiet. Jacob carefully studied their faces and was finally satisfied.

"All right! Since no-one has spoken otherwise, I'm going to assume that you're all still with me. Now let's get down to business. First, I'm going to tell you what Lone Elk has recommended; then you can tell me what you think and then I'll make the final decision."

After relating his grandfather's vision and his insistence that he take only two warriors along with him, he put the subject up for discussion. Running Deer was the first to speak.

"No way! It's insane to go in there with only yourself and two of us! We won't stand a chance! I think we should all go!"

"Actually, I agree with you. But there is one problem. I really should check them out first and that would be a lot easier with just three of us. The rest of you could be in some backup position, ready to assist when needed. In fact, we really don't have to discuss this any further at all. I've decided and that's the end of it! There's just one other thing I need to tell you. Some of you were with me the night of the barn dance, so you might remember the red-haired woman who was there with her friends. She's one of the vacationers going on the wilderness tour. Do any of you know who I'm talking

197

about?"

With a gleam in his eye, Three Bears was the first to answer.

"Are you kiddin'? Who could ever forget her? What a knock-out!"

Hawk had something to add.

"Yeah, I remember her. Some guy was tryin' to carry her outa there by force. I could hardly blame the guy; I wanted to take her home, myself. Now there's a white girl I could warm up to real easy!"

Everyone laughed, except Jacob. His face clouded over and his eyes somehow appeared even blacker. Everyone immediately quieted down as Jacob confronted Hawk with a menacing glare.

"Don't even think about it! She's off limits to all of you! There are only two things you need to know about her. First, her name is Shannon and second, the most important part of your job is to make absolutely certain that nothing happens to her! Have I made myself clear?"

Without saying a word, they all stared at Jacob. Their silence was more eloquent than anything they could have said.

"Good! I'll take that as a 'yes'! By the way, the two who will accompany me are Running Deer and Two Eagles. Make the usual preparations; we leave at dawn!"

With those words, Jacob abruptly left. The warriors stood by the crackling fire a while longer and talked quietly among themselves. Owl stood apart, apparently lost in thought until, finally, he was ready to speak.

"Well, I guess we all know what his 'be good to the whites' speech was all about! It's pretty clear the Falcon has found his mate! You know what this means, don't you? We're all going to be in deep shit unless we learn to accept her and I mean really accept her! It's impossible to fool him; he'll know in a flash whether or not we're sincere. I don't know about the rest of you, but I'm not about to get on his bad side. I suggest you all make a serious effort to forget that she's white. One more thing, did you notice that he left without telling the rest of us when to follow them into the danger zone. Unless someone has a better idea, I think we should go in about two days behind them and we'd better pray that nothing happens to her!"

They all agreed with Owl and silently nodded their assent. Then, without so much as a word, they moved to their ritual positions around the fire. At this unspoken signal, the drummers began the tribe's ancient battle song and the men slowly began to dance. As the tempo increased, the valley soon echoed with the sound of their chanting and the beating of their drums. While they leaped and swayed around the fire, the flames shot high above their heads, the bright flashes accenting their exotic moves and costumes. In their tribal dress, they looked for all the world like warriors from another century! Unknown to them, Jacob watched from a nearby hilltop and smiled to himself. Whenever his warriors did the battle dance, he was momentarily transported back to a time where he really belonged and his world finally felt right.

CHAPTER 20 ROCK CABIN CAMP

In the darkest hour before the dawn, Shannon lay tossing and turning in her bed, unable to get back to sleep. She had no idea what had awoken her. Thinking that it might have been some noise, she listened carefully, but heard nothing out of the ordinary, only some light snoring from Tony and Cat. Feeling restless, she decided to get up and take a short walk. Taking care not to disturb the others, she quietly dressed and stepped out of the motorhome, gently closing the door behind her. While she stood for a moment, pondering which direction to take, the early morning chill caused her to shiver. Snugly wrapping herself within her warm jacket, she decided to hike the relatively short distance to the cafe; a hot cup of coffee was just what she needed. Glancing at her watch, she realized that the cafe should be open by the time she arrived, so she left a note telling where she'd gone and departed with a brisk stride. As she walked, she slowly became aware of a heavy silence, a quietude so profound that it was unnerving. After a short time, she couldn't shake the feeling that she was being followed. Worried, she began looking over her shoulder, but neither saw nor heard anything unusual. Upon approaching a huge oak tree, she realized that she was over halfway there and sighed with relief. Stepping beneath the shelter of the massive, old oak, she was startled by the hoot of an owl in a branch just above her head. Involuntarily, she shuddered and began to run down the road until she felt silly and forced herself to slow down. Chiding herself for being so foolish, she gradually noticed the lights of a vehicle approaching from behind her. She stopped and turned to face the oncoming lights, wondering if she should have hidden behind a tree until she knew who it was. It was too late to hide now, so she stood and waited, filled with a prickly sense of unease. An old Dodge pickup slowly pulled up beside her and the man inside offered her a ride. Warily, Shannon stepped up to the passenger side and looked in the window, prepared to politely decline the offer. She gasped out loud as she found herself staring into the eyes of the man from the barn dance; trembling, she could still feel his hands on her breasts! Shaken to the core, she turned to run down the road toward the safety of the cafe, when his pickup lurched forward and cut her off. Frozen with fear, she stood, watching with bated breath, as he leaped out of his truck and ran over to her. Unable to speak, she just stared at him and awaited the inevitable. To her amazement, Mathias stopped directly in front of her and just stared back at her with the strangest look on his face; he didn't even attempt to touch her. Looking into her green eyes, Matt once again felt those strange, new feelings wash over him, leaving him bewildered and, for the first time in his life, at a loss for words. The morning sun was just beginning to peek over the rim of the mountains, streaking the sky with banners of red, gold and fuchsia, colors which were caught and reflected by Shannon's glorious, wavy, red hair. Matt thought she looked like some kind of goddess. She was entirely too beautiful to be real! Hesitantly, he reached out to touch her hair and assure himself that she wasn't just some dream he had conjured up as an antidote to his extreme loneliness. While he stroked a lock of her hair, Shannon felt a chill go down her spine and she carefully studied his face for some clue as to what to expect from him. While she braced herself for the worst, he only continued to stroke

202

her hair and gaze at her with an almost imperceptible longing. Then, he shocked her by actually speaking.

"I'm sorry about the other night. I drank too much and lost control. I'm not tryin' to make an excuse; it's just a fact and I'm real sorry. It won't happen again. If you need a ride, I'll give you one. If you don't, I'll leave you alone. Just let me know what you want."

Shannon knew what it cost him to say that. The words hadn't come easily to him. The look in his eyes convinced her that she would be safe with him, so she decided to take pity on him.

"Thank you for the apology; consider it accepted, along with your offer for a ride."

Stunned that she had actually forgiven him, he found himself stammering, while he rushed to open the door for her.

"Hop in! Where are you goin'......I mean, where do you want me to take you?"

Shannon laughed nervously.

"I'm just going to the cafe for a cup of coffee. I couldn't sleep, so......"

Matt quickly interrupted her.

"I know just what you mean. I have trouble sleepin' all the time! Coffee sure sounds good right now. Do you feel like company?"

"Sure! Why not?"

The old pickup creaked to a stop as they reached the cafe. Matt rushed around to open her door and she flushed as their eyes met. Shannon suddenly realized that he was quite attractive, in spite of the long scar on his cheek. She wondered how it had happened, but was afraid to ask. All her instincts told her that he was dangerous, yet she somehow felt safe with him. Even so, she knew enough to keep her questions to herself. He held out his hand to help her out of the truck and she was shocked by the electrical charge that raced between them. Breathlessly, she removed her hand from his and quickly headed for the cafe. As they stepped through the doorway, Matt took her by the arm and led her to a secluded table. He pulled out her chair and she sat down without meeting his eyes, a fact which wasn't lost on Matt. He began to feel the first stirring of hope well up inside himself. Who knows? Maybe he would actually get lucky! For the very first time, he thought of his life in terms of a future, instead of just living for today. Maybe, just maybe......

"Okay, folks, what'll you have?"

Startled, Matt stared at the waitress for a moment. He hadn't even noticed her walk up to them. He looked at Shannon and shrugged.

"Just coffee? Or would you like some breakfast? Get whatever you want."

Shannon flashed him a radiant smile and nodded.

"Okay! You twisted my arm! Bacon and scrambled eggs, please, and some black coffee."

"Me too! I'll take the same as the lady."

Feeling her nervousness fade away, Shannon smiled at Matt.

"You know what? I just realized that we don't actually know each other! Perhaps we should introduce ourselves."

"Don't tell me your name; let me guess! I'll bet it's Shannon!"

Shannon was amazed.

"How did you know my name?"

"I made it my business to find out. I wanted to know who I had to apologize to."

His remark instantly brought back the events of the evening of the barn dance, causing her to flush and look away. Matt felt something wrenching at his heart and hastened to continue.

"I'm sorry! I didn't mean to embarrass you! Let's

start over. My name is Mathias, but you can call me Matt. Everybody else does. Let's make this official and shake hands."

Shannon gingerly offered her hand and watched him apprehensively as he grasped her soft hand with his large, strong one. Once again, she felt as though she had been struck by high voltage and tried to disentangle her hand from his, but his grip was firm and he only released her after several long seconds, while he enjoyed the obvious effect he had on her. Annoyed by the smug look on his face, Shannon forced herself to stare right back at him, her eyes ablaze with a green fire. She wasn't about to let him think that she was intimidated by him!

"Well? I thought you wanted company. Why don't you tell me a little about yourself? How long have you lived here and what kind of work do you do?"

Matt couldn't help smiling to himself; she was so determined to keep things casual. Of course, he wasn't about to let that happen! She would soon realize that he always took control of any situation.

"Oh, yeah! I'm in the mood for company, all right, 'specially yours. As for your other questions, I've been hangin' around these parts for a fair time, long enough to know my way around. You might say I sort of help people find what they're lookin' for. In fact, I guess you could say I'm some kind of explorer. How about you? What are you lookin' for? Maybe I can help you find it."

"I don't believe the lady needs your assistance. I'm sure I can supply all the help she needs!"

Startled by the interruption, Matt looked up to find a very angry Trevor Thompson standing by their table. Trying to appear calm, Trevor turned to Shannon and nodded.

"I see you've arrived ahead of the others. Would you mind if I join you for a cup of coffee while we wait for them?"

Shannon nodded her assent, feeling greatly relieved not to be alone with Matt any longer. It seemed as though all his remarks were filled with sexual innuendoes. She found him both aggravating and fascinating, but, most of all, she considered him dangerous. It was pretty clear that Trevor also found him irritating; in fact, she was puzzled by the depth of his anger.

"I'd be pleased to have you join us! Allow me to introduce you, or do you two already know each other?"

Matt leaned back in his chair and shot Trevor a sly look.

"Sure we do! It's a small town; everyone knows everybody around here. How's it hangin', Trevor? Ain't seen much of you lately. Where you been hidin' out?"

"As a matter of fact, I've been tending to business. Maybe you ought to try that yourself, sometime. I'm really surprised to find you in town. I thought you were supposed to be doing some job in the back country. Aren't you afraid your boss will fire you?"

"Nah, not a chance! He ain't nothin' but a Goddamn wimp! He wouldn't have the guts to fire me. Besides, he'd never get the job done without me! But thanks for the warning, Trevor; that's real nice of you."

Before Trevor could answer, they were interrupted by the waitress bringing their breakfasts.

"Here you are, folks! How about you; do you need a menu?"

"No thanks! Just some black coffee would be fine."

With an icy stare, Trevor turned back to Matt.

"Yeah, I guess I'm just a nice guy! Seriously, though, if I were you, I'd get back to work as fast as I could. Otherwise, you might not have enough time to finish your job, and that could cost you more than you

206

know!"

Matt laughed out loud at the thinly disguised threat.

"Fortunately, you're not me! So I guess I'll just go ahead and enjoy my breakfast along with the company of this beautiful young lady. After that, I'll mosey on out to the job in my own good time. Meanwhile, maybe you could find somewhere else to sit, so's the lady and I can finish our conversation."

Growing angrier by the moment, Trevor was finding it increasingly difficult to restrain himself. Unaware that his hands were knotted in a fist, he spoke through clenched teeth.

"I believe it's up to the lady whether or not I stay, not you!"

Instantly, Matt flew out of his chair, knocking it over as he lunged at Trevor and grabbed him by his collar! Strangling, Trevor tried to remove his hands, to no avail! Matt towered over him and was easily twice as strong as he was. Trevor knew that he wouldn't stand a chance without a gun.

"Wrong guess, little man! It's not up to the lady; it's up to me! Now get your ass outa here before I bounce it off the street!"

With those words, Matt shoved Trevor away and waited to see what he'd do. Matt was praying he'd try to pull a gun on him; he knew he could flatten him even before he managed to aim it. But Trevor didn't have his gun with him and would never have attempted to use it, anyway, in such close proximity; he knew Matt far too well to try that. Besides, they were in a public place; the timing was all wrong. But his day would come and, when it did, he'd be prepared. Matt was dead meat; he just didn't know it yet! Rubbing his neck, Trevor slowly backed away, with a bitter smile on his face.

"This must be your lucky day, Matt. It's the wrong

place and the wrong time, but we're not finished yet. You and I still have a long way to go before we're done. Be sure to watch your back; you never know who'll be comin' up behind you!"

Speechless, Shannon watched as Trevor slowly left the cafe. Then, she turned and stared at Matt, waiting for some kind of explanation. Trying to appear calm, she attempted to lift her coffee cup, but her hands were so shaky, she spilled it all over the table. Embarrassed, she quickly set the cup down and picked up her napkin in order to clean up the mess. Before she could do so, Matt leaned over and grabbed her hand, holding her still. Unable to meet his eyes, she just sat there while he scooted his chair over and sat right beside her. He put his hand just under her chin and gently raised her face, forcing her to look at him. Nervously, she studied his face and was amazed to find the anger gone from his eyes. How quickly he changed moods! She was disconcerted by the tender way in which he was looking at her, almost with a touch of pity. She had the distinct impression that he thought he could do anything he wanted with her, but chose to be merciful. Once again, she felt a chill go down her back. She had never before realized that danger could be so intoxicating! While she looked deep into his eyes, she found herself unable to move, almost unable to breathe! It was Matt who finally broke the silence.

"I'm sorry about that ugly scene. You must think trouble follows me around like a lonesome dog. Go ahead; you can tell me what you really think of me. And you don't have to look so scared! I'm not goin' to hurt you. In fact, I wouldn't ever do anything to you, unless I thought it was somethin' you might like."

Pushing his hand away from her, Shannon bristled with indignation!

"Do you really want to know what I think of you?

Fine! Then I'll tell you. You're entirely too smug! That's what I don't like about you. You think you can just take whatever you want in life, but that's not the way things work! You have to earn what you want, whether it's respect, love or money. By the way, I don't know what's going on between you and Trevor, but if you thought you were impressing me by threatening him, then you've got a lot to learn about women! And now, I'm going outside to look for Trevor!"

As she started to rise, Matt grabbed her by the arm and pulled her uncomfortably close. While she struggled, Matt just smiled knowingly and held her all the more tightly.

"You dare to call that the truth? I'll give you the truth! I'll tell you what you really think of me; you know, the good stuff that you won't admit, even to yourself! You like dangerous men, the kind who know what they want and take it! And, in your heart, you'd love to be taken by just such a man, but you won't dare admit it, 'cause ladies ain't supposed to have such wicked thoughts! I'll bet you never had a really good fuck; you know, the kind that sets your whole body on fire and makes you beg for more! That's the kind I'm gonna give you! Not right now, but soon, I promise you. And when the time comes, don't even bother fightin' me, 'cause we both know you want it as bad as I do!"

Then he grabbed her hair and tilted her face upward, staring deep into her green eyes. Unable to move, she was forced to submit to his long, passionate kiss. Against her will, she found herself strongly aroused by him and instinctively returned his kiss. When they finally pulled apart, Shannon was visibly shaken and just stared at him, breathlessly. Matt could hardly believe the effect she had on him and was even more shaken than she was, although he'd die before he'd ever admit it! With one last look at her lovely face, he abruptly released her and walked out of the cafe, without so much as a backward look! Trevor was standing outside and watched as Matt climbed into his pickup and drove away. Only then did he walk back into the cafe and approach Shannon's table. As he sat down, he noticed that she was extremely agitated. In fact, she didn't even seem aware of his presence. He reached over and lightly touched her hand, instantly causing her to jump back ever so slightly.

"Oh, Trevor! I'm sorry! I didn't realize it was you who had touched me. I must have been lost in thought."

"Shannon, what's wrong? What did he say to you? He'd better not have laid a hand on you! Well, did he?"

With a stricken face, she answered him without words.

"That bastard! I swear I'll kill him yet! I'm sorry, Shannon; I should never have left your side. Whatever you do, stay away from him! He's a sick man! I promise he'll never touch you again!"

Trevor called the waitress over to get them some fresh coffee; Shannon looked like she needed some. While they sat quietly drinking their coffee, Trevor studied her face and thought she appeared much calmer. She was somewhat of a paradox; he'd never met anyone quite like her. When he first met her, she struck him as strong and self-reliant. But right now, she seemed incredibly vulnerable. He wondered what on Earth she was doing with that wimpy husband of hers. She was so beautiful, she could have anyone; so why him? What was his name? Larry, that was it! The town gossips were buzzing with the way he'd acted on the night of the barn dance. Evidently, he was quite a coward, hardly the right man for a woman like Shannon! He wondered if she secretly wished she were rid of him. They were about to take a long tour in the wilderness;

anything could happen. Who knows? Her wish just might come true!

Shannon was also lost in thought as she slowly drank her coffee. She was filled with self-doubt and more than a little shame. How on Earth could she possibly be attracted to a man like Matt? He was arrogant, bossy, abrasive and disgustingly smug! He represented everything she disliked in a man. He thought he was so macho, so exciting and so sexy! The trouble was that he was absolutely right! When he kissed her, he awoke such a hunger within her that all she could think of was instantly going to bed with him! When he told her what he would do to her, she could almost feel him inside her and desperately wished to be taken at that exact moment! But how did he know she wanted him? Was her wanton need written all over her face for anyone to see? How embarrassing! She felt like she was losing control; what in the world had happened to her? She used to be the picture of respectability! She had always looked down on promiscuous women. She considered them nothing more than sluts and now she had somehow turned into one of them! She really had no idea what had brought about such a change in her. Shannon was just beginning to find out that she was only human, after all, and that sexual desire didn't necessarily always go hand in hand with love, not even for her. That was only a man-made rule; it definitely wasn't one of Mother Nature's!

While Trevor and Shannon were finishing their coffee, Eric and the rest of the group entered the cafe. Larry rushed directly over to Shannon. He looked nervously at Trevor; he didn't like the idea of Shannon sitting there alone with him. He especially didn't like the way Trevor was looking at her. But the thing that troubled him most of all was the fact that Shannon

211

seemed to have lost all interest in making love with him. He couldn't even remember the last time they'd had sex. Last night, after the others had fallen asleep, he snuggled up against her back and started kissing her shoulder. She didn't say anything, but he could feel her tense up. Then he reached his hand around and began to gently squeeze her breast. She quickly grabbed his hand and pushed it away, saying she was just too tired. Ordinarily, he would have forced her, but something told him that wouldn't be too wise this time, so he rolled over and tried to sleep, but sleep was a long time coming.

"Honey, you had me worried when I woke up and found you gone. You should have waited for me! I don't think it's safe to take such a long walk all by yourself at that hour."

"It's all right, Larry! I'm fine, really. Why don't you sit down and order some breakfast? It'll be your last meal in a restaurant for some time."

Eric and Tony pushed some of the tables together and they all sat down and ordered breakfast. Eric made certain that he was sitting between Shannon and Trevor; he wasn't about to let him get too close to her! Elaine sat on Eric's other side and was the only one there who didn't feel the tension in the air. Eric glared at Trevor and wondered what they had talked about before he arrived. He couldn't wait to get Shannon alone; he wanted to make certain that Trevor hadn't tried anything with her.

Trevor was amused by the look on Eric's face. It was obvious that Eric considered him quite a threat and he probably didn't know just how correct he was. One thing was certain; if it were the last thing he ever did, Trevor was determined, somehow or other, to get Shannon alone and spend a whole night making love to her!

While they were all eating breakfast, two of

212

Trevor's men stepped into the cafe and signaled that they needed to speak to him. He motioned them over to the table and stood to greet them. They seemed a little surprised by his good humor at this early hour, until they caught sight of Shannon. Then they smiled knowingly at each other.

"Good morning, boys! You're right on time. Let me introduce you to these good folks. This tall, skinny one here is Jesse and the little feller there is his younger brother, Mitch, but he'll answer to the name of Tadpole. He was the runt of the litter, so his family took to callin' him by that name. But make no mistake; these two boys are plenty tough and they'll do a good job of lookin' out for you! Listen up, boys, so you'll remember their names! Those two over there are Tony and Cat Salerno, in the middle we have Larry and Shannon Larsen, and last, but not least, are Eric and Elaine Taylor. Now, if you'll excuse us, the boys and I are goin' outside to check on the supplies. We'll all take off in about fifteen minutes."

As soon as they left, the three couples all began to talk at once. None of them were too pleased with the two brothers. Finally, Tony managed to be heard above all the noise.

"Quiet, everyone! Shut up and listen, will you? I know those two aren't exactly crowd-pleasers, but I don't think there's a Hell of a lot we can do about it, unless you all just want to call it quits and head for home. As for me, I vote for making the best of it and going on with our vacation. After coming this far and spending all that money, are we going to let a couple of weird-looking guys spoil our trip?"

Tony could tolerate almost anything, except spending money for nothing! And he was well aware that they wouldn't get any refund if they backed out at the last minute. He looked at the rest of them and saw that they shared his thoughts on the matter. Oddly enough, it was Elaine who spoke up.

"I agree with Tony! Why should it matter what those two look like? They're only the hired hands and I strongly doubt that either one of them would bother any of us. I vote in favor of our vacation."

For a moment, they were all taken aback by hearing such a positive statement from Elaine. Then they all agreed to continue and began to file out of the cafe. As they stepped through the door, they noticed that the chill of the morning had given way to a warm, gentle breeze, a prelude to the summer heat soon to descend on them with a vengeance! Eric saw Trevor standing off to the side, obviously engrossed in a serious conversation with the two brothers. He appeared to be very upset about something and even made a threatening gesture toward Jesse, who looked equally angry! Eric didn't like what he saw, so he decided to check things out. Trevor wasn't even aware of Eric's approach until he was almost upon them. He quickly flashed a look of warning to Jesse and turned to face Eric with an annoyed stance.

"What do you want? I'm pretty busy with the men right now, so make it quick, okay?"

"It looked to me like you were having some kind of a problem, so I thought maybe I should offer my help."

His remarks irritated Trevor even further. He couldn't restrain a snide laugh.

"You've got to be kidding! Let's get one thing straight, right now! I won't ever need your help for anything! I've never had a problem that I couldn't solve! So why don't you just mosey on back to your friends and get your gear together and allow me to take care of my business, okay? We're leaving in just a few minutes, so you'd better hurry!"

Then he abruptly turned back to the two brothers

214

in an obvious dismissal of Eric. But Eric wasn't quite so easily dismissed. Annoyed, he grabbed Trevor by his shoulder and spun him back around!

"Just in case you didn't notice, I wasn't through speaking! And maybe you'd better get this straight, right now! When I talk to you, you'd better listen and when I ask a question, I expect an answer! Understand?"

As angry as he was, Trevor knew the trip was too important to push Eric any further at this time, so he just nodded, while Jesse and Tadpole looked on, astonished. They'd never seen anyone talk to Trevor like that and get away with it.

"Good! Now maybe you can answer my question. Why were you yelling at Jesse? I want to know exactly what's going on with you guys!"

Trevor shot a quick, unfathomable look to the two brothers and then turned to answer Eric. By this time, the rest of the group had noticed that something was going on and had walked over to join Eric.

"It's nothing! They forgot some of the supplies, that's all. Don't worry about it! I'll just have to send one of them back later to pick up what we need."

Eric found that hard to believe.

"Are you serious? That's all you were yelling about? Why don't we just wait around and pick up the stuff when the store opens?"

"Because the store won't open for two more hours and we can't spare the time. We have to be at Rock Cabin Camp by then in order to meet up with the man who's bringing out our horses and we can't be late!"

"So what happens if we're a little late? Will he turn into a pumpkin or something?"

Trevor was quickly losing patience.

"All right! Enough of this bullshit! Who's in charge here, anyway, you or me? Am I going to have to fight you over every little decision, or are you going to

215

allow me to call the shots?"

"Seeing as how you put it that way, I guess I'll let you call the shots, at least for the time being. But if the time ever comes that I don't like your decisions, then we're going to change the rules!"

Everyone held their breath, waiting for the inevitable explosion between the two angry men; even the morning breeze had abated while everyone stood in a silence so intense that it was deafening. Finally, Tony stepped forward and put his hand on Eric's shoulder.

"All right! I'm glad that's settled! Come on! Let's pack our gear on the bus. I still have to find a place to park the Winnebago. I sure hope somebody has a suggestion!"

Trevor forced himself to ignore Eric and respond to Tony.

"You can park it on the side of that barn where they had the dance. It'll be safe there. The rest of you get your stuff loaded on the bus; then we'll pick Tony up at the barn. Let's go! We're burnin' daylight!"

Without further incident, they finished loading their gear, picked up Tony and were finally on their way. In spite of the unpleasant scene outside the cafe, they were all aglow with a happy excitement, that wonderful feeling which only comes with the start of a new adventure! As they drove along the quiet country road, each of them was filled with his or her own private expectations of this wilderness trek.

Cat saw this trip as a chance to get off by herself and really be alone in a primitive forest. All her life, she had always been surrounded by other people, her parents, her school friends, her husband and their children. Sometimes, she felt so overwhelmed by it all, that she would pray for an opportunity just to be by herself for a while. It wasn't enough to be alone for a few hours in her own home, because then she was still at the mercy of the telephone and Tony could always surprise her and come home early. No, she had to be alone with nature for a while; maybe then, she could finally find herself. She hoped Tony would understand her wish and respect it.

With a smile on his face, Tony leaned back in his seat and tried to visualize the wonderful fishing that awaited him. He loved to fish more than anything else in the whole world! Well, almost anything else. If he really had to choose, sex came first, but fishing was a very close second. That's what was so great about this trip! For once in his life, he'd get plenty of both! The first chance he had, he'd take Cat out for a walk and get the first mountain piece he'd had in years! Wow! Wasn't life great?

While Elaine jabbered incessantly in his ear, Eric was trying to figure out a way to get Shannon off alone with him. There was something in her eyes, whenever she looked at him lately, that left him feeling very unsettled. Something had definitely changed between them, but he didn't know exactly what. He felt a desperate need to talk to her! If he could only feel certain that she really loved him, his world would be all right again!

Completely unaware that Eric hadn't been listening to her, Elaine finally ran out of things to say and stared out the window at the passing scenery. She was glad they'd all decided to continue with their vacation. She thought it was important that she and Eric spend some quality time together. Lately, he seemed to have lost all interest in her; he no longer even pestered her for sex. Since she considered sex an extremely distasteful chore, she was partially relieved by his sudden lack of interest. Still, she was well aware that he did enjoy it, so she knew something was very wrong. Her mother always used to tell her that, unless you forced yourself to have sexual relations with your husband, he would definitely find someone else to accommodate him. She wondered if he were having an affair and, if so, with whom? It was much too painful to think about such things; she was beginning to get a severe headache. She lay back and tried to doze for a while. As she slowly drifted off, buried memories of her childhood came back to haunt her. She remembered being locked in a dark closet for the longest time......she yelled and screamed and swore she'd obey if he would just let her out of the closet! Finally, he opened the door, yanked her out by her arm and dragged her into his bedroom. He was her sixteen-year-old cousin and he was supposed to be watching her while their parents were at a dance. She was only nine years old and she was terrified of him. She begged her parents not to leave her with him, but they never listened to her. They both laughed and told her she was just being a silly goose; Nathan was such a good boy! He was good all right! He was good at fooling grownups, but he didn't fool her for a second. Even at her young age, she knew he wanted to do something really bad to her. She didn't know what, but she knew it was bad. He took her clothes off and threw her on the bed; then he undressed and lay on top of her. She was too afraid to struggle; she just lay there, frozen with fear! Then he grabbed that big thing hanging between his legs and he started poking her with it. He poked harder and harder until it was all the way inside her. It hurt so bad, but she was afraid to scream because she knew he would lock her in the closet again. She just lay there, with tears streaming down her face until, finally, he was done with her and had filled her with something sticky. When she went to the bathroom, she saw that she was bleeding and then something just snapped in her; she screamed and screamed and screamed.......and then, suddenly, someone was shaking her!

"Elaine! Wake up! It's all right; I'm here. Good Lord! What on Earth were you dreaming about?"

Mercifully, Elaine had no memory of her dream.

"I don't know, but it must have been scary!"

She was grateful that Eric was right there beside her. She lay her head on his shoulder while he comforted her. Whenever he held her gently like this, her world was all right again.

Larry looked over at Elaine and couldn't help shaking his head. That woman was definitely a basket case! He wondered if he were the only one aware of it. Thank God he had a normal wife! If only he could hang on to her! He wondered what it would take to rekindle her love for him. If only he hadn't blown it at the barn dance! But, dear God! What did she expect from him? If he had tried to fight that guy, he would have been torn to pieces! He never would have stood a chance! Didn't she know that? There was really nothing he could have done, not without a gun, anyway. He needed to talk to Shannon about all this, really talk to her. Maybe then she'd understand and give him one last chance. That's all he needed, just one last chance to prove himself. He knew that all women secretly wanted a hero; that's what he really needed, the chance to do something heroic! Maybe there'd be an opportunity for that, once they were in the wilderness, just maybe......

Shannon sat quietly watching the passing scenery; she seemed to be the only one truly interested in the countryside around her. As long as she could remember, she always had a need to be outdoors. She positively glowed with joy at the thought of being in the mountains. All her life, she knew that was where she really belonged. She watched with anticipation as the road took them in an easterly direction. Just before they left the valley floor, the road took a sharp left turn around an old lumber mill. Shannon noticed sprinklers running on top of the piles of logs, keeping them wet. Then the road narrowed and climbed for about a mile and a half, twisting its way to another valley, about two hundred feet higher than the one they'd left behind. When they were about halfway through the long valley, Shannon caught sight of a huge, old barn just off to the left. The sweet smell of fresh grass was wafting on the breeze. This upper valley was so beautiful, she knew she'd never forget it. Finally, the road led out of the valley and they suddenly found themselves driving through a heavily forested area, so dense that it was like going through a jungle, with a rich, musky odor emanating from the heavy foliage. Now they were all watching the scenery. There was something hypnotic about a jungle-like atmosphere; no-one was immune to it. After a mile or so, the road led them through a dry, rocky area, which seemed almost ugly compared to the beauty of the dense forest. Shannon found herself getting sleepy. She lay her head back, intending only a short rest. She didn't want to fall asleep and miss out on any of the drive. However, against her will, she began to doze off......just as she entered the misty realm of dreams, she saw Jacob's face; he appeared to be calling to her. She tried to follow him, but he kept getting further and further away, until she could no longer see him. Filled with despair, she turned around to leave and suddenly he was there, right in front of her. Without a word, he removed her clothing, pushed her down on the grass and made love to her, right there in the forest! Oh, God! It felt so good! She wanted more, still more......she moaned in her sleep with the ecstasy of it! The last thing she remembered before she awoke was his voice telling her that she belonged to him! She came to in a cold sweat, breathing hard. Dear God! She'd never had a dream that felt so real! She looked around nervously to see if anyone had been watching her, but they were all wrapped up in their own thoughts. She wondered if her dream were some kind of omen; she certainly hoped so! She just couldn't get Jacob out of her mind or her soul! He was the only man she'd ever met that she absolutely had to have, even if only for one night. Although she found other men attractive, Jacob was the one man who could make her forget all about the others. She knew he would be that satisfying; somehow, she just knew!

As they approached the bridge across the Eel river, Shannon saw the Middle Eel Work Center just off to their right. According to what she had been told, that was where the California Conservation Corp. workers had been housed, back when they were cutting the trails throughout the Yolla Bolly wilderness area. Shannon really enjoyed learning about the history of her surroundings. Just after crossing the bridge, the road took a sharp left and began to climb through a dry, brushy area. They were still on a paved road, but it was very rough and dotted with potholes. The bus driver kept swerving to miss the deep holes, causing the passengers to feel more than a little queasy. As if that weren't enough, everyone on the bus was also beginning to suffer from the summer heat. They opened their windows, but felt little relief as they were assailed by a hot, dry wind. For the next five or six miles, they climbed slowly, but steadily, until they found themselves driving through another densely wooded section. Their surroundings had changed so dramatically, it was as though they had entered a whole, new world! The air was crisp and fresh and had the most delightful aroma. The dry heat of the brushy area had given way to a refreshingly cool breeze, nature's own air conditioning at its finest! The passengers breathed a collective sigh of relief as they reveled in the almost sensual beauty of this primeval oasis. Their relief was short-lived. As they left the deep forest, Shannon suddenly realized the road was no longer paved. Now they had to contend with more than just potholes; there was a horrible washboard effect to the dirt and gravel road, which made it absolutely essential to crawl along at a snail's pace. Every single mile felt like ten. If she closed her eyes, Shannon could easily imagine herself riding along in a covered wagon; this must have been exactly how it felt, bumpy and slow going, with layers of dust carried by the breeze, covering everyone and everything inside. As they rounded a corner, the bus driver suddenly had to veer sharply off the road in order to miss a logging truck which was bearing down on them, with no apparent concern about crashing into them. In the hasty effort to avoid the truck, the right front tire of the bus hit one of the deep potholes with a loud crash, further jolting the already weary and shaken passengers. For the next ten miles, the road began to climb steadily again, until it finally reached a high plateau. At this point, the driver stopped the bus so everyone could stretch their legs and enjoy the view. As they looked to the southwest, they could see the lovely Round Valley, but were unable to see the little town of Covelo. From that distance, the valley looked primitive and uninhabited. As they turned and looked in the opposite direction, they could see the Eel river winding its way before them, in a northeasterly course. The view was both exhilarating and humbling, all at once. Trevor watched the three couples and knew exactly what they were experiencing. Even after all this time, he was struck anew by the majesty and grandeur of what appeared to be an infinite wilderness. As far as the eye could see, there was no sign of civilization, just the soul-satisfying beauty of raw nature, land as it was meant to be, land as it was in the days of our forefathers. What a sight to behold! Trevor didn't care much for people in general, but he had a deep and abiding love for the land.

"All right, folks! I think we've spent enough time admiring the view. Let's get back on the bus; we have a schedule to keep."

Reluctantly, they all climbed back into the bus and took their seats. Tony sat with his arm around Cat; he was feeling very sentimental.

"Well, babe, you're mighty quiet! A penny for your thoughts, okay?"

Cat smiled at him and leaned her head on his shoulder. She was happier than she had been in a long time, happier than she had thought possible.

"I was just thinking what a wonderful time we're going to have on this trip. The closer we get to the first camp, the more real it all seems. For such a long time, it was just an idea and now it's real. You know, Tony; you were right about us needing time alone without the kids. I miss them and yet I don't; you know what I mean? I'm enjoying this so much, I almost feel guilty."

"But not too guilty, right? Listen, babe; I don't want you feelin' even a little bit guilty. We both love the kids, but we really need this time together. I don't know about you, but, for me, it's like a new beginning. It feels almost like we're meeting for the very first time, all over again. I feel like I'm being given a second chance with you and I don't want to blow it. I know I probably don't say it often enough, but I really love you. I don't know what I'd do if you ever decided you couldn't put up with me anymore."

He tilted her face up to kiss her and was surprised to see her eyes filled with tears. Embarrassed, she quickly brushed them away and looked down at her lap.

"This dust is just terrible! I can't seem to keep it out of my eyes."

Tony just smiled gently at her and pulled her head against his chest, holding her close. Even Tony knew enough to be quiet at a time like this.

Shannon looked back at the two of them and smiled to herself. She was so pleased to see them like that. She loved them both dearly and was happy they had found each other again. She watched Larry as he dozed off and was again filled with pity for him. She hoped he wouldn't take it too badly when she finally told him it was over between them. Lost in thought, she gradually became aware of someone watching her. She looked up to see Trevor carefully studying her. Happy to catch her eye, he smiled and nodded to her. She smiled and politely nodded back to him, but she didn't feel comfortable with him. There was something about the way he looked at her; she couldn't put her finger on it, but he made her feel very uneasy. Just then, the bus made another violent lurch to the right, as another logging truck driver claimed the full center of the road, blasting away on his horn and narrowly missing them! Shannon was amazed that they hadn't been sideswiped! Then the road continued for several miles going up a grade and then down, then up, then down, over and over, until it seemed to go on forever. Finally, they approached the bridge that crossed Rattlesnake Creek, a major tributary which funneled into the Eel river. The bridge was an unusual sight, in that it was a modern, cement structure with dirt roads on either end of it, making it look rather out of place in such primitive surroundings. The bus driver slowed, pulled off the road and parked in a turnout just before the bridge. After they came to a stop, Trevor called for their attention and made an announcement.

"Listen up, everyone! This is about the last chance you'll have to wash off the dust before we reach Rock Cabin Camp. We'll be staying there for the rest of the day, while you all get used to your horses. Then we'll have a nice meal and bed down for the night. The following morning, we'll take off bright and early for some serious riding. Meanwhile, you might just as well grab your swimsuits and enjoy that nice deep pool over there. I think you're really going to enjoy the water. I make it a point to stop here with every tour group and they always love it. There's even a really nice waterfall that pours right into the pool! So, come on! I want to see everyone havin' a great time!"

The passengers grabbed their swimsuits and towels and gratefully disembarked. Wearily, they just stood for a moment, drinking in the beauty of Rattlesnake Creek. They were all hot and sweaty and coated with the dust from the dirt road, thus making the beautiful pool of water exceptionally inviting. Eric headed for a big boulder to hide behind while he changed into his swimsuit.

"C'mon, guys! We'll change over there and the ladies can change on the bus."

After they had all changed, they eagerly rushed down to the pool. As they dove in, they found the water to be refreshingly crisp and extremely clear. Oh, to be clean and cool again, it was delightful!

"Cat, come here! Look what I found!"

Cat couldn't see him, but his voice came from behind the waterfall. She swam toward it and found Tony standing behind the falling sheet of water.

"Oh, Tony! This is beautiful!"

Hearing their voices, the rest of the group soon joined them. They all stood in a hushed silence and just listened to the sound of the falling water. It had the most hypnotic effect, especially on Elaine; she felt as though she could remain there forever, safe and secure from the rest of the world. While the others returned to the pool to swim, Elaine stayed behind, just for the

225

pleasure of being alone with her daydreams.

Jesse and Tadpole looked at the group happily cavorting in the water and decided it was time to join them. As they walked toward the pool, they made a strange-looking pair; they were about as different as two brothers could possibly be. Jesse was tall and thin, with a thick mop of curly, sandy-blonde hair and sky-blue eyes. In spite of his slender build, he was surprisingly strong and had an intense way of looking at people, which left them feeling extremely wary; his was a face one would never forget! Tadpole was just the opposite; he was short, of average build, with stringy, brown hair and hazel eyes. He always had a guilty air about him and never quite looked anyone in the eye; except for this one peculiar habit, his face was quite forgettable. In spite of their extreme difference, they were unusually close. They cared deeply for one another and always watched each other's back. A fight with one of them would guarantee a fight with the other! Standing at the water's edge, Jesse noticed that Elaine was missing. He figured she had to be behind the waterfall and decided to check there. He just looked at his younger brother and nodded in that direction, then quietly slid into the water. Tadpole immediately understood the unspoken message and carefully watched to make sure that no-one noticed Jesse heading for the waterfall. No-one did. Jesse approached Elaine so quietly that it took a moment for her to realize that he wasn't a part of one of her daydreams. She looked at him quizzically and then politely smiled at him, wondering what he wanted. When he didn't say anything, she automatically dismissed him and returned to her own private world. Jesse studied her closely, fully aware that she was lost in her own dreams. He realized that she was different from the others, someone who didn't quite fit in with ordinary people, and it was precisely that which so intrigued him. Being pretty much a loner, himself, he felt as though he had finally found a kindred spirit, someone who might understand his secret yearnings. He was pleased that she was so attractive; he'd always enjoyed collecting pretty things. He had a beautiful collection of butterfly wings; he had spent many happy hours catching the prettiest butterflies and methodically tearing off their wings. It always made him feel sad to hurt them, but how else could he keep them? Besides, he knew he was actually doing them a favor; in this way, their beauty would be preserved for all time. He would love to show his collection to Elaine; he just knew she would like it! She was so pretty; he could hardly wait to get her alone. He would have to be patient for a while longer; now was not the time. His chance would come somewhere on the trail. Taking one last look at her full breasts, he thought about how nice they'd feel in his hands. Then he leaned over and gave her a gentle kiss on the lips, a fact of which she seemed blissfully unaware. Slipping away as quietly as he had arrived, he was completely unnoticed by anyone except Tadpole.

"All right, folks! Time to go! I hate to break this up, but we're running a little late, so let's get a move on!"

After a last bit of splashing in the water, they all reluctantly left the sparkling pool and headed back for the bus. Eric looked around and noticed that Elaine was missing. He quickly dove back in and swam toward the waterfall. As he came up beside her, he noticed that she seemed unusually oblivious of his presence.

"Elaine! Come on! We're leaving! What's the matter with you? Don't you hear me?"

Still receiving no response, he tapped her on the shoulder, snapping her out of her reverie.

"Oh, dear! You startled me! What is it? What do

you want?"

Worried, Eric just looked at her for a moment. For the first time, he realized that she was beginning to lose it, slowly but surely slipping further and further away from reality. He was greatly saddened by the vacant look on her face; she was no longer the girl he had married. He felt an infinite pity for her and very gently put his arm around her.

"Come on, Elaine. It's time for us to get back on the bus. Everyone's waiting for us."

"Oh, dear! I hope they're not upset with me. I didn't mean to keep them waiting. Eric, I just had the sweetest daydream. I was a princess in Camelot and there was a blond knight on a white horse; he came up to me and kissed me! He was such a nice young man. Oh, well, come on; we'd better hurry!"

They quickly joined the others and the bus sluggishly pulled back onto the dirt road, taking them upon the modern, cement bridge which crossed Rattlesnake Creek. Shannon took one last look at the swimming hole and knew that, before the day was done, they'd all be wishing they were back in that cool, clear water.

Once they had crossed the bridge, the road began a steep climb up the side of the mountain until it finally reached a large, grassy meadow, which was about half a mile wide with a gradual, upward slope. The road led them on a zigzag course all the way across the meadow. While they drove, they saw numerous cattle and even some deer grazing in apparent harmony. Then the road straightened out and continued through a somewhat dry, rocky terrain. Although it seemed much longer, they had only gone about three miles from the crossing at Rattlesnake Creek, when suddenly they found themselves in a beautiful, lush forest. Once again, the air was filled with the delightful fragrance of nature's sweet perfume. In that one moment, all the trials and irritations of the hot, dry, dusty road were forgotten, as the passengers reveled in this lovely, green paradise. After they had gone about two more miles, they saw an old cabin off to the right, which was called 'Indian Dick Station'. Finally, after another mile, was the turn leading to Rock Cabin Camp. The group smiled in eager anticipation as they pulled in to their first camp and saw a pole corral filled with several fine-looking horses. As the old bus creaked and groaned to a stop, Trevor once again called for their attention.

"All right, folks! This is it, the real beginning of your vacation! I know you're anxious to get off the bus and start relaxing, but I need a few words with you first. I'm certain you're all going to have the time of your lives, just so long as you mind our few rules."

En masse, the crowd started to groan. Trevor quickly silenced them by raising his hand.

"Don't worry! We don't have to go over the rules right now; I just wanted you to be prepared to discuss them first thing in the morning. The only thing we really have to do this afternoon is match you up with your horses, so you can all get used to them. Okay, I guess that's it for now. I'll meet you over by the corral in about one hour."

While the three couples looked around the beautiful campsite, they found their tents already set up by some of Trevor's men. They had been placed around an open fire pit filled with wood which would be set ablaze just prior to nightfall. After stowing their gear inside the tents, they wandered over to the corral to check out the horses. Jesse and Tadpole were leaning against the poles along with two other hired hands. They were debating which of the horses had the most spirit. Jesse was convinced that the grey Arabian had no equal.

"Listen here, you two dimwits! It's clear to me neither one of you knows shit about horses! I've seen that Arab in action before and I'm tellin' you he can't be beat! Don't you know nothin' about these animals? Arabs are famous for their 'git up an' go'! Those other mounts are quarter-horses; they ain't never gonna keep up with no Arab! Ain't that right, Tad?"

"Damn straight! We seen all these horses in action, time after time, and that Arab was always in the lead. None of the others ever got close enough to sniff his ass! You two boys must be a couple of flat-landers! Anyways, you're both too new around here to know diddly-squat about these horses!"

Bristling with anger, Pedro stepped toward them with clenched fists, only to be jerked back by his friend, Dillon, who quickly whispered something in his ear. Whatever he said seemed to calm Pedro down, as he slowly nodded, with an evil grin on his face.

"Okay, muchachos! My friend here has a very good idea. He says we should challenge you to a race between your precious Arab and a quarter-horse of our choice. What do you say to that? Are you willing to put some money where your big mouths are?"

Jesse and Tad smiled at each other, their eyes gleaming with the anticipation of easy money.

"Yeah, I think me an' Tad could muster up a small wager. Exactly how much do you fellas have in mind?"

"If it's not too steep for you boys, we figured about fifty apiece would be a fair bet."

Unable to restrain himself, Jesse snorted derisively.

"Cut the bullshit! I wouldn't make no bet about nothin' fer less'n a hundred bucks each! Of course, I'll understand if you two wanna back out of this deal, seein' as how you don't know shit about horses,

230

anyways."

Glaring at the two smug brothers, Dillon quickly conferred with Pedro, who silently nodded in agreement and handed over his share. With an icy stare, Dillon approached Jesse with their two hundred dollars.

"All right! We have a bet! Just remember; we get to pick the quarter-horse! And one more thing, it's not that we don't trust you boys, but we'd like to pick who's going to hold the money."

At that point, Trevor stepped over to the four of them. He'd been watching them the whole time and thought the race was a great idea. It would entertain his tour group and give two of the most spirited horses a good workout.

"If you're all agreeable to the idea, I'd be pleased to hold the money for you. By the way, see that meadow right over there? It's about a quarter of a mile long and would be perfect for your race. There's a young pine tree right at the end; the horses could circle that and race back to the starting point. How does that sound?"

The four men were surprised to find Trevor in such good humor; he was usually rather impatient and all business. Without a word, they walked over and handed him the money. Then Pedro and Dillon stepped aside and discussed which quarter-horse they would choose. Pedro favored the high-stepping, sixteen-hand buckskin, with the white star on his forehead.

"Listen to what I'm telling you, amigo! I know horses; I grew up with them and this buckskin can run. Just look at his formation; look at the strength in his legs! Look at his eyes; this one has spirit. He can beat any horse here! Can't you tell, hombre?"

Dillon was dubious. He preferred the sorrel with the four white stockings. His ears were pricked forward and he was watching the men intently. He was

231

long-legged and also about sixteen hands. He snorted and waved his head in the air, looking for all the world like he was raring to go.

"I don't know what you have against the sorrel. He looks like he's just itching to run!"

"That's exactly the problem! He's too spooky! Look at his eyes. Can't you see he has the wild eyes? Trust me, amigo! I know horses better than you do and I know the buckskin is the right choice!"

Dillon was still dubious, but he knew his friend well and had seldom found him to be wrong.

"All right, Pedro, you win! But the horse better win too, or you're gonna owe me one, a big one at that! I can't afford to lose that much money and you know it."

"Don't worry, amigo! We're not going to lose; they are. Maybe I should ride the horse. After all, I am lighter than you and I have ridden all my life. What do you say?"

"You'll get no argument from me there, friend. I know you're the better rider. Come on; let's go saddle him up."

Jesse and Tad eagerly watched to see which horse they would choose. When they saw the buckskin being led out of the corral, they looked at each other, a bit puzzled. They both considered the buckskin a good, stable mount, but hardly the right choice for racing. Then the two brothers looked over at the Arab and were instantly reassured by the sight of the handsome steed nervously prancing around the corral, swinging his head and snorting with the obvious desire to get out and run. What a contrast between the two horses! What they didn't realize was that they had only seen the calm quarter-horse under trail-riding conditions and had no way of knowing his true potential. They'd never seen a good quarter-horse being raced and that's exactly what this one was, a good quarter-horse! It would be a much closer race than Jesse or Tad could possibly imagine!

Pedro tied the buckskin, appropriately named Star, to one of the poles and saddled him, speaking gently to him the whole time.

"You can do it, Star! I know you can run like the wind. Vamos, amigo; let's show them what you can do! I'm giving you the chance to live up to your name; you'll be the star of the show!"

While Pedro was sweet-talking Star, Jesse and Tad brought the Arab out and saddled him. His name was Raja and he did indeed look like royalty as he pranced in placed and swung his head majestically, looking down his nose at them. It was decided that Tad would ride him since he was extremely light and also an outstanding rider. He mounted Raja and brought him to the designated starting point. It was more than a little difficult holding him still while they waited for Star.

"Take it easy, Raja! I'll turn you loose in just a second and you can make that old nag eat your dust!"

Trevor walked over and made sure they were both behind the starting line.

"All right, boys! You both know the signal; when I fire the gun, take off! I'll wait right here to judge who crosses the finish line first. Good luck to both of you!"

The intelligent buckskin seemed to know just what was expected of him and pranced in anticipation, looking sideways at his opponent, as though telling him to beware! Tad looked nervously at Star; he'd never seen him act that way before! For the first time, he felt a little worried about the outcome of the race. Irritated by the proximity of Star, Raja snorted imperiously at him and angrily leaped about in place so that Tad could barely control him! Then Trevor fired the gun and the ricocheting sound of the shot echoed throughout the mountains as the two horses blasted away from the starting line! Jesse could hardly believe his eyes! With his powerful haunches, Star streaked ahead of Raja with an incredible burst of speed, his thundering hooves churning the hard ground and leaving the Arab in a cloud of dust! By the time Star whipped around the pine tree, Raja was a third of the distance behind him. Seeing his horse slip further and further behind, Tad desperately quirted Raja until he seemed to erupt with a frenzy of energy! He tore around the pine tree and slowly but surely began to gain on Star. With a hundred yards left to go, he was only about two feet behind the Buckskin! Jesse and Dillon were watching with clenched fists, their knuckles white with the tension, as Raja continued to narrow the gap! Seemingly determined not to let the Arab win, Star found his second wind and lengthened his stride. They crossed the finish line with Star about six inches in the lead! The crowd of onlookers let out a roar of applause in appreciation of the magnificent race!

Amazed and dejected, Jesse walked over to Tad as he climbed down from the lathered horse.

"Tad! What the Hell happened? You musta done somethin' wrong fer that old nag to beat Raja!"

"You're dead wrong, Jesse. I like'ta beat that horse to death, but there weren't no way he could win that race! Don't that just beat all? I never knowed a quarter-horse could run like that!"

Tad unsaddled the Arab and walked him out in order to cool him down. Jesse just sat on a log, trying to figure out what had gone wrong, while he grumpily watched Dillon pick up his winnings from Trevor. Dillon looked at Jesse out of the corner of his eye and gave him a wide berth as he walked over to Pedro to split up the money. Pedro was smiling happily as he brushed down the powerful buckskin.

"Well, amigo, what do you say now? Do I know

my horses or not? I told you this one would win and I was right! This is a magnificent animal! Aye, caramba! I'll take a good quarter-horse over an Arab any day!"

"Right on, my friend! You sure as Hell do know your horses! I'll back you on a bet, anytime!"

Listening to the two of them, Trevor couldn't help laughing out loud! They were mighty happy winners! He noticed the crowd looked awfully happy, too. He was glad they had enjoyed the race; happy people rarely cause any problems and it was extremely important not to have any problems on this trip!

The three couples had been absolutely thrilled by the race! They were all talking at once about it until Tony managed to drown them out.

"Wow! What a race! This trip is startin' out with a bang, isn't it? I have a feeling this is going to be the best vacation of our lives! Was this a great idea or what?"

The rest of them groaned en masse and Cat just shook her head at him.

"If that isn't just like you, Tony! I can't believe you, trying to take credit for Shannon's idea! This trip was her idea, not yours, moron!"

"Hey! Watch out who you're callin' a moron! I just said it was a great idea; I didn't say it was mine!"

Before they could continue their argument, Trevor broke into their conversation.

"Sorry to interrupt, folks, but I think it's time to match you up with your horses. They're all up for grabs except for Raja; I always ride him. Star will go to the best rider among you, so will you kindly tell me who that might be?"

They all turned at once and pointed to Eric. He was a little embarrassed by the attention, but there was no way he could deny that he was the best rider, so he just looked at Trevor and shrugged. Trevor gave him an unfathomable look and nodded.

"All right, hotshot! I guess Star goes to you. Just be sure to take good care of him. Try not to ride him too hard; I wouldn't want him to have some kind of accident and get injured. You know what I mean?"

Eric gave him a long, steely look.

"Yeah, I'm sure I know exactly what you mean. But don't worry about it; I never have accidents!"

Shannon noticed there was always an undercurrent of tension between those two, even in the smallest discussions. She decided to break into their conversation.

"Believe it or not, I think I'm the second-best rider here! What horse do you have in mind for me?"

Trevor turned to Shannon and stared as the sun's rays sparkled in her gorgeous hair. He couldn't help thinking, 'Oh baby, if you only knew what kind of a ride I have in store for you!'

"I'm not at all surprised to hear that you're a good rider; you look like a natural to me! How would you like the Appaloosa? He's quite spirited, but extremely well-trained and his name is Sundancer. I think he'd be an excellent mount for you. Well, what do you think of him?"

Shannon stared at the Appaloosa with open admiration. He was the most striking horse she'd ever seen! He was jet black with the most beautiful white blanket and four perfectly matched white stockings. At fifteen hands, he was even the right height for her and he had the most intelligent look, with his ears pricked forward while he stared right back at her. She was delighted with him!

"Oh, Trevor! I'm absolutely thrilled! He's the most wonderful horse I've ever seen! I just know he and I will get along famously. I can't thank you enough for him!"

Her green eyes were gleaming with happiness! Trevor was extremely pleased by her reaction and thought to himself, 'Don't worry, sweetheart; I know exactly how you can thank me!' Eric saw the way Trevor was looking at her and was instantly annoyed! Before he could say anything, he caught Tony flashing him a look of warning. He forced himself to calm down and decided to say nothing at the moment, but he knew it was just a matter of time before he'd have to settle things with Trevor.

With Trevor's help, Elaine, Larry, Tony and Cat all found appropriate mounts. They were good, dependable horses and very mild-mannered.

"Listen up, everyone! My men are going to help you saddle your horses and make certain that you're all completely familiar with the procedure. Then, I want you to take a short trail ride this afternoon so you'll get used to being on horseback. Believe me, a short ride today will make tomorrow's ride a lot easier on you. Jesse and Tad will be your escorts; they both know their way around, so just relax and have a great time! Your supper will be waiting for you by the time you get back."

As they all began to saddle their horses, Jesse and Tad offered their assistance to those who needed it. Most of the horses remained still, making the job quite a bit easier, but Tony's horse seemed determined to aggravate him. Every time Tony put the blanket on his back, he would casually turn his head back, grab the blanket with his teeth and toss it in the air. Tony was beginning to gnash his teeth in frustration. Finally, he exploded in a torrent of curses!

"Damn this stupid horse! What the Hell's the matter with him, anyway? I thought these horses were supposed to be well-trained!"

Jesse and Tad grinned at each other, trying unsuccessfully to suppress their laughter. Jesse walked

237

over to the horse, picked up the blanket and put it on his back. When the horse leaned back to grab it, Jesse whacked him sharply on the side of his head. The horse instantly realized that this man wouldn't put up with his antics, so he immediately turned his head back around and became the picture of docility. Without any more trouble, Jesse tossed the saddle on him and began to tighten up the cinch.

"He is well-trained! He's just a little on the stubborn side and that's how we handle a stubborn horse. I sure hope you were takin' notice, 'cause that's what you're gonna have to do! Now you know why we call him Jack; it's short for Jackass! He's the most stubborn animal we got, but he's still a good trail horse; you just got to let him know who's boss. Once you done that, he'll settle right down and do a good job for you. Now, d'ya think you can take 'im from here?"

Tony was feeling a little embarrassed. It seemed like he was the only one who ever had trouble with horses.

"Yeah, sure! I can handle him from here on. If he gets out of line, I'll just whack him over the head like you did!"

Everyone else seemed to be doing all right, except for Elaine. Tad had put the blanket and saddle on for her and was trying to teach her how to tighten the cinch. But she was so afraid that the horse would try to kick her, that she couldn't make herself get that close to him. Jesse watched them for a moment and quietly nodded to Tad, who instantly understood his brother's silent signal and moved on to help someone else. Confused, Elaine just looked from one to the other, wondering which one would help her. Jesse slowly approached her, speaking ever so gently.

"Just you watch how I do this, Miss Elaine, and then we'll let you have a try at it. See here? As long as

238

you go real slow and steady, the horse feels safe and he won't try to kick you none. There! He's all cinched up and rarin' to go! See how easy that was? Are you ready for me to undo it and let you have a stab at it?"

Elaine shuddered and shook her head.

"No! I mean......that's all right! I'll just learn next time, okay?"

Jesse gave her a long look and thought how easy she'd be to control. He gently patted her on the shoulder, causing her to wince and involuntarily take a step back.

"It's all right, Miss Elaine; you don't have to learn how to do that at all, if you don't want to. I'll always be close by so's I can help you. I think I'll just make you my own special project for this trip. How's that sound to you?"

Elaine visibly relaxed. She felt extremely relieved and was very grateful to the nice young man. However, she also felt a little puzzled as she stared at him; he looked just like that blond prince in her daydream about Camelot. What a sweet coincidence! She gave Jesse a shy smile.

"Thank you! It's very nice of you to be so willing to help me. I hope I won't become a nuisance to you!"

Jesse gave her a kind, reassuring smile and once again patted her on the shoulder. This time, she didn't even flinch.

"Don't you worry yourself none, Miss Elaine; there ain't no way you could ever be a nuisance to me. I'm right happy for the chance to help you. Before this trip's over with, I'll be able to teach you all sorts of things! Well, I guess we better git you up on your horse so's you can try him out. And don't you worry none; I'll stay real close to you while you ride."

Elaine was deeply touched by his thoughtfulness. She couldn't remember ever meeting such a considerate young man! Even in the beginning of their marriage, Eric had never treated her with such deference. Come to think of it, that's exactly what was wrong with their marriage! She was the only one who ever showed any consideration; in fact, Eric hardly even gave her the time of day! Well, she'd show him a thing or two! She'd just start giving her attention to this nice young man; he seemed to appreciate her a lot more than Eric did! Now, if she could only gain the courage to climb up on her horse. Goodness! He looked so tall! She turned and looked beseechingly at Jesse.

"Here, Miss Elaine, let me help you up there. Just put your left foot in my hand and I'll give you a boost. Okay, are you ready?"

He gave her a quick push upward, but she couldn't seem to hold her left leg steady; it collapsed beneath her and she fell heavily back into his arms. He caught her just beneath her breasts and held her close for a moment as he tried to steady her. She felt the strangest tingling sensation building deep within her body; she'd never felt that way before and didn't quite know what to make of it. She flushed with embarrassment and quickly stepped away from him, finding herself unable to meet his eyes.

"Maybe we should just forget about this! I don't think I'll ever be able to ride that horse! Look at everyone else; they're all riding up and down that meadow already. They make it look so easy, but it's not easy for me. I have a good idea! I could just stay right here at this camp and wait for everyone to come back from the long trip. How about that?"

Jesse smiled gently at her.

"I have a better idea! Let's try it one more time; I know you can make it. Come on over here and don't be scared. Here, put your left foot in my hand again, only this time keep your leg stiff and swing your right leg over the saddle."

Afraid to move, she just looked at him somewhat vacantly. Jesse didn't want her slipping into her dream world again, so he stepped over to her, grabbed her gently by her arm and led her back to the side of the horse. She nervously put her foot in his hand and he once again gave her a quick boost upward. This time it worked! She landed safely in the saddle and rewarded Jesse with an adoring, grateful smile! Jesse patted her on the leg and gave her a smile of approval. Then he quickly mounted his own horse and they headed for the meadow to join the others. Jesse was careful to maintain a slow pace so as not to frighten her.

"There now, you see, Miss Elaine! I knew you could do it! Before too long, you're gonna be one of the best riders here. You know what? I'm kinda curious about somethin'. If you ain't familiar with horses, how come you decided to take a horseback vacation?"

"Well, actually, I have been around horses before, but it was way back when I was around ten years old. We used to have family reunions at my grandparents' ranch and I always loved watching the horses run in their pasture; their lives seemed so free and easy to me. But I was too scared of them to try riding; they looked so huge and uncontrollable! Then, one time when I was leaning against the fence watching them, my older cousin rode his horse right up beside me. I was so frightened I started to climb up on the fence, but I didn't dare climb all the way over because then I would be in the same pasture with all the horses. While he came closer and closer, laughing at me, I looked around for someone to call for help, but we were all alone; there wasn't anyone to help me. So I just hung on to the fence, frozen with fear, until he reached out and pulled me off the fence! Then he threw me over the horse in front of him and galloped all the way to a nearby orchard! I can still remember how the ground looked as we raced away; it was all churned up, with clods of dirt flying up in the air. With my head hanging down around the horse's mid-section, I was sure one of the dirt clods would hit me right in the face! I was so terrified that it's a miracle I didn't just pass out cold!"

"That sounds just awful, Miss Elaine! No wonder you're so nervous around horses! What happened then? Did he git the lickin' of his life when you got back? I sure as heck hope so!"

Elaine looked thoughtful, her eyes slightly misting and beginning to cloud over with a partially vacant look.

"Actually, I don't remember what happened after that. I'm not sure why, but there's a lot about my past that I can't remember at all. Every time I try to recall something, I get horrible headaches, so I finally just quit trying!"

Jesse studied her expression and knew all in that moment that her childhood must have been tragic. He would never again ask her any questions about her past. He smiled reassuringly at her and reached over to pat her hand.

"Well, Miss Elaine, you won't have no reason to be scared of horses on this trip. I'm gonna take special care of you and make sure you're safe! Anyways, that horse of yours is called 'Pokey' and there's a good reason for that name; he's real slow and easy-goin'. Fact is, I don't recall ever seein' him run, not for no reason! So you'll sure never have to worry none about him takin' off with you. How d'ya feel about that?"

Elaine gave him a grateful smile; he managed to cheer her up like no-one else ever had, not even Eric. Just then, while she was thinking of him, Eric came loping up to her and stopped right beside her.

"C'mon, honey! Why don't you ride along with the rest of us? We're going to start circling the meadow and I'd like to make certain that you can keep up."

"No, Eric, I'd rather not. You're all going to want to go fast and I would definitely slow you down. With Jesse here to help me, I'll be just fine; he's giving me some slow, easy lessons and that's what I really need right now. So you go on back to the others and don't worry about me."

Trying not to show his relief, Eric gave her an encouraging smile, nodded his thanks to Jesse and happily galloped back to his friends, catching up with them just as they began to circle the meadow. He came from behind and quickly overtook the lot of them, leaving them all in a cloud of dust. What a great horse! He had never before ridden such a magnificent animal and he was drunk with power as they flew through the lush, aromatic grasses of the long meadow. Once again, he had that wonderful feeling of stepping back into time, back into the world of his choice, the world of which he alone was the master! At this moment, he truly felt there was nothing he couldn't do! As they raced along, Eric saw a fallen log off to the side of the meadow. Turning Star in a long circle, he galloped directly back toward the log!

"Yahoo! C'mon, Star! Let's show 'em what we can do!"

The others were just getting close to the huge log when Eric and Star approached it at a full gallop from the opposite direction. With a lump in her throat, Shannon stared at them fearfully as Star made a powerful leap, clearing the gigantic log with only inches to spare! They landed in a thunder of hooves as horse and rider galloped away! Then, after another large circle, Eric and Star returned to the stunned group. Shannon was the first to break the silence.

"Eric! That was an insane thing to do! You could have been killed! You had no way of knowing whether or not your horse could actually make that jump!"

Eric flashed her a triumphant smile.

"Sometimes you just have to go for it! Besides, I do know horses and I knew Star could do it! And I was right, wasn't I, baby?"

Eric leaned over and patted Star on the head. The others just stared at him, still shocked into silence. While they watched, Jesse approached, dismounted and took a close look at Star's legs, making sure that he hadn't been injured. After reassuring himself that the horse was all right, Jesse slowly stood and studied Eric for a long moment, wondering if he should chew him out for pulling such a stunt. Trevor had told him to keep his eye on Eric; it was almost as though his boss expected Eric to try something foolish. Jesse decided not to say anything and just let it slide on by this time; after all, there hadn't been any damage done. He just gave Eric a sly grin and thought to himself, 'What the Hell! If it ain't broke, why fix it?' Besides, he admired courage and Eric obviously had plenty of that!

"Well, everything looks okay here! I guess I better git back to Elaine; she tends to git a little frightened when she's left by herself. I saw all this commotion over here and figured I better check it out. You folks got about a half hour to finish your ridin'; after that, supper will be waitin' for us. See y'all back at the camp!"

Eric watched him lope back to Elaine and wondered for the first time if Jesse's interest in her wasn't a little more than it should be. Nah......Eric decided he couldn't possibly be interested in Elaine; she was just too boring! He had forgotten that age-old rule, 'one man's poison is another man's pleasure'.

While the group rode around the log, still amazed by the size of it, Cat noticed a trail leading into the forest.

244

"Look, everyone! See that trail over there? Who feels like exploring it with me?"

Tad quickly intervened.

"I'm sorry, but I don't think we got time to follow that trail. It goes through the forest for a ways and then it cuts around the side of the mountain. It gits pretty steep along that part; I don't know if y'all are ready for that kind of ridin' yet. Anyways, our supper's almost ready and I'm gittin' pretty danged hungry! Let's just ride around the meadow some more and call it a day. Is that okay with you folks?"

Cat nodded and smiled at him.

"Sure, that's okay! Besides, if it's all that steep, maybe I should just think about hiking on the trail, instead of riding. Maybe there'll be time to go exploring after supper."

"You're right! After we're all done eatin', you folks will have plenty of time to check out your surroundings. Y'all are free to hike wherever you please; just don't git yourselves lost! Let's head back to the far end of the meadow; we got enough time for a couple more go-arounds."

After they were done circling the meadow a few more times, they slowly rode back to the corral and dismounted. While they were unsaddling their horses, Tony caught the tantalizing scent of barbecued ribs and baked beans wafting on the air.

"Holy cow! Do you guys smell that! I think we're in for some good chow!"

They all completed the chore of unsaddling in record time and rushed over to the fire where the ribs were sizzling on a rack. Watching hungrily, they also saw beans and biscuits, already done and waiting for them.

Trevor walked up to the group and motioned for their attention.

"All right, folks! I can see you're all starved, so grab a plate, get in line and the cook will serve you. After that, you can take a seat right over there where we've got logs set up for the occasion. Bon apetit!"

After they had finished their delicious meal, they were all feeling pretty lethargic and just sat around chatting. Cat stood up and stretched.

"Tony, I need to walk off some of that food. Let's go for a hike! We still have over an hour of daylight left. I'd like to explore that trail I saw off to the side of the meadow."

Tony groaned and rubbed his stomach.

"Cat, we just finished eating! Can't you give me at least a few minutes for my food to settle?"

"Okay, lazybones! You had your chance! I guess I'll just go for a walk by myself. You know where to find me if you change your mind."

With those words, she started walking in the direction of the trail. A little worried about her going alone, Tony started to rise, then groaned aloud and stretched back out on the log.

"Jesus Christ! That woman's going to drive me nuts! Why does she have to do everything now, right now? She never wants to give me five minutes to rest! What do you think, Eric? Will she be safe hiking by herself for a while?"

"Shit, yeah! We're only in a national forest, you know; it's not exactly outer Mongolia! Besides, it's still broad daylight and I'll bet she won't walk that far, anyway."

"You're probably right. I think I'll just rest for half an hour or so and then I'll go out and meet her when she's on her way back. That way I won't have to walk so far. Hey, am I smart or what?"

"Or what!" The entire group chorused together.

"All right!   Just for that, I'm going to relax in my

tent. So there!"

Tired but happy, Tony headed for his tent and wearily stretched out on his sleeping bag. He'd intended only a short rest, but instead was fast asleep within a short span of minutes.

Cat waited for a while at the head of the trail, expecting to see Tony trying to catch up with her. After five minutes had passed, she realized that he really wasn't coming. She was surprised, but also a little relieved, since this would be one of her few, precious chances to be alone. She happily began to hike down the trail, humming to herself. After walking for about ten minutes, she realized that she had reached the steep section that Tad had mentioned. The mountain went straight up on her left and dropped off sharply on her right. The trail seemed to be carved into the side of the mountain and, at this point, appeared to be climbing rapidly. The path was quite overgrown, with vines stretching back and forth across it. It was tedious walking through the vines; they were difficult to see in the declining light and her feet kept getting tangled in them. She had badly misjudged the time; dark was falling much sooner than she had expected. She was beginning to tire and paused for a minute to catch her breath, when all of a sudden a chill went down her spine as she realized that it was just like her dream! She froze for a moment and listened carefully for any strange sounds, but heard absolutely nothing. In fact, the forest seemed unnaturally quiet. The only sound she could hear was the violent beating of her own heart! Berating herself for being so foolish as to believe in omens, she slowly turned to walk back to the camp. And then she heard it! An ominous, crashing sound coming from somewhere behind her! It sounded exactly like someone or something was chasing after her!

Back at the camp, the huge evening fire had been

lit by one of Trevor's men. The group sat around the fire pit, hypnotized by the shooting flames and spiraling sparks, a striking contrast against the rapidly darkening sky. They had all been lulled into a serene sense of security, when suddenly, with a worried expression on his face, Eric bolted upright and looked around the camp!

"Hey! Where's Cat? She never came back, did she? And I'll bet Tony's snoring away in his tent! I'd better go check on the two of them!"

He raced over to the tent and, sure enough, Tony was sound asleep! Eric quickly shook him awake.

Still groggy with sleep, Tony sat up and rubbed his eyes.

"What? Huh? What's goin' on?"

"C'mon, Tony, wake up! It's almost dark and Cat's still not back! Quick! Get up! We have to go find her!"

Tony bounded up, fully awake!

"Wait a second! I've got to find the flashlight! Okay, I've got it! Let's go!"

They rushed out of the tent and ran all the way to the trail. As they raced up the path, they heard a piercing scream and ran even faster. The steepening trail narrowed and was covered with vines, causing them to stumble as they tried to hurry forward. They heard another scream and called out Cat's name! Then they saw a huge creature, outlined by the moonlight, bending over a figure lying on the ground. As they approached, they could see that the figure was Cat and the creature was a large black bear! Suddenly the bear rose to its full height and roared in defiance of the new intruders! Tony and Eric rushed forward, screaming at the bear and shining the flashlight in his eyes! After one last deafening roar, the bear turned and ran back up the trail, to the extreme relief of the three terrified people!

Tony knelt down to comfort Cat, who was crying hysterically! Eric stood, his heart beating like a drum, and tried to calm himself as he carefully watched and listened for any further sign of danger.

"Jesus Christ, Tony! What in the Hell would we have done if that bear hadn't decided to retreat? I'd feel a lot safer if we had a gun with us!"

"Amen to that, brother! I think I'd also feel a lot safer if we got the Hell outa here! C'mon, Cat! You can finish cryin' back at the camp! Let's go!"

He pulled her to her feet and they quickly retraced their steps down the path. Once they reached the open meadow, they saw the huge campfire, which seemed to beckon to them like a beacon of safety! They finally reached the perimeter of the fire, thoroughly disheveled and breathing so hard that their friends rushed over to them to see what was the matter! The mesmerizing fire had so lulled them into a false sense of security that they had forgotten the three of them were even missing!

After the trio had recounted their harrowing experience, they sat around the fire discussing their lack of weapons. Larry spoke up strongly in favor of being armed.

"I think it's outrageous that any of us should be at such risk on a vacation! Where the Hell do they get off forbidding us to bring guns? We should never have agreed to such a ridiculous rule! It's just too damned dangerous to be in the wilderness without weapons!"

Eric studied him for a long moment and then decided to let them all in on his secret, even Larry.

"Make sure you don't breathe a word of this, but I did bring a gun with me, a forty-five automatic! I should have brought it with me when we were looking for Cat, but it just never occurred to me that she might actually be in danger. I was just afraid she might have wandered off the trail and gotten lost. One thing's for sure; I won't be without it again!"

With visible relief on their faces, they all looked at Eric with open admiration. All except for Larry, that is; his eyes were filled with naked jealousy! No matter how hard he tried, it seemed to him that Eric was always the one who was considered the hero and he was getting damned tired of it! There must be some way of getting rid of Eric! He had to be alone for a while; he needed time to think, in order to devise some type of plan. He was missed by no-one, as he silently headed for his tent.

The others continued the conversation in a low monotone, so that none of Trevor's men would hear them. Cat appeared unusually thoughtful as she looked from Eric to Tony and back again. Finally, she just had to ask the question!

"Eric, there's something I must know! Were you the one who decided to come after me, or was it Tony?"

Eric looked her right in the eye and, without the slightest hesitation, lied for his friend.

"I'd like to pretend it was me, but it was Tony. He noticed it was getting dark sooner than we thought it would and he was worried about you. He asked me to go along with him, in case we had to split up to find you."

Her eyes instantly filling with tears of happiness, Cat gazed at Tony adoringly. She walked over to him and wrapped her arms around him, burying her face against his shoulder while her whole body quietly shook. With silent gratitude in his eyes, Tony looked over her shoulder at Eric and ever so slightly nodded his thanks. Eric just shrugged and turned back to the fire, wearily leaning back against a log while he watched the crackling flames reach for the sky. He felt the sensation of someone watching him and looked up to see

Shannon studying him with an unreadable look on her lovely face. If only he knew what she was thinking; he sensed admiration, gratitude and something else, something indefinable. He wished they could be alone for a while; he had an aching need to hold her once more, at least once more. Please, God, don't let it be over with yet!

One by one, the small group retired to their tents and slept the deep slumber of the truly weary. Trevor's men were also fast asleep, even the two who were supposed to be on guard duty. Only God in his Heaven and the creatures of the forest kept watch that night. Tomorrow would dawn a bright new day and, when they embarked on the next leg of their journey, Rock Cabin Camp would slowly fade into memory.

CHAPTER 21 SOLDIER RIDGE

In the still of the night, the forest appeared deceptively peaceful. While the three couples lay snuggled in their sleeping bags, deeply asleep, a mountain lion silently stalked his prey as he padded along the very trail where Cat had encountered the huge, black bear. Halting every few feet to cautiously sniff the air, the intended victim was a young, black-tailed deer. Sensing no danger, he stopped for a while and grazed on some of the succulent grasses which grew in abundance throughout the forest. Savoring every delicious morsel, the young spike was completely unaware of the huge mountain lion stealthily approaching, his yellow eyes gleaming with the anticipation of a fresh kill. Suddenly, as though warned by some sense of premonition, the deer nervously jerked his head upright and looked around, but saw nothing out of the ordinary. His heart hammering incessantly, he listened carefully, but the forest was silent, too silent. Except for the tensing of his muscles, the cunning feline had immediately ceased all movement. Hiding behind some low brush, he awaited just the right moment to close in for the kill. He didn't have long to wait, as the deer responded to his primal instincts and bolted in a desperate attempt to flee! Unleashing the power of his taut muscles, the mountain lion exploded from his cover and quickly closed the gap between himself and his hapless victim! Violently bringing him down in a deadly frenzy, the lion clamped his powerful jaws around the deer's neck, instantly crushing his wind-pipe with a horrible, crunching sound!

While the young spike lay shuddering in the agonizing last throes of his untimely death, a nearby owl observed the savage scene with a stoic silence. At almost the same moment and not too far away, a fox was feasting on an unlucky rabbit. Countless such killings occurred throughout the wilderness on a nightly basis. Mother Nature's basic law of survival was cruel but simple; some must die that others might live!

As they slept beneath the waning moon, the three couples were peacefully oblivious to all the carnage. The only sound to disturb their slumber was the beautiful, soothing birdsong which slowly spread throughout the forest even before the first, golden rays of the morning sun began to ease the coal black of the night.

Shannon almost jumped out of her sleeping bag as the clanging of the breakfast bell brought her fully awake. Sleepily rubbing her eyes, she gently nudged Larry.

"Come on, sleepyhead; it's time for breakfast."

Larry just rolled over and groaned.

"I know; I know! Go ahead without me; I'll be along later."

"Larry, get up! You can't go later! We have to do everything on a schedule. Besides, Trevor wants to discuss the rules with all of us, remember?"

"All right! I'm getting up! Satisfied? This is all ridiculous, anyway! Since when do we need a stupid schedule on a vacation? Shouldn't we just be doing things as we feel like it? I can't believe this! I thought a vacation was for relaxing!"

Shannon looked at him with a mixture of pity and irritation.

"You know what's wrong with you? You're the kind of person who just doesn't know how to relax and have fun. You're too busy complaining! Besides, if you're feeling so tired, why didn't you go to bed a little earlier? Why were you up so late last night? What were you doing, anyway?"

Larry looked at her with an oblique expression.

"Just thinking, that's all. Why do you ask? Since when are you interested in what I'm doing?"

Disgusted, Shannon just shook her head and left their tent. As she stepped into the morning chill, she shivered and wrapped her sweater tightly around herself. The first rays of sunlight were peeking through the branches of the tall pines encircling the tents. A squirrel in a nearby tree stared at her and chattered indignantly before racing to a higher branch. The various birds were trilling in a cacophony of song as they joyously greeted the day. Shannon smiled happily, positively reveling in the sights and sounds of the wilderness. She couldn't understand Larry; she wouldn't have wanted to miss one moment of this glorious morning! She decided to look for a private area to use as a restroom before having breakfast. She noticed a thick, tightly-knit grove of trees just west of the camp and headed in that direction. Unaware that someone else had entered the heavily-forested area ahead of her, she stepped behind the largest of the trees just as Eric was zipping up his pants. Startled, he just stared at her for a moment, forcing her to speak first. Shannon flushed as she stared back at him.

"I'm sorry! I didn't know anyone else was here. I'll leave and let you finish."

Before she could turn away, Eric quickly stepped over to her and grabbed her by the arm.

"I'm already finished and you're not going anywhere! We need to talk!"

Stammering, Shannon wrenched her arm away.

"I'm sorry, Eric, but nature calls! We'll just have to talk later."

"That's all right! I'll wait right here and stand guard for you. You can go over there behind that brush. Then we'll talk!"

She knew by the look in his eyes that she wouldn't be able to put this off. She would have to talk to him. While she tended to her personal needs, she wondered what on Earth she could possibly say to him to ease the extreme tension between them. When she was finished, she slowly walked back to him, her eyes betraying her reluctance.

"It's pretty obvious that your feelings about me have changed. Maybe you'd like to explain just what in the Hell's going on! Well? Go ahead! I'm listening!"

"Eric, that's exactly the problem! My feelings toward you haven't changed at all! Oh, what's the use of trying to explain things to you? You probably wouldn't understand, anyway!"

Completely confused, Eric stared at her.

"I don't get it! If you really do feel the same about me, then what's the problem? And why have you been avoiding me? It has something to do with that Goddamned Indian, doesn't it?"

Stricken, Shannon just looked at him with an ashen face and quickly turned to leave. Once again, Eric seized her arms and roughly pulled her to him, forcing her to look into his eyes.

"Wait a minute! We're going to finish this! You just said your feelings haven't changed. Goddamn it! Do you love me or not? Maybe I'm just some plaything for you, something to appease your appetite because asshole Larry's no good in the sack! Is that it?"

Flushed with anger, Shannon managed to pull one arm free and slapped him hard across the face! Instantly, Eric caught her wrist and held both her hands behind her back as he crushed her body against his own and savagely kissed her, forcing her lips apart while his

256

tongue invaded her mouth. Shannon was held captive more by her own overwhelming, primal urges than by the strength of his vise-like grip. Her anger was soon all but forgotten as she returned his kiss with such a fiery depth that Eric groaned aloud in frustration. After partially releasing her, they stared at each other with a palpable hunger, until Shannon could no longer bear the yearning look in his eyes. She tried to pull completely away from him, but was unable to break free of his embrace.

"Please, Eric! Let me go! We both know this is impossible right now!"

"Right now, maybe, but not later! I'll only release you if you swear to meet me tonight, after everyone else is asleep!"

"Okay, okay! I swear it! Now let me go before someone finds us!"

Finding herself abruptly freed, Shannon turned and almost ran all the way back to the camp. As she joined the breakfast line, her distraught manner was noticed only by Trevor. He looked over in the general area from which she'd come and saw Eric approaching from the same direction. Well, well, well! How interesting! Evidently, Eric had done something to distress the young lady. Maybe he should look into that situation; perhaps the young lady would appreciate a gentleman coming to her aid, and he just might find a suitable way for her to show her appreciation. When Shannon reached the front of the line and Trevor handed her a plate, she could only wonder what on Earth he was grinning about so smugly! As she took her plate from him, she decided just to ignore him and walked quickly away to sit with Cat and Tony while they ate.

"Well, kitten, it's about time you caught up with us! Since you're usually such an early-bird, I thought you'd be the first one in line!"

"I just decided to take a short walk before breakfast. By the way, have you two seen Larry yet?"

"Yeah, we saw him. In fact, he was here just a minute ago. He had his plate with him and everything. I thought he was going to sit down and eat with us. Did you see where he went, Cat?"

"He muttered something about not being able to live without his Sweet'n'Low. I think he went to look for some in the supply wagon."

They all looked in that direction just in time to see Larry searching through some of the supplies. At that same moment, Trevor also caught sight of him and angrily motioned to Dillon to get his ass over there and handle the situation. Dillon quickly sprinted to Larry's side and tapped him on the shoulder.

"Tell me what you're lookin' for, friend; maybe I can help you find it."

"As a matter of fact, I'm looking for some Sweet'n'Low, but I haven't found any yet. Do you know where it is?"

"I know where it ain't! The fact is; we haven't got any. Sorry about that! Is there anything else I can get for you?"

Larry gave him a long, sardonic look.

"No, but thanks anyway. You've already been more than helpful."

Disgusted, Larry walked back and sat with Shannon, Cat and Tony, arriving just as Trevor called for the group's attention.

"I know you're all anxious to get on with your vacation, so I'll make this short and simple. Basically, we have very few rules. The most important one is that no-one touches the supplies except for my men or myself. The reason for this is that everything is neatly organized into exact portions for each day of the trip and

I really don't want my system all messed up. If you need something, just ask any one of the men and they'll be glad to bring you whatever you need. Another rule is that you always let us know before you decide to take off on your own for a while. Also, we have to know which trail you'll be on and about when to expect you back. Obviously, this rule is for your own safety. Each day, when we've arrived at the next camp, there'll be plenty of time for you to explore and ride around by yourselves. We don't want any of you getting lost, so be sure to stay on whatever trail you've chosen. That way, if anyone gets injured or doesn't return in time for supper, we'll be able to find you and assist you. I sincerely hope none of you has any problem with these few rules; as long as you abide by them, I'm sure we'll get along just fine and you'll all have the time of your lives! Okay, folks, that's pretty much all I have to say. Any questions?"

Without uttering a word, the entire group merely watched him.

"All right! I guess no-one has any questions. Well, eat hearty! Just as soon as you're done, we'll pack up and head out on the first long ride of the trip. We'll be on the trail for about five hours until we reach the next camp. I'll meet all of you at the corral in about half an hour."

Larry stirred his coffee one last time, tasted it, then angrily tossed it aside. His mood as black and bitter as his discarded coffee, he glared testily at the rest of the group.

"Rules, rules, rules! I can't believe this! Am I the only one who feels like he's back in kindergarten? This is some vacation! I can't even get a decent cup of coffee!"

"Hey, buddy! Lighten up, will you? Just pretend you're some kind of explorer going through this part of the country for the first time, all right? We're here for the excitement, not the chow! Cat and I weren't exactly thrilled about our grub, either, but you don't hear us complaining, do you? The only time you'll get a complaint out of me is if the trip turns out too dull. I don't know about the rest of you, but we're here for some thrills and chills, something to tell our grandkids about!"

"Hah! You'd better speak for yourself, Tony! After that run-in with the bear last night, I've had enough excitement for the whole trip! I'm hoping the rest of our time will be spent in peace and harmony. I could stand a little boring relaxation."

Everyone laughed except Eric, who seemed lost in thought while he quietly watched Shannon. Their eyes met just for a fraction of a second before they both quickly looked away and stood to join the others as they all headed for the corral. That brief look was lost on everyone except Larry, who forced his way ahead of the others, his mood even darker than before.

Intently watching the group approaching them, the horses moved around restlessly and softly nickered to each other in anticipation of leaving the corral. They appeared to be every bit as eager to get on their way as the riders were. While they all saddled their own mounts, Jesse quietly led Elaine's horse off to the side where he could personally take care of the job. The horse he had chosen for Elaine was a mild-mannered mare by the name of Daisy. In fact, she had such an incredibly calm disposition, everyone just called her Lazy-Daze. Even Elaine had noticed how quiet she was and seemed unafraid of the animal. As soon as Jesse finished saddling her mare and his own horse, a tall buckskin by the name of Buckaroo, he called Elaine over to assist her in mounting. She walked around to the left side of Daisy and smiled nervously at Jesse.

She chattered incessantly to him while he gave her a boost into the saddle.

"You haven't forgotten your promise, have you, Jesse? I mean......you really will stay by my side all the time that we're riding, won't you? I hate to be such a nuisance, but you do know how scared I am of horses, don't you?"

Jesse quickly mounted his own horse and, with a gentle smile, turned toward Elaine.

"Now you just quit all that frettin'! You ain't any nuisance to me; I'm right happy to stay by your side and help you out anyway I can. That's why I picked out this sweet little mare for you instead of that horse you were ridin' yesterday. You remember Pokey, don't you?"

"Of course I do! I'm glad you picked out a different horse for me; I was a little frightened of Pokey. He was so tall!"

"That's just what I figured! Well, what d'ya think of old Lazy-Daze? I'll bet you're not scared of her!"

Elaine laughed out loud, a soft, lilting kind of laugh that was ever so pleasing to Jesse's ears. He smiled broadly at her, his eyes wrinkling at the corners while he studied her.

"Miss Elaine, you're so purty when you laugh. You ought to do that more often."

Elaine's face turned a deep scarlet as she blushed with pleasure and embarrassment. Just then, Trevor called for everyone's attention and they all turned to face him.

"Listen up, everyone! I have just a few more things to tell you and then we'll take off. Dillon and I will take the lead; the rest of the men will be interspersed among you in case anyone needs assistance along the way. We'll be riding single file and it's very important that you all keep up with me, so try hard to maintain whatever pace I set for you. However, if anyone absolutely has to stop for a moment, please make it brief and catch up with us as quickly as possible. Oh, by the way, in case anyone's interested, the name of our first trail is Soldier Ridge."

Always interested in history, Shannon was curious about the name.

"I wonder why it's called Soldier Ridge. Was there some Indian war fought in that area? I'll bet that's it, right?"

Although she had addressed her question to Trevor, it was Jesse who responded. His sky-blue eyes were filled with melancholy as he spoke.

"Uh......that ain't exactly it, ma'am. Fact is; I'm not so certain you'd wanna know the real story. I mean......it's kind of a sad story an' it's liable to sour your whole trip."

"Actually, Jesse, I'd really like to know, although I do appreciate your concern. How about the rest of you? Would you like to hear the story?"

Eager to hear the tale, they all nodded their assent.

"Well, it's goes like this; way back in the eighteen-sixties, when lots of settlers were comin' into California, they didn't much wanna share the land with the Indians, even though it belonged to them in the first place. A bunch of big-shots got together and decided to herd over four hundred fifty Indians from somewheres around Sacramento all the way to the Round Valley Reservation in Covelo. Now, y'all understand them soldiers were ridin' horses, but the poor Indians were afoot an' they were havin' one heck of a time tryin' to keep up. Course, they weren't able to since they were hikin' through some purty rough mountains. By the time they all got up to this here ridge, the soldiers were gittin' pissed off about the Indians goin' so danged slow an' they decided to do somethin' about it. Well, to make a long story short, they started killin' off the slow ones, the old men, some women an' even some babies. So's they could save their bullets, they used their bayonets on everyone 'cept the babies. They just snatched the babies out of their mothers' arms and bashed their tiny heads against a tree! By the time they got to the reservation, there was only a little over two hundred seventy Indians still alive! Them soldiers were just a bunch of rotten, no-good sons-o-bitches! I wish to Hell I was around back then; I'da taught them soldiers how it feels to git butchered an' I woulda enjoyed every minute of it!"

Without even realizing it, Jesse had unsheathed his long, Bowie knife and was slashing through the air with it, his eyes glazed over as he pictured himself in the heat of battle. The silence was intense as everyone stared at him in amazement. Those closest to him warily stepped back a pace or two, all except Elaine, who moved even closer and spoke softly to him.

"Jesse, you were right. That's a very sad story and I wish you could have been there to help those poor Indians. But that all happened a long time ago and now it's time for us to leave. Jesse, did you hear me? Are you ready to go?"

Elaine's soothing voice slowly brought him back to reality and he answered with a nervous start.

"Huh? Oh, yeah! Course I'm ready to go!"

Jesse quickly sheathed his knife and took his place behind Elaine. Trevor had been quietly watching him the whole time with a very worried expression on his face. Finally, he just shook his head and looked over at Dillon, who silently nodded. He fully understood the mute order; he would keep a close eye on Jesse. Trevor took one last look around and motioned everyone to fall in behind him. Thus, they quietly embarked on their journey. Not with a shout and a

263

hurrah, but with a tangible silence, did they leave their familiar world behind and enter a remote, new environment, fraught with unimaginable dangers. Never again would any of them be quite the same person as before, their lives to be forever changed by events beyond their control.

Riding single file along the ridge, Trevor maintained a slow pace while Raja showed his impatience by snorting and tossing his head. The Arab's behavior was contagious and the rest of the horses soon appeared equally restless. The day was young and the air delightfully crisp as the horses pranced in place, their hooves kicking up small dust clouds while their heavy breathing turned into steam against the morning chill. Tony was having a problem controlling Jack, who kept erupting with a series of small bucks and appeared to have a keen desire to throw his inept rider as far as he possibly could.

"Stop it! You stupid, Goddamned horse! What's the matter with you? Just calm down or I'm gonna turn you into dogmeat!"

Ignoring his threats, Jack continued to hump up in preparation for a serious round of bucking when Tony finally gained his attention by whacking him sharply across the head. Jack immediately became docile and calmly proceeded along the trail as though bucking off his rider was the farthest thing from his mind.

"Well, I'll be damned! It worked! I actually controlled this beast. Cat! Did you see that? I think I'm finally turning into a decent rider! What do you think?"

"I'm proud of you, sweetheart. Now, will you please shut up so we can enjoy the view?"

Feeling slightly miffed, he turned to check out the scenery and was instantly overwhelmed by the panoramic vistas on both sides of the ridge. The entire group was filled with awe as they watched silvery patches of morning mist swirling throughout the canyons before giving them up to the heat of the day. Through the mists, they could see the glorious colors of the various wild flowers which covered the meadows in an array of purples, pinks, reds and golds. Shannon looked upon nature's beauty and found it difficult to reconcile with thoughts of the soldiers' cruelties committed on this very trail. The morning breeze was just beginning and Shannon's long, red hair billowed softly behind her, vibrant with the highlights of the sun's golden rays. She felt a chill go down her back, but it wasn't from the cool breeze. It was from the sound caused by the wind as it gained in speed. Winding its way around the tall pines, the wind created an eerie wail, so soft in tone that it reminded Shannon of an infant's cry. Upon approaching a stand of the taller pines, the wailing sound increased in pitch ever so slightly, until Shannon just had to turn Sundancer off the trail and stop for a moment. Listening intently, she could vividly imagine an Indian infant being ripped from the arms of his sobbing mother, his cries silenced forever as his head was smashed against a tree by one of the soldiers. Eric caught up with Shannon just as her entire body was racked by involuntary shivers.

"Shannon! What's the matter? You look like you just saw a ghost!"

Shannon stared at him, her green eyes filled with a deep sadness.

"I believe I did, Eric, but I don't want to discuss it right now. Come on; let's rejoin the others."

Uncomprehending, Eric just nodded and they fell in behind Tony and Cat, who looked back at them quizzically, but said nothing.

After riding along quietly for about ten minutes, Trevor was startled to find himself being hailed by several riders coming up the trail from the opposite direction. He motioned the others to stop and shielded his eyes from the sun while he tried to identify them. With the sun directly behind them, this was an impossible feat until the strangers were almost on top of him. Finally, Trevor recognized them as that group of environmentalists involved in the showdown with the loggers. Damn! What the Hell were they doing in the wilderness area?

"Hello, there! Aren't you the James Randolph I saw back in Covelo? I thought you and your friends were supposed to be checking out all the damage caused by the logging industry. You boys must be lost; I don't believe they allow any logging in the Yolla Bolly, so what are you doing here?"

James Randolph smiled and nodded to the group in general as he removed his hat and wiped the sweat from his brow.

"Actually, friend, we're mixing a little pleasure with our business. We've never been in the Yolla Bolly before, so we thought we'd check it out along the way. It's truly delightful! Perhaps one of these days, I'll sign up for one of your guided tours. You are Trevor Thompson, right?"

"That's right, old-timer! Look, I'd really like to stick around and chat with you some more, but we've got a schedule to keep, so we'd better mosey along. It's been nice talkin' to you; you boys be careful and don't get yourselves lost."

"Thanks for your concern, but I'm sure we'll be all right. It's been a pleasure talking to you; maybe we'll run into each other again on your return trip."

Trevor watched quietly as Randolph and his group rode on past them. When they were out of earshot, Trevor turned to Dillon and just shook his head.

"I sure hope those fools keep out of our way. The last thing I need is an unsupervised group of flat-landers wandering around our territory!"

"Amen to that, Boss! But I wouldn't worry too much about them. They seemed to be on their way out, so we probably won't see them again."

"I sure as Hell hope not! Well, let's pick up the pace a bit. It's time to break these folks in to some real riding!"

Dillon turned around and motioned to the others to hurry up and the members of the group soon found themselves riding along at a light trot. Although it was a rather jarring gait, no-one complained except Elaine, who was riding at the rear with Jesse right behind her.

"Oh, dear! I don't know how much longer I can keep this up. My stomach hurts and my back, too! Jesse, why do we have to go so fast? Can't we just slow down and catch up with the others later? Let them go fast, if they want to!"

"All right, Miss Elaine! I guess there ain't no harm in that. Let's you and me slow down a bit and enjoy the purty scenery. See them purple flowers over yonder? You just set still for a minute and I'll go pick you some. Would'ya like that?"

Before she could even answer, Jesse jumped off his horse and ran to pick some of the flowers for her. In the midst of gathering the purple ones, he noticed some pretty, star-shaped, red flowers and added them to the bouquet, which he then shyly presented to Elaine. While she admired and smelled the flowers, Jesse stared at her golden hair and tried to imagine her undressed; he wondered if all her hair were golden.

"Jesse, why are you staring at me like that? Is my hair a terrible mess?"

"Oh no, Miss Elaine, not at all! You got the purtiest hair I ever seen!"

Flushed with pleasure, Elaine smiled at him and then began to dismount. It was the first time she had tried it on her own and Jesse was worried that she might fall. He reached out to help her down just as her left foot got tangled in the stirrup and she half-fell into his arms. Staring up at him, she flinched as he tightened his grip on her and looked into her eyes with an unbearable longing. Unable to look away, she suddenly realized that he was as lonely as she was and that they somehow belonged together. All at once, she felt her fears dissolve as he pulled her close for a long, gentle kiss. How delightful! It was just like that kiss from the prince who visited her in her dreams. Then it dawned on her; he was her prince! How wonderful! How perfect! She just knew they would live happily ever after! She clung to him and returned his kiss with a fierce passion she had never before experienced. While she wrapped herself around him, she held him tightly with all her strength until it seemed to Jesse as though she were trying to climb into his very soul! Aching with desire, he shakily pried her away and held her at arms' length.

"Miss Elaine, we can't be doin' this right now 'cause the others might come lookin' for us. But don't you worry none! Our time's comin'! Purty soon, we'll be together for always!"

Her eyes moist and gleaming with happiness, she nodded and smiled at him adoringly. After stroking her silky, golden hair one last time, he helped her back on her horse and quickly remounted his own. Although their little excursion had taken only a few minutes, he knew it was important to catch up with the others right away.

"Miss Elaine, do you s'pose you could keep up with me if we lope along for a short while? A lope is a lot easier on your back than a trot, so I don't think it'll hurt you none. Just give ole Lazy-Daze her head and she'll keep right up with my horse, okay?"

268

For the first time in her life, Elaine was in such a state of exhilaration that she had completely forgotten her fears. At that moment, she would have followed Jesse anywhere, without the slightest hesitation. She nodded silently and soon found herself enjoying the smooth, loping gait of her mare. She was so grateful that she had met Jesse! Without him, she would never have been able to conquer her fears and experience the simple pleasure of horseback riding. She was fairly certain that he would soon teach her other, more basic pleasures, as well. She wished for all the world that they were completely alone on this trip, just the two of them. While she happily day-dreamed, they quickly caught up with the rest of the group, only to find that they hadn't even been missed. Jesse noticed that Trevor was maintaining a slower pace; the horses were no longer trotting. Smiling to himself, Jesse could well imagine the flat-landers protesting the jarring gait. He leaned forward in the saddle as he caught the tail-end of a conversation between Cat and Tony.

"Goddamn it, Cat! You never listen to me. I'm telling you I must have wrenched my back! It's killing me! That dumb shit, Trevor! Why in the Hell did he make us trot, anyway? He should have known better! After all, most of us are pretty new to all this riding!"

"Tony! I'm sorry you're in pain, but will you please shut up? There's nothing we can do about it right now, so be quiet! When we get to the next camp, I'll give you a good back rub. In the meantime, I'd like to enjoy the trip, okay?"

As they continued along their way, the summer heat descended on them with a vengeance and tempers became short. Cat thought Tony was a pain in the ass and Tony was annoyed by her uncaring manner. Elaine felt insulted that Eric hadn't even noticed when she had left the trail and was anxious to get rid of him for good.

269

All she really wanted was to be alone with Jesse, anyway. Jesse was frustrated by the lack of opportunity to be alone with Elaine. He didn't know how much longer he could be around her without taking her. He had nothing against Eric on a personal basis, but he wouldn't hesitate for a moment to kill him if it became necessary to do so. He would let nothing come between him and Elaine! His forehead was furrowed with lines as he desperately tried to come up with a foolproof plan to keep Elaine with him for all time. Feeling himself watched, Eric turned around to find both Elaine and Jesse glaring at him. What in the Hell was the matter with those two idiots? Jesus Christ! That's all he needed! Harassment by imbeciles! As if he didn't have enough problems! Deciding to ignore the two of them, he turned forward and stared at Shannon. Now there was a real problem. If only he could succeed in holding on to her, his world would be right. He didn't know what he would do if he lost her! He didn't even want to think about it. Larry had been furtively watching Eric and his blood boiled whenever he caught him staring at Shannon. Goddamn it! She belonged to him and he wasn't about to let Eric steal her away! He had pretty much concluded that he would have to kill Eric in order to keep Shannon. But it would have to look like an accident! How in the Hell was he going to arrange that? Lost in thought, he was quite unaware that hours had passed and he had altogether missed out on the beauty of Mother Nature's original landscapes, which were unsurpassed by any artist.

For the next half-hour, they all rode quietly, when the trail suddenly began to curve downward through an ever-thickening forest. Single-file, the horses plodded slowly along as the path wound around tall pines and Douglas firs. Interspersed among them were stately, old, white oaks, their branches laden with a thick moss

270

hanging low across the trail in veil-like strips. Eric reached up and grabbed a handful of the soft, feathery moss, which fell apart in his hands and drifted away on the breeze. All of a sudden, Eric felt a chill go down his spine! Looking carefully around, he couldn't shake the feeling that he was once again being watched, but not by Elaine and Jesse. He could have sworn he had seen a flash of movement in the forest, but, when he stared into the thicket, he saw only the forest itself. Nevertheless, his instincts bade him be wary and he remained alert. He knew something was out there, even if it were only an animal. Once again looking upward, Eric saw that the tightly interwoven branches allowed only a small amount of filtered sunlight to reach them and light their way, bathing the entire area in a soft, ethereal glow. It was so lovely, he just had to signal to Shannon and make certain she wasn't missing any of this. As he did so, she looked back at him and smiled, her eyes as green as the forest and glowing with a serene happiness. Did he detect some sign of promise in her eyes? He fervently hoped so! While he looked around, he noticed the forest was filled with birdsong, but the birds were hidden from sight by the dense foliage. At this moment, that was exactly how his life seemed to him, as though happiness itself were all around him and ever so close, yet somehow elusive and impossible to hold. The group quietly continued along the way, the majesty of the forest bidding them all to maintain their silence. After a while, the trail steepened sharply downward, causing the riders to lean back in their saddles and brace themselves as the horses took slow, cautious steps, their hooves clanging against an occasional rock. The trail cut back at sharp angles and their descent was fairly rapid. Before long, Eric noticed a change in the terrain; the forest was becoming less dense. He was able to see large patches of sky through

271

the branches and found them filled with dark clouds. How strange! Where did they come from? The sky had been clear when they started their ride. And there was the unmistakable smell of rain in the air. It was evident that a summer storm was about to descend on them. Trevor looked up nervously and then halted Raja while he quickly conferred with Dillon.

"I don't like the look of that sky! It's gonna open up on us anytime now! Fortunately, we're pretty close to the next camp. You'd better go on ahead with some of the men and set up the tents. And be damned quick about it! It'll be a miracle if you get done in time! Get goin' now!"

Dillon called the men together and they rushed on to the next campsite. They'd no sooner finished with the tents when the sky erupted with a fury, shooting hailstones the size of marbles down on the weary riders! For a while, it was complete chaos as everyone scurried to unsaddle the skittish horses while they nervously pranced about and neighed to one another. With the horses finally secured, the riders all ran for the protection of the inviting tents. The three couples headed for the nearest one and crowded in together, heedless of which tent belonged to whom. In a tightly knit group, they all stood at the entrance and stared at the violent storm in a stunned silence while the hail collected in deep drifts. The irritations which had so plagued the small group during their long, hot ride were temporarily forgotten as they stood close together, shivering in the sudden chill. As streaks of lightning split the sky, the reactions evoked by the storm were widely varied. Shannon and Eric were enthralled by the sudden onslaught and reveled in the delightful crispness of the air. They loved the sound of the rolling thunder, even the deafening echoes. While they listened, each rumble became louder than the previous one, until it seemed to be directly over their heads! Elaine began to whimper; she had always been scared to death of thunder. Taking pity on her, Cat held her close and spoke to her soothingly. Larry just looked at Elaine and shook his head in disgust. In his eyes, she was nothing but a blubbering idiot! He was equally annoyed by the storm; he considered it a tremendous inconvenience and silently cursed the ill wind which had brought it to them. Completely unnoticed by the others, Tony stood almost in a trance as the evocative storm momentarily transported him back in time. All of a sudden, the hail wasn't hitting the ground in front of him; it was bouncing off his windshield on that fateful trip to Nicole's home. He could still feel the electricity in the air as he put his arm around her and pulled her close for that first kiss. A chill went down his spine as he remembered the feel of her petite, sensuous body and he shuddered involuntarily. While he stood, lost in the past, the intense storm suddenly abated. Before their very eyes, the churning clouds broke apart and drifted away on the wind. Once again, the rays of the summer sun bathed the earth with a warm, golden glow. Small puffs of steam were rising from the quickly diminishing drifts of hail. In short order, the thirsty ground absorbed almost all of the moisture, leaving hardly a trace of the unseasonable downpour. Eric was the first to step out of the dark tent into the dazzling glare of the sunshine. He squinted his eyes as he looked around, drinking in the radiant beauty of the storm's aftermath. Bits of hail nestled in the branches of the tall pines and sparkled like diamonds as they caught the sun's rays. The fresh air was intoxicating; Eric could feel his worries disappearing right along with the last of the hail. He laughed out loud as he watched the others still standing inside the tent.

"Hey! What's the matter with you people? Are

you a bunch of wimps or what? C'mon! It's beautiful out here!"

The rest of the group gingerly stepped outside, almost as though they expected another storm to catch them off guard. Trevor and his men also left their tents and they all stood quietly for a moment, shielding their eyes as they adjusted to the blinding glare of the sun. Almost without exception, each person stood in awe of the spellbinding beauty of the gleaming forest, fragrant with the most tantalizing of scents. After a while, Trevor called for everyone's attention.

"Listen up, folks! The boys and myself are going to be busy for a while, taking care of some chores and preparing your meals. In the meantime, you're all free to do some exploring and have fun. You already know the rules; don't get lost and get back in time for supper, which will be right around dusk. That leaves you plenty of time to be on your own, a good four hours or so. There are two trails that lead out of camp; pick either one and stay on it so you can find your way back. I guess that's about it. Have fun and be careful!"

Trevor and his men dispersed, leaving the three couples to entertain themselves. Tony immediately made it clear that he wanted to be alone with Cat.

"Honey, is this country gorgeous, or what? It makes a guy feel downright romantic! How about the two of us goin' for a walk, all by ourselves?"

His mood was contagious; Cat smiled at him and nodded. They quickly chose the upper trail and soon disappeared from view, leaving their four friends to share an uncomfortable silence. Already out of sorts, Larry looked from Shannon to Eric and back again, his mood visibly darkening .

"I'm feeling rather tired; I think I'll just rest up until it's time to eat. How about you, Shannon? Do you want to kick back with me?"

"Actually, Larry, I feel more like exploring. I think I'll walk down by that creek over there."

"I don't see any trail leading in that direction. Remember the rules? You're supposed to stay on a trail. Aren't you afraid of getting lost?"

Eric couldn't resist a snide remark.

"Don't worry about it, Larry! I'll be right beside her; she'll be safe with me."

"Oh, yeah? And who's going to protect her from you? Elaine?"

Elaine instantly burst into tears and started to walk away. Eric quickly caught up with her and tried to put his arm around her, but she pushed him away with a surprising amount of force.

"Just leave me alone, all of you! I'm going for a walk by myself! And just for the record, not that anyone's interested, I'll be on the lower trail!"

With those words, she stalked off in a huff! Eric watched until she disappeared from sight and then returned just in time to hear Shannon chewing out Larry.

"That was just great, Larry! You really made her day, didn't you? Why in the Hell can't you think before you speak? Or do you just enjoy being cruel? C'mon, Eric! Let's get out of here! I can't stand the sight of him!"

Glaring smugly at Larry, Eric paused for a moment before joining Shannon, just to make certain he didn't try to follow them. He needn't have worried; Larry wasn't quite prepared for a serious confrontation. He only watched bitterly as Shannon and Eric headed downstream and disappeared from his sight.

Only a short distance away, Jesse and Tad had been tending the horses and overheard the entire argument. When Elaine fled the scene, Jesse tensed up and quickly glanced at his brother. Tad gave Jesse a knowing look and quietly nodded in response to the unspoken question. Knowing he could count on Tad to cover for him, Jesse took a circular route around the edge of the camp, being careful not to be seen, and quickly picked up Elaine's trail. Although he didn't look like one, Jesse was part Indian and he took great pride in the fact that he could walk through the forest as quietly as any of his Indian ancestors. In order to keep Elaine from screaming in surprise, he silently approached her, stepping right behind her while he grabbed her around the waist with one hand and covered her mouth with the other. She struggled briefly until she discovered who it was and then collapsed into a dead faint. Looking carefully around, Jesse tossed her over his shoulder and carried her deep into the forest. She was light as a feather; he hardly noticed her weight at all as he strode along at a brisk pace, searching for a certain, familiar, dense thicket. About fifteen minutes into his search, he found it, the exact, same thicket he'd used to hide from his brother over two years ago. He chuckled to himself as he recalled the look on Tad's face when he'd surprised him by suddenly leaping out of the dense foliage. He'd thought for sure his kid brother would have a heart attack! He knelt down and gently lay Elaine upon a thick bed of pine needles. She stirred slightly and moaned ever so softly as she began to waken. Jesse sat quietly by her side and tenderly took her small, delicate hand within his large, callused one. Her eyes fluttered open and she gave Jesse a dazzling smile as she suddenly recognized him.

"Oh, Jesse, thank God you're here! I should have known you'd come looking for me!"

"I hope I didn't scare you too bad, Miss Elaine. I just didn't want you to scream none! I was scared somebody would hear you and come after us. All I really wanted was for us to be by ourselves for a while."

"It's all right, Jesse. I'm not scared anymore. Besides, this is exactly what I've been praying for, a chance to be alone with you."

She looked at him with such a hunger that he instantly scooped her into his arms and kissed her long and slow. She wrapped her arms around him and pulled him back down on the ground, moaning softly with a newly found passion as she did so. As eager as she appeared, Jesse's instincts warned him to go very slowly with her. Shaky with desire, he started to unbutton her blouse, working awkwardly with one hand. Finally, he was down to the last one when, suddenly, she brushed his hand away and ripped it apart by herself. The last button went flying in the air as her blouse fell completely open, exposing full, voluptuous breasts almost bursting the seams of a black, lacy bra, which opened in the front. Jesse quickly unhooked the bra and then stared hungrily at her breasts as they fell free of their bondage. The look on his face was priceless while he stared at them for a moment, almost at a loss as to which one to grab first. Elaine laughed happily as he finally took one in each hand and nestled his whole face between them, positively reveling in the feel of them. Then his need became so great that he dared not wait much longer. He slid his hand down and unsnapped her jeans, then quickly unzipped them. As he slid them down over her hips, he noticed that her private area was covered with beautiful, golden ringlets. So intrigued was he, that he stopped dead with her pants only halfway off and instantly ran his fingers through the soft, silky curls. Unable to wait for him to finish, Elaine kicked her jeans off by herself and wrapped her legs around him, begging him to take her. Responding to her desperate need, Jesse hurriedly removed his pants, exposing a huge, throbbing penis. Elaine stared in shock, fear written all over her face!

277

"Jesse! I didn't know you were so big! I mean......I don't think this will work!"

"It's gonna be all right, Elaine! I promise I won't hurt you none. I'll put it in little by little, an' you just holler when you can't take no more, okay?"

He was so gentle with her, never forcing his way, that she trusted him implicitly. She could literally feel her fear melting away. There was a lump in her throat as she silently nodded her acquiescence. First, he lowered his face down to her silky mound, gently spread her apart and began to lick her with his tongue. God, she tasted so good! He pushed his tongue as far inside her as he could and stroked her relentlessly with it, until her fear was long forgotten and she groaned in desperation. Finally, Jesse mounted her, sliding his cock in ever so slowly until he felt himself at an impasse. Restraining himself, he backed off and stroked her only up to that point. Elaine sensed his restraint and shocked him by begging for more. Instantly obliging her, he forced his entire cock inside her, causing her to shudder with a depth of passion she had never imagined possible! At first it hurt, but she wanted him so badly she just had to have all of him. With every stroke, she was less aware of the pain as she became consumed by a constant, burning thrill, until, suddenly, her whole body was aflame and began to jerk convulsively while she experienced an earth-shattering orgasm, the very first of her entire life! Sensing her climax, Jesse came right along with her, planting his seed deep within her as he pushed himself further and further inside her! Their passions finally spent, they clung to each other, their bodies still shuddering with leftover tremors. Jesse thought he'd surely died and gone to Heaven! He'd never had a sexual experience to equal this one. And Elaine lay staring up at the tall pines, the most blissful expression on her face! She

278

was absolutely stunned by the depth of her feelings! She finally understood why others considered sex such a beautiful act. Dear God! What if she had never met Jesse? She would never have known what she was missing! How could she ever give him up? Jesse studied her sweet face and somehow read her mind.

"Don't worry yourself none! I got plans for us. I ain't never givin' you up! I just need a little more time an' then you an' me are takin' off together."

Her worries instantly vanished! He was her prince and she knew he would take care of everything. Her eyes damp with tears, she gave him a radiant smile and snuggled against his warm body.

"I just have one question; how soon can we do that again?"

Jesse laughed out loud, then held her tightly and showered her with kisses. After a while, he gently disentangled himself and leaned on one elbow, carefully studying her body as if to memorize it for all time.

"I can't hardly believe my eyes, Elaine. You got the purtiest body I ever seen in my whole life!"

"That sounds like quite a compliment, Jesse! Exactly how many naked ladies have you been with, anyway?"

"None that mattered, that's for sure! And now that I've been with you, them others are fadin' fast. I can't rightly recollect any of 'em right now!"

Her eyes misted slightly with tears of happiness.

"That's the sweetest thing anyone ever said to me! And Jesse, there's something I want you to know; you're the only man who's ever given me pleasure, absolutely the only one!"

She uttered those words with such vehemence, that he hadn't the slightest doubt as to the truth of her statement. Besides which, Jesse was extremely intuitive and he had strongly suspected it was the first time she

279

had ever experienced real passion. For all practical purposes, he knew this encounter had been with a virgin. He smiled tenderly at her and began to lightly fondle her full breasts. He was pleased to see the nipples instantly harden with a renewed desire. He had a strong hunch he had awakened an insatiable appetite. He leaned over and sucked on first one nipple and then the other, delighting in the sound of her light moans. Oh, yes, he would be kept very busy for quite a while! He reached down and played with her soft, golden ringlets, still damp where a little of his come had leaked out of her. He ran his fingers through the curls, lightly tugging on them, causing her moans to increase dramatically as she arched her back and rubbed against him. He spent the better part of an hour fondling and teasing her until she again begged him to take her. She reached down and seized his penis, which quickly hardened in her hand. Still holding onto it, she very deftly pushed him over on his back and climbed on top of him, guiding his erect member inside herself. She gingerly came down on him, gasping with pain and pleasure until he was completely inside her. While she rode him, he grabbed her hips, forcefully bringing her down against him as he pushed himself even more deeply within her. Letting out a yelp of pain, she hunched over slightly, her heavy breasts brushing against his lips in a tantalizing fashion. Unable to resist, he clamped his mouth tightly around one of her nipples and hung onto it while he continued to impale her with his huge cock! Suddenly overwhelmed by the onset of a violent climax, she almost screamed with pleasure as he pumped another load into her. He finished a little ahead of her and he could feel her sucking every last drop out of him as her orgasm continued. Finally satisfied, she shakily collapsed on top of him and they held each other close, both of them bathed in sweat and breathing hard.

"Oh, Jesse! That was so wonderful! You thrill me out of my mind! I want you to make love to me every single day!"

Jesse chuckled as he gently stroked the small of her back, delighting in the feel of her body. Oh, yes, she would keep him extremely busy!

"Darlin', as much as I'd like to stay inside you, I think we better git ourselves back to camp. Otherwise, somebody just might come a lookin' for us!"

Jesse kissed her tenderly one last time and then gently separated himself from her. They both collected their clothes and hurriedly dressed.

"Oh, dear! I can't close my blouse all the way! I completely forgot about breaking off that last button! What am I going to do? I can't go back to camp looking like this!"

"Now, honey, don't git yourself all worked up over nothin'! I can fix it just fine."

He grabbed the two ends of the blouse and tied them together just beneath her bust, western-style.

"There now, darlin', you look purty as can be!"

"Do you really think so? I always want to look my best for you! Thanks, Jesse, for fixing my blouse. It seems like you're forever coming to my rescue! I love you so very much!"

Looking at him with a glowing smile, her entire being radiated the happiness she felt. A light breeze stirred the branches above them, allowing some filtered sunlight to shine down on them. Her golden hair caught the light, which shimmered like a halo about her head. Rendered speechless by her angelic beauty, Jesse was filled with awe as he stared at her. Although his life had been filled with various encounters, he had never before actually been in love. This was his very first time and he somehow knew it would also be his last. He would never again feel this way about another woman.

"Let's go, darlin'. It's time to start back. We can walk together for a ways, but when we get close to camp, we better split up. It just wouldn't look too good if we show up at the same time."

Her eyes glistening, Elaine nodded and they stepped out of the dense thicket together, walking hand in hand. As they hiked along, Elaine noticed that the forest was exceptionally beautiful! She wondered why she had never noticed it before. And the smells! The incredibly delicious smells! All at once, everything seemed so new and perfect! It was as though her life had only just begun and she was seeing the world for the very first time! She felt reborn; her previous world no longer existed. Jesse was all that mattered to her now, nothing else! She would never again worry about her future. She didn't care where or by what means they lived, just so long as they were together. Suddenly, she just had to hug him once more! Stopping in her tracks, she wrapped her arms around him and held him tightly, catching him completely off guard. Worried, he instinctively held her at arms' length.

"Whoa, gal! We're a mite close to camp to be doin' this! What if someone sees us?"

Seeing the hurt look on her face, he immediately relented and pulled her back into his arms, holding her close to his heart.

"Woman, what have you done to me? I guess I'm just gonna be your slave for the rest of my life!"

Looking at her tenderly, he gently tilted her face up and kissed her passionately. So wrapped up were they in each other, that they were completely unaware of Dillon watching them from behind some trees......

"Boss!......Boss!......Guess what......Guess what I saw!"

Almost out of breath from running back to camp, Dillon could barely get the words out without wheezing!

"Jesus Christ! Calm down, man! What in the Hell are you talkin' about?"

"It was Jesse! He was all wrapped around that Elaine broad! I think those two are gettin' it on!"

"Shit! That's what all the yelling's about? You dumb fuck! What the Hell do I care if he's humpin' some broad?"

Dillon looked dismayed.

"But, Boss, you told me to keep an eye on him and report back to you."

"Yeah! But only if it's something important, like messin' with the goods or stealin' from us! You know, stuff like that! Or gettin' mad and carvin' up somebody with that knife of his! Understand? Don't bother me with any more small shit! I got work to do! Go on; get outa here!"

Trevor was still mumbling angrily to himself when he saw Elaine approaching the camp from the lower trail. Even from that distance, he could see that she looked disheveled and something about her blouse seemed different. Her demeanor had also somehow changed; she no longer appeared nervous. She strode toward her tent with a confident air. Now, that was unusual! He looked back at the lower trail just in time to see Jesse returning to camp. He didn't look nervous either, but then he never did! He was one of those rare types who could handle any situation life threw at them. Trevor gave Jesse a knowing grin as he approached.

"Hey, Jesse, how was she?"

With an air of nonchalance, Jesse merely looked at him.

"What're you talkin' about?"

"C'mon, Jesse! You can level with me. I know you been fuckin' that Elaine broad. I just wanna know how she was; maybe I'll get a piece off her, too! You don't mind sharin', do you?"

With extreme control, Jesse managed to remain calm. He was even able to give Trevor a leering grin of his own.

"Hey, man, keep your voice down, will you? I don't want her old man to hear us! C'mon; let's walk out a ways an' I'll tell you all about it!"

With a nasty smile on his face, Trevor took a short walk with him into the woods, just far enough to get out of earshot. As soon as they stopped and Trevor turned to face him, Jesse slammed him against a tree and held his huge, Bowie knife against Trevor's neck! Almost gagging on the bile rising in his throat, Trevor could feel the razor-sharp knife slicing into his skin ever so slightly! Unable to control himself, he could feel his own piss running down his leg. Jesse glared at him with unwavering, icy, blue eyes and looked quite undecided about whether or not to finish him off! Finally, with evident self-restraint, Jesse decided to let him off with a warning.

"If you ever talk about Miss Elaine like that again, you're dead meat! I'll cut you into so many pieces, nobody'll ever find hide nor hair of you! I'd just as soon hack you to bits right now, but we got a job to do an' we're damn well gonna finish it! D'ya understand what I'm sayin'?"

Terrified out of his mind, Trevor nodded only a tiny bit, lest he cause the sharp edge to cut any deeper. Only then did Jesse relax his grip and sheathe his knife. He stepped back a pace or two and sneered as he watched Trevor slump all the way to the base of the tree, taking ragged breaths while he clutched at his throat.

"And don't waste your time tryin' to git back at me! Right now, you can't do without even one less man! Anyways, me an' Tad are gonna be watchin' you real close. One wrong move, an' you're history!"

Trevor just nodded and looked down at the spots of blood on his arm. When he looked up again, Jesse was gone! He hadn't even made a sound as he disappeared into the forest. 'Just like a Goddamn Indian!' Trevor thought. 'He must have Indian blood in him, that bastard! I'm not done yet, by God! We'll just see who's still alive when the job's over!' He tried to stand, only to have his legs buckle beneath him as he fell back to the ground. He decided to wait a little longer before returning to the camp.

The only person to notice Jesse's return was his brother. Tad walked over to him and knew by his expression that he'd had a serious run-in with someone. Still trembling with an inner rage, Jesse fixed his gaze on Tad and they both stood silently for a moment. Little by little, the cold bitterness left his heart and was slowly replaced by a warm affection for his younger brother. Seeing the change in his expression, Tad playfully punched him in the arm, his hazel eyes glowing with admiration for Jesse. Reaching out to brush Tad's stringy, brown hair out of his eyes, Jesse instead grabbed him around the middle and brought him down to the ground in a surprise move, pinning his shoulders down and bursting into laughter all at once!

"Hey, kid, ain't you learnt nothin' yet? How come you're still fallin' for that ole trick? I guess I'm just gonna nail you every danged time, huh?"

"We'll just see about that, Jesse! I ain't finished yet!"

Tad tried desperately to break out of the hold, to no avail. Finally, rocking back and forth, he felt Jesse's grip weaken ever so slightly. With one magnificent effort, he managed to dislodge his brother and turn the tables on him. Smiling victoriously, he sat astride Jesse and laughed hilariously!

"What d'ya say now, big brother?   It looks like I

git the last laugh after all!"

Jesse grinned up at him, more than satisfied to see his little brother come out on top.

"All right! You win! Now let me up, you big bully!"

Tad moved off of him and gave him a hand up. As he stood, Jesse tousled his brother's hair and then gently pushed him away.

"C'mon, kid! You an' me better go check on the horses. By the way, it wouldn't hurt none for us to keep a close watch on Trevor an' his asshole buddies. You never know what they might be up to!"

Tad stared intently at his brother. So that's who he was fighting with! He had a hunch what it was about.

"Sure thing, Jesse! I'll keep a close eye on the lot of 'em! Maybe it wouldn't hurt none for me to watch out for Miss Elaine, too."

Jesse smiled gratefully at his brother. Tad was so intuitive, he almost didn't have to tell him anything. He always seemed to know exactly what was going on. He felt extremely fortunate to have such a bright, loyal brother!

While Jesse and Tad were taking care of the horses, Eric and Shannon were still enjoying their walk down by the creek. They had been moving slowly along when Eric noticed an inviting deer trail leading into the forest.

"Come on, Shannon! Let's do a little exploring. Haven't you seen enough of that creek by now?"

Shannon shook her head and smiled knowingly at him.

"Not a chance, Eric! You think I don't know why you want to get me off alone in the woods? Don't even think about it! I'm staying right by the creek where it's open and rocky and way too uncomfortable for you to get out of line!"

"All right, woman! Have it your way! If you want it in the rough, I'm happy to oblige you!"

With those words, he stepped right beside her and started to undo her blouse. Laughing, she quickly ripped the fabric out of his hands and ran up the deer trail, with him hot on her heels. Just a short distance into the forest, she tripped over a branch and he fell right on top of her, both of them bursting into laughter simultaneously. Their smiles slowly faded as they felt the heat from each other's body. He started to kiss her, but she quickly covered his lips with her hand.

"No, Eric! Please! We can't be doing this anymore!"

"Why not? You know you want it just as much as I do!"

"Eric, I mean it......"

He drowned out her words with a searing kiss, from which there was no retreat, only surrender! Filled with impatience, Eric tore her blouse open, all the buttons flying into the thick grass! Leaning back, he ripped her jeans from her body in one fluid motion, her boots sliding right off with them. Desperate to be inside her, he mounted her roughly, almost savagely. It had been such a long wait since the last time, too long! Filled with the same pressing hunger, Shannon wrapped her legs around him, holding him tightly while he stroked her relentlessly! Shakily, he forced himself to slow down a little; he didn't want this to end too soon. His cock throbbing inside her, she moaned desperately while he removed her bra and grabbed both her breasts, squeezing them gently and sucking on each nipple in turn. Her moans increased as she felt herself beginning to come. Sensing her urgency, he began to fill her with his seed, pumping it into her over and over in a lengthy, burning climax! Finally, their passions spent, Eric remained inside her for a while, continuing to fondle and suck on her breasts, enjoying the feel of the leftover tremors coursing through her body. She was the most passionate woman he had ever known, with orgasms that seemed to go on forever! Dear God! How he loved this woman! He moved his lips from her nipples to her mouth and began to kiss her deeply, his tongue invading her mouth until she began to moan all over again. His member remained firm inside her and he could feel her sucking on it with a renewed vigor! Sensing that she was about to come for the second time, he pushed himself even further inside her until her body once again convulsed into spasms while he continued to stroke her. After her tremors subsided for good, he looked down at her tenderly and brushed her lustrous, red hair back from her forehead. She was a true, natural redhead. Her pubic hair was also a beautiful, burnished copper. Her green eyes mirrored the forest and held such a look of satisfaction that he just had to chuckle out loud!

"What? What are you laughing about?"

"That look of pure satisfaction on your face, that's what! You remind me of the cat who ate the canary! Tell me again how you really can't be doing this anymore. I want to see if you can keep a straight face while you say the words!"

Flustered, Shannon began to stammer.

"You don't understand......I really did mean what I said, but......once you're inside me, I lose all control......I mean......Oh! What's the use? No matter how hard I try to explain, you just refuse to understand!"

"Be quiet, woman! This is all I need to understand, right here and right now! I'll never give you up!"

He then covered her mouth with his and gave her another long, passionate kiss, which she instinctively returned with a fiery depth. Slowly releasing her, he gazed down on her possessively when, all of a sudden, the sound of a twig snapping broke the silence! Startled, they both looked in the direction from where the sound had come, but saw nothing. While they continued to stare into the forest, Eric could have sworn he saw a flash of movement through some distant trees. Worried, he silently motioned for Shannon to get dressed and he quickly did the same. Signaling her to remain behind, he sprinted in the direction of the noise. Stopping at the point where he thought he had seen something, he suddenly became aware of an extreme silence all around him. His heart pounding, he looked warily in all directions, but there was nothing to be seen or heard. Had it occurred to him to look upward, he might have spotted Two Eagles hiding in the tall pine tree directly over his head. Instead, he slowly returned to Shannon, all the while knowing he was being watched by someone. He didn't just feel it; he knew it!

"We'd better get back to camp, just as quickly and quietly as we can. I didn't see anyone, but I know there's somebody out there! Whoever it is could be watching us right now. Hurry up, Shannon! It's starting to get dark."

They hurriedly ran back down the deer trail until they reached the creek. As they headed upstream, they were forced to slow down a little due to the rocky terrain. Dusk was falling quickly and it was becoming difficult to see the path. Eric kept looking over his shoulder, almost certain he would find someone following them, but all he saw were shadows. He kept trying to hurry Shannon along, but she just couldn't keep up with him. Finally, in desperation, he half-carried her until they were almost there. Just short of the camp, an owl hooted directly over their heads, causing Shannon to almost leap into his arms! Eric laughed with relief as he suddenly realized the eerie silence had ended. He knew they were safe now! He held Shannon close and kissed her one last time before they strode into camp.

Upon entering the clearing, they noticed the others were already eating their supper and chatting around the evening fire. As they approached, the entire group suddenly quit eating and stared at them in amazement! The two looked at each other in confusion until they realized that, in their haste to return to camp, they had forgotten to clean up. Shannon had hastily tied her blouse together, but, with all the buttons gone, it was quite revealing. And they were both covered with some of the grass on which they had made love. There could be no question as to what they had been doing! Embarrassed, Cat and Tony looked down at their food and said nothing. His face suffused with a dangerous anger, Larry threw his plate down in disgust and stalked off into the forest! Her mind filled with thoughts of Jesse, Elaine was dreamily looking into the fire; she was completely unaware of their return. Even Trevor was at a loss for words as he enviously stared at them. Absent-mindedly fingering the kerchief around his neck, he tried to imagine making love to Shannon. Jesus, God! Was her body perfect or what? If it was the last thing he ever did, he was determined to get some of that! With a knowing smile on his face, Jesse was the only one who seemed pleased with the situation. After all, Eric was married to Elaine, his Elaine! Now it was obvious that he would have no problem in taking her away from him. Actually, he rather liked Eric and was quite pleased that it would be unnecessary to kill him.

CHAPTER 22 EVENING MIST

The sun had long since made its final descent of the day. The dwindling light of dusk slowly faded into the pitch black of night. While crickets chirped and a few mocking birds filled the air with their defiant melodies, the remainder of the group sat around the fire. Only Larry and Elaine were missing. She had retired right after supper and Larry hadn't been seen since he had angrily disappeared into the forest. Eric stirred the dying embers of the fire with a long stick, causing a whole stream of sparks to spiral into the heavens.

"Well, I guess there aren't any more secrets around here. Oh, the Hell with it! He had to find out sooner or later, anyway."

Tony looked nervously around the outskirts of the camp.

"Yeah? Well, for my money, I wish it could have been later! If I were in your shoes, I'd be watchin' my back from here on out!"

"Shit! You think I'm scared of that wimp? I could take him with one arm tied behind my back! Besides, he doesn't have the guts to face me, not without a weapon anyway. And I'm the only one with a gun around here, remember?"

"Yeah, far as you know! How do you know these guides of ours aren't packin', huh? I sure as Hell wouldn't put it past old Larry to swipe one of their weapons, even if it's only a knife! Didn't you see that humungous Bowie that Jesse's carryin'? I'd sure hate to face that thing in the dark!"

"Yeah, right! I'm sure Larry's going to walk right

up to them and take their weapons away! You must be losin' it, Tony!"

"Oh, yeah? We'll see about that! They all have to sleep sometime! And you'd better start sleepin' with your gun in your hand!"

"Shhh! Will you two pipe down? Somebody might hear you! C'mon, Tony! I'm tired; I want to get some sleep!"

"All right! Cool it, will you? I'm coming! As for you, Eric, you'd better be damned careful! You haven't seen the end of this!"

Lost in thought, Shannon had been sitting quietly the whole time, her lovely red hair reflecting the light of the fire. Eric was struck anew by her flawless beauty. Although it had been only a few hours, he felt a sudden, overwhelming need to once again hold her in his arms. She was like quicksilver, always on the verge of slipping away. Something in her expression made her appear unusually vulnerable. He moved close to her and put his arm around her shoulder, drawing her near. With silent tears, she leaned against him, taking comfort from the warmth of his body. He was always there for her, always seemed to know when she needed him most. If only she were able to love him in the way he deserved. She almost wished she had never met Jacob. Common sense told her she would probably never see him again, anyway. But, in her heart, she knew that wasn't really true. All her instincts told her that she and Jacob were irrevocably bound together. He'd aroused feelings in her that she'd never before experienced. That was why she felt so guilty about Eric; she felt as though she were using him. She loved him, but not enough and not in the right way. She kept trying to explain that it was over between them, but he refused to listen. Instead, he used every opportunity to get her alone and take advantage of the sexual hold he had over her and, dear

God, what a hold it was! With a little forceful persuasion, he knew she would melt every single time. There was a strong, physical attraction between them, but she knew it wouldn't be enough in the long run. There's more to love than just making love and she didn't want to settle for the wrong man. She'd made that mistake once and she didn't want to repeat it.

"Hey! Are those tears I see? Shannon, there's nothing to cry about. Believe me; I can handle any problem with Larry! I won't let him harm you, if that's what you're worried about. Is that it, sweetheart?"

"No, that's not it! It's just that I'm feeling very confused right now. I need some time to myself so I can think clearly. At the end of tomorrow's ride, I'd really like to go exploring on my own for a while. I hope you understand, Eric."

As much as he wanted to spend every minute with her, he knew he'd better give her some space or he'd lose her for good.

"Sure, honey, I understand. But what about tonight? I'm just a little concerned about how Larry might treat you when he returns! Maybe I should stay in your tent with you. Elaine won't even know I'm missing."

"Are you crazy? You must have some kind of death wish! I'm positive that he would never hurt me, but we both know he'd like to kill you! Especially if he finds you in our tent! That would be such a slap in his face, that he could never ignore it! As strong as you are, Eric, you'd be at his mercy if he sneaked up on you while you were asleep!"

"Yeah, I guess you're right. Maybe it's just that I wanted to snuggle up with you tonight. You're very addictive! I'm afraid you've spoiled me for all other women for all time!"

Shannon instantly put her hand to his lips.

"Don't say that, Eric! It's very dangerous to love

293

anyone that much! It's too easy to get hurt!"

He moved her hand aside and gazed into her green eyes.

"It doesn't matter how dangerous it is! It's too late for me! I already love you that much and I always will!"

With those words, he pulled her close to him and kissed her long and hard. Struggling against him only for a moment, she quickly succumbed to the instant desire he always aroused in her. Locked in a passionate embrace, they were totally unaware of Jesse watching them from the shadows of a dense thicket, smiling smugly to himself. They were equally oblivious of being watched by Two Eagles and Running Deer, who were carefully hidden in the branches of a tree not too far from Jesse. An owl stared into the eyes of the two warriors, hooted at them and flew away to another tree. Startled by the owl, Shannon broke away from Eric for just a moment.

"Eric, please, someone might see us! Besides, it's late and we have to get up early. You have to let me go!"

"All right, you win! C'mon; I'll walk you to your tent."

On their way to her tent, they heard the bubbling sound of a small waterfall. They walked over to the creek and watched as the water splashed against the rocks, creating a fine mist that shimmered and sparkled in the soft moonlight.

"Oh, Eric! Look! Isn't that just the loveliest sight you've ever seen?"

With a gentle smile, Eric shook his head.

"No, Shannon. You're the loveliest sight I've ever seen!"

He kissed her one last time and then reluctantly released her. After watching her step into her tent, he walked into his own and looked down at Elaine, who was peacefully sleeping with a slight smile on her face. He wondered if anyone could possibly be as content as she appeared. She seemed so different lately; he couldn't quite put his finger on it, but she just wasn't the Elaine he remembered. He quietly wrapped up in his sleeping bag and was almost instantly asleep. Shortly afterward, Larry finally returned to his tent. He stood quietly and stared at Shannon while she slept. After watching her intently for a few moments, he retired to his own sleeping bag, but sleep was a long time coming. As the sky slowly lightened with a faint rosy glow in the eastern sky, Larry was still wide awake, making plans for his revenge against Eric. By the time Larry finally fell asleep, Two Eagles and Running Deer were well on their way to a pre-arranged meeting site with Jacob.

"There's no way I'm going to break the news to Falcon! If you want to tell him about Shannon, be my guest! At his best, he can be difficult and you know it! Do you really want to put him in a bad mood? Just do it my way, Running Deer. We'll tell him we saw her and let it go at that. There's no reason to mention any details. Understand?"

"Oh, sure! You make it sound so easy. What about the fact that he always asks specific questions? Huh? What are you going to do then? Lie to him?"

Two Eagles was becoming increasingly annoyed.

"Oh, shut up! I don't want to talk about this anymore! We'll just have to meet with him and play it by ear. But you better get one thing straight! I'm still not going to be the one to give him any details!"

Just as the sun broke through some low clouds hovering over the mountains to the east, Running Deer and Two Eagles were approaching the cave where Jacob had spent the night. Unknown to the two warriors, the deep cave had two entrances. The first one faced the upper part of a small meadow and was carefully camouflaged by a dense thicket of manzanita growing directly in front of it. There was a steep ridge along the top of the cave and the second entrance opened into a rocky crevice at the back. It was a narrow opening; only a slender person could get through, but it made an excellent escape route in case of an emergency. Once through, a person could skirt around the back side of the mountain until it once again was covered with dense trees. Jacob knew the land like the back of his hand and he was extremely talented in disappearing silently into the forest without a trace. While Two Eagles waited just outside, Running Deer squeezed past the manzanita and stepped into the cave, peering intently as his eyes adjusted to the dark.

"Falcon! Where are you? I can't see you! Speak up so I'll know that you're here. Come on! This is no time to play games! We have news of your woman!"

Finally, his eyes focused and he could see that he was alone in the dark cave. Feeling foolish, he walked back through the entrance to return to Two Eagles, only to find that he had disappeared. Frustrated, he carefully looked around, but saw no sign of a scuffle.

"All right, I've had enough of this crap! Come on, Falcon! We've been up all night and I'm not in the mood for any......"

In the middle of his sentence, he was tackled and brought to the ground by Jacob, who sat astride him victoriously with an evil gleam in his eyes.

"You're damned lucky it's me! How many times have I told you to approach silently and stay out of sight? You act like we're the only ones in the forest!"

Glaring, Jacob stood without offering his friend a hand up. Quickly standing, Running Deer flushed angrily and glared back at Jacob.

"Just for the record, your enemies aren't around here. They're all back at the camp preparing for the day's ride. I thought you already knew that!"

"And just how do you know you weren't followed? If you're not careful, you could get us all killed! I hope you were at least a little more cautious when you watched their camp!"

"We were very discreet, all right? And we weren't followed! So just relax! Now, do you want to hear our news, or not?"

Jacob curtly nodded. Two Eagles and Running Deer looked nervously at each other, each hoping the other would speak first. Disgusted, Jacob glared at both of them.

"Come on! Spit it out! When you're that nervous, it's either about something really important, or you've screwed up in a big way!" Still, they hesitated. "Well? Which is it?"

Two Eagles was looking extremely agitated!

"Damn it! You'd better start talking, Running Deer! I told you I wasn't going to be the one to tell him anything!"

With a smug grin, Running Deer just shook his head.

"You're the one with the perfect vision; I never saw a thing. We were too far away! I have only your word for what you saw, so it's all up to you. I have nothing to say!"

"Goddamn it! One of you better tell me the news and I mean right now!"

Looking resigned, Two Eagles finally relented.

"All right! Just don't take it out on me when you get all pissed off about what I'm going to say!"

"If you don't hurry up, I'm going to throttle you without even hearing the news! Understand?"

"Yeah......well, it's like this. The leader of the trail ride is a guy named Trevor and he's always watching Shannon with......with a certain look on his face. You know what I mean......he wants to, uh......what I mean is......"

"What you mean is, he wants to fuck her! Jesus Christ! Can't you even speak English?"

"Uh......yeah! That's pretty much what I was going to say."

"You mean, that's it? Shit! What else happened? Did he do anything to her? Did he hurt her? Come on! There has to be more to it than this!" He looked at them both suspiciously. "What are you leaving out?"

"Nothing! Nothing at all! I mean......she wasn't exactly in our sight the whole time! After all, you told us to keep an eye on everyone, not just her!"

Jacob stared at them through obsidian eyes that somehow became blacker with each passing moment. After several seconds of intense silence, he spoke to them in a low, menacing tone.

"Exactly where was she heading when she left your sight? And with whom did she go?"

Two Eagles and Running Deer broke into a sweat as they looked at each other. Finally, Running Deer spoke, almost defiantly.

"She walked along the creek for a ways and then followed a deer trail into the forest......she was with some guy named Eric."

After several more long seconds, Jacob glared at Running Deer.

"I see. They were completely out of your sight, but you were somehow magically able to figure out which trail they took! How interesting! Perhaps it is you and not I who should be the one to follow Lone Elk and become our next medicine man! Did anything else

298

occur that you didn't see, but just happen to know about?"

Unable to look Jacob in the eye, Running Deer looked down at his feet and spoke quietly.

"Nothing that we'd care to discuss. Anyway, it has nothing to do with what we're trying to accomplish."

Fully expecting Jacob to fly into a rage, the two warriors were both surprised and relieved to see that he remained calm. In fact, he seemed more than calm; he appeared to be completely lost in thought. While they stared at each other in confusion, he was remembering the look on Eric's face when they'd talked about Shannon. It had been obvious that he loved her deeply. He could well imagine what had taken place in the forest. No wonder his two friends were afraid to tell him. He could hardly stand the thought of her in anyone's arms but his own, but he felt no hatred for Eric. Instead, he felt a strong determination to cure Shannon of her infatuation with the man. She wasn't meant for anyone but himself and he had no intention of sharing her. He knew it was only a matter of time, but he felt a desperate need to hold her right now, this very moment! Somehow or other, he would have to find a way to be alone with her before the passing of another day. With an unfathomable look in his dark eyes, Jacob turned and faced his two friends.

"There's been enough said about this situation. Let's just forget about it and get on with what we have to do! The rest of our men are expecting to meet with us at this cave, but we dare not wait any longer for them. I've left instructions for them inside, telling them our general direction. I'm sure they won't have any problem catching up with us later. Right now, the important thing is for the three of us to catch up with Trevor's group and maintain a close watch. Sooner or later, he'll have to send some of his men to meet with the growers and it's imperative that we know exactly when that occurs! Let's go! We'll be lucky to catch up with them by the time they make camp this afternoon. By the way......you both did an okay job of checking on all of them yesterday."

Astonished, Running Deer and Two Eagles just looked at each other, neither one willing to break the silence as they all mounted their horses and slowly began the long trek to the next camp. Zigzagging back and forth, the trail led them to the crest of a ridge just as the sun's rays began to bathe the mountains in a golden glow. The morning chill still held the land in its cold grip, but the three warriors felt only an inner warmth as they thought of the battle yet to come. They were determined to rid their forest lands of drug dealers once and for all and they knew there was no choice but to kill every last one of them! Simultaneously, they all recalled their last tribal council; they could still see the sad expression on Lone Elk's face as he spoke to them. Indeed, his words still rang in their ears......

"My children, this is a sad occasion for us to meet. I have fervently prayed that the actions you're about to take would prove unnecessary. Unfortunately, one's prayers are not always answered. We have only one choice; we must annihilate the enemy and cover all traces! We know all too well that turning them over to the law will solve nothing. They, or others like them, would return in the blink of an eye. Word travels swiftly in the underworld and that will prove to be a great benefit to us. When they learn what we do to their kind, other drug dealers will not be so willing to enter our forests and grow their evil crops. There is great risk in what you are about to do, so act with extreme caution and do not get caught! I will stay behind and aid you in whatever ways I can. Remember; I am always with you in spirit!"

.......The three friends glanced at one another and

knew they shared the same thoughts. Running Deer was especially contemplative; certain parts of their plan deeply concerned him. He ran his fingers through his long, thick, black hair and impatiently tossed his head as a huge blow-fly hovered around him. Jacob watched him and chuckled silently.

"You know; if you'd braid that mop of yours, it would be a lot easier to control!"

Slightly irritated, Running Deer looked sharply at him.

"Don't let it worry you! I'll braid it just before the battle! You'd do well to take care of your own hair. I notice it's been blowing in your face all morning!"

This time, Jacob laughed out loud!

"All right, what's on your mind? You only get this crabby when you're really worried about something. What is it?"

"It's the flat-landers! I know how worried you are about Shannon, but what in the world makes you think we can really protect any of them when we're in the middle of an all-out fight? Our enemies aren't just ordinary, average guys; they're dangerous, professional gunmen with no qualms about killing! Make no mistake! This isn't just a battle; it's a war! And the only way we're going to win it is by ignoring the innocent bystanders and fighting the way we're supposed to, concentrating only on the enemy, with no holds barred!"

Jacob was silent for a while as he considered the problem.

"You're absolutely right, Running Deer! There is no way to guarantee their safety, short of scrapping our entire mission and I'm not willing to do that. But I do have an idea that should at least protect Shannon. After they make camp this afternoon, I'm going to try to get her alone and talk to her. Obviously, I can't tell her everything, but I will let her know that they're all in some

301

danger and to be very cautious around Trevor and his men. We'll arrange some kind of warning sign, so she'll have a chance to break away before the battle begins. Well, what do you think?"

His two friends looked aghast! Two Eagles stared at Jacob as though he'd lost his mind.

"You can't be serious! If you actually tell her they're all in some kind of danger, she'll certainly warn the others and they'll all start acting really wary around Trevor and his men. And I suppose you think they won't notice that strange behavior! Hell! You might just as well send one of us in to tell him that we're about to do battle with him and that he should be on guard! Oh well, so much for the idea of a surprise attack!"

Annoyed by his sarcasm, Jacob glared at him for a long moment, but then realized the truth of his words. He was guilty of letting his feelings for Shannon color his judgement. He wouldn't let it happen again. Besides, Lone Elk had told him to have faith in his vision. If it should indeed come true, she would survive the battle. The real question in Jacob's mind was whether or not he would also survive it.

"You're right; it was a bad idea. All right, so it was a rotten idea! Let's just forget I ever suggested it. How about this? When I give the signal, we'll descend on them like warriors from Hell and let the chips fall where they may! Destiny will decide who lives and who dies! Every man will take his chances, and every woman too. We'll at least have the advantage of surprise. They don't even suspect that we're in the forest and that's the way we're going to keep it! For now, we'd better concern ourselves with catching up with them by the time they make their next camp. We're wasting time! Let's get a move on!"

With those words, the three warriors kicked their mounts into a light gallop and they all quietly loped along, the only noises being the heavy breathing of the horses and an occasional rock thrown by one of them. In the chill of the morning air, small clouds of steam danced around the horses' heads with every breath they took. The grasses were still moist and gleaming with a heavy dew. As they rode, they instinctively kept a low profile, staying well beneath the skyline. After a while, they made a gradual descent from the side of the ridge and took an easterly route through fragrant, tall pines and huge, old, white oaks. The dense forest afforded them excellent cover as they silently and steadily whittled away the distance between themselves and their enemies' next campsite.

Early that same morning, Trevor had awoken in a cold sweat from a nightmare that seemed entirely too real. In his dream, he had been sleeping peacefully when he suddenly felt the sharp edge of a Bowie knife at his throat. Only half-awake, he jerked upright, clutched at his throat and nervously looked around. In the bleak, greyish blackness just before the dawn, he thought he saw a figure slip out of his tent. His heart beating violently, he couldn't be certain if he'd really seen someone, or if it were just a fading fragment from his nightmare. A chill went down his spine as he remembered Jesse's warning about being watched. He suddenly realized that either Jesse or his brother could have been in his tent and he wouldn't have heard the slightest sound. Those Goddamned assholes! They must have Indian blood in them! You just never could hear either one of 'em comin' up behind you. They knew the forest inside out and they were better trackers than any Indian he'd ever known. And they were thick as thieves! You didn't dare get one of 'em mad or the other one would be lookin' to kill you! He wished to Hell he'd never hired them! What he really needed were more men like Dillon and Pedro. They took their orders, kept their mouths shut and stayed respectful. All they really cared about was their cut of the action. They'd dance with the Devil himself if there were enough money in it! With men like that, where money was always the bottom line, you knew exactly what to expect from them. But Jesse and Tad were a different story. They had their own strange code of ethics. You never quite knew what that code was and you definitely never knew exactly where you stood with them. Somehow or other, he'd have to find a way to get rid of them before he left the wilderness. There are some enemies you dare not leave alive! While he considered his problems, his thoughts turned to Mathias, another man he didn't trust. He was supposed to report in at the next camp, but God only knew if he would show up. He was far too unpredictable and extremely dangerous! Trevor wished he could get rid of him right along with Jesse and Tad. Unable to get back to sleep, he quickly dressed and left to rouse Dillon and Pedro so they could get an early start on breakfast. He knew he'd feel calmer once they were back on the trail; he only really felt at home when he was in the saddle.

The sound of the breakfast bell brought Eric out of a fitful dream, leaving him with an uneasy feeling as he slowly sat up and looked around the dimly lit tent. Trying to remember the quickly fading nightmare, he was barely able to recall shadowy images chasing after him in the forest, before the dream evaporated into thin air. Even after he was fully awake, he was left with the strong conviction that it was more than just a dream; he was positive that someone was following them! He decided to keep his feelings to himself until he had some kind of proof. Rubbing his eyes, he looked over at Elaine's sleeping bag and was surprised to find her gone. She was a night person and always had trouble getting up in the morning. She was usually the last one to show up for breakfast. He wondered if it had anything to do with his and Shannon's appearance last night at supper. At the time, Elaine hadn't seemed to notice them, but one never really knew what she was thinking. Feeling a little worried, Eric quickly dressed and stepped from his tent into the faint light of the pre-dawn. There was a biting chill in the air and it seemed much too early for breakfast. Warily looking around, he noticed that Cat and Tony were already seated at the fire with their plates in their laps. There was no sign of Elaine or Larry, but Shannon had just returned from her morning walk and was heading for the breakfast line. Eric ran to catch up with her.

"Shannon, have you seen Elaine yet this morning?"

"No! Why? Is she missing?"

"Not exactly. It's just that she was already gone when I woke up. I'm not used to her getting up before me. Oh, well, she'll probably show up any minute. What about Larry? How's he taking things? He didn't give you any trouble last night, did he?"

"No, he didn't. In fact, I never even heard him come back. He must have stayed out really late. He was still asleep when I left the tent. If he doesn't get up pretty soon, he'll miss breakfast. I wonder why we're eating so early this morning; is it a longer ride to the next camp? What do you think, Eric?"

"I don't know. We'll have to ask Trevor. C'mon; let's grab our food and join Cat and Tony. Maybe they already have some answers."

They sat with their friends around the fire, its warmth a welcome relief from the chill of the morning. Tony gave a knowing smile to the two of them and just shook his head.

"Well, well! I was wondering if you two love-birds would be brave enough to show your faces this

305

morning!"

"Knock it off, Tony! I'm not in the mood for any of your bullshit! Listen; I'm a little worried about Elaine. She was already gone when I woke up and I figured she was just using the great outdoors for a restroom. But, even so, she ought to be back by now. Have you two seen her at all?"

"Nope! She must have gotten up before I did and I was up pretty early. My back was hurtin' me and I couldn't sleep any longer. Hey! If she left that early, then she's been gone for quite a while! How about you, Cat? Did you spot her when you went off for a walk?"

"No, I didn't! This isn't like her to just disappear! I think we'd all better go search for......"

As her voice trailed off, they all turned to look in the direction in which she was staring and were quite relieved to see Elaine emerge from a thick growth of trees across a small clearing. Amazed, they all watched as she walked with a buoyant step and a glowing expression. She looked positively radiant! As she approached them, they just stared at her, amazed at the difference in her demeanor. She gave them all a cheerful smile and nodded to them.

"Hello, everyone! Isn't it an especially beautiful morning? I just love getting up before the sun! Everything smells so good then!"

As she walked away to get her food, Eric was astonished.

"I can't believe this! She's always hated the mornings! What in the world's gotten into her?"

Shannon and Cat stared at each other, both of them with identical thoughts. All in that instant, they knew exactly what was different about Elaine! With the same idea, they both turned as one and looked in the direction from which Elaine had come. They watched for a few minutes, but saw nothing. Then, just as they

306

were about to give up, they caught sight of Jesse coming out of a different group of trees and crossing the clearing from a slightly different angle. Oh, yes! They knew exactly what had gotten into Elaine!

Tony and Eric had continued talking and weren't paying any attention to the girls, when Tony suddenly realized that neither one had said a word. He looked at both of them quizzically.

"What's with you two? Why so quiet, huh?"

Cat flashed Shannon a warning look.

"Nothing! We're just enjoying our breakfast; that's all. Scoot over my way, Tony and make room for Elaine. She's coming back now. And don't bother her with a bunch of questions, either! She looks happier right now than she has in a long time. Let's just let her relax and enjoy herself, okay?"

"Jesus! What did you think I was gonna do? Interrogate her? For Christ's sake! Can't you give me a little credit for manners?"

"All right! I'm sorry! Now hush or she'll hear you!"

Cat needn't have worried. Their conversation was no more than a buzz in her ears. She took a seat slightly removed from them and dreamily contemplated her delightful, morning tryst with Jesse. She was so lost in thought that she never even noticed them all watching her. When they were all finished eating, Trevor joined the group to explain a few things about the morning's ride.

"Good morning, everyone! Sorry about getting you all up so early, but today's ride will be a little longer than usual, probably another two hours or so. We're heading for a place close to Fern Point, which is sort of a landmark. There used to be an old, suspended, cable bridge at that point. It's too bad it's gone now; it was quite a sight! Well, anyway, our next camp is close to

307

that area and I think you're really going to enjoy yourselves! There's a beautiful pond not too far from camp; it's located where two forks of the Eel river come together and it's great for swimming! I don't know if we'll make it in time for you to swim today but, if not, you can go sometime tomorrow. It's the major camp on this trip, so we'll stay there for a couple of days and give you plenty of time for fun. By the way, the fishing's great if you go upstream for a ways. As you can see, there'll be plenty for you to do, so let's get going. The sooner we leave, the sooner we'll get there! I'll meet you all at the corral in about fifteen minutes."

The group all returned to their individual tents to finish their last bit of packing. Shannon warily stepped inside hers and was surprised to find Larry all packed and just sitting on his sleeping bag. He looked at her with an unnerving intensity and didn't utter so much as a word.

"I see you're all ready to go, Larry, but you missed breakfast! I brought you some extra biscuits to eat along the way. It'll be a while before we stop to eat again and I was afraid you'd be starved. Here, put these in your pocket."

She held them out to him and he took them without a word, giving her another long, unfathomable look. Then he picked up his things and left the tent. Shakily, Shannon sat down on her sleeping bag for a minute while silent tears filled her eyes. Dear God! Why did life always have to be so difficult?

Waiting at the corral, Trevor stood with Pedro and Dillon. He was giving them some last-minute instructions when they all noticed Larry approaching, his eyes filled with a dark, silent rage. He stalked past them without speaking, went straight to his horse and began to saddle him. His mount was a fifteen-hand, black quarter-horse named Dandy. His disposition was

308

usually calm, but, on this particular occasion, he seemed to sense Larry's anger and shied away from him at the last moment, causing him to drop the saddle. It was the last straw! Something just snapped in Larry and he lunged at Dandy, spewing curses while he viciously kicked him! The frightened horse reared and tossed his head, almost snapping the reins that were snugly looped around the top rail of the corral. Enraged, Larry continued his attack on Dandy in spite of the danger from the animal's deadly hooves! Horrified, Trevor and Dillon ran to grab Larry and managed to drag him away before he could be completely trampled! While he struggled to get away from them, Pedro ran over and sat on him. Even with the other two holding him, it took all three of them to make him lie still. Trevor's shock gave way to anger as he glared at Larry.

"You stupid idiot! Are you insane? Another minute of fightin' with that horse and you woulda been buzzard bait! Don't you have any brains at all? That horse was tied to the fence! And a trapped animal always fights back! This might come as a surprise to you, but one that size usually wins! So the next time you're pissed off 'cause your wife hops in the sack with another guy, try fightin' the man she's screwin' with instead of your horse! You'll have a lot better shot at stayin' alive! Got it?"

"Yeah! I've got it! Now let me up!"

The three men looked at one another, wondering if they should release him.

"I'm all right now! I was just blowin' off some steam. It won't happen again. I mean it! C'mon; let me go!"

Trevor gave him a long look and then nodded to his men. As they stepped back from him, he slowly sat up and rubbed his wrists where they had gripped him. By this time, the entire crowd had gathered and Larry could feel them watching him. Refusing to acknowledge any of them, he gathered himself up with all the dignity he could muster and returned to his horse, speaking calmly while he saddled him. With a wary look in his eyes, the intelligent quarter-horse realized the danger was over and submitted to his rider's authority. While Larry cinched up the saddle, the crowd slowly dispersed and headed toward their own horses. Eric quickly saddled Star and walked him over by Sundancer. He was in a hurry to help Shannon with her horse; he intended to keep her well away from Larry. He kept remembering the look on his face when he lay struggling on the ground; he looked like someone who had gone completely over the edge! Whatever happened, Eric was determined that Shannon would not be harmed! Looking around, he noticed that Larry had already left the corral, pointedly removing himself from the others until they were ready to ride. Good! That's just where he wanted to see him, from a distance! Keeping one eye on Larry, he quickly began to saddle Sundancer, finishing just as Shannon walked up to him. Her eyes were just a little too bright; he knew in an instant that she had been crying.

"That Goddamned, good-for-nothing bastard! That does it! I'm gonna kill the son of a bitch!"

As he turned to walk away, Shannon quickly grabbed his arm and spoke to him in a hushed tone.

"No! Eric, stop it! He didn't do anything! Just leave him alone! He's not crazy enough to do anything to me!"

"Oh, yeah? So he's not crazy, huh? Where were you when he attacked his horse and had to be held down by three guys? You missed all the action! I'm tellin' you; the guy's nuts! I don't want you anywhere around him! Understand?"

Shannon's face visibly paled. She remembered

the strange look on Larry's face just before he left the tent and realized that Eric was right. She would avoid Larry; in fact, she would no longer sleep in the same tent with him. Tonight, after the others were asleep, she and Eric would sneak away and sleep together in the forest! She knew she would be safe with him. And Elaine probably wouldn't even notice that he was missing. Larry wasn't the only one who'd gone around the bend. Flashing Eric a grateful smile, she reached up to whisper in his ear.

"All right, you win! I'll stay away from him, okay? Tonight, I'll stay with you, if you can find us someplace safe in the forest, away from all the others. Of course, that's after I've had some time to myself. I still need to be alone for a while after we reach the next camp. I hope you understand."

Overjoyed by the prospect of being alone with her, Eric looked at her longingly and nodded.

"Sure, honey, I understand. And I'll keep an eye on Larry while you're gone. I'll make sure he doesn't bother you. Just you hurry back to me safe and sound. I can't wait until tonight!"

Giving her arm a gentle squeeze, he helped her to mount Sundancer, holding her hand just a little longer than necessary. They were unnoticed by everyone except Trevor, who was unable to get Shannon out of his mind and found himself always checking on her whereabouts. He kept picturing her as she'd appeared last night, her glorious hair in wild disarray and her open blouse revealing almost everything. With a green fire burning in her eyes, she looked like some wild creature of the forest. Christ! What he wouldn't give to possess her for at least one night! Maybe, just maybe, if he played his cards right, he'd find some way to get her off alone at the next camp. That's all he needed, just some time alone with her. His natural charm would do the rest. He'd never met a woman who could resist him when he was at his most charming! His thoughts drifted back to a pretty, young, Mexican woman he'd met at a dance some years back......

He was sitting at a table, drinking with two of his men, Quinn and Gus, when he first noticed her on the dance floor. She was the prettiest girl there, with long, wavy, black hair and the darkest eyes he'd ever seen. She was doing the mambo with a dark-haired, young man and her slender hips swayed provocatively to the beat of the music. After a few more drinks, he found his heart beating to the same tempo! Every time she got up to dance, he stared at her relentlessly until, finally, she could feel his eyes upon her and she returned his stare with the same intensity. Knowing he'd just made another conquest, he swaggered onto the dance floor, rudely stepped right in front of her partner and began to dance with her in a most suggestive manner. The young man took immediate offense and grabbed him by the shoulder, in an attempt to spin him around. It was a very bad mistake! Before he could even complete his move, he found himself being picked up and hauled away by Gus, the larger and more dangerous of Trevor's two men. Being surly by nature, Gus always welcomed a fight and was severely disappointed when his victim only ran away after being thrown out on the street. When he returned to their table, Gus found Trevor fondling the girl while she sat on his lap.

"Hey, Boss! You won't have to worry none about her chicken-shit boyfriend! He just ran for cover after I threw his ass out!"

The girl started giggling; she'd had a few too many drinks.

"You silly gringos! That wasn't my boyfriend. That was my husband, Tobias!"

There was only a moment of shocked silence

before they all started laughing, louder and louder! Suddenly, they noticed everyone else staring at them. Trevor abruptly stood up, the girl all but falling off his lap.

"C'mon, guys! I don't think we're wanted here! Besides, it's time to party and we're gonna need a motel room for that! What's your name, sweetheart?"

"Juanita. What's yours?"

"You don't need to know that, darlin'! Just tell me where I can find the closest motel and I'll teach you all you need to know!"

He gave her a quick swat on the ass, causing her to jump and start giggling again.

"There's one about two blocks from here. I know the place very well."

"I'll just bet you do, honey! Okay, boys! You heard the little lady; let's get movin'!"

As soon as they entered the motel room, Trevor started tearing her clothes off. With a shocked look, she tried to push him away.

"No! Wait a minute! Not in front of them! It's supposed to be just you and me! Por favor, send them away!"

Trevor just laughed and motioned to Gus to hold her still while he continued to undress her.

"Now darlin', you don't understand. These boys are my partners. We share and share alike! Just you cooperate, sweetheart, and we might even give you a little bonus when we're finished with you. Okay, boys! You know the rules. I'm the boss, so that makes me first. You two will just have to toss for second place!"

She struggled to no avail while he continued to remove her clothing. As he began to pull off her panty-hose, she kicked violently at him, momentarily knocking him backward. In a rage, he lunged at her and slapped her hard across the face! With tears streaming

313

down her face, she knew better than to scream and silently submitted to their demands. With a triumphant look, Trevor savagely mounted her, causing her to cry out in pain as he pumped himself into her, going deeper with each stroke. Gus was laughing while he held her hands.

"That's the way, Boss! Give it to her! Women don't enjoy it none without feelin' some pain!"

"Jesus! I'm about to come! If you don't want to get hurt, girl, you better wrap your legs around me and hold me in tight while I fill your pussy! Comprende?"

She nodded and wrapped her legs tightly around him while he planted his seed deep within her. He stayed inside her just a little longer while he sucked on both her breasts. Almost drooling, Quinn stared at them hungrily. Gus was visibly sweating and getting more impatient by the moment.

"Lordy! Ain't you done, yet? C'mon, Boss! I'm about to cream my pants!"

"Goddamn it! How can a man enjoy a good fuck with you hurryin' him up all the time?"

"Sorry, Boss! It's just that I ain't gonna last much longer!"

Finally, Trevor pulled his cock out of her and grinned at Gus.

"All right, big guy! She's all yours!"

With sweat literally dripping off him, Gus tore his own clothes off, revealing a huge, throbbing penis. Juanita took one look at it and passed out cold!

......Smiling to himself, Trevor could still remember her petite body and the feel of her breasts in his hands, even after all these years. Oh, yes! With his charm, he could have any woman he wanted! And Shannon was the one he wanted now. All he needed was a little time alone with her. He was brought out of his reverie by Dillon, tapping him on his shoulder.

"Boss! Didn't you hear me? Everyone's ready to go! I even saddled Raja for you."

Trevor quickly mounted his horse and faced the crowd.

"All right, folks! You already know the rules; if anyone has to stop for any reason, just don't go far from the trail and catch up with us as fast as you can. We have a long way to go, so let's get a move on!"

With those words, he took the lead, followed closely by Dillon, and set a fairly quick pace. It was a rather somber group that followed behind him, Larry's terrible scene still weighing heavily on their minds. Tony and Cat rode close together, speaking in hushed tones.

"Tony, I'm worried about Shannon! Larry looks downright unbalanced. There's no telling what he might do to her! I don't think she should sleep in the same tent with him anymore."

"You're right, babe! Maybe we better have her sleep with us tonight. And I don't want you anywhere close to him, either. He's obviously gone psycho on us and we'd all better be damned careful around him! This trip sure hasn't turned out like I expected. I'm beginnin' to think I'll be glad when it's over!"

"Yeah, me too. I just hope we all come out of this without any bloodshed!"

"Well, we can at least be grateful for one thing; he doesn't have any weapons. Besides, did you see how quick Trevor and his men jumped him? I wouldn't worry too much about any bloodshed, but, just to be on the safe side, I still don't want you to get too close to him."

Cat laughed nervously.

"Believe me; that's the last thing you have to worry about!"

Eric and Shannon were riding directly behind Cat

315

and Tony. They couldn't hear every word of their conversation, but they heard enough to get the general idea. They just looked at one another and nodded, both sharing the same thoughts. They knew how concerned their friends were. Eric was very relieved that he was the only one with a weapon. He'd make certain it was right by his side while they were sleeping tonight.

Elaine was riding further back in line, just in front of Jesse. She was also very anxious for this trip to end, but only so that she and Jesse could get away by themselves and be together forever. As far as Larry was concerned, she was quite unaware of any tension regarding him. Her thoughts were centered only on Jesse and herself; the others barely even existed in her mind. All she could think of was Jesse and once more being held by him. He was almost too good to be real! Every now and then, Elaine felt a sudden, sharp need for reassurance that he wasn't merely a figment of her imagination. Looking back at him, she would then flash him a relieved smile. The day stretched endlessly in front of her; she could hardly wait for nightfall. Looking around, she was once again overwhelmed by the beauty surrounding her. They were riding across a small meadow just as the morning chill began to dissipate. The lush grasses sparkled as bits of dew caught the sun's rays. And the smells! Elaine delighted in taking deep breaths of the delicious odors. As she sighed contentedly, the trail took them through a dense section of the forest, winding its way around tall pines, Douglas firs and majestic, old oaks. From the sound of the birdsong, it seemed to Elaine that the trees were filled with a thousand birds, all of them harmoniously singing a haunting melody. It was as though Mother Nature were putting on her very best show just for Elaine and Jesse. She looked back once more, giving him another adoring smile. With a silent chuckle, Jesse smiled back at her.   He knew exactly what she was thinking. That woman would be the death of him yet! He'd never seen such an affectionate, love-starved woman!   But, dear Lord, what a way to go!   He could hardly wait for nightfall. Feeling eyes upon him, he quickly glanced back and caught Larry staring at him with a strange expression.   Caught in the act, Larry abruptly looked away, feigning interest in the view.   With a dark look, Jesse continued to watch him for a while before turning back around. He knew that one would bear watching. He really didn't care what he did to the others, so long as he didn't come close to his beloved Elaine. God pity him if he ever did, because Jesse sure as Hell wouldn't!

Trying to appear nonchalant, Larry still seethed with an inner rage, which only intensified when Jesse scowled at him. If he'd had any idea why Larry had been staring at him, he would have been even angrier! It was Jesse's huge Bowie knife!   Larry needed a weapon and the knife would do just fine.   If only he could manage to get it away from him......there must be a way! After all, Jesse had to sleep sometime. While he was pondering his problem, he couldn't help but notice the way Jesse and Elaine looked at each other. He could hardly believe that Jesse was actually interested in her.   Good Lord!   Didn't he realize the woman was a basket case?   Oh well, there's just no accounting for some people's taste!

As they quietly rode along, the gentle coolness of the morning slowly gave way to a fierce, summer heat. Without a doubt, it was the hottest day they had yet encountered. Even before noon, they found the blazing heat almost unbearable. Already irritable, the horses soon became even more so as they found themselves being harassed by clusters of gnats and occasional blow-flies. The relentless insects got in their eyes and crawled into their ears, causing them to violently shake their heads and flatten their ears in anger. Even the riders were pestered by the gnats and they were constantly brushing them away from their eyes, while beads of sweat formed little rivulets through the dust on their faces, further adding to their misery. Suddenly, the trail led them up a steep incline and they gradually left the dense forest behind as they began to climb Shale Mountain, heading for a dry, rocky ridge, high above them. Zigzagging back and forth, the riders were all leaning over their saddle horns as the horses used the strength of their massive muscles to push themselves all the way to the top. Finally, the riders and their mounts, all dripping with sweat and covered with dust, found themselves on a high, wind-swept plateau. By some unspoken understanding, they all stopped for a while and rested the horses and themselves as they stood in a whistling, welcome wind. While the swift breeze cooled their overheated bodies, they all stood in awe of the panorama spread before them. They saw deep, mysterious canyons far below and row after row of majestic mountains that seemed to shimmer in the sizzling, summer heat. Trevor had made this trip many times, but was just as awe-struck as the newcomers. He always felt a pang in his heart when he stood on this particular plateau; he somehow felt that it belonged just to him. He had never felt close to a human being; the wilderness was his one, true commitment. He loved the land almost as much as the Indians did, but with a slightly different point of view. He had never considered it wrong to use the land for growing marijuana; after all, it wasn't as though they were burning down the forest or actually harming the land. In his mind, it was just business and it pleased him that he was able to conduct his business in such beautiful surroundings. As for the effect the crops would eventually have on the people who used them, he felt absolutely no remorse. He had no feelings for people in general and really didn't give a damn what happened to them. As far as he was concerned, let the buyer beware! So what if lots of them were only school kids? The Hell with them all! As he looked around, he noticed Shannon standing close to the edge, with her beautiful, red hair blowing wild in the wind. He was as impressed by her exotic beauty as he was by the wilderness. With her mesmerizing, green eyes, she looked for all the world like some goddess descended from the heavens. He had never desired a woman as he desired her! Maybe, at the next camp......there had to be some way to get her alone. Frustrated, he turned to the others with a scowl on his face.

"All right, that's enough dawdling! Everyone mount up; we're movin' on!"

Without even waiting for the others, Trevor mounted Raja and took off without so much as a backward glance. Startled, the others quickly followed suit and soon they were all riding along the ridge at a brisk pace. With the wind blowing in their faces, the riders were no longer bothered by any flying insects and were beginning to really enjoy the trip. Even the horses seemed rejuvenated and were more than willing to pick up the pace when Trevor quirted his horse into a lope. Eric found the ride exhilarating as the wind whipped through his hair and wailed its own haunting melody. The trail was wide along the ridge and he was able to ride abreast of Shannon. Watching her ride gave him infinite pleasure as he thought of the night to come. He could hardly wait for nightfall!

Upon approaching the end of the ridge, they slowed to a walk and began the steep descent down the side of the mountain. The trail led them on a zigzag course through rocky terrain. The going was slow and tedious as the horses took cautious steps in the slippery shale, sliding every few feet, then scrambling to regain their footing. The wary riders leaned far back in their saddles, braced against the possibility of their horses sliding out of control. When they were almost two thirds of the way down the mountain, the trail veered to the right and rounded a point, suddenly leveling off and leading them into a whole different world. All at once, the ground had changed from dry shale to a rich, moist soil and they were happily surprised to find themselves riding through a jungle of fragrant, yellow flowers. They grew on tall bushes that were so tightly interwoven, they formed an impenetrable wall. As the riders followed the damp trail through the shoulder-high flowers, their senses were assailed by a heady, sweet aroma, so strong that it was positively breath-taking! Without a word, the entire group came to a stop and admired the bright beauty of the flowers. Looking upward, they noticed the heavy growth actually began about two thirds of the way up, but only on this side of the mountain. Evidently there was a spring which started at that high point, supplying water for the lovely flowers which grew all the way down like a pyramid. While they took deep breaths of the delicious fragrance, they slowly became aware of a steady, vibrating hum. With a shock, they realized they were surrounded by thousands of wild, mountain honey-bees! As they nervously continued on their way, they were extremely relieved to find themselves totally ignored by the bees, whose only interest was the bountiful nectar. Still a little concerned about the proximity of the bees, the riders were unwilling to break the silence and rode quietly along, the only sounds being the constant droning and the clopping of the horses' hooves as they splashed through an occasional puddle of water. Finally, after what seemed like an eternity, the trail rose slightly and then dropped over the edge of the outer rim, taking them out of the jungle of flowers and down into a dense forest. Free at last from any worry over the bees, Elaine let out an audible sigh of relief, echoing the sentiment of the entire group. She had been stung by bees many times as a child and had developed almost a phobia of them, but she soon found her extreme tension disappearing right along with the awful, droning sound. As they entered the deep forest, she turned around and was comforted by the loving expression in Jesse's eyes. She felt safe and happy again and anxiously awaited their arrival at the next camp.

Riding at a slower pace, the trail led them through a dense thicket of cedars; the air was rich with their distinctive, intoxicating odor. Without even realizing it, the entire group had slowed almost to a walk, delighting in the beauty of the tall trees. Annoyed by their inability to keep up, Trevor looked back and suddenly realized how dirty and tired the riders appeared. Although he was loath to stop, he knew he'd have to give them a real rest or they wouldn't be able to continue. He came to a complete halt and spoke to them briefly.

"Listen up, everyone! We've been riding for several hours and I know how tired you all are, but if you can hang in there for about ten more minutes, we'll be at a wide section of the Eel river and you can all go swimming. In fact, we'll stay long enough for you to eat a bite of lunch and have a real break. How does that sound?"

Except for Larry, they all cheered and whistled! Dillon grinned at Trevor and they both just shook their heads. Smugly riding along at a faster gait, Trevor thought to himself how simple it was to manipulate others. As tired as they were, he had been able to hurry them along with only a few, choice words. All his life, it had been almost too easy for him; people were just putty in his hands. He sensed that Shannon was somewhat more of a challenge. He had yet to find the magic words to work on her, but find them he would! Lost in thought, he was soon brought back to reality by the shouts of the riders as they spotted the river in the distance, at the end of a long, lush meadow. As they started to mill around, both horses and riders appeared antsy. In fact, they acted like they were going to break loose any second and make a run for it. Trevor tried to yell at them over all the noise.

"Calm down, everyone! Just take it easy! I know you're all anxious, but I have something important to tell you! Stay in line and don't get off the trail, because, if you do......"

It was too late! They hadn't really been paying attention to him in the first place and his last words were completely drowned out by the excited neighing of the horses and the loud voices of the people talking to each other. It was one of those things that just had to happen! Challenges were being tossed in the air, not so much verbally as by the looks in the eyes of the riders and the attitudes of the horses! Eric could feel Star tensing up beneath him; the powerful quarter-horse was dying to run! Jesse's horse, Buckaroo, was feeling the same desperate need for an all-out gallop! Shannon saw the looks flashing between the two men and decided to beat them both to the punch! Equally anxious to break loose, Sundancer seemed to sense what Shannon was up to and responded to her subtle leg pressure by blasting off from behind the two men and tearing past them like a streak of lightning! Startled, Jesse and Eric stared at each other for just a fraction of a second and then tore out after her! Even Larry was affected by the mood of the others and, determined not to be out-done, spurred Dandy into his fastest run, his powerful hooves tearing up the ground! As the others streaked by him, Raja almost went crazy with desperation! Instead of fighting him, Trevor decided to throw caution to the wind and turned him loose! Halfway across the meadow, he was closing on the others with a furious need to win! Star and Raja reached the water in a dead heat, with the other three horses right behind them! Laughing, they all turned around to see if the others had caught up, only to find themselves witnessing the strangest scene. The other horses all appeared to be trying to buck off their riders! Trevor just shook his head; he was the only one who knew what had happened. There were hornets' nests on the ground not too far from the trail and one of the racing horses must have stepped on one, stirring the occupants into a stinging frenzy! By the time the hornets had come out, bent on revenge, the racers had already gone by and the slower horses were just coming into range. The hapless horses were attacked en masse by the furious, stinging horde! The riders themselves had the good fortune not to be stung and had no idea what was causing their horses to buck. Caught off guard, Tony had his right foot out of the stirrup and was leaning dangerously to the left side! Screaming at his horse, he kept trying to regain his footing while Jack spun around in little circles, bucking all the time!

"Cut it out, you stupid horse! Whoa! I said whoa! Goddamn it!"

Finally, Tony flew off the horse and rolled over and over in the lush grasses! Still bucking, Jack headed straight for the water and immediately rolled in it, saddle and all! Concerned about Elaine, Jesse galloped back to her and pulled her off of Lazy-Daze, who suddenly didn't appear lazy at all! As soon as she was free of Elaine, she also headed for the river and rolled in the water. Too frightened to speak, Elaine just held onto Jesse with all her strength and shook uncontrollably!

The rest of the riders jumped off of their horses as soon as they could and watched them all head for the water. Trevor was still sitting on Raja, laughing so hard he could barely speak!

"I tried to warn all of you, but......you wouldn't listen! I hate to say it, but......you all brought it on yourselves! Next time, you'd all......better listen to me!"

His laughter was contagious; pretty soon, they were all laughing hysterically, even Elaine! As everyone gradually returned to normal, they all took care of their horses, changed into their swimsuits and rushed into the cool, inviting waters of the sparkling river. Laughing and splashing one another, they looked more like one large, happy family than a mixed up group of dangerous drug-dealers and naive flat-landers! Watching them all together at that moment, one would never have been able to predict what would happen to them in the very near future!

After a nice, refreshing swim, they sat around talking while they waited for their gear to dry out. Trevor's men brought everyone some energy bars to snack on while they rested. Stretched out on the thick grass, they all looked extremely comfortable. Some of them even appeared in danger of dozing off, especially Tony as he lay with his head on Cat's lap, his eyes peacefully closed and the most blissful expression on his face. Shannon sat close to them and was weaving some long blades of grass into an intricate pattern while Cat looked on in fascination.

"That looks really neat! How did you learn to do that?"

As soon as Cat spoke, a few others looked over to see what Shannon was doing. A little embarrassed by all the attention, she quickly made light of the subject and handed the grass weave to Cat.

"It's nothing! I was just playing around. Here!

You can have it."

With a bemused expression, Trevor had been watching all of them, especially Shannon. He found it interesting that she didn't enjoy being the center of attention. He thought perhaps the knowledge would come in handy. He considered it important to know as much as possible about her. Sensing that he was studying her, she quickly looked up and their eyes met for a brief second, just long enough for her to feel uncomfortable. With a flash of irritation, she looked away and tried to ignore him. He always made her feel uneasy; it was almost as though he knew more about her than he should. There were times when she would have sworn that he could read her most private thoughts. She didn't like it one bit and was tempted to complain about him to Eric, but she knew he'd lose his temper and do something foolish! The last thing she wanted was another scene! She'd just have to handle things by herself. Besides, as much as Trevor annoyed her, he couldn't do her any real harm by staring, so she decided just to forget about him for the time being. Knowing she wouldn't look his way again, Trevor decided it was time to leave.

"Well, folks, I think we've all had enough rest. We still have quite a ways to go, so we'd better get moving. As it is, there'll only be about two hours of daylight left after we make camp. C'mon, everyone! Let's hustle!"

With some audible groans, everyone reluctantly got up and went to saddle their horses. Jesse quickly saddled Buckaroo and then hurried to take care of Daisy for Elaine. While he helped her into the saddle, he squeezed her hand and spoke to her in a low voice.

"We're gonna be ridin' at the back at of the line and I want you to keep an eye open for my signal. After we been on the trail for an hour or so, we're gonna slip away from the others for a while. I need to talk to you 'bout somethin' real important. Okay?"

Puzzled, Elaine nodded, wondering what on Earth could be so important. His serious expression worried her; she hoped it wouldn't be bad news. Seeing her concern, he quickly looked around and then gave her a comforting pat on the leg, before mounting his own horse.

"By the way, you did just great when old Lazy-Daze was buckin' away! I'm right proud of you!"

Glowing with pride, she gave him one of her dazzling smiles and then they both turned to join the line of riders. Moving out slowly, they all took one last look at the beautiful river, already wishing they were back in the cool, clear water. No-one spoke as the trail gradually took them away from the meadow and led them into an unusually dense section of the forest. It took a few moments for their eyes to adjust to the sudden darkness. It was a dramatic change from the glaring sunlight they had just left! It seemed unnaturally quiet; there was absolutely no birdsong, in fact, no noise at all, other than the horses' hooves crunching through thick layers of pine needles. They all found themselves looking around warily; there was just something eerie about this part of the trail! Even the horses appeared subdued as they nervously looked around with their ears pricked forward to catch the slightest sound. Positive that someone or something was watching him, Eric peered carefully into the branches just above him and off to his left. Then he saw it! He was barely able to discern the face of a large mountain lion as it stared down at him with menacing, yellow eyes, its mouth curled in a silent snarl. Slowing his horse almost to a standstill, Eric turned around, signaled Shannon to keep quiet and pointed up at the tree. For just a moment, she was confused; she didn't understand what he was trying to show her.   So perfectly camouflaged was the mountain lion that only with the closest scrutiny could one distinguish him from the tree.   All of a sudden, Shannon realized she was staring into the eyes of a terrifyingly huge mountain lion and tried unsuccessfully to stifle a shriek! The horses hadn't yet picked up the animal's scent, but they had sensed that something was wrong and Shannon's strangled yell sent them all into a frenzy! The herd instinct ran strong in the fear-crazed horses and they all bolted at once, pushing themselves down the narrow trail and ramming into the lead horses! With a hard jerk on the reins, Trevor tried desperately to control Raja, but was unable to restrain him as the nervous Arab took the bit in his mouth and flew down the dark trail and out into open country! Finally free from the confining, scary part of the trail, the horses began to calm down and their riders were able to bring them to a halt.   Stopping long enough to catch their breath, horses and riders alike were still feeling more than a little shaky. Simultaneously puzzled and irritated, Trevor approached the group.

"What in the Hell happened back there? Why did the horses suddenly go crazy?"

Looking a little guilty, Eric stepped forward.

"Actually, it was my fault! I saw a mountain lion in a tree and pointed him out to Shannon without......"

His last words were drowned out by Shannon.

"No, it was all my fault! When I saw the mountain lion, I just couldn't help screaming! I'm sorry for causing such a stampede, but he was so big and so close and he was staring right at me!"

An involuntary shudder went down her spine as she remembered the evil gleam in his yellow eyes. Surprised, Trevor just stared at her for a moment. He had come to think of her as a brave, young woman. Seeing her so fear-stricken came as quite a revelation to him! So she did have her secret fears after all! For just a fraction of a second, he actually felt a twinge of compassion for her, but the feeling was quickly replaced by the thought of using her fear to his advantage.

"Don't worry about it, Shannon! It could happen to anyone. I'll let you in on a little secret; if a mountain lion caught me off guard, I'd probably scream too!"

Surprised by his kind words and relieved that he wasn't angry with her, she flashed him a grateful smile. Returning her smile, Trevor nodded to her and then spoke to all of them.

"Well, folks, I guess it's time to move along. One thing's for sure; we've all had our share of thrills and chills for the day! I can't even imagine anything very exciting happening after that! But at least something good came out of it; the rest of the trip's going to seem a quite a bit shorter now. The way I figure it, with that all-out run, we were makin' great time without even planning on it!"

With those words, Trevor turned and took his place in the lead. There were a few scattered laughs among the crowd as they fell in behind him. Before long, they found themselves climbing again, heading up a steep ridge into a dry, brushy area. As they rode along, silhouetted against the skyline, it never once occurred to them that they were being watched. They were in such a remote area that it was hard to imagine anyone else being close enough to see them. Of course, they had no way of knowing that three brave warriors, relentless in their pursuit, had ridden hard since the break of day and were even now closing on them. In fact, Jacob, Two Eagles and Running Deer had come even closer than they had intended. As he watched the line of riders drop off the end of the ridge and disappear into the trees, Jacob decided it would be wise to hold back for a while and take a small break.

After all, he didn't want to get too close to them this soon. He turned and looked at his two friends and they both nodded to him, fully understanding his mute decision. Without a word, they all dismounted where they stood and looked for something to lean against while they rested.

Completely unaware that they were being followed, the group had left the hot, dry ridge and entered a lovely stand of pines and oaks. Slowing their pace a little, the riders welcomed the cooling shade of the tall trees. Jesse had stayed at the back of the line with Elaine and decided this would be a good time to slip away from the others. After carefully looking around, he signaled her to hang back with him. Riding slowly, they watched the others drifting further and further ahead until, finally, they dropped completely out of sight. After waiting for just a moment, Jesse motioned Elaine to follow him and they rode down a small incline into a dense thicket which he had spotted from the trail. Well hidden and safely out of earshot, he helped her dismount and held her tenderly for a while. Then he gently lifted her face and looked into her eyes.

"Elaine, I got just two questions I need to ask you. Do you for sure an' certain wanna stay with me for all time and do you completely trust me?"

"Oh, yes! Of course I do!"

"That's just what I was hopin' you'd say. Now you listen to me real good, sweetheart, 'cause this is very important! I got a plan for us to git away from the others when the time is right. The only thing is; I don't know for sure when that'll be! We'll just have to play it by ear. I want you to stay where you can see me at all times and watch real close for my signal. When I let you know it's time to go, then you better be ready to hightail it outa camp with me that very second! You got it? There won't be no goin' back in your tent to git somethin'; you just come a runnin' for me lickety-split! You can't go tellin' nobody 'bout this, neither, 'cause they'll sure as shootin' try to stop us! Do you understand all this, Elaine?"

She had never seen him so serious! It made her a little nervous; she felt like there was something he wasn't telling her.

"Yes, I understand! And I'll come running to you whenever you call me! But why are you telling me all this right now? We'll be together tonight; why didn't you just wait and tell me then? Unless......it's supposed to happen tonight......that's it; isn't it?"

"Elaine, it might be tonight or it might be a different night! All I know for certain is that it's gonna be soon. You'll just have to trust me, honey. I'll know when the time is right; you just be ready to run the second I give you the signal, okay?"

Looking up at him with trusting eyes, she just nodded and lay her head on his shoulder. Dear God, she loved him so much! She would follow him anywhere!

Jesse held her for just a moment longer, then tilted her face up and gave her a long, tender kiss. Before releasing her, he kept her at arm's length for a few seconds, staring hard at her lovely, innocent face as though to memorize it for all time. Jesus! How he loved this woman! He would do whatever necessary to keep her and God pity anyone who tried to stop him! Finally, he helped her back on her horse and quickly mounted his own.

"Let's go, honey! We better git back as quick as we can! I sure hope nobody noticed we was gone!"

Loping most of the way, they made good time and caught up with the others in only a short while. As they fell in at the back of the line, Jesse was relieved to find they had been missed by no-one. In fact, the weary

330

riders were thinking of nothing except making it to the next camp and getting some rest. Tony was especially impatient and had been loudly complaining.

"Criminy! Aren't we supposed to be there by now? I thought he said we'd have a good two hours of daylight left after we made camp! Just look at that sun, Cat! The way I see it, we've only got about two hours of light left right now! So why in the Hell aren't we there yet, huh?"

"Tony! Will you please shut up? I don't know why we're not there yet! Why don't you go ask Trevor and quit nagging me?"

"You know what? You really piss me off! Every time I ask you a simple question, you try to make a fight out of it!"

"Oh, yeah? Well, here's a news flash for you! You're not asking questions; you're just nagging! You've been bitching and complaining for the last twenty minutes and I'm sick and tired of listening to you! So why don't you just shut up?"

Annoyed, Tony just glared at her, determined not to speak to her until she apologized. He wasn't the only one in a bad mood; most of the others were also tired and crabby. They simply weren't quite as vociferous about it.

After another ten minutes of riding, the trail led them up a small hill where Trevor stopped for a moment and signaled for the group's attention.

"There it is, folks, right down there in the middle of those Cedars. You're really going to love this camp; it's everyone's favorite!"

Standing on the hilltop looking down on the lovely campsite, the entire group quickly forgot the various discomforts of the long ride. Gone was the memory of the blazing heat, replaced instead by a happier recollection of swimming and splashing in the cool, refreshing waters of the beautiful Eel river. The memory of the scary stampede away from the mountain lion was somehow changed into a thrilling, adventurous ride through a primitive, lush forest. As with almost all experiences in life, memories are imperceptibly altered to accommodate the needs of the person, which explains why very few people ever remember things in exactly the same way. As Trevor led the suddenly rejuvenated group down the hill into the camp, they were all filled with high expectations of wonderful times. Even Tony was cheerful and completely forgot that he wasn't speaking to his wife.

"Cat! Just look at this camp! Is this beautiful country or what? Aren't you glad I talked you into coming on this trip?"

With a bemused expression, Cat smiled at him.

"Yes, honey, I'm very glad. You always have great ideas! Now let's go find our tent, okay? I think I'll just stretch out and rest until dinner's ready."

Tony looked amazed.

"Really? You're actually gonna just sit around and do nothing on a beautiful day like this? Well......if you really want to rest, maybe I'll get the guys together and we'll go fishing. By the time we get unsaddled and go upstream, it'll be close to dusk and that's the perfect time to land some steelhead! Are you sure you don't mind, babe?"

"Of course not! Go and enjoy yourself! All I want is some peace and quiet so I can rest."

After they'd all seen to their horses, they unloaded their belongings in their tents and then walked around the camp together, finally stopping to talk by the edge of a lovely stream which eventually flowed into the Eel river.

"Well, who wants to go fishing with me? Trevor says the steelhead are just waiting to bite! What do you say, guys?"

Eric was all for it. "Sounds great to me! Let's go!"

Larry looked dubious. Tony was okay, but he really couldn't stand the thought of being around Eric. That smug bastard! Then again, there was always the off chance that they might find themselves going over some steep terrain and maybe, just maybe......with one quick shove, anything could happen! All of a sudden, it didn't sound like such a bad idea, but he didn't want to appear too eager.

"I don't know, Tony. Fish don't really start biting until dusk and that would make us a little late for supper."

"Late for supper! Hell, man, we'll be catching our supper! Didn't you hear Trevor? He said his men will cook up whatever we bring 'em. I guess they like steelhead too! C'mon, guys; it'll be fun! But we better hurry! If we head upstream right now, Trevor says we'll be at the best fishing spots just in time for the big ones!"

Agreeing to go, they rushed back to their tents, picked up their fishing gear and the three of them were soon on their way.

Grateful that Tony was out of her hair for a while, Cat stretched out on her sleeping bag, basking in the peace and quiet. Intending only a short rest, she was sound asleep within minutes. Pretending that she was also going to rest, Shannon stayed in her tent for about ten minutes, then grabbed a towel and headed for the deep swimming pool that Trevor had mentioned. As she left the camp, she looked carefully around to make certain that no-one was watching her. Finally feeling safe, she slipped away through a thick growth of trees, catching the main trail a little further away from camp. Exhilarated to be alone at last in the wilderness, she strode happily along, delighting in the beauty of the forest and the sweet birdsong that filled the air. She was so relieved to be on her own for a while that her spirits weren't even daunted by the sweltering heat that still lay across the land like a scorching blanket. In fact, it would only serve to make her swim all the more refreshing.

Unknown to Shannon, Trevor had caught sight of her only moments before she disappeared into the trees. With the towel in her hand, he knew exactly where she was going. His heart suddenly beating at a faster pace, he tried to stay cool. He knew he might never get another chance like this. Casually looking around, he ascertained that no-one else had noticed her. Wondering how long he should wait before he followed her, he allowed his gaze to linger on Jesse. He was relieved to see that he was momentarily tied up with Elaine, the two of them deeply engrossed in conversation. It was pretty obvious that Jesse was totally bananas over that broad. Good! Let her keep him busy! While he prepared to sneak off after Shannon, Trevor suddenly noticed a familiar, deadly look fill Jesse's eyes. Instant fear forming a knot in his stomach, he cursed himself for staring too hard at him! You just never knew what would set off that maniac! Braced for the worst, he could feel the bile rising in his throat as Jesse abruptly stood, all but dismissing Elaine! While his knees turned to rubber, Trevor suddenly became aware that Jesse was staring at someone approaching from the far side of camp. Wait a minute! That was Mathias riding into camp! Why was Jesse glaring at him? While he watched, he saw Matt stop dead just a few feet away from Jesse and stare at him with a palpable, open hatred! If looks could kill, they'd both be dead! Stepping back a pace without even realizing it, Elaine stared from one to the other and turned white as a sheet! Never had she seen such a cruel-looking face as Matt's! Suddenly realizing that Matt was carrying a rifle, she was terrified for Jesse's life! Amazed and shocked by the hostility between the two men, Trevor quickly grabbed his own rifle from his tent and slowly approached them, determined to avert any bloodshed between the two. This just wasn't the time for it! Later, maybe, but not now. Their eyes never leaving each other's, Jesse's hand was on his large, Bowie knife while Matt kept his finger on the trigger of his rifle! Glancing from one to the other, Trevor nervously walked over to them.

"It's good to see you, Matt. You know what? You're a whole day ahead of schedule. That's great! Come on over to my tent and let's talk."

His eyes remaining on Jesse, Matt answered in a menacing tone.

"Yeah, that's a good idea! I need to get away from this piece of trash anyway!"

Finally dismounting, Matt slowly walked his horse to the corral. He was accompanied by Trevor, who felt extremely uncomfortable and kept glancing over his shoulder from time to time. Matt looked at him and just shook his head.

"Relax, you big chicken-shit! He ain't gonna do nothin' to you! I'm the one he'd like to kill, or couldn't you tell?"

"Yeah, I noticed that! What's with you guys, anyway?"

"None of your fuckin' business, that's what! Listen; I ain't here to pass the time of day with you! I'm gonna grab a bite to eat, sack out for a couple of hours in your tent and then I'm outa here! You just make sure you got them pack-mules ready for me! You got all that?"

"Yeah, I got it! For your information, I already took care of that; the packs are all loaded and ready to go whenever you are! So there's no need for you to get all bent out of shape! As for my tent, just help yourself! It's still so damned hot; I'll probably just sleep outside somewhere."

"Great! Then I won't have to see your ugly mug again 'til I come back with the goods!"

With those words, Matt stepped into the tent while Trevor took a last, long look around camp. Reassuring himself that he had been seen by no-one, he cautiously slipped away through the trees and hurried after Shannon. His heart racing with thoughts of her naked body, he suddenly became aware that he still had his rifle with him. Since he was on foot, he wasn't too happy about carrying the heavy weapon, but maybe it was for the best. In case he ran into any of the others, he could always pretend he was out hunting. Yeah, that would work! Of course, with everyone else doing their own separate thing, he probably wouldn't run into anyone other than Shannon, but still, better safe than sorry. If only Matt hadn't shown up when he did. Talk about bad timing! Oh, well, she was only about fifteen minutes ahead of him. He could just picture her already undressed and standing by the edge of the water, her beautiful red hair sparkling in the last rays of the dwindling sunlight. He couldn't wait to get his hands on her!

As Shannon approached the inviting waters of the crystal-clear pool, she was stunned by the incredible beauty of the setting. The pool was so large that it resembled a small lake and it was surrounded by deep forest on all sides. There was a huge, flat boulder that jutted far out into the water, which would be perfect to use for diving or simply for sunbathing. Realizing that there wasn't much daylight left, she decided to go for a quick swim and then bask in the sun for a while on top of the boulder. Stripping off her clothes, she tossed

336

them aside and stood looking down into the water, wondering how deep it was. The boulder was warm beneath her bare feet; it had been soaking up the sun's rays all day long. Shannon suddenly shivered, thinking how good that warmth would feel after coming out of the cool water. While she stood, trying to build up her nerve to jump in all at once, she was completely unaware that she was being watched from only a short distance away.

Trevor wasn't the only one who had seen her leave. Jacob and his two warriors had arrived at the camp just behind the main group and the three of them had been keeping a close watch on Trevor's activities. As soon as Mathias had shown up, Jacob assigned Two Eagles to keep an eye on him and follow him wherever he might go. He then sent Running Deer to find the rest of the warriors and hurry them back to the camp. That left him free to follow Shannon, which he quickly did, silently stalking her through the forest. He arrived at the pool just as she began to undress. Hidden by some thick foliage along the water's edge, Jacob watched Shannon through obsidian eyes that slowly followed every curve of her shapely form. Her hair glowed with the fire of the sun and her emerald eyes mirrored the forest. He was hypnotized by her flawless beauty and continued to stare as she leaped from the tall boulder and dove into the water, her glorious red mane flowing behind her. She looked for all the world like some magical water nymph; she was entirely too beautiful to be real! Almost without realizing what he was doing, Jacob removed his clothing and very quietly slipped into the water without being seen by Shannon. Immediately diving at a steep angle, his strong body cut through the current like a knife as he headed straight for her. Having heard the splash from his dive, she looked in that direction, but saw nothing. All at once, she felt something brush against her leg and let out a small yell as Jacob surfaced directly in front of her! And then something magical did indeed occur. As though in a trance, they looked deeply into each other's eyes, both of them realizing, all in that instant, that they had found their destiny! Treading water, Jacob reached out and brushed a lock of hair from her shoulder, then pulled her close for a long, slow kiss. Locked in a passionate embrace, they were completely unaware of yet another pair of eyes peering through the heavy foliage at the water's edge.

Sneaking up on Shannon, Trevor had arrived with great stealth and was standing in the exact spot where Jacob had undressed. Puzzled at first, he picked up Jacob's leggings and stared at them. Who would wear such things? And then it dawned on him! Not only was there another man on the scene; that man had to be Jacob! His heart pounding with a jealous rage, he looked toward the water and saw Jacob and Shannon wrapped around each other. Goddamn that bastard! Throwing the leggings aside, he silently crept forward until he reached an old log lying close to the water. Kneeling down, he used the log as a rest for his rifle, took careful aim and slowly pulled back the hammer. While he looked down the sight, waiting for a clear shot, he was suddenly overwhelmed by a tingling sense of premonition as a foreboding chill crept down his spine. With the strongest feeling of imminent danger, Trevor looked up just in time to see a heavy evening mist forming above him. There was something eerie about the mist; it seemed almost alive as it somehow changed into a thick fog before his very eyes! Astonished, a deep fear gripped him as it dropped down, wrapping its icy tentacles around the branches of the nearest trees, steadily advancing on him. All of a sudden, the hunter had become the hunted! Petrified, he was unable to move and just lay there in a cold sweat, watching the

338

mysterious fog close in on him while a deafening silence engulfed the land. There was absolutely no sound at all! His heart beating wildly, he stared in horror while the frigid, slimy tentacles slithered across his body and began to encircle his throat! Prodded by his desperate need to flee, his legs shakily responded as he forced himself to stand. Frantic with fear, he blindly ran from the treacherous mist, tripping and stumbling in his crashing flight through the forest! When he finally broke free of the fog, Shannon and Jacob were the last things on his mind!

Far removed from that terrifying scene, Lone Elk sat in his ceremonial teepee with an extremely satisfied smile on his weathered face. While he sat before a crackling fire, repeating a sacred chant over and over, an evening mist, borne on the wind, silently entered his domain and swirled directly over his head for a few moments before suddenly evaporating into thin air. Having put all of his energy into this particular rite, Lone Elk was suddenly overwhelmed with fatigue and, against his will, began to doze. Before entering the grey realm of dreams, his last vision was of Jacob and Shannon embracing in the lovely pool of clear water.

While the shadows lengthened and twilight softly approached the forest, Jacob carried Shannon from the water into a dense thicket of trees and gently set her down. So entranced were they by one another, they hadn't even noticed the mysterious evening mist. Alone at last with the red-haired vision from his dreams, he felt strangely removed from the rest of the world. Completely forgotten were the drug dealers and the fight yet to come. Gone also were any thoughts of his warriors and even his grandfather. His only concern was the lovely, young woman standing before him, in all her naked glory!

As Shannon returned his gaze, all worries left her

mind. Her husband, her friends, even Eric no longer existed for her. Her entire past had somehow disappeared, replaced instead by a whole, new world she saw in Jacob's haunting, black eyes. Enthralled by the thought of a future with such a dangerously exciting man, involuntary shivers ran up and down her spine. With a need to reassure herself that she wasn't dreaming, she tentatively reached out and lightly stroked his chest. Her soft touch instantly raised goosebumps on his flesh as a wave of electricity raced back and forth between them. Filled with a sudden, desperate need to hold her, Jacob pulled her close and kissed her tenderly. Feeling her body trembling against his, he became slowly overwhelmed by the strongest sense of their belonging together. Never had a kiss tasted so sweet, nor felt so completely right! Struggling with the enormity of his emotions, Jacob felt a lump in his throat as she nestled even more closely in his arms. Almost drunk with the feel and the smell of her, he wanted the moment to last forever. Gazing into her eyes, he recalled a recent conversation with his grandfather. Lone Elk had told him about the very first time he'd met Jacob's grandmother, how he'd known in an instant that she was the right woman for him. He'd said that it had taken only one look into her dark eyes to know that she was his destiny. Only now, as he felt himself consumed by the green fire in Shannon's eyes, did he realize how absolutely correct his grandfather had been. The eyes are indeed the pathway to a person's soul and Jacob knew with a certainty that he was seeing his own future in hers. His heart soaring with ecstasy, he knew he could never again have such a depth of feeling for another woman; a love such as this could occur only once in a lifetime. Reaching up, she pulled his face down to her inviting lips for yet another kiss. Lost in the sensation of caressing her sensuous body, Jacob felt a stirring begin deep in his loins and lay her gently down upon a thick blanket of grass. As he knelt over her, she once again had that feeling of losing her very soul in his dark eyes. Just as he began to cover her body with his own, they were both startled by a sudden gust of wind whipping through the surrounding trees. Looking up, they were able to see the night sky through the swaying branches. Shining down upon them, the stars sparkled like diamonds in the heavens; it was as though Mother Nature had planned this beautiful sight just for their pleasure. The soft wail of the wind mingled with the sound of a nearby waterfall to create a haunting melody, one the young lovers would never forget. In the soft and gentle setting of the ancient forest, Jacob and Shannon soon became lost in their own private world, a place where time itself seemed to spin out of control, leaving them with an endless night to consummate their love.

CHAPTER 23 PROPHECY

Trembling with fear, Trevor was gasping for breath when he finally reached the outskirts of camp. His legs buckling in protest, he collapsed on the ground in a tattered heap and groaned aloud in pain. His clothing was torn and his arms and face were covered with scratches from stumbling through the manzanita in his desperate flight through the forest. His entire body shuddering uncontrollably, he could still envision that horrible fog as it chased him through the trees, surrounding him at every turn, trying to strangle him with a cold, slimy hand! He couldn't understand where it had come from or why it had finally released him. Fearfully looking around, he could no longer see any remaining remnants of the fog, only shadows in the waning light. It would soon be completely dark and he desperately wanted to be safely inside his tent by that time. Attempting to stand, he rose unsteadily, trying with shaky hands to brush some of the debris from his clothing. All of a sudden, he realized that he was still holding his rifle; it was a miracle that he hadn't dropped it along the way. Then he realized what a sight he'd make walking into camp. How would he explain his battered appearance? No-one would ever believe the truth! Maybe he should claim that he'd been out hunting and had to run from a bear. They'd probably never believe that either, but at least it sounded more plausible. As the last glimmer of light slowly faded from the sky and dusk descended upon the land, Trevor decided to wait a few more minutes and enter the camp under the welcome guise of semi-darkness. With a little luck, he would be able to steal into his tent without even being seen. As he stealthily approached the outer ring of the camp-site and stood beneath an old, white oak, he was completely unaware of Tad staring down at him from one of the branches. He cautiously continued around the edge of the camp until he was close to his own tent and then he made a run for it, slipping inside before anyone else was able to spot him. Panting with relief, he threw his rifle aside and made a dive for the welcome refuge of his sleeping bag. Unfortunately, he had completely forgotten about Mathias, who had borrowed his bag and was sound asleep until Trevor landed right on top of him! There was a brief moment of confusion while Trevor tried to figure out exactly what was squirming beneath him. In the very next second, Trevor realized the magnitude of his error as Mathias exploded from the bag in a fury of curses and knocked him flat!

"You dumb fuck! What the shit d'ya think you're doin'? I oughta beat you senseless! You Goddamn fag! If you're that hard up, you better go find your asshole buddy, Dillon! Now get the Hell outa here so I can get some shut-eye, you stupid moron!"

"Hey! Take it easy! I just forgot you were there, okay? Go ahead and get some more sleep. I'm outa here!"

In a heartbeat, Trevor was outside the tent, angrily mumbling to himself. "Goddamn it! If I didn't have bad luck, I probably wouldn't have any luck at all!"

While Trevor stood huddled beside a tall, fragrant cedar in the early evening chill, the three members of the fishing party were clambering over the last ridge on their way back to camp. Tony was tired and his back was killing him, but it was worth it; he'd caught more fish than the other two put together. And he wasn't about to let them forget it, either.

"Hey, you guys! Will you please slow down a little and wait for me? I can't go as fast as you two. I have this humungous load of steelhead to carry! Remember?"

Eric and Larry just looked at each other and walked faster, leaving Tony even further behind.

"Come on, guys! It's almost dark and we're supposed to stay together. You know, safety in numbers and all that crap! Hey, I know! I've got a great idea! Why don't both of you carry some of my catch and then you won't look quite so pathetic walking into camp? How about it, boys?"

At that last remark, Eric stopped dead in his tracks and gave Tony a withering look.

"What's the matter, Tony? Just a little scared of the dark, are you? I guess I'd better stay by your side 'til we get back to camp. Otherwise, some bear might come along and decide to have you for dinner and your fish for dessert!"

Dropping sharply from the ridge, the steep, rocky trail became increasingly difficult as it wound around huge boulders, which all but engulfed the weary hikers. After slipping and sliding around several twists and turns, the trail finally led them to a small, grassy meadow with a stream running through it. Feeling uneasy, Tony warily looked around in the dim light and came to a dead stop.

"Wait a minute, Eric! I don't remember this meadow. And Larry's nowhere in sight! We must have taken a wrong turn somewhere. Shit! Have you gotten us lost, or what?"

"Relax, Tony! We're perfectly safe; all I did was take a short-cut. See the tall cedars on the other side of that stream? We'll take a short hike through those trees and wind up right in the middle of camp. In fact, we'll get there way before Larry. What a shame he didn't wait for us."

"Yeah, I can see you're all broke up about it!"

Laughing, the two friends hurried along and soon found themselves approaching the area where the camp supplies were kept. Looking in the direction of the evening camp fire, they saw everyone sitting around, eating their dinner. Tony was irritated.

"Hey! I thought they were going to wait for us! I guess they didn't want fresh fish for dinner after all. Oh well, it's their loss! C'mon, Eric; let's dig out some flour and fry up these babies all by ourselves."

Searching for the flour in the shadowy light of dusk, Tony inadvertently knocked over two of the packs which had been carefully placed to one side, causing the contents to slide out on the ground.

"Shit! What a mess! C'mere, Eric. Give me a hand with all this, okay? Hey! You know what? I totally forgot! We're not supposed to be messin' around with this stuff, so we better hurry before that asshole Trevor sees us and starts bitchin'!"

While they felt around to retrieve the spilled contents, it simultaneously dawned on them that what they were picking up were bundles of hundred-dollar bills. After a long moment of staring at each other in shocked silence, Eric finally spoke in a low voice.

"Jesus Christ! Tony, there's thousands and thousands here! Do you know what this means? This means trouble, big trouble! C'mon! Let's put this shit back before anyone knows we've seen it! Hurry up! We've gotta get out of here and I mean right now!"

Feverishly cramming the money back into the packs, they quickly finished and put them back in place, then rose silently and nervously looked around. Before making a move, Eric once again spoke in a hushed tone.

"Let's go. We'll circle around and enter the camp

from the other side. We'll pretend we just got back."

As they carefully back-tracked, they were unaware of Trevor watching them with a cold, hard look in his eyes. He had caught sight of them just as they had finished with the packs and he immediately knew what they had found. He stayed close to the large cedar while he decided how to handle the situation. In the dim light, he was almost indiscernible from the base of the tree and he remained there until they were completely out of sight. No longer concerned about his own appearance, he broke from his cover and headed directly for Dillon's tent. He should still be asleep because he'd been assigned the late watch for the night. Abruptly entering the tent, he leaned over and shook Dillon, who woke with a start, mumbling to himself while he rubbed his eyes.

"What is it? Is it time for my shift already?"

"No, it's not! In fact, you're not taking a shift tonight. I've got something more important for you to do. I want you to accompany Matt to the base camp tonight. You have to give a special message to the men without Matt's knowledge. Now listen carefully, because this is critical. Just a few minutes ago, two of the flat-landers found our money while they were snooping through the supplies......"

Horrified, Dillon interrupted.

"What?!!? You've got to be kidding! What the Hell were they doing in the supplies? They know it's not allowed and......and...... Hey! What the shit happened to you? Did you get in a fight with them?"

"Damn it! No! I didn't fight with them! They don't even know I saw them! Now just shut up and listen! We don't have a whole lot of time. I want you and Matt to get to the base camp just as quick as you can. When you get there, find some excuse to get off alone with Gus and Quinn and tell them what happened. Make certain they understand that I want the whole bunch of them to hurry right back here along with you and Matt. I want them to take care of these damned flat-landers! And while they're at it, I want them to get rid of Matt, Jesse and Tad at the same time. They're nothing but trouble-makers and I don't trust a single one of them! And listen! Don't let them deal with Matt over there; I don't want the sound of any gunfire carrying back here to spook the others. I want them all taken care of right here at the same time, so you make sure that Matt's out of ear-shot before you say anything to the boys! You understand? Any questions?"

Stunned into silence by all this news, Dillon only nodded. Deep within himself, he couldn't help but wonder if the time might ever come that Trevor would get rid of him in the same manner.

"No questions? Good! Hurry up and get dressed! I'll go wake Matt and the two of you can get on your way. While you're travelin', you'd be wise to keep a poker face. Matt's no fool and he picks up right away on a guy's expression, so you'd better be damned careful!"

Stepping out of the tent, Trevor looked up at a sky filled with stars. Looking off to the side, he was pleased to see a beautiful, full moon just beginning to rise; his men would be able to make good time on the night trail. With that happy thought, he re-entered his own tent and heard Matt snarl at him.

"Shit! Are you back already? I might as well hit the trail! A man sure as Hell can't get any sleep with you wanderin' in and out all night long!"

Glaring at Trevor, Matt got up and stalked out of the tent. Trevor warily followed him to the corral where Dillon was waiting for them, his horse already saddled. Matt turned around and looked at Trevor suspiciously.

"What the fuck's goin' on? Dillon ain't goin'

348

anywhere with me! I travel alone!"

"Actually, he is going with you. You're carrying too much money this time and I don't feel easy about it. You just might need the extra protection that Dillon can give you. I'm still the boss and that's the way I want it. You have a problem with that?"

Looking at Trevor with a deadly expression in his eyes, Matt's face slowly broke into an evil grin, causing Trevor to instantly break into a sweat.

"Nah! I ain't got any problems that I can't handle. Besides, like you say, you're still the boss, far as anyone knows. I guess Dillon just better make sure he keeps up with me. Wouldn't want this boy gettin' lost now, would we? I'd feel downright awful if somethin' bad happened to him."

While Matt saddled his horse, Dillon glanced nervously at Trevor, who only shook his head and flashed him a look of warning. With a resigned expression, Dillon mounted his horse and led the pack mules over to the supplies. Just as he began to load the mules, Matt caught up with him and they quietly finished the job together and remounted their horses. Noticing that Dillon was careful not to look directly at him, Matt walked his horse right in front of Dillon's, forcing him to make eye contact. He didn't like what he saw. He read something more than just fear in his eyes. Suspicious by nature, Matt decided to keep a close eye on Dillon.

"Relax, boy! Don't pay any mind to what I said back there. I ain't gonna let nothin' happen to you. I was just playin' games with Trevor. It's fun gettin' 'im all riled up!"

Laughing nervously, Dillon nodded and smiled sheepishly at Matt.

"I'll have to take your word for that. I never had the guts to try it!"

"Hell! You can't be scared of that wimp! Besides,

it don't take guts to rile that chicken-shit! Everything pisses him off! But if you're worried about him, you can relax. Long as you're with me, you're absolutely safe. It's like I said, kid; I ain't gonna let nothin' happen to you. I don't plan on lettin' you outa my sight."

With those words, Matt and Dillon began their trek to the base camp, traveling beneath a full moon and a sky filled with stars. Although the night trail was fairly well lit, Matt kept them at a slow pace. Finally, Dillon could no longer keep quiet about it.

"Shouldn't we be going a little faster? At this rate, it's going to take forever!"

"Don't sweat the small stuff, kid! We're doin' just fine. Ain't no reason to hurry, anyway; is there?"

"Well......no, I guess not. It's just that......I think Trevor wanted us to move right along."

"Well, just between you and me, kid, I really don't give a shit what Trevor wants! So just kick back and relax; we're in for a real peaceful trip, just the two of us."

Unknown to Matt, there was a third person making the same trip. Carefully keeping out of sight, Two Eagles followed only a short distance behind. Matt was in a rare, talkative mood and decided to share one of his favorite stories with Dillon.

"See that big dipper up there? I'll bet you ain't got any idea why there's a big dipper and a little dipper."

"Huh? What're you talking about? They're just a bunch of stars; that's all!"

"Just as I thought! I figured you didn't know nothin' about it. Well, boy, tonight's your lucky night, 'cause I'm gonna explain the whole thing to you. It goes like this; a long, long time ago, when the first man and the first woman lived on this here planet, they were unhappy 'cause the night sky was pitch black. The woman used to cry herself to sleep every night 'cause she was so scared of the dark. In fact, she was so unhappy, she flat refused to sleep with her man. He was upset about not gettin' any, so he tried real hard to cheer her up, but nothin' worked. After a while, the Supreme Maker realized there weren't gonna be any babies unless he did somethin' about that dark sky. So he took two dippers, a big one and a little one, and filled them with all the sparkly rocks he could find on this here planet. He put the biggest rocks in the big dipper and the little ones in the little dipper. Then he took those dippers and flung all the rocks up in the sky, where they started to burn and turned into stars. Of course, the big rocks made the big stars and the little ones made the teeny, little stars. Then he put both the dippers up in the sky so they'd be handy in case the stars ever burnt out and he had to do it all over again. Well, kid, how'd you like the story?"

"You want the truth? I think it's ridiculous! Where in the Hell did you ever hear a dumb story like that?"

"As a matter of fact, an old Indian squaw told it to my cousin and he told it to me."

Dillon snorted derisively.

"That figures! Most Indians are just a bunch of retards, anyway!"

Matt rode quietly for a few seconds and then stopped right in the middle of the trail. Turning slowly around, he fixed Dillon with a steely gaze and then spoke in a low, menacing tone.

"Well, I wouldn't know about that, kid. You see; the old squaw was my cousin's mother and he never said nothin' about her bein' retarded."

Dillon was speechless as their eyes remained locked for a long moment in the deathly quiet. Finally, Dillon found his voice and began to stammer.

"I'm sorry........I mean........I'm really sorry! I.........I didn't mean it like it sounded!"

"Sure you did, kid! But don't worry about it. What you think don't matter a Hell of a lot to me, anyway!"

With a last, hard look, Matt turned back around and kicked his horse into a canter. Letting out a pent-up sigh of relief, Dillon resolved to keep his big mouth shut, then kicked his horse into a lope so he could catch up with Matt. Pretty soon, the stars appeared to be rushing by them as they galloped along beneath the big dipper.

Riding behind them, just out of sight, Two Eagles thought about the story. He'd been able to hear every word and was surprised at how closely the story resembled the tales of his youth. He found it sadly ironic that one of his enemies was probably related to his very own people.

While the three men rode down the moonlit trail, Shannon and Jacob were talking quietly as he walked her back toward the camp. Abruptly stopping, he pulled her close for one last embrace.

"This is as far as I go, Shannon. I must leave before anyone sees me. You'll have to walk the rest of the way by yourself. It's only a short distance and you have the full moon to guide you. When you speak to the others, say nothing of our meeting. Just remember that you are mine! When next we meet, you will leave with me, understand?"

As his dark eyes held hers in a penetrating gaze, she felt a chill go down her spine. Unable to speak, she nodded her acquiescence and stared, spellbound, as he pulled her even closer for a long, deep kiss that left her breathless! Then, without the slightest sound, he disappeared into the forest. Listening carefully, she heard nothing except the evening breeze, whistling through the tall pines. It was as though he had vanished into thin air. Without the searing memory of being crushed in his arms, she might have thought it

352

had all been a dream. Smiling to herself, she hummed a favorite tune as she approached the camp, blissfully unaware of the nightmare yet to come. Realizing she was late for dinner, she hurried through the trees and entered the camp just in time to see Eric and Tony arrive from the other side. Waving, she walked over to join them.

"Hi, guys! I'm glad to see I'm not the only one late for dinner! We'd better grab a bite before they put everything away. C'mon; you can tell me all about your fishing trip while we eat."

Without waiting for a response, she turned and headed toward the cook fire. Eric and Tony looked at each other for a brief moment and then followed her; they knew it was the wrong time to tell her their news. While they stood in line with their plates, the cook grinned at all three of them.

"It's about time you dudes showed up! You came mighty close to goin' to bed hungry. Hey! What do I smell? Don't tell me you boys actually caught some fish! Just leave those babies right here an' I'll fry 'em up for tomorrow's breakfast."

While the three of them sat around the fire, eating their dinner, Shannon wondered why the two men were so quiet.

"Well? I thought you were going to tell me about your fishing trip. C'mon, guys! There must have been something exciting about your trip! And where's Larry? I thought he went with you."

A little puzzled, Eric and Tony looked around for a moment, but Larry was nowhere in sight. Giving Tony a guarded look, Eric was the first to speak.

"He did go with us, but he got back to camp a little ahead of us. He's probably already in his tent. Do you want me to check on him?"

"No! Actually, I'm relieved that he's not here.

He's been acting so strangely and I'm really not in the mood to deal with him. I'm feeling very happy right now and I don't want anything to spoil it, so why don't you two tell me all about your wonderful excursion?"

Looking at each other almost contritely, Eric and Tony were hesitant to relate their news. Again, in a very low voice, it was Eric who spoke.

"Shannon, I have something very important to tell you, but not here. There are too many other people around and I can't risk anyone hearing me. As soon as we're done eating, I want you to go for a walk with me. I'll explain everything as soon as we're alone, all right?"

Misunderstanding his intent, Shannon blushed and couldn't quite meet his eyes.

"Eric, if you don't mind, I'd really rather not be alone with you tonight. I have a lot on my mind and I'm just not ready for......any complications."

Realizing what she meant, Eric tilted her face up and looked into her eyes, hoping she would recognize the importance of the situation.

"No, Shannon, you don't understand. It's not what you think! Something extremely serious has come up and we have to talk about it. Tony's going to find Cat and the four of us are taking a walk. Quit looking at me like that! I don't want anyone else to think anything's wrong, okay?"

Sensing a note of desperation in his voice, Shannon was worried and curious all at once. Trying to appear casual, she forced herself to smile at him, nodded and then quickly finished her dinner. Just as the three of them stood to leave, Cat came walking up to them.

"Well, it's about time you three showed up! I was beginning to worry!"

"Cat! You must be reading my mind, babe! I was just going to look for you. I want you to take a walk with us, okay?"

"Are you serious? You just got back! I should think the last thing you'd want is more walking! Why don't we just relax around the fire for a while and then turn in early?"

Grabbing her hand, Tony pulled her along with him.

"C'mon, Cat! We're goin' for a walk and that's all there is to it! Who's the boss around here, anyway?"

Laughing, Cat allowed herself to be pulled along. As soon as they felt they were a safe distance away from camp, Tony and Eric stopped and carefully looked around before speaking. Puzzled, Cat looked from one to the other.

"What's the matter with you two? Why so serious?"

"Listen, babe! We've got a big problem! We found money! Lots and lots of money! If they find out about it, we'll be in deep shit! In fact, we might be in deep shit, anyway! You understand?"

More confused than ever, Cat shook her head and looked at Eric beseechingly.

"No, I don't understand! Eric, what on Earth is he talking about?"

"Everyone just calm down and I'll explain. When we first got back to camp, we decided to fry up the fish by ourselves. We were looking through the supplies for some flour when Tony accidentally knocked over some packs filled with money, serious money! I'm talking about thousands and thousands of dollars! Fortunately, no-one saw us, so we put the money back and got the Hell out of there! Then we back-tracked, circled around and came into camp from the other side, pretending we'd just arrived. As you can see, we're in real danger!"

Horrified, the two girls looked at each other in disbelief. Finally, Cat broke the silence. "I don't get it!

If nobody saw you, why are we in danger? All we have to do is pretend we don't know anything about it and just act normal, right?"

In the still of the night, Eric stared at her for a long moment.

"Cat, don't you understand the implications of that money? People who deal in that amount of money can only be drug dealers."

"My God! You mean Trevor and his men are........ are........"

"Yes, Cat, that's exactly what I mean! I'll bet they're growing marijuana somewhere around here and they're probably bringing money and supplies in and taking their crop out on the return trip. Anyway, that's my guess! I don't know about the rest of you, but I sure as Hell don't feel safe around men like that! Think about it! What if one of them had seen us with that money? You can believe we'd all be dead right now!"

Feeling more than a little frightened, Shannon interrupted.

"What are you suggesting, Eric? What can we possibly do about the situation?"

"All we can do is stay cool and be careful! And definitely keep out of the supplies! By the way, I purposely didn't include Elaine and Larry in this discussion because I wasn't too sure how they'd react. The four of us will just have to watch out for them, okay?"

They all nodded in agreement and then Cat spoke to Shannon.

"Speaking of Larry, Tony and I have been extremely worried about his behavior. We'd feel a lot better if you'd sleep in our tent tonight. What do you say?"

With an oblique glance at Eric, Shannon quickly responded.

356

"Thanks, Cat! I think I'll take you up on that offer. Sure you won't mind, Tony?"

"Of course not! You're welcome in our tent anytime, kiddo! Let's start back now, okay? Even with all this excitement, I'm feelin' beat. I've gotta get some sleep."

As the four of them quietly walked down the moonlit trail, they were all lost in their own private thoughts. Cat and Tony were both anxious for this trip to end. All they wanted was to be safely home with their beloved twins.

Although Shannon was concerned about the drug dealers, her mind and heart were filled with thoughts of Jacob. She could still feel the touch of his burning hands on her bare skin, still see his black, mysterious eyes boring into her very soul while he made love to her. Never had she been so consumed by passion. She knew her fate was forever sealed by that one encounter. When she was very young, she had asked her mother how she would recognize true love. Her mother had smiled and told her that it was impossible to explain, but that she would just know. For the first time, she understood exactly what her mother had meant. When she was with Jacob, she had absolutely no doubts. Her world felt completely right when she was in his arms. She felt terrible about hurting Eric, but she could never again be with anyone but Jacob. She hoped he would understand and someday find the right woman to fill his life with a happiness to equal her own. He was a wonderful man and she would always have a deep affection for him.

Eric's heart was heavy because Shannon had made it abundantly clear that she wouldn't spend the night with him. He couldn't escape the feeling that she was once again slipping away from him. He was beginning to wonder if she would ever realize that they truly belonged together. His extreme preoccupation with Shannon pushed his worries about the drug dealers to the back of his mind. As he watched her walking in front of him, her beautiful red hair shimmering in the soft moonlight, he swore that he'd die before he'd ever let her go!

While the four friends were walking back to camp, Jesse had just returned from an evening tryst with Elaine. After walking her to her tent, he joined Tad on the far side of the fire.

"I'm right glad you're back, Jesse! I been wantin' to talk to you real bad! There's been some strange things goin' on around here. Just before dark, I was hidin' up in a tree, keepin' an eye on Trevor like you wanted me to. While I was up there, I saw Eric and Tony nosin' through the supplies and you can be certain that Trevor saw 'em too. Well, they musta found the money, 'cause they backed outa there like scared rabbits. Now listen to this, 'cause this is where it gits interestin'! After they skedaddled outa there, Trevor went rushin' over to Dillon's tent like his ass was on fire! Now I don't rightly know what all he said to Dillon, but the next thing I see is him headin' for the corral, while Trevor goes back to his own tent. Then, all of a sudden like, Mathias goes rushin' off to the corral with Trevor hot on his heels! I couldn't hear 'em, but it sure looked like they was havin' some heated words down there. Then, before you know it, Dillon and Mathias are over at the supplies, loadin' up the packs and I'll be danged if the two of 'em don't go ridin' off together! Don't that beat all?!!?"

"You got that right, brother! Specially since Mathias always insists on ridin' alone! You done a good job of keepin' watch, Tad. I'm right proud of you."

Beaming with pride, Tad sat quietly while Jesse pondered the situation for a few minutes. Finally, with a decisive look, Jesse spoke.

"Listen good, little brother! I think it's about time we made our move. At the break of dawn, we're gittin' outa here, you, me an' Elaine. I don't rightly know what Trevor and his asshole buddies are up to, but it sure as Hell can't be nothin' good! I better git back to Elaine and tell her what we're doin' so she'll be ready to go. Oh! One more thing, brother, when we leave tomorrow, you be sure to watch your back! I don't think anyone's gonna see us leave, but, just in case, you be careful. I don't want nothin' happenin' to you, understand?"

Touched and a little embarrassed by his brother's words, Tad grinned and playfully punched Jesse in the arm.

"Shucks, Jesse! Ain't nothin' gonna happen to me! I'm way too quick for one of them jerks to do me any harm! So don't you worry none about me. You just watch out for Miss Elaine and I'll watch out for the both of you. See you in the mornin', brother."

As Tad walked off to their tent, Jesse watched him until he was out of sight. He deeply loved his brother and felt uneasy about the following morning. Something was eating at him, but he couldn't quite put his finger on it. He'd feel a lot better when they were all well on their way. Filled with concern, he headed for Elaine's tent.

While Jesse was explaining his plan to Elaine, Mathias and Dillon were just arriving at the base camp. Two Eagles watched them closely from a thick grove of trees as Matt hailed the cabin in a loud voice. In an instant, a half dozen men erupted from the cabin door in a pushing, shoving mass, with one of them tripping and falling flat on his face. Gus, a large, burly man with a violent disposition, angrily kicked the fallen man in the ribs before stepping over him.

"You dumb shit! If you can't stay on your feet,

then keep the Hell outa my way!"

Groaning, the man just lay there and said nothing. Matt looked at him for a moment and then stared at Gus with a venomous look.

"I see nothin's changed around here! You morons are still too stupid to keep a watch outside the cabin! I'd sure like to know what the Hell you woulda done if this'd been some kind of bust! It'll be your head, Gus, if anything goes wrong around here! I'll bet you plumb forgot you're the one in charge of this place, seein' as how you're so busy kickin' the shit outa anyone weaker'n yourself! One of these days, you really oughta try pickin' a fight with someone your own size, just to see how it feels to get the crap beat outa you!"

Before Gus was able to respond, Dillon quickly interrupted by walking his horse between the two men.

"Jesus Christ! Don't you guys have anything better to do than fight? C'mon, Gus; get your men to unload the packs and then you and Quinn can help me take these animals to the corral, okay?"

As much as he enjoyed a good fight, Gus wasn't overly anxious to trade blows with Matt. He was well aware that there are some men who should never be challenged and Matt definitely fell in that category. The scariest thing about Matt wasn't his obvious strength or his brutal reputation; it was the cold, remorseless look of death in his eyes. One had only to stare into them for a moment to see the relentless killer lurking behind them.

"All right, boys, you heard the man! Git those packs unloaded and haul 'em into the cabin! Matt, why don't you go on inside and take it easy for a spell while me and Quinn give Dillon a hand with the mules? And don't you worry none about your horse; I'll tend to him myself."

Deigning no reply, Matt silently dismounted, letting the reins fall to the ground as he scornfully dismissed Gus and entered the cabin. Looking around, he noticed an old, wooden table filled with playing cards and poker chips. Chuckling to himself, he walked over and checked out a couple of the hands. Two of the players had full houses and, interestingly enough, each one of those hands held three aces! Not at all surprised by the cards, he could only wonder which of the two men were cheating. As he picked up a third hand and saw two more aces, he laughed out loud! Just as he put the hand down, one of the men came into the cabin, his arms filled with three of the packs. It was the one who had fallen, a skinny, young man with a pock-marked face. His name was Riggs. That was it, just Riggs; no-one ever knew if it were his first name or his last, because he refused to discuss it. Giving Matt a cautious smile, he spoke in a hesitant manner.

"Thanks for taking my side out there! I really appreciate it."

"Don't flatter yourself, kid! I wasn't takin' your side; I was only statin' the obvious. One of these days, that big lard-ass is gonna pick on the wrong guy and I sure as Hell hope it's me!"

Flustered by Matt's hostile response, Riggs nervously looked around, searching for a safe topic of conversation.

"Uh, we were just starting a poker game when you showed up. You'd be more than welcome to join us. We're always happy to have new players!"

Matt snorted in disgust.

"Yeah, I'll bet you are! I'm sure you can always use some fresh blood in this game! I think I'll pass, though. I'm not quite in the mood for bein' ganged up on by a bunch of blood-thirsty vampires! Just for the record, kid, which hand is yours?"

Puzzled, Riggs picked up a hand which appeared to have honest cards. With such a lousy hand, he

361

obviously wasn't one of the card sharks. Shaking his head, Matt decided to give him some free advice.

"I've got a question for you, kid. By any chance, have you been losin' a lot of money at these games?"

"Yeah! How'd you know? I've had a horrible run of luck! I just haven't been catching the cards! It seems like no matter what I get dealt, there's always someone with a better hand. Oh well, I'm hanging in there. My luck's bound to change! You know what they say about luck coming in streaks and I'm way overdue for mine!"

"You think so, huh? Well, I got some bad news for you, kid. Sometimes old Lady Luck decides she ain't never gonna visit you! Your friends sure as Hell ain't waitin' around none for her! Looks to me like they just took the matter into their own hands. Take a gander at some of these cards, boy; maybe that'll wake you up."

Bewildered, Riggs stared at all the aces and then looked up at Matt with a bitter expression.

"Those assholes! I'm going to make them give me my money back!"

"Nah, I don't think so, kid. Ain't a one of 'em gonna admit to cheatin'! They'll just accuse each other and end up in a big brawl. And you still won't get your money back. Better just chalk it up to experience and stay the Hell outa these games!"

"Yeah, I see what you mean. Well, at least I didn't have time to lose any money tonight. Thanks for the advice. I owe you one."

"You can skip the thanks, kid! I don't want anyone beholden to me, 'specially not a greenhorn like yourself. Just put up those supplies while I see what's keepin' the others."

Stepping outside, Matt noticed some packs sitting on the ground with one of them already open. Three of the men, Mick, Dawes and Gator, had found the booze and were standing around, passing a bottle between them.

"What's the matter, boys? Been a long time between drinks? Maybe you'd best take care of the packs before you start hittin' that stuff."

Although Matt spoke in a friendly enough voice and he wasn't officially their boss, none of them was willing to argue the point and they quickly put up the rest of the supplies without comment.

Matt followed the men back into the cabin and watched as they continued their poker game. While they were all relaxing inside, Dillon was reluctantly discussing Trevor's plan with Gus and Quinn, who seemed all too anxious to carry out Trevor's orders. In fact, Gus appeared downright gleeful!

"Let's see if I got this straight, Dillon. Trevor wants me and the boys to take care of them flat-landers, which just happens to include three women, right? And we can handle them any which way we want to, right? Tell me about them women! What do they look like? Any of 'em got big tits? What's the matter, boy? Cat got your tongue? C'mon! Talk to me!"

Dillon was finding it difficult to answer them. He'd gotten to know the women and wasn't happy about their impending doom. Damn! If only the money hadn't been found! Of course, he knew Trevor was right; they couldn't be left alive! But the thought of those women being assaulted by Gus and his men made him sick to his stomach! Trembling, he could feel himself breaking into a cold sweat while Gus and Quinn stared at him, almost drooling in anticipation. In the still of the night, Gus leered at Quinn.

"Jesus! Lookit that boy sweat! Them women must be somethin' else! I think Dillon wants 'em all to hisself! What do you think, Quinn?"

"Won't do him no good, Gus! He knows the rules; we share an' share, alike. Hell! We're all

363

partners, ain't we? Besides, if we have to take care of them women, the least we can do is show 'em a good time before we finish 'em off! It's the Christian thing to do, by God!"

Watching them laugh raucously, Dillon tried to hide his feelings.

"Yeah, I guess you're right. I shouldn't be stingy; after all, there's plenty of women to go around. Let's get back to Trevor's orders for a minute. I want you to keep in mind that you're also supposed to take care of Matt, Jesse and Tad at the same time. They can be pretty dangerous, so I think they should be taken care of first. What do you think, Gus?"

In the back of his mind, Dillon was hoping there'd be some way to save the women while Gus and his men were taking care of Matt and the two brothers. For the first time in his life, Dillon was thinking about people instead of money. In his heart, he knew he was only grasping at straws; there was almost no possibility of saving the women. At the very least, he'd shoot them himself before he'd allow Gus and his men to torture them! If they didn't kill him first! Unfortunately, Dillon knew that was a very big 'if'!

His laughter abruptly subsiding with the sobering thought of confronting Matt, Jesse and Tad, all thoughts of the women instantly vanished from Gus' mind.

"You're right about them three bein' dangerous! Why wait 'til they're together? I'd just as soon do Matt while we got 'im here all by his lonesome! Don't that make sense to you?"

"No can do! Trevor gave explicit orders! He doesn't want the sound of any gunfire carrying back to the other camp."

"Who said anything about guns? Ain't you never heard of usin' a knife? All I gotta do is sneak up on 'im while he's sleepin'."

"Sneak up on Matt with a knife and live to tell about it?!!? You've got to be kidding! That man has the instincts of an Indian! Before you even knew what hit you, he'd be all over you like horseflies on shit! And he's vicious! He'd rip that knife out of your hand and carve you up with it! From what I've heard about him, he'd probably chop off your privates and stuff them in your mouth before finishing you off! Trevor swears he did that to someone only two years ago! If I were you, I'd wait until we're back at the other camp and use a gun. You're going to need all the edge you can get!"

Bathed in sweat, Gus and Quinn were both staring at him. Too shocked to speak, neither one uttered a word. In the deathly quiet, Dillon had to stifle a grin. He'd wanted to get their minds off the women and he'd obviously succeeded. Of course, there had been rumors about Matt committing that particular atrocity and, when asked about it, Trevor swore that it had actually happened. But Dillon didn't really trust Trevor's word on anything and had taken his statement with a grain of salt. Before returning to the cabin, he had one last thing to say.

"I hope you both realize that we have to leave early enough to arrive just before dawn. That's the way Trevor wants it. Any questions?"

Still unwilling to speak, Gus and Quinn only nodded and the three men silently walked back to the cabin, completely unaware that Two Eagles, safely out of sight, had heard their entire conversation. Even before the men entered the cabin, Two Eagles had quietly backtracked and was just beginning the long ride back to the other camp. He was anxious to meet with Jacob and warn him about the coming attack. He fervently prayed that Running Deer would return in time with the rest of their warriors. If not, Two Eagles hated to think of the possible consequences. As he rode beneath the full moon, he thought about the atrocity attributed to Matt and wondered if it were true. It had been his experience that white men lied quite often. Indians were just the opposite; they would rather die than live without honor. No wonder the whites feared death with such a passion! How could they possibly be prepared to meet the Supreme Maker with so many lies against them? He had to smile as he imagined Heaven populated only with Indians. Looking up at the stars, he saw the big dipper and was reminded of the tale that Matt had told. There was a paradox! He found it hard to believe that a man who would tell such a story could ever be capable of committing the act of which he stood accused. Personally, Two Eagles didn't approve of torture. If one had to deal with an enemy, he considered a clean kill far more honorable. All of a sudden, he frowned as he recalled a story he'd heard over two years ago about a white man rescuing a young Indian girl and torturing her attacker. He wondered if that man could possibly be Matt.

While Two Eagles continued on his way, lost in thought, Matt had fallen asleep in a back room of the cabin and was tossing fitfully as a recurring nightmare returned to haunt him. Bathed in sweat, he jerked upright as he came to with a start. While he shook his head to clear away the fading fragments of the dream, he found himself reliving the events of two summers ago which had caused it......

On one of his runs to the base camp, Matt had taken a different trail. It was an early July morning and he was riding slowly along, in no particular hurry, when he suddenly heard a strangled scream in the distance. Wondering if one of the boys were playing a trick on him, he dismounted and silently moved through the trees, determined to catch whoever it was in the act. Unfortunately, it wasn't one of the boys and the act he witnessed was one he would never be able to forget. A young Indian girl was writhing in pain while being raped by a local hunter, a piece of white trash who hated all Indians. In the midst of raping her, he was using his hunting knife to slice off her left breast. Working slowly so as to torture the poor girl, he had imbedded the blade about an inch deep by the time Matt reached him. Using one hand to grab his knife away and the other to grip the man in a strangle-hold, Matt drug him away from the injured girl with the blade cutting into the man's throat ever so slightly. Matt was determined not to let him die too quickly! Savagely throwing the man at the base of a small pine tree, Matt stared down at him with a lethal look while the petrified man whimpered and begged for mercy. With a look of pure contempt and one swift blow, Matt knocked him unconscious, quickly got some rope from his saddlebag and tied the man securely to the tree. Then he rushed to the girl's side and carefully checked her wound. She was barely conscious and had lost some blood, but, with proper care, would be all right. Matt took a clean T-shirt out of his pack and cut it into long strips. While he wrapped them tightly about her chest, she moaned and tried to speak to him.

"My brothers......I came here with them......they're hunting......I stayed in camp......that man......he came up behind me and......"

"It's all right, girl! He ain't goin' nowhere! Don't you worry yourself none; I'll take care of 'im for you! I guarantee he won't be botherin' anyone ever again! I'm sorry about wrappin' this cloth so tight around you, but I had to do it to stop the bleedin'."

With a hysterical note in her voice, the girl attempted to sit up.

"Bleeding?!!? What bleeding?!!? What did he do to me?!!?"

"Calm yourself, girl! It ain't nothin'; it's just a

small cut. You're gonna be fine. I'll see to that! If you can remember the way to your camp, I'll take you there, nice and easy. I'll bet your brothers are there right now wonderin' where you're at. You feel strong enough to travel?"

Nodding weakly, she shakily pointed to the east and then collapsed back on the ground. Picking her up with great care, Matt slowly approached his horse, speaking softly to him all the while. Wide-eyed, with his ears pricked forward, the tall, black gelding stared apprehensively at the girl and snorted his displeasure!

"Easy, Satan! Calm down! Everything's okay. We're just gonna take this girl for a little ride; that's all."

"Satan! Why do you call him by that name? Is he dangerous?"

Chuckling, Matt continued to talk in a low, comforting tone as he gently placed the girl in the saddle and mounted directly behind her.

"Now, honey, don't start frettin' about Satan. He ain't dangerous; he's just fast! When I turn 'im loose, he runs like his ass is on fire, like he's got the devil himself inside 'im! Matter of fact, I ain't never seen any horse beat 'im yet."

Making no response, the girl just slumped in his arms, her head rolling against his shoulder. Worried that she might be going into shock, Matt gently shook her, causing her to shake her head in confusion.

"Hey! Don't you drop off on me, girl! You gotta stay awake so you can show me the way to your camp. Are we goin' in the right direction? By the way, what's your name?"

Looking around to gain her bearing, she answered in a weak voice.

"Yes, we are........and I am called Chin-chaw."
"That's a pretty name. What does it mean?"
"In the Yuki language, it means 'bird'."

368

Upon approaching a small meadow, the girl suddenly pointed to a deer trail on their left.

"There! We must follow that trail! Our camp lies only a short distance ahead!"

Weakened by her ordeal, all the talking left her exhausted and she once again slumped against him.

"Don't give out on me now, Chin-chaw! Hang in there, girl!"

Finally reaching the camp, they were warily greeted by her two brothers. Helping her dismount, they carried her to one of the sleeping bags and kneeled beside her, listening carefully while she whispered to them. She had barely managed to relate what had been done to her before completely passing out. Slowly rising, both brothers stared accusingly at Matt. The older brother quickly glanced at his rifle, which was leaning against a tree only a few feet away. Giving him a deadly look, Matt rested his hand on his own rifle and spoke in a menacing tone.

"Don't even think about it! Anyway, I ain't the one you want. It was someone else done that to her. If I hadn't come along, she'd probably be dead by now, or worse!"

As the full realization of Matt's meaning dawned on him, the older brother spoke with a barely controlled rage.

"Where is he? I'll show that bastard how to use a knife! Before I'm done, he'll beg for death!"

"Don't worry yourself none about that! He ain't goin' nowhere; I left 'im tied to a tree. For right now, you better tend to your sister and make sure she's okay. Then you can deal with that piece of trash!"

After telling the two brothers approximately where the man was tied, Matt quickly left, determined to do a little carving of his own! In his haste, he gave Satan his head and the horse, living up to his name, bolted down

369

the narrow trail, seemingly Hell-bent on returning to the scene of the crime! Within minutes, they arrived and slowly approached the whimpering captive. Staring up at them, the man was horrified to see both horse and rider glaring down at him with the same malevolent look! It was almost as though Satan knew exactly what Matt had in mind and couldn't wait to see it done!

"Please, mister! Don't hurt me! I was just havin' a little fun with the girl and......and......I got carried away! That's all! If you just let me go, I won't never do nothin' like that again! I swear it!!"

His eyes hardening with a look of pure evil, Matt slowly dismounted and unsheathed a solid foot of razor-sharp steel! His eyes bulging with fear, the man was rendered speechless as he stared at the blade. Kneeling in front of him, Matt stared directly into his eyes and uttered the last words the man would ever hear.

"You got that right, you son of a bitch! You won't never do that again!"

As the sizzling summer heat slowly invaded every nook and cranny of the forest, Chin-chaw's two brothers were on the deer trail leading to the general area of her attacker. Burning with an inner rage, they were impervious to the outer temperature. Their only thought was to destroy the filth who had almost killed their sister. While they searched for the tied man, they noticed that an unnatural stillness had settled upon the land. As they made their way through the dense foliage, the only sound they heard was the drumming of their own hearts. All of a sudden, their ears were assaulted by a loud, insistent buzzing as they broke out into a small clearing. Following the noise, they soon found the dead captive. Fighting the urge to vomit, the two brothers stared in shock at the horde of flies hovering and crawling over his gaping wound!

......His heart racing and his body covered with sweat, Matt couldn't understand why that particular nightmare plagued him so often. After all, the man deserved to die; there was no question about that! Sometimes, even in the middle of the day, the pleading look in the man's eyes would come back to haunt him. All right! So he had begged for mercy! So what? He sure as Hell wouldn't have shown any mercy to the girl, so why should he have gotten any? It was the only time in his entire life that Matt had killed someone in cold blood and it had left him with a very bad feeling!

While Matt had been reliving his nightmare back at the cabin, Two Eagles had finally reached the high plateau over-looking the camp wherein the tour group lay sleeping. Expecting to find only Jacob waiting for him, he was amazed and relieved to find the entire band of warriors waiting with him. They were all in war-paint and looked eager to fight! With men such as these, there was no longer any reason to dread the dawn; instead, Two Eagles could hardly wait for the first golden rays of the sun.

While Two Eagles told Jacob all that he'd heard at the base camp, Jesse was preparing to leave with Elaine and Tad. After sending his brother to get the horses, he headed for Elaine's tent. Stepping inside, he found Eric and Elaine sound asleep. Closely watching Eric, he carefully woke Elaine, keeping one hand over her mouth just as a precaution. Her eyes nervously fluttering open, she relaxed as soon as she recognized Jesse. Smiling down at her, he motioned for her to get up. Quietly rising, she picked up a small pack with her belongings and nodded to Jesse that she was ready to go. Just before stepping outside, she took one last look at Eric and was surprised to feel a small pang in her heart. She didn't realize that, when two people have loved and shared their lives as they had, at least one tiny piece of that love will survive. Dismissing the feeling, she responded to Jesse's tug on her hand and hurried outside into the chilly air of the pre-dawn. Taking no chances on waking the others, Tad had led all three of their horses into a heavily treed area just across from the tents. Looking carefully around, Jesse and Elaine paused for just a moment before rushing across the small clearing to meet him.

"Good work, little brother! I see you already got 'em saddled. Take care of these two packs for me while I help Elaine mount her horse, okay?"

Happy to oblige, Tad quickly loaded the packs on Jesse's horse and then turned to mount his own. A look of concern clouded his eyes as he stopped abruptly and stared in the direction of the lower trail leading into camp, the very one they'd planned on taking.

"Tad! Hurry up! We gotta high-tail it outa here! What's the matter with you?"

"Shhh! Listen! There! Did'ya hear that? I think someone's comin' up the trail!"

"Yeah, I do hear somethin'. It must be Matt and Dillon comin' in early with the goods. Damn! We shoulda left sooner! Now we're stuck here 'til we git a chance to take off without bein' seen. All we can do is keep the horses quiet and look for a break."

Frightened, Elaine whispered to Jesse.

"Isn't there some other way we can go? If we wait, I'm afraid someone will find us and stop us! Jesse, I don't ever want to go back; I want to stay with you!"

"We ain't got no choice, Elaine. We got to stay on the lower trail at least long enough to git clear of the camp. The growth is just too thick around here. If we try to cut our own trail, they'll hear the horses crashin' through the brush for sure and certain! We'll just have to wait 'em out. But don't you worry none, sweetheart; we'll still manage to git away. I ain't about to lose you

372

now, girl; it took me too danged long to find you!"

While the two brothers and Elaine watched intently, Matt and Dillon rode into camp and stopped in front of Trevor's tent. As they dismounted, Matt was surprised to find Trevor coming out of his tent to greet them.

"Well, it looks like you boys made good time! How was the trip? Did everything go as expected?"

Matt didn't miss the fact that Trevor's last remark was aimed at Dillon. Silently watching them, he found it quite interesting that Dillon's response was only a nod. Instantly suspicious, Matt angrily confronted Trevor.

"You're up to somethin' and you'd better tell me what the fuck it is! And I mean right now, you Goddamn......"

Interrupted by the sound of horses coming up behind them, Matt turned just in time to see five riders approaching. Staring at the two in front, he recognized Gus and Quinn only a split second before he heard a familiar clicking sound and felt a gun barrel pressed against his back.

"Get your hands up and keep your mouth shut, asshole! You'll find out what I'm up to soon enough!"

Slowly raising his hands, his face darkened with an almost uncontrollable rage as he glared at Trevor with a lethal expression.

"Better watch your back, Trevor; this ain't over yet! I'll see you in Hell before I let you get away with this!"

His rifle in hand, Gus dismounted and stood between Matt and Trevor.

"That's where you're wrong, Matt. As far as you're concerned, it's over and then some! We can handle things from here on, Trevor. My men have got 'im covered. You and your boys go ahead and take the shipment out. This mess'll be all cleaned up by the time you git back."

"Thanks, Gus! I knew I could count on you! I'll have a nice bonus for you when I return. As for you, Matt, you probably will see me in Hell, but you'll get there way before me! Adios, sucker!"

At that moment, Pedro rode up, bringing Trevor's horse with him. Quickly mounting Raja, Trevor headed out of camp, with Pedro leading the pack mules and Dillon bringing up the rear. Just before they lost sight of the camp, Dillon turned around and took one last, long look. With a sick feeling in the pit of his stomach, he realized he'd only been kidding himself about saving the women. Once he saw the men all together, their guns drawn, he knew any rescue attempt would be both futile and suicidal. All he could do was look out for himself; there wasn't a Goddamned thing he could do about the women. When it came right down to it, his own welfare was still the bottom line.

With the three of them out of the way, Gus decided it was time to have some fun.

"Well, boys, I think it's time to party. Quinn, you go wake up them flat-landers! I wanna check out them ladies real personal-like. Go on! Bring 'em out here and tell 'em they don't need to bother gittin' dressed!"

While the men laughed in eager anticipation of the morning's fun, Quinn appeared worried.

"Gus, I thought Dillon said we should take care of Matt, Jesse and Tad first. Remember him sayin' how dangerous they are?"

With a loud guffaw, Gus shoved Quinn toward the tents.

"What's the matter with you? Lookit this asshole reachin' for the sky! He don't look so dangerous, now, does he? I think we'll just tie him and the other two up and let 'em watch us pleasure the women-folk. Maybe they'll learn a thing or two before we do 'em in. Go on!

374

Bring them bitches out! I'm gittin' a hard-on just thinkin' about 'em!"

With obvious reluctance, Quinn motioned for Mick and Dawes to help him and each of them simultaneously entered a tent. In short order, Larry, Shannon, Eric, Tony and Cat found themselves herded together in the midst of some very unsavory, dangerous men! Unprepared for the sight of a woman as beautiful as Shannon, the men were silent while they stared at her with obvious intent. Her green eyes filled with fear, she shivered as goose bumps raced up and down her spine. His shock giving way to anger, Eric stepped in front of Shannon, keeping himself between her and the men. Staring at the guns in horror, Larry seemed rooted to the ground, frozen with fear. As Cat clung to him, sobbing, Tony looked nervously at the sinister group surrounding them. While a palpable tension held everyone in its relentless grip, Jacob and his warriors were on the ridge above them, waiting for just enough light to attack!

There was a deathly quiet in the early July dawn. The eastern sky was beginning to show streaks of fuchsia and deep purple. The pre-dawn chill hadn't yet released the land. Jacob was lying flat amidst the grasses that lined the ridge, peering down upon the people in the camp just beneath him. The smoke from their night fire floated gently in the breeze, covering the entire scene in an ethereal haze. In spite of the chill, Jacob was bathed in sweat. Staring down at the dangerous drug dealers, he knew there would be no room for error. The thought of Shannon being at their mercy sent a chill down his back. As he caught sight of the tents poking through the morning mists, just for a moment, they resembled the tops of covered wagons. Shaking his head to bring himself back to reality, he was filled with the dread of premonition. It was as though he'd gone back in time to fight a very familiar battle. The prophecy of his dream was about to be fulfilled!

All of a sudden, the silence surrounding the captives was broken by Gus' booming voice.

"Hey! There's only two women here! Where's the other one? And where in the Hell are those two brothers? Damn it, Quinn! I told you to fetch everyone!"

"I did! I brought you everyone from the tents! I don't know where the others are!"

"You dumb shit! They hafta be around here somewhere! Go find 'em!"

Hearing those words, Jesse and Tad nodded silently to each other and then turned to Elaine. Very quietly, Jesse whispered to her.

"This is it, Elaine! Stay right behind me and ride like Hell! Remember what I told you; stay low on your horse and don't look back. Now!!!"

With those final words, the three of them burst from their cover, trying desperately to reach the lower trail before the men got a fix on them!

Startled, Gus and his men stared at the riders for a split second before they realized what was happening. Dawes was the first to react, lifting his rifle and taking careful aim at the departing trio. His first shot ran wild, but the second one caught Tad in the middle of his back, causing him to slump forward in the saddle. By that time, the others were taking shots as well, but they were too late. While the valley echoed with the sound of gunfire, Jesse, Elaine and Tad were safely out of range and riding hard down the lower trail.

At that moment, Jacob's savage cry filled the air, instantly rousing the rest of the war party, their cries mingling with his! Mounting his horse with a single leap, Jacob rushed headlong down the steep incline with his band of warriors! They descended in a huge dust cloud, the earth churning beneath the horses' hooves.

376

Astonished, Gus and his men stared in shock at the attacking horde of Indians. Using the moment to his advantage, Matt sprinted past Gus, ripping the rifle from his hand as he did so. Without breaking his stride, he raced for the shelter of the deep forest. Two Eagles saw him running, took deadly accurate aim, then purposely hesitated for only an instant before firing. Just as he reached the trees, Matt could hear the whistle of a bullet whizzing past him, narrowly missing its mark. Unknown to him, his distant relationship to the Yukis had saved his life. His heart pounding, he continued to run, heading in the same direction that Trevor had taken.

With the Indians almost upon them, Gus pulled out his pistol, grabbed Shannon as a hostage and started slowly backing away with her. Snapped out of his shock, Larry committed the only truly brave act of his entire life as he made a desperate lunge for Gus. Without the slightest hesitation, Gus fired point-blank! Larry was dead before he hit the ground! Screaming, Shannon kicked Gus as she fought to escape, but it was to no avail. In a crushing grip, he continued to drag her away. Horrified, Eric stared at Larry's bloody corpse and found himself strangely unable to move. He'd been in his share of fights, but never anything even remotely like this. All of a sudden, two of the drug dealers, Dawes and Gator, fell right in front of him, their bodies riddled with bullets. He'd never seen anyone killed before and was in a mild state of shock as he vacantly stared at the blood pouring from Gator's head. Seeing his uncomprehending gaze, Tony instantly understood the situation and tackled his friend, bringing him to the ground amidst a hail of bullets. "C'mon! We've gotta get out of here!"

Half dragging Eric, Tony managed to bring both him and Cat to safety as they crawled behind the tents and hid behind a huge log. Jacob saw Shannon being carried away and quirted Tomahawk while they galloped in her direction. With horse and rider almost upon him, Gus threw Shannon to the ground and fired his pistol at Jacob, who gritted his teeth as the bullet burned into his shoulder! Leaping upon Gus from his horse, the momentum sent them both sprawling to the edge of a small plateau which dropped sharply down a steep, rocky incline to the river below. Weakened by his wound, Jacob knew he was in serious trouble as they wrestled for position. His enemy was huge and unusually strong. He managed to slash Gus' shoulder with his knife, but it didn't even faze him as he knocked the knife from Jacob's hand. Then, with a murderous bellow, he picked up Jacob and threw him off the cliff! He heard Shannon's scream as he catapulted straight toward the sharp rocks below! Just a few feet below the edge, he managed to catch hold of the branch of a Tamarack growing out of the bank. Taking only a moment to catch his breath, he quickly climbed back to the top, pushing himself over the edge just in time to see Shannon running toward the forest with Gus hot on her heels. Scooping up his knife as he ran, Jacob raced after Gus, catching up with him only a few feet from Shannon. With a flying leap, he brought Gus to the ground and they rolled in a heap. Crashing against a small boulder, Jacob hit his head and once again lost his knife. Struggling to remain conscious, he lost the battle as his vision faded and his mind fell into a deep, black abyss.

As the echo of the last shot slowly faded away, a penetrating silence descended upon the forest. After motioning Cat to stay hidden, Tony cautiously peered over the top of the log. Neither seeing nor hearing anyone, he then crept to the corner of the nearest tent and slowly looked around the edge. Shocked by all the carnage, he spoke out loud without even realizing it.

"Oh, my God! Jesus Christ!"

Unable to restrain herself any longer, Cat burst from behind the log and ran to Tony's side. He tried to block her view, but it was too late. Moaning in horror, she backed away a few steps, sank to her knees and threw up, over and over, until there was nothing left but dry heaves. Finally coming out of his stupor, Eric stood and walked over to Tony, both of them silently staring at the dead bodies strewn around the camp. Looking up, Eric saw a band of painted warriors who, except for their rifles, appeared to have come from some ancient time. Confused, Eric watched apprehensively as one of them rushed over with a look of concern.

"Are you people all right? What about her? She didn't take a bullet, did she?"

"No! She's okay; all of us are, except for him." Pausing for a moment, he pointed to Larry's body and then continued. "Who are you and where in the world did you come from?"

"All I can tell you is that we've been after these drug dealers for quite a while and you people just happened to be in the wrong place at the wrong time. Sorry about your friend; it just couldn't be helped."

While the warrior returned to the rest of his group, Eric looked across at the edge of the forest and saw Shannon sitting on the ground leaning over a fallen warrior. Puzzled, he walked in their direction. Halfway there, he stopped dead in his tracks when he realized the warrior was Jacob.

As he slowly came to, a face appeared out of the mists and Jacob found himself looking into beautiful, green eyes filled with tears. A lovely, young, red-haired woman was trying to comfort him. Recognizing Shannon, he smiled with relief. The prophecy was fulfilled!

CHAPTER 24 MYSTIC MOMENT

Standing behind Shannon, Jacob's two best friends were grinning down at him. With an evil gleam in his eye, Running Deer was shaking his head as he spoke to Two Eagles.

"You know what really pisses me off? We always do all the work and Falcon always gets the girl! You ever notice that?"

"Yeah, you're right! I wonder how he manages that?"

Laughing, Jacob gingerly stood, pulling Shannon up with him.

"All right, which one of you two clowns is going to tell me what happened to him?"

Looking down at Gus' body, Two Eagles responded.

"Oh, you mean him? I can explain that. While you two were wrestling around, anyone could see that you were in complete control. I mean; with him on top, strangling you and all, I could tell right away that you were only toying with him. The trouble was, you took too long! I got tired of waiting, so I shot the bastard! Sorry about spoiling all your fun! By the way, you got lucky with that bullet; it went through nice and clean. All it needed was some bandaging and Shannon took care of that. Now, if you can tear yourself away from your girlfriend for a while, you'd better decide what you want to do about the bodies."

With a long, grateful look at Two Eagles, Jacob realized all at once how very close he'd come to dying. Holding Shannon close to him, he spoke to his two friends.

"Tell the men to take them into the forest and bury them in a common grave. Make certain to cover any sign that they were ever here. While you're doing that, I'll explain everything to Shannon's friends."

Confused, Shannon looked at Jacob.

"Why did they call you Falcon?"

"It's my tribal name; it's what they've always called me. Except for my grandfather, only outsiders call me Jacob."

"What should I call you?"

Laughing, Jacob tilted her face up to his.

"Anything you damned please!"

Then he kissed her with a passion that left her breathless.

Watching Shannon return Jacob's kiss was like a knife in Eric's heart. Filled with bitterness, he turned away and headed for his tent. He couldn't forget the blissful glow in her eyes while she gazed adoringly at Jacob. That one look told Eric more than words ever could. For the first time, he realized that it was truly over between them. For a moment, he almost wished that one of the bullets had found him. It couldn't possibly have been as painful! While he gathered up his belongings, Tony stepped into the tent and stood quietly until Eric finally turned to face him. The naked grief on Eric's face reminded Tony of the day Nicole had told him they could never again be together. He knew that his own face must have mirrored Eric's tragic expression. Haltingly, he tried to find the words to console his friend.

"Listen, buddy, I know exactly what you're goin' through. Believe it or not, things will finally get better. It just takes time! I know, because...... Oh, Hell! You'll just have to take my word for it."

With an anguished look and a lump in his throat,

Eric was slow to respond.

"I know you mean well, Tony, but, as far as time goes, I don't think there's enough time in the entire universe to make me quit loving her."

"No, Eric! You don't understand! I never said you'd quit loving her. That kind of love never dies! I just meant, with the passage of time, it gets bearable. I know it's hard to believe right now, but you finally learn how to live with it. You learn to appreciate others. Eventually, you even find love again, with someone else. Trust me! I know what I'm talking about."

Staring at his friend, Eric was unable to speak and only nodded as he turned to finish his packing. All of a sudden, Cat rushed into the tent and grabbed Tony by the arm.

"Tony! Those Indians are hauling all the bodies away! They want to know what we're going to do with Larry's body. C'mon! You have to talk to them!"

Stepping outside, Tony saw Jacob approaching with Shannon, a look of pure ecstasy on her face. He knew she had found her one true love. He was as happy for her as he was sad for Eric.

Stepping up to the others, Jacob quickly explained all about the drug dealers. When he finished, Shannon suddenly remembered Larry and turned to look for his body. Rushing to block her view, Tony grabbed her and turned her back around.

"Listen, kiddo; I don't want you lookin' at him right now! It's better for you to remember him the way he was, okay? That's the least you can do for him! After all, he died trying to save you."

With an anguished look, Shannon buried her head on Tony's shoulder while silent tears streamed down her face. Jacob took a step toward them, but Tony just looked at him and shook his head. Realizing what close friends they must be, Jacob backed off, waiting patiently for her to calm down.

At that same moment, Trevor, Pedro and Dillon were well on their way to Rock Cabin Camp, the distance from the last camp being no longer than four hours by horseback. The entire vacation tour was a circuitous route, beginning at Rock Cabin Camp and ending there. The three men were on the last leg of their journey and anxious to have it behind them. They rode quietly, all of them engrossed in their own private thoughts. After leaving the previous camp, the trail had taken them steadily upward, winding around the steep edge of a mountain. Stopping for a moment to take one last look down the ravine, they heard the sound of gunfire echoing throughout the forest. Trevor's instant reaction was pure satisfaction! Once and for all, he was rid of Matt, Jesse and Tad, the stupid assholes! They should have known better than to mess with him. No-one had ever gotten the best of him and no-one ever would, by God! His only regret was that he'd never succeeded in bedding Shannon. In the last seconds before leaving the camp, he'd considered taking his pleasure with her, but something deep inside his gut warned him away. She was one of those rare women who could really get a hold on a man if he weakened, even for a moment. A smart man would be far better off to avoid her kind, altogether. Besides, if he took her by force and then left her to die, he knew those green eyes would haunt him for the rest of his life. Oh well, there were plenty of other women to take her place. All in all, he considered the executions a job well done. As he continued to ride, he wore a very pleased expression.

Pedro's reaction was a little different. He wasn't comfortable with the idea of the women being killed, but he understood that it was necessary. With that realization, he was able to put it from his mind and concentrate on the money. He wondered what would happen to the share that belonged to Matt, Jesse and Tad. It seemed only fair that it be divided among the rest of the men. He would have to ask Trevor about that. Frowning, he kicked his horse as they continued their climb.

Unable to forget the sound of the gunfire, Dillon shuddered as he imagined the women's fate. He could easily envision them stripped and thrown to the ground as Gus and his men took turns with them, humiliating them before everyone. With her defiant attitude, he hated to think of the punishment Shannon must have endured before Gus forced her to submit. Cat probably cried and screamed, begging for mercy from men who didn't know the meaning of the word. He almost couldn't bear to think of Elaine, sweet, gentle Elaine. He pictured her retreating even further into her protective shell, lying completely still with a vacant stare, only vaguely aware of her surroundings. At least, she probably died without any knowledge of what was happening. Oh, God! Those poor women! And what about the huge amount of gunfire? What did those bastards do? Pump a hundred rounds into each person? Jesus Christ! How could he ever live with this knowledge? With a look of pure anguish, Dillon knew he couldn't continue in this business. He'd just take his cut and disappear. For the first time, he finally realized that money wasn't everything. It could never justify what had happened today. Suddenly aware that Trevor and Pedro were out of sight, he spurred his horse to catch up with them.

Not too far behind them was Mathias. From the moment he'd sprinted away from the camp, he never looked back. He just kept on running until, finally, he fell to the ground in exhaustion. His heart pounding and his legs throbbing, he listened carefully for any sign of pursuit, but heard only the fading echoes of the gunfire, followed by an eerie silence. While he lay there, breathing hard, he wondered if Gus or any of his men had survived the Indian attack. It hardly seemed possible, but he desperately hoped that Gus had somehow gotten away, so he could find him and kill the bastard himself! Well, at least he knew that Trevor, Pedro and Dillon were still alive and they shouldn't be too far ahead of him. With the pack animals, they were forced to stick to the trail, whereas Matt had the distinct advantage of being able to cut straight through the forest. It was a rugged way to go, but it was his only chance of catching them, since they were riding and he was on foot. Forcing himself to continue, his legs soon began to throb again, but he ignored them, thinking only of what he would do when he caught the three men. First, he would shoot them in the knees to disable them; then the real torture would begin! With a sadistic grimace, he forged ahead, determined to capture his prey. God pity them when he caught up with 'em, 'cause he sure as Hell wouldn't!

While Matt was heading in the direction of Rock Cabin Camp, Jesse, Elaine and Tad were going in the opposite direction, racing toward the base camp. As they galloped along, Tad tried desperately to stay in the saddle, but was steadily weakened by the bullet in his back. About a mile down the trail, his vision began to blur and he slowly fell from his horse. Elaine looked back just in time to see him hit the ground.

"Jesse! Come quick! Tad fell off his horse!"

Twisting Buckaroo around in one fluid movement, Jesse raced back to Tad, leaping to the ground even before his horse had completely stopped. Kneeling by his brother, he saw where the bullet had entered and knew in a heartbeat that Tad couldn't possibly survive. Fighting to hold back his tears, Jesse scooped Tad into his arms, holding him gently while he looked into his eyes.

"Little brother, I told you to watch your back! You don't mind worth a damn! I shoulda made you ride in front where I could keep an eye on you."

"Shit! Listen to you! It was always me who had to watch out for you! Jesse, I ain't feelin' so good. I won't be able to go with you. You two better git outa here while you still got a chance."

"There ain't no way in Hell I'm leavin' you behind! Besides, it's only a scratch; you're gonna be fine!"

Almost too weak to continue talking, Tad merely nodded. His face bathed in sweat, he called to Elaine in a ragged whisper. Her face covered with tears, she knelt close to him and took his hand in hers.

"You gotta promise me.....look out for Jesse.....he don't do so good on his own......"

Unable to go on, Tad slumped in Jesse's arms. Holding him all the more tightly, Jesse rocked back and forth with him, refusing to accept his death.

"Don't worry, Tad! You're gonna be all right. I won't let nothin' happen to you. Listen! Do you hear that birdsong? It's your favorite, the Meadowlark. Don't that sound purty? It's gonna be a beautiful day! The sun's just peekin' over the mountains......and the valley's all misty......"

His face streaked with tears, Jesse looked, bewildered, at all the beauty surrounding them. His brother couldn't possibly die on such a glorious day! But the forest sounds continued as usual and the sun rose even higher in the heavens, bathing the earth with a warm, golden glow. In spite of all the trials and tribulations of mankind, Mother Nature abides. In the wilderness, death is acknowledged only as a minor part of the daily routine. It was all so unfair!! No longer able to contain his grief, Jesse let out such a scream of primal rage, that all the creatures of the forest froze simultaneously. In the eerie silence that followed, Jesse screamed his curses, venting his wrath upon God himself for daring to let his beloved brother die! Sobbing, Elaine put her arms around both of them, wishing her touch could somehow bring Tad back to life. Instead, her touch gradually lessened Jesse's pain and slowly brought him back to reality. Little by little, the forest sounds returned to normal. A small squirrel scampered up a nearby tree and chattered indignantly. It was as though nothing unusual had happened. Slowly rising, Jesse carried Tad to his horse and gently tied him across the saddle. Then he turned to Elaine.

"We better hurry. I don't know how much time we got before someone comes after us. There's a few things I have to take care of and then we'll bury Tad in a place that was special to him."

Elaine nodded and they mounted their horses. Jesse took the lead, pulling Tad's horse behind him, and they headed into the sun.

While Jesse and Elaine rode down the trail, Jacob was carefully checking out the campsite. When he was finally satisfied that all evidence of the drug dealers was completely obliterated, he called his warriors together.

"Two Eagles, I want you and the rest of the men to go to the base camp, cut down all the marijuana plants and stack them in the cabin. After the first rains, we'll come back and burn the place down. I'll take Shannon and her friends out to Rock Cabin Camp and we'll wait for you there."

"What about Trevor? He and two of his men left earlier and took that same route. They might still be at the camp."

"Yeah, you're right. Just to play it safe, I'll take two of the men with me. The rest of you better get going. You've got a lot of work to do."

While the two groups headed in opposite directions, Jesse and Elaine finally arrived at the base camp. As they approached, Riggs walked out the cabin door, staring at them with a puzzled look.

"Hey, Jesse! What're you doing here? And who's the girl?"

From the innocent expression on his face, Jesse instantly understood that Riggs knew nothing about the set-up. Fidgeting nervously, he seemed pathetically awkward and......and there was something else about him. Jesse couldn't quite put his finger on it, but he had some quality that reminded him of Tad. He decided to give the poor kid a break.

"We ran into some trouble at the other camp. Some Indian vigilantes decided they didn't want us in their forest anymore, so they shot most of the guys......"

Shocked, Riggs interrupted him.

"What?!!? Oh, my God! That's Tad across the saddle!! He's dead, isn't he? Jesus Christ! They'll be coming here next, won't they?"

"Yeah, I'd be willin' to bet on it! Listen good, Riggs! We ain't got much time. We gotta git outa here, but we don't dare show our faces in Covelo! So we'll go in the opposite direction, over those far mountains. The trip'll take four or five days, so we better pack enough grub to last a week. Git three of the pack mules out of the corral and bring 'em over here. Me and Elaine'll start layin' out the supplies. Go on! Git a move on!"

Almost in a daze, Riggs headed for the corral. At the same moment, Jesse hurried Elaine into the cabin and pointed out the supplies to her.

"We're gonna have to hurry, Elaine. Start throwin' together whatever you think we need and Riggs will help you load the stuff. I've got somethin' else to take care of."

While Elaine began to sort through the supplies,

389

Jesse rushed into the back bedroom and dragged from the closet a huge wooden chest with a padlock. Staring at the lock for just a second, he ran outside, grabbed the splitting mall and raced back into the bedroom. Puzzled, Elaine followed him, entering the room just as he took a mighty swing at the padlock, sending it crashing against the wall. His hands trembling, he opened the lid and Elaine gasped out loud as they stared down at an ocean of green.

"Oh, my God!! Where did all that money come from?"

"Elaine, I ain't got time to explain right now! There's over three and a half million dollars in this box and we're takin' it with us! Go git me some of them green plastic bags from the kitchen and I'll start fillin' 'em while you finish your job. Hurry up, gal! We gotta move!"

His words filling her with a sense of urgency, Elaine rushed the bags to him and then hurried back to the supplies. He and Elaine completed their packing just as Riggs finished saddling his horse and the mules. As he led them to the railing in front of the cabin, he saw Jesse approaching, carrying a green plastic bag and two gunny sacks filled with supplies.

"Here, Riggs, this is for you. Don't spend it all in one place!"

Confused, Riggs took the bag and curiously looked inside. Rendered speechless by the sight of so much money, he stared at Jesse with a bewildered expression.

"Go on, kid; take it! There's three hundred grand in that bag and it'll take you a long ways if you're careful. Just make sure you don't go flashin' it around; you understand?"

With a grateful look, Riggs nodded his thanks and carefully loaded the money and supplies on one of the mules, then took a step toward the cabin to help with the rest. Quickly blocking his way, Jesse shook his head.

"It's okay, kid; we'll load our own mules. You're all set, so you might as well take off. I want you to go north; me and Elaine are headin' east."

"Wait a minute! I thought we were all leaving together!"

"Uh-uh! It'll be safer if we part company. If we git lucky, it might confuse anyone followin' us."

Stricken with fear, Riggs looked apprehensively at the trees beyond the trail.

"You figure they're coming after us, don't you?"

Seeing how frightened he was, Jesse tried to calm him.

"I don't figure nothin' of the sort! It just pays to be cautious; that's all. You git goin' now and quit worryin'! Things'll be just fine. Go on; git!"

Reluctantly, Riggs mounted his horse, took one last look at the cabin and headed north. Just before he reached the big trees, he turned and waved to Jesse, then disappeared into the forest. His heartache somewhat lightened by helping Riggs, Jesse turned to Elaine and smiled.

"C'mon, darlin'! Let's git our stuff loaded and high-tail it outa here!"

In a matter of minutes, Jesse and Elaine loaded the other two mules, mounted their horses and headed east. Slowly making their way through the forest, they climbed steadily, following a deer trail which finally brought them to the edge of a high meadow overlooking the valley below. They couldn't quite make out the cabin, but they had a clear view of the trail leading down to it. While they watched, Jacob's warriors suddenly came into sight, riding hard on their way to destroy the marijuana crop. His heart skipping a beat, Jesse realized they'd gotten out of there just in time. Seeing the worried look on Elaine's face, Jesse gave her an encouraging smile.

"Don't worry, honey; we're safe. They don't know we're up here and there ain't no way they can spot us against the trees. We better keep goin', though; I still have to find Tad's special place."

His heart wrenched anew by merely speaking his brother's name, Jesse's eyes clouded with grief and he quickly turned the animals back to the dense forest. With tears stinging her eyes, Elaine silently followed him as they continued their search for Tad's final resting place.

While Jesse and Elaine made their way through the forest, Trevor and his men were finally approaching Rock Cabin Camp. The men were jubilant as they caught sight of the corral, lying just on the outskirts of the camp. Breaking into a canter, even the horses were happy to be at the end of the trail and neighed excitedly to one another. In their cheerful mood, the three men let their guard down and were completely unaware of being watched by Mathias, who had reached the camp at the same moment, but from a slightly different angle. Winded from his long run, he was bathed in sweat and breathing hard as he hid in the dense growth. Waiting just long enough to catch his breath, he watched while the men dismounted and tied the horses to the railing. When they stepped into the open, he slowly raised the rifle and took careful aim at Trevor's knees. Within a hair's breadth of pulling the trigger, he heard the men being hailed by Sheriff Stanton as he drove up in his Chevy Blazer. Silently cursing, he lowered the rifle, warily watching as the Sheriff got out and walked up to the men. While Matt stared in amazement, they all shook hands and then started loading the marijuana into the Blazer. Shocked, Matt couldn't help mumbling to himself.

"Son of a bitch! Don't they look friendly?!!? No wonder Trevor ain't never been caught! He's in cahoots with the Sheriff! Oh well, any friend of Trevor's sure as Hell ain't any friend of mine. So fuck 'im! I'll just shoot 'em all!"

With an evil grin slowly spreading across his face, Matt once again raised the rifle. Taking careful aim, he was suddenly interrupted by the sound of several jeeps approaching.

"Damn! What now?!!?"

While Matt watched, seething with irritation, James Randolph and the rest of his group climbed out of their jeeps and nonchalantly walked up to Trevor, who stared at them with obvious annoyance.

"Listen, old-timer! I don't mean to be rude, but if you stopped to ask about one of my tours, you picked a bad time for it. I'm really busy right now, so you'd better catch me in town later and we'll discuss everything then, okay?"

"No, sonny, it's not okay! I think I'll just 'catch' you right now!"

Bewildered, Trevor and his men stared in confusion as Randolph pulled out a badge while his men drew their pistols.

"Wait a minute! What do you want with us? I thought you were checking out the logging around here! Aren't you that Randolph guy?"

"You're partly correct; my name is James Randolph, but I'm with the Drug Enforcement Agency. Trevor Thompson, you and your men are under arrest for murder and drug dealing. You have the right to remain silent. Anything you say can and will be used against you......"

Trying to appear calm, the Sheriff interrupted him in a booming voice.

"That's all right, Randolph; I can take it from here. I was just about to wrap things up when you fellows showed up. You see; I've had these boys under surveillance for quite a while and it finally paid off."

"I'm sure it did! In fact, I would imagine that it paid quite handsomely! However, I find it rather odd that they were so willing to help you load the evidence in your vehicle, especially since they were not being held at gun-point. Having witnessed that act through a tele-photo lens, I believe we've caught you with your pants down, so to speak. Of course, once you're in jail, I'm sure you'll be caught with your pants down quite frequently! And that's exactly where you're headed, directly to jail, right along with these other chaps. Let's see, now; where did I leave off? Oh yes, anything you say can and will be used against you......"

Trembling with fear and sweating profusely, Dillon cut him short, his voice crumbling as he spoke.

"Hold on! You can't arrest me for murder! I didn't murder those women! Trevor's the guilty one! He told Gus to kill them! He even had some of his own men killed! I didn't have anything to do with it! Do you hear me?!!? I'm innocent!"

Enraged, Trevor kicked Dillon squarely in the stomach, knocking the wind out of him and sending him sprawling to the ground.

"You dumb fuck! Keep your mouth shut! If I go down, you'll go way before me! Hell, you're the one who told Gus what to do! I wasn't even there, you stupid asshole!"

While two of Randolph's men quickly grabbed Trevor and cuffed him, Dillon attempted to rise, grimacing with pain as he did so. Randolph studied him for a moment and then helped him up.

"Listen, young man! If you're willing to testify in court about Trevor Thompson arranging to have people

394

killed, that testimony would probably work in your favor. Do you understand what I'm saying?"

Glaring at Trevor with pure hatred burning in his eyes, Dillon nodded.

"Yes, I do understand and I'll co-operate one hundred per cent, whether or not it helps me. If it's the last thing I ever do, I want that bastard behind bars!"

With a look of satisfaction, Randolph nodded to Dillon and then called over four of his agents.

"Ryan, see that the others are cuffed and finish reading them their rights. Then I want you and Brad to load them into the Sheriff's vehicle and drive them to Ukiah; Jameson and Curtis will follow in their Jeep. The rest of us will patrol these back roads just a bit longer to see if we can find any of their friends."

Hidden by the dense foliage, Mathias watched with bated breath as the sobering scene unfolded before him. His heart hammering in his ears, he had to listen carefully in order to hear. The word 'jail' sent a shock wave of emotions through him. He shuddered as he realized how close he'd come to being arrested right along with them! Then he felt cheated! Now he would never be able to kill Trevor! While he lay there, drenched in sweat, a persistent fly kept buzzing about his face. All of a sudden, every sound seemed magnified. The buzzing was driving him crazy, but he dared not move. Trying desperately to concentrate on something other than the fly, a picture flashed through his mind. A malevolent smile crept across his face as he imagined Trevor in prison, being gang-banged by other convicts. Maybe things were turning out all right after all! After a seemingly endless wait, the last Jeep finally drove away and Mathias cautiously stepped into the open and looked around. Seeing and hearing nothing unusual, he decided it was safe to head for the corral. As he approached Trevor's horse, Raja, Matt recalled how strongly Trevor had always favored the animal. Smiling with the sweet satisfaction of taking Trevor's prized Arab, Matt quickly mounted him and rode him next to one of the pack mules. Grabbing the lead rope, he pulled the mule along as they headed back down the trail. Worried about the possibility of running into Jacob and his warriors, Matt rode hard until he reached the point where a less-used trail branched off from the main route. Once he was safely down the new trail, he came to a dead stop and listened carefully. Carried along on the morning breeze was the faint sound of voices. Certain that it was Jacob and his band of Indians coming up the main trail, Matt's heart skipped a beat as he realized he'd once again barely escaped a dangerous confrontation. With a feeling of great relief, he urged Raja down the narrow trail and rode east into the sun.

While Matt was making his way east, Jacob was leading Shannon and her friends up the main trail to Rock Cabin Camp. He purposely maintained a slow pace so that the rest of his warriors wouldn't be too far behind them. Concerned that Trevor and his men might still be there, Jacob took Running Deer aside and spoke quietly to him.

"You'd better go on ahead of us and check out the camp. If you see Trevor and his men, get your ass back here on the double! Otherwise, just signal me from the lookout point."

Nodding, Running Deer urged his horse up the trail for a short distance, then suddenly veered off into the forest, taking a narrow deer trail the rest of the way. Annoyed by their private conversation, Eric angrily confronted Jacob.

"What's with the secret talk, huh? I think the rest of us have a right to know what's going on!"

His black eyes turning even darker, Jacob just

396

looked at Eric for a long moment and said nothing. Turning to the others, he spoke quietly.

"If anyone needs to stop for a while, tell me now. Otherwise, let's keep moving."

No-one uttered a word, not even Eric as he noticed Shannon watching him with an unfathomable expression. With an oblique glance at the two of them, Jacob once again urged Tomahawk up the steep trail, with the somber group following along in an awkward silence. While the sun blazed a path across the sky, heading for high noon, the weary riders were engulfed by a searing heat which made the trip seem even longer. With tedious twists and turns, the trail slowly carved its way around the side of the steep mountain. Already irritated by the long, hot climb, the horses flattened their ears and violently shook their heads as a cloud of relentless horse-flies descended upon them. At long last, the trail made one, final cut to the right, bringing them within sight of the lookout point. To Jacob's relief, Running Deer was standing on the edge, waving to the group. That simple act seemed to dissolve the extreme tension that had kept them all in a silent turmoil. Turning to look at the others, Jacob's eyes immediately found Shannon's and they both smiled as everyone began to speak at once. Knowing they were almost back at the main corral, the horses neighed excitedly and instinctively quickened their pace. With a sense of tremendous relief and widely varying emotions, the small group finally returned to Rock Cabin Camp.

As they rode by the meadow where they'd raced the horses, Cat looked warily down one of the side trails. Shuddering with the memory of the huge, black bear, its terrifying roar still echoed in her mind. Yet, as horrifying as that experience had been, it paled in comparison to the harrowing scene at the last camp. As long as she lived, Cat would never forget the looks on the faces of the men who had held them at gunpoint. Of all God's creatures, there could be no doubt that man was the most dangerous of them all.

Tony's memory of the bear incident differed from Cat's. He considered it more exciting than terrifying. In his mind, he could still hear the bear's frustrated roar as it turned and ran back up the trail. The thrill of chasing the bear away made him feel like some kind of conquering hero. As long as he lived, Tony would never forget the adoring look on Cat's face just before she ran into his arms. For the first time in their married life, she had looked upon her husband as her protector. Tony wasn't used to being admired and smiled as the gratifying sensation swept over him anew. In the extremely dangerous situation with the drug dealers, he was proud that he had managed to pull both Cat and Eric out of the line of fire and hide them behind the huge log. That had been a far more serious confrontation than the one with the bear! One thing was very clear to Tony; of all God's creatures, man was the most dangerous of them all.

Looking across the meadow, Eric bitterly recalled the feeling that had washed over him when he and Star sailed over that huge log. For that one sweet moment, he had felt as though he held the world in his hands, as though nothing were beyond his reach, not even Shannon. What a fool he had been! All through the trip, he'd constantly felt as though she were slipping away from him. His gut instinct had told him something was wrong, but he'd refused to believe it. His love for her ran so deep, he just hadn't been able to accept the truth, not until he'd seen her with Jacob at the last camp. As long as he lived, he would never forget the way she had looked at him. It cut him to the quick to see the two of them together. All of a sudden, another picture flashed through Eric's mind; it was the look on Jesse's face whenever he looked at Elaine. How could he possibly have missed what was happening between those two? He was probably the last one to find out. At least no-one had said anything about them riding off together; he really wasn't in the mood to deal with any further embarrassment.

As they approached the main corral, they were surprised to find Trevor's bus still there. Jacob directed a questioning look at Running Deer, who shrugged as he spoke.

"Yeah, I know exactly what you're thinking. If they didn't take the bus, then where in the Hell are they? All I can tell you is they're definitely not around here. I checked the entire area very carefully before I signaled you from the lookout point."

Their conversation interrupted by the sound of approaching vehicles, Jacob and his two warriors grabbed their rifles and warily looked down the road. While they all watched in silence, Randolph and his men arrived in a cloud of dust. As the group stared apprehensively, the agents approached with their guns drawn. Jacob instantly stepped in front of Shannon, shielding her with his body. In that same moment, Running Deer and Owl flanked their leader, the three of them presenting a united front with their rifles held waist-high. No-one spoke as the two groups silently appraised one another. Finally, after carefully noting Jacob's wound and the dead body tied across one of the horses, Randolph stepped forward, motioning for Jacob and his men to lower their rifles, which they reluctantly did.

"A most wise decision, gentlemen! After all, we do have you a bit out-numbered. It would appear you people have run into a spot of trouble along the way. Anyone care to clarify the situation for me?"

Glaring through obsidian eyes, Jacob spoke in a

menacing tone.

"I make it a point never to explain myself to anyone stupid enough to aim a gun at me. Besides which, it's none of your Goddamned business!"

"That's where you're wrong, young man. As you can see by these credentials, it's very much my business!"

Displaying his badge, Randolph had to stifle a smile at Jacob's frustrated expression. He recognized him from the confrontation with the loggers back in Covelo. It had been obvious even then that he was not accustomed to taking orders from anyone. All of a sudden, an ominous silence descended upon the camp. As Randolph and his men nervously looked around, they realized that all sounds had ceased, even the ever-present birdsong. With a quick glance at Jacob, Randolph was puzzled by the strange expression on his face. Then all Hell broke loose! Amid savage screams and the thunder of hooves, fifteen warriors erupted from the forest, instantly surrounding Randolph and his five agents! Bathed in sweat as their hearts pounded in protest, the six men found themselves staring into fifteen rifle barrels! No longer feeling quite so smug, Randolph let his pistol fall to the ground, his men immediately following his example. With a satisfied grin, Jacob nodded to his men and they relaxed ever so slightly. His voice dripping with sarcasm, Jacob threw Randolph's words right back in his face.

"A most wise decision, gentlemen! After all, we do have you quite out-numbered! And unless you're ready to deal with more than a 'spot' of trouble, you'd better do a little 'clarifying' of your own!"

"Yes, I believe you're right! Perhaps it would help if I explained exactly why my men and I are here. For some time, we've been trying to apprehend some drug dealers who were thought to be operating out of the wilderness area. Unfortunately, in our endeavors, some of my best men have completely disappeared. Therefore, I'm sure you can understand our need for caution. This morning, our luck seemed to change for the better. We caught three of the suspects loading their cargo of drugs into a sheriff's vehicle. We arrested the men right along with the sheriff, of course. Then, upon returning to this camp......"

Smiling broadly, Jacob interrupted him.

"Wait a minute! Did you say you arrested a sheriff?!!? His name wouldn't happen to be Stanton, would it?"

"Yes, as a matter of fact, that was his name! Why do you ask?"

"No particular reason, just curious. Go on."

"As I was saying, upon returning to this camp, we expected to find some more of the drug dealers. Instead, we found you and, quite frankly, we didn't quite know what to make of the lot of you. In fact, I still don't, especially with your men pointing their rifles at us!"

With only a slight change of expression, Jacob signaled his men to lower their rifles. The fact that they didn't sheathe them wasn't lost on Randolph or his agents.

"Now I'm going to explain a few things to you. For one thing, we aren't drug dealers. In fact, I can almost guarantee that you'll never see another drug dealer in these parts. Now that you've got that straight, I think it would be wise for you and your men to get the Hell out of here!"

"Actually, I quite agree with you. It is time for us to leave, but there is one thing that bothers me just a little. What exactly happened to that unfortunate, young man draped across the horse?"

"Hunting accident! Any other questions?"

"Yes, what about you? You appear to have

401

sustained an injury. How did that occur?"

His lips curled in a slight sneer, Jacob carefully enunciated his response as he spoke in a challenging tone.

"Hunting accident!"

"I see......another hunting accident. You people must have been doing a great deal of hunting! Did you bag everything you went after?"

"Yes! Every single thing! That's the nice thing about being an Indian. Indians never miss!"

"Odd you should mention that! I was just thinking the very same thing! In fact, I'm so impressed with your expertise that I have a proposal for you. Since there is now a vacancy, perhaps you would be interested in running for the sheriff's position! What do you think?"

His dark eyes blazing with irritation, Jacob's voice was filled with impatience.

"I think you're crazy! There's no way in Hell that the white population would ever vote for an Indian! You might not have noticed, but there's a lot more of them than there are of us!"

"Let me put it this way; I head an organization that has a lot of political clout. You'd be surprised at the many ways in which we could help with your campaign! You don't have to answer right now; just think about it. A man like you could do a great deal of good in these parts!"

His black eyes filled with an unfathomable expression, Jacob just stared at him, obviously anxious for him to leave. Realizing he would receive no further response, Randolph nodded to his men.

"Well, I suppose it's time to leave. I doubt there's any further need for us to linger. It would appear that all the loose ends have been neatly tucked away. Good day to all of you! And please, do think about that proposal!"

Jacob and the others watched quietly as Randolph and his men drove their Jeeps down the dusty road. Only when they were completely out of sight did Jacob speak to his warriors.

"I'll take Shannon and her friends back to Covelo in Trevor's bus. While the rest of you are riding straight to the reservation, you can take the spare horses and Larry's body with you. Shannon will take care of the final arrangements by tomorrow. Tell Lone Elk that I must first drive these people to their motorhome, but then we'll meet with him as soon as possible."

Nodding, his men turned to collect the horses. With a puzzled expression, Shannon followed Jacob as he walked over to the bus.

"Unless Trevor left a key behind, how would you manage to start the motor?"

Amused, Jacob stopped for a moment and put his arm around her.

"Believe me, Shannon; these old buses can usually be started with or without a key. Trust me on that, okay?"

"Fine, but I have another question for you. Who's Lone Elk and why are we going to see him?"

"He's our tribal medicine man and also my grandfather. He knows more than you could ever imagine and he's very anxious to meet you. You'll understand once you get to know him. Come on; let's check out the bus!"

While Jacob was driving the small group back to Covelo, Jesse was putting the last rock on Tad's grave. He had buried his beloved brother in his favorite place, a high plateau overlooking the Yolla Bolly Wilderness. While he looked at Tad's final resting place, Jesse recalled the last time they had stood together upon this ground. It was almost a year ago, in the fall, but it seemed like yesterday......

403

They had been hunting when an early storm caught them unaware. In one moment the dark clouds were only dots on the far horizon, barely discernible. Then, all of a sudden, carried by an ominous wind, they were swirling and crashing together directly over their heads. As the thunder claps became deafening and streaks of lightning hit the ground with a vengeance, Jesse looked around nervously, worried about their dangerous exposure.

"C'mon, Tad! This ain't safe! Let's head for the deep forest!"

With the wind whipping through his hair and an air of supreme confidence, Tad merely grinned at his brother.

"Hell, Jesse! There ain't no place safer'n this! Nothin' can ever harm me up here, 'cause I own this piece of ground! God can have the rest of the whole, danged world, but this here mountain top belongs to me! And you're safe so long as you're by my side. Even God knows better than to mess with my brother!"

......Looking down at Tad's grave, Jesse's eyes filled with tears.

"Rest in peace, little brother. I wish to Hell I'd watched out for you as good as you did for me! I won't never forget you, Tad. Me and Elaine are gonna name our first boy after you. And when he's old enough, we'll bring 'im up here to put flowers on your grave. That's a promise!"

Allowing Jesse a private moment with his departed brother, Elaine stood a short distance away when she suddenly caught sight of a rider emerging from the edge of the forest, leading a pack mule behind him. At first she thought it must be Riggs. Not until he was halfway across the plateau did she realize that it was Mathias. Hearing her frightened gasp, Jesse turned and watched Matt slowly close the distance

404

between them. Her heart beating frantically, Elaine watched with extreme fear as the two men silently stared at one another, neither one yet making a move for his weapon. Finally climbing down from his horse, Matt stood with his hand resting on his rifle. Amazed that Jesse had still not unsheathed his huge, Bowie knife, Elaine could only assume that his grief had left him vulnerable. If necessary, she was prepared to throw herself in front of Jesse, giving him the time needed to pull his weapon. She would do anything to protect him. While these thoughts raced through her mind, Mathias spoke to Jesse almost in a whisper.

"Jesse, I'm real sorry about Tad. It's a Goddamn shame! I'm sure as Hell gonna miss 'im!"

"Yeah, me too. He was more than just my brother; he was my best friend in the whole world!"

Both of them momentarily unable to continue, they stepped forward and gave each other a quick hug, then, feeling slightly embarrassed, broke apart just as quickly.

"I know it don't help much, Jesse, but I wanted you to know; the asshole that shot Tad is dead!"

"I'm right glad to hear that! Did you nail the bastard yourself, Matt?"

"I wish to Hell it had been me, but it wasn't. Right after you three rode away from the camp, a bunch of Indians came stormin' in, shootin' and hollerin'! I took off runnin' and barely made it to the deep forest when a bullet sailed right by me! I was damned lucky to get away! Gus and the others are dead for sure, 'cause those savages made it real clear they weren't takin' any prisoners!"

Amazed that the two men were being so friendly with each other, Elaine cautiously walked toward them and stood beside Jesse.

"Honey, I'm sorry! I kinda forgot my manners.

Elaine, I want you to meet my cousin, Mathias."

"Your cousin!! But I thought......I mean, back at that other camp......"

"That was just an act we was puttin' on. We didn't want nobody to know we was related. You see; we had it planned all along to git that money away from Trevor's gang and we didn't want 'em watchin' us too close, like they always did me and Tad. In the end, I guess it didn't matter none, 'cause our plans got all screwed up. I'm just glad Mathias thought to look for me up here. Now we can divvy up the money and take off for a new life somewhere. Looks like it'll be a fifty-fifty split instead of three ways."

"No way, Jesse! I don't want any of Tad's money! Looks like you found yourself a good woman, so just give his share to her. I think that's how Tad would've wanted it. Have you decided whereabouts you'll be headin'?"

"Well, I ain't discussed it with Elaine yet, but I was thinkin' about buyin' some land in Idaho and tryin' my hand at raisin' horses. How does that sound to you, Elaine?"

"It doesn't matter where we go, Jesse, as long as I'm with you!"

Feeling just a little awkward, Matt looked away for a moment while Jesse held Elaine in a close embrace. Finally, clearing his throat, Matt broke the silence.

"I don't suppose the two of you are interested in havin' someone go in partners with you on that horse ranch?"

With a twinkle in his eye, Jesse grinned at Matt.

"You mean someone...... like a cousin, maybe?"

"Well......yeah!"

"Why not? We could use the help. You know, Elaine; he ain't too smart, but he's plenty strong! We could always use 'im for the heavy work!"

With a quick tackle, Matt brought Jesse to the ground and the two of them rolled over the soft grasses, finally coming to a stop with Jesse pinned to the ground.

"Shit! Looks like I'm smart enough to catch you off guard, cousin!"

Her eyes glowing with happiness, Elaine watched while the two of them lay there laughing. She was very pleased that Jesse would have a close family member to help relieve his heartache over losing his brother. While Elaine took one last look at Tad's grave, Matt helped Jesse up and they brushed themselves off. As they mounted their horses and headed for the deep forest, Jesse stayed behind just long enough to wish his brother a final farewell. Looking toward the west, he saw what appeared to be small, dark clouds looming on the far horizon. While he watched intently, an ominous wind suddenly descended upon the mountain top, sending a chill down his spine. With the wind whistling around him, a deep sense of peace slowly settled in Jesse's heart as it dawned on him that this was God's way of paying his final respects to Tad. His eyes filled with grateful tears, Jesse kicked Buckaroo into a gallop and he quickly caught up with Elaine and Matt at the edge of the forest. While the sky darkened with swirling clouds and the sound of thunder echoed throughout the valleys, the three riders disappeared into the wilderness.

At that same moment, Jacob had finally reached the small town of Covelo with his weary passengers. There was a strained silence as he drove the old bus down the main street. Only the three of them, Jacob, Shannon and Eric, were still awake. Tony and Cat had long since fallen asleep and were lightly snoring. The only other sound to disturb the quiet was that of the rain relentlessly pelting the windshield. Shannon couldn't wait to get out of the bus; the return trip had seemed unbearably long, especially with the tension between Eric and Jacob. Thank God it was finally coming to an end! All three felt great relief as they made one last turn and pulled in beside Tony's motorhome. Eric stepped to the back seat and gently shook his sleeping friends.

"Huh? What's going on? Where are we? Oh, wow! We're back already? Boy, that was quick! Wake up, Cat!"

Sleepily rubbing her eyes, Cat looked around in disbelief.

"How did we get here so fast? It seems like we just barely left!"

With a slight smile, Jacob just shook his head and spoke quietly to them.

"Funny how a nice, sound sleep shortens a long trip. Well, Tony, I hope you won't mind driving me out to the reservation. My grandfather, Lone Elk, is really looking forward to meeting all of you."

"Are you kidding?!!? Of course I don't mind! After the way you saved our asses, I figure we owe you a Hell of a lot more than that! Hey! Look outside! It's hailing!"

While they were talking, the torrential rain had turned into a hailstorm. All of a sudden, the roof of the bus was being battered by hail the size of small marbles. The noise was deafening! Awestruck, they watched in silence as the ground turned white before their eyes. Then, almost as fast as it had begun, it was over! With unbelievable speed, the dark, ominous clouds separated and blew away on the wind. As they stepped out of the bus, they were amazed to find the sun shining down on them out of a bright, blue sky. Stretching their legs for a moment, they all reveled in the sight of the beautiful, sparkling, ice crystals and the smell of the delightfully fresh air. To speak amidst such beauty somehow seemed a travesty, so they all stood quietly as they stared at the breathtaking landscape. Finally, by unspoken agreement, they retrieved their belongings from the bus and carried them into the Winnebago. As soon as they had put everything away, Tony spoke to the group.

"I don't know about the rest of you, but I think we'd all better get cleaned up a little before we meet Jacob's grandfather. Otherwise, we just might not be too welcome!"

Laughing, they all agreed and took turns using the motorhome's small shower. Only a short while later, feeling clean and refreshed, they headed for the reservation.

Knowing his guests would soon arrive, Lone Elk waited patiently in front of his ceremonial tepee. Standing on either side of him were Two Eagles, Running Deer and most of the other warriors. Hovering nearby, the women of the tribe were extremely curious and more than a little annoyed about the white woman who had stolen Jacob away from their own eligible maidens. They knew better than to show any sign of resentment, but they were all prepared to dislike her. As Tony drove up in the huge motorhome and parked, all eyes were fastened on its doors, waiting to catch sight of the red-haired woman. The moment she set foot on the ground, Shannon realized she was the object of intense curiosity and felt herself blushing while she struggled to maintain her dignity. Choosing to ignore the impolite stares, she held her head high and proudly walked arm in arm with Jacob, making her claim on him abundantly clear. As the small group approached Lone Elk, Jacob also ignored the rest of the tribe. Looking only at his grandfather, he anxiously awaited his reaction to Shannon. When they were finally face to face, Lone Elk stared into her hypnotic, green eyes for a few, brief moments and then, with a slight nod, flashed a quick look of approval to his grandson. In that split second, everyone in the tribe understood and accepted Lone Elk's obvious approval and the palpable tension that had prevailed instantly dissipated. Jacob's heart filled with relief and extreme pride as his people's stares mirrored open admiration of Shannon's exotic beauty. A little puzzled that no-one had yet spoken a word, Tony took a step forward and was about to say something, but was stopped in his tracks by Cat as she gave him a quick jab in the ribs and glared at him. Only then did Jacob finally break the silence.

"Honored Grandfather, my heart is gladdened by the sight of you. Standing before you is Shannon, soon to be my wife. The other three are her friends, Eric, Tony and his wife, Cat."

With a disarming smile, Lone Elk acknowledged his guests.

"You are all a most welcome sight for this old man's eyes! Please do me the honor of sitting with me in my tepee so that we may become better acquainted."

Lone Elk led the way so that he could show them where to sit.   Upon entering the tepee, they were amazed by the spacious interior; it hadn't seemed that large from the outside. After motioning his four guests to sit across from him, Lone Elk had Jacob sit beside him, with Two Eagles and Running Deer on either side and slightly behind them. Noticing their obvious interest in various items which were used in special ceremonies, he invited questions from the small group. There was an awkward moment of silence before Tony burst forth with the first question.

"Uh, we've been told that you're a medicine man. Exactly what does that mean? Do you perform some kind of magical rites, or what? My wife, Cat, wants to know, but she doesn't have the nerve to ask."

Mortified, Cat almost shrieked his name and

lightly punched her errant husband on the shoulder.

"Tony!! I can't believe you actually said that! I'm sorry; he had no right to ask such a rude question!"

With a gentle smile, Lone Elk attempted to calm her.

"There is no cause for concern; your husband's words have not offended me. In answer to the question, I do indeed perform various rites. Whether or not they are magical would depend on one's interpretation. Now, if you don't mind, I have a question for you. I notice that you are called Cat, a charming and most fitting name, for you move with the grace of a feline. However, I am much surprised that your parents chose to name you in the Indian fashion, after one of God's creatures! How did that occur?"

With a nervous laugh, Cat quickly answered before Tony could interrupt.

"Actually, Cat is only my nickname; it's short for Caitlin. But I'm glad you like the name; it's what I've always been called. If it's all right to ask, I'm curious about the Indian way of choosing names. For instance, why are you called Lone Elk?"

A sudden silence descended on all of them as a myriad of memories flashed through Lone Elk's mind. Finally, with a far-off look and an almost imperceptible smile, he answered Cat in such a hushed tone that everyone had to strain to hear his words.

"You do me a great honor in asking about my name, but the explanation would involve a lengthy tale from a time long ago. If none of you is in a hurry to leave, I would be most pleased to share that small part of my personal history."

Almost as one, the small group assured him that they had all the time in the world and would love to hear his story. While they watched with rapt expressions, the smile slowly faded from Lone Elk's weathered face and his dark eyes seemed to look inward upon another dimension, a place wherein he would soon lead his eager audience.

"In order to properly explain my name, I must first tell you about my ancestors. There was a time in the far distant past when Round Valley and all the mountains encircling it were inhabited only by the Yuki Indians, the Ukomno'm. Their numbers were such that, in the evening, anyone standing upon a high plateau at the entrance to the valley would have seen thousands of campfires dotting the valley floor and all the surrounding mountains, almost like clusters of fire-flies. The winds would have carried the echoes of their drums and chanting across the valley and into the forests, sending a chill down the spine of anyone who might chance upon their domain. Their creator and supreme being was Taikomol, 'he who walks alone'. He spoke with thunder and it was understood that Taikomol wanted his people to lead good and useful lives. Their daily routine was simple but fulfilling and they lived by very few rules. Mother Earth provided all their needs in great abundance, so they lived happily and worried little. Other than an occasional skirmish with a neighboring tribe, they faced no extreme dangers, especially since they were almost always the winners of any tribal wars. From the earliest of times, the Yuki had the reputation of being a fierce, warlike people who were intensely proud of their fighting skills. One had only to witness one of their war dances to understand why they were able to strike such fear in the hearts of their enemies! A typical war dance would begin with the warriors assembling behind a small hill where they would strip naked; then they would smear their bodies with a sticky substance and cover themselves with white eagle-down. Upon their heads they would place bushy plumes or large feathers. Thus adorned, they would burst from the top of the hill and come screaming down upon the plain with unearthly cries to join in a spectacular dance. As they whooped and leaped about, brandishing their weapons over their heads, the mountains and valleys would slowly begin to vibrate with the terrifying sounds of their war-chants! From that time so long ago, preserved within our tribal lore, is the tale of one particular battle which began with just such a dance as I have described. The Yuki were preparing for battle because one of their maidens had been kidnapped by an enemy war party from a neighboring tribe. The lovely, young girl was called Cat Climbing, because she could climb a tree as swiftly and easily as any mountain lion. She was the daughter of a powerful shaman and was also the fairest maiden in the tribe. She was adventurous by nature and had chosen to walk alone in the forest on the eve of her wedding when she had been surprised by enemy warriors. They were just returning from a successful raid on a weaker tribe and were all too happy to return with yet another captive. Cat Climbing had succeeded in letting out a blood-curdling scream before being knocked unconscious and carried away in the dusk of twilight. Her father, who had been quietly meditating within his tepee, sat bolt upright at the moment of her abduction; he had felt her scream rather than heard it! Fearing for his daughter, he rushed outside, calling her name over and over as he followed the path she had taken. Alarmed by his yells, the Yuki warriors swiftly caught up with the distraught medicine man and they all searched for Cat Climbing, but she had disappeared into the night. In the waning light, all they found were signs of a scuffle and they knew she had been taken captive by one of the neighboring tribes. Realizing they would have to continue their search at dawn, he sent the men back to their camp and told them to prepare for the morning's battle. In despair, he remained behind, wishing to be left alone. While he stood, lost in thought, he stared at the heavens as though seeking help from Taikomol. But his God was silent; there was no thunder in the night sky, only the thousands of brilliant stars blinking down at him. While he stared, riveted by their bright light, it seemed as though several of the stars were suddenly plummeting to earth. Astonished, he watched as they fell from the sky and disappeared behind a nearby hill. Running as fast as he could, he climbed to the top of the hill and stared, breathless, down into the valley below. Carefully scanning the area, he expected to see fallen stars burning brightly on the ground, but his eyes beheld only a soft glow emanating from a group of mist-shrouded trees just a short distance away. As he warily approached, he noticed shadowy figures watching him from the mist. Something in their eyes bade him stop in his tracks and come no closer. As he stared at their strange appearance, he realized they must be from a tribe he had never before encountered. Mesmerized, he lost all track of time and even his will to move, standing motionless while his mind was flooded with a myriad of images, some recognizable and others of an alien nature. And there was something else, an intangible sense of being given specific orders regarding the future, thoughts upon which he would dwell for the rest of his life. The last of the countless pictures flashing through his mind were of his daughter. All of a sudden, he knew exactly where to find her. Elated by the knowledge, he forgot all about the shadowy figures with the hypnotic eyes and raced back to his tribe. He ran so fast that he would later be unable to remember his feet ever touching the ground. As he approached the warriors, they were dancing around the huge tribal fire, its light casting eerie shadows on their leaping, twisting bodies. Interrupting their war dance, he summoned them to immediately

414

leave with him to rescue his daughter. Confused, one of the warriors found the courage to question the medicine man's judgment.

"Honored Shaman, I do not understand how we will be able to find any tracks in the blackness of night. Would it not be wise to wait until first light as you had earlier decided?"

With a strange light in his eyes, the medicine man smiled benevolently at the mystified warriors.

"I know it is difficult to believe, but I have seen Cat Climbing in my mind and I will lead you directly to her. But we must hurry, or we will be too late to save her. She was taken captive by an enemy war party and they are even now arguing over whether to burn her at the stake or use her for their pleasure. There is no more time for talking; we leave now!"

From that point, there ensued the greatest victory the Yuki tribe had ever known. They caught their enemies completely unprepared, for none could even imagine being tracked in the deep blackness of night. For the first time, no Yuki warriors were lost in battle, nor even injured, but instead wrought a terrible vengeance on their enemies, who were annihilated without mercy.

On the following day, the entire tribe celebrated as Cat Climbing became mate to Gray Eagle, son of the Yuki chief. The wedding rites were performed by her father, the great medicine man known as Lone Elk. As time progressed, he came to be revered for his ability to see things which had not yet happened. He was the first shaman to possess such an ability and he used it wisely, according to some inner credo that had developed within him since the night of the falling stars. Whenever he spoke of that night, the people would sit in awe as he related the story, but any true meaning was lost on them, for there were no words to accurately describe what had taken place. Lone Elk, himself, was never quite certain as to what had actually happened; he knew only that he had uncanny visions which enabled him to see bits and pieces of the future. He also learned that the visions were always correct, unless he made a false interpretation.

As time continued its relentless march across the span of centuries, the ability to receive visions would always skip a generation and pass directly from a medicine man to the grandson who would succeed him. When I was born, my grandfather foresaw that I would be the first medicine man to possess an additional power, the ability to harness the forces of nature. Thus did he decide to bestow upon me the name of my honored ancestor, the original Lone Elk, since we were both the first to receive certain powers. Sometimes I wonder who will be the third medicine man to carry the name and what new power will be involved. Who knows? Perhaps it will be the grandson of Falcon and Shannon."

With those words, he smiled at his grandson and then at the rest of his audience. He had to suppress a chuckle at the obvious expressions of disbelief worn by Cat and Tony. As their eyes met, Cat instinctively knew that the old man read her thoughts and she quickly looked away, feeling quite embarrassed. Lone Elk reached out and took her strong, young hand within his old, wrinkled one. Looking up at him, Cat found his eyes filled with kind understanding as he spoke to her in a reassuring tone.

"It's all right, Cat. You needn't feel badly about not being able to believe my story. Except for the fact that I am the one afflicted with such powers, I would also find it almost impossible to believe. I use the word 'afflicted' because, sometimes, it does indeed seem like an affliction, but that is another story for another time.

For now, this tired old man thanks you for honoring him with your visit and your patience in allowing him to rattle on about a time so long ago."

While his audience quietly watched, the light in Lone Elk's eyes slowly dimmed and Cat felt her hand being gently released as the venerable, old medicine man silently drifted off to sleep. Jacob looked fondly at his grandfather for a few seconds and then motioned the others out of the tepee. Standing outside, the small group noticed that it was almost dark. There was an awkward moment of silence as Cat and Shannon stared at one another, all at once realizing how much they would miss their close friendship. With tears threatening to spill from their eyes, they tried to blink them away while they hugged each other and promised to write often.

Feeling slightly embarrassed by the women, Tony reached out and shook Jacob's hand.

"These women act like we're never going to see each other again! But, hey! Covelo isn't that far away! We'll just have to take the time to get together now and then, right?"

"That's right, friend! And neither of us would let you miss our wedding! Right, Shannon?"

Wiping her eyes, Shannon still couldn't speak and rushed over to Tony, wrapping her arms around him and hiding her face on his shoulder while her body shook with silent sobs.

"Hey, kiddo! What's with all this crying, huh? We're not that easy to get rid of! You're going to be stuck with our visits for years and years and years! Got it?"

Gently disentangling himself, Tony tilted her face up to his and gave her a kiss on the cheek. As she looked into his eyes, Shannon managed to laugh through her tears.

"You talk mighty tough, mister, but your eyes are looking a little damp right now, too! And you're definitely not getting away with a little peck on the cheek!"

Before he could move, Shannon planted a long kiss right on his lips, leaving him infinitely embarrassed!

"Okay, that's enough of this mushy stuff! C'mon, Cat! We're getting out of here before she rapes me right on the spot!"

Everyone except Eric was laughing as Tony rushed Cat over to the motorhome. Feeling his eyes upon her, Shannon glanced at Eric and saw a look of pure anguish on his face. While they stared at each other in silence, Jacob tactfully turned away in order to give them a private moment to say farewell. While Jacob stepped back into his grandfather's tepee, Shannon walked over to Eric, desperately hoping they could part as friends.

"I'm truly sorry, Eric. I never meant to hurt you. Can you ever forgive me for the pain I've caused you?"

With a lump in his throat, Eric took a moment to compose himself.

"What's to forgive? I'm a big boy; I can handle a little pain. Besides, you know that old saying, better to have loved and lost than......"

Unable to speak, Shannon just looked at him while a stray tear coursed down her cheek. His eyes filled with tenderness, Eric reached out and gently wiped it away.

"Listen to me, Shannon; this is important! Lone Elk is a nice, old man and I'm sure he believes in his visions. But no-one can actually read the future, so if you're marrying Jacob because of some Indian prophecy, then I think you're making a big mistake! Even in the best of relationships, time has a funny way of playing tricks on people; sometimes things just don't

418

turn out the way they hope. I guess what I'm really trying to say is this......if the time ever comes that you think you've made a mistake......if you ever need me......ever......for any reason, just call and I'll be at your side so fast your head will spin! I'll always be there for you, Shannon......always!"

At that moment, Tony revved his motor and honked the horn, waving at Eric to hurry up! The noise brought Jacob out of his grandfather's tepee just in time to see Eric pulling Shannon close for one, last, tender kiss. As they broke apart, their gaze momentarily locked, Shannon knew that one small part of her heart would always belong to Eric. Then, almost before she realized it, they were gone, the motorhome leaving a trail of dust as it jolted down the dirt road. While she stared after them, tears streaking her face, Jacob silently came up behind her and wrapped his arms around her, comforting her without any words at all.

As Tony, Cat and Eric left the small town of Covelo behind them, the last rays of light quickly disappeared from the sky. The long, straight road leading to the base of the mountains stretched before them, somehow seeming longer that its actual distance of only a few miles. No-one spoke as the black mantle of darkness covered the land, brightened only by the stars glittering in the heavens. Only when the road began its steep climb out of the valley, did Tony finally break the silence.

"You know; listening to that old man really makes a guy think. I mean; wouldn't it be great if you really could see into the future?"

Frowning, Cat shook her head in disagreement.

"I don't think it would be great at all! Just think how boring life would be if you always knew what was going to happen! I'm glad it's not actually possible to see into the future!"

Even as she spoke the words, a small seed of doubt crept into her subconscious. There was something about the look on the old medicine man's face when he told his story. It was obvious he believed in the power of his visions, no matter what anyone else thought of them. And what about that other power, the ability to harness the forces of nature? What on earth did he mean by that? While she sat, lost in thought, Tony continued the conversation.

"Well, I'll say one thing for that old man; he's one Hell of a story-teller! I know it was all bullshit, but I really enjoyed listening to him. The Indian culture is fascinating, isn't it? Just think about it! They pass those legends down, generation after generation, until, somewhere along the way, they actually start believing in them! If our culture worked the same way, I guess, by now, we'd all have to believe in Santa Claus and the tooth fairy and all that crap! You know what? I think I just figured out the major difference between our two races! Don't get me wrong; I'm not prejudiced or anything, but I think we're just more evolved than they are. Once they reach our level, they won't be able to swallow that bullshit anymore! Time will finally cure them of believing fairy tales handed down from the past. You know what they say; time cures everything!"

With the tires squealing in protest, they all felt themselves swaying sideways as Tony took another switchback just a little too fast. Feeling nauseated by Tony's erratic driving, Cat angrily snapped at him.

"Tony! Quit talking and watch the road! You know how sick I get every time you corner like that! Thanks to you, my stomach's going in circles!"

Feeling contrite, Tony instantly slowed down.

"I'm sorry, babe! When we get to the top, I'll stop for a few minutes and we can all stretch our legs; that'll make you feel better!"

Finally reaching the top, Tony parked his motorhome at the lookout point and the three of them stepped outside to a crystal-clear night filled with stars and the sound of crickets chirping. As they silently looked down upon the vastness that was Round Valley, there were only a few lights to designate the small town of Covelo. Other than that, the rest of the valley and the mountains that encircled it were dark and foreboding, causing Cat to snuggle closely against Tony's warm body. While they stood looking over the edge, reveling in the beauty of the still, summer night, an evening mist began to creep through the valley, filling every nook and cranny before their very eyes. Within minutes, they were looking out upon an ocean of fog and there was not a sound to be heard, not even the chirping of a single cricket! Puzzled, all three warily looked around, wanting to leave, but somehow unable to move. While they watched, spellbound, the thick fog suddenly began to break apart and float away on a gentle breeze. As Round Valley once again became visible, they were stunned to see the lights of thousands of campfires dotting the valley floor and all the surrounding mountains, almost like clusters of fire-flies! With chills racing up and down their spines, a strange, vibrating sound reached their ears as the haunting echoes of drums and chanting spread across the valley and into the forests, leaving its imprint upon their hearts and souls forever.

Far from that hypnotic scene, Lone Elk sat before a crackling fire in his ceremonial tepee. While he repeated a sacred chant, an evening mist, borne on the wind, silently entered his domain and swirled over his head for a few moments before suddenly evaporating into thin air. No longer able to fight the relentless exhaustion steadily invading his body, he began to doze. Before entering the shadow world of dreams, his last vision was that of Tony, Cat and Eric looking down upon thousands of campfires. As the vision slowly faded, a very satisfied smile crept across the weathered face of the Mendocino Medicine Man.

ABOUT THE AUTHOR

A native Californian, Carol Douglas Tillotson was raised in Antioch, California and graduated with honors from Antioch High School. After attending the University of California at Berkeley, she married Don Tillotson and they raised four sons in Placerville, California. Living on a large ranch with registered quarterhorses, she acquired an affinity and appreciation for horseback riding. On one of their vacations, they loaded six of their horses into a trailer and took them to the Yolla Bolly Wilderness Area in northern California. The entire family rode along the very trails described in this novel. Haunted by the beauty of the ancient forests of Mendocino County, she was left with the burning desire to write a novel centered around that area. Years later, with her children grown, she finally had the opportunity to do so. She is currently working on the sequel to Mendocino Medicine Man.